Of Vikings and Voyageurs

Of Vikings and Voyageurs

Jack Salmela

NORTH STAR PRESS OF ST. CLOUD, INC.
St. Cloud, Minnesota

Copyright © 2008 Jack Salmela

All rights reserved.

ISBN-10: 0-87839-288-2
ISBN-13: 978-0-87839-288-9

This is a work of fiction. Names, characters, places, and incidents are the products of the author's imagination or are used fictitiously. Any resemblance to actual events or persons, living or dead, is entirely coincidental.

First Edition: July 2008

Printed in the United States of America

Published by
North Star Press of St. Cloud, Inc.
P.O. Box 451
St. Cloud, Minnesota 56302

northstarpress.com

info@northstarpress.com

DEDICATION

Sir Alexander Mackenzie, 1764 – 1820
&
David Thompson, 1770 – 1857

Mackenzie and Thompson were not only legendary figures of the North West Company, they were the greatest European explorers of the North American continent from Hudson Bay and the Great Lakes to the Pacific Ocean.

ACKNOWLEDGMENTS

The author wishes to thank the following people for their help in producing this novel.

Catherine Crawford, Voyageurs National Park - voyageur history
David Geister - front and back cover paintings
Lindsey Hall - French translation
Jeremy Kingsbury - voyageur history
Candy Rousse - manuscript review
Steven D. Smith - graphics, cover concept images
Staff at the Duluth Public Library - research assistance

The author also wishes to acknowledge . . . Carl Gawboy, for his theory that the pictographs on North Hegman Lake depict how the Ojibwe had interpreted late-winter constellations; David Kovala—if one wishes to explore the wilderness canoe country known as the Quetico/Superior, then one should first find a canoe partner as good as David; Richard Nielson and Scott F. Wolter, for their groundbreaking book, *The Kensington Rune Stone: Compelling New Evidence*, which was of utmost importance in the author's research; and "Clarence Louis Mitchel," a random conversation with whom has made all this possible.

Of Vikings . . .

". . . fierce, foreboding omens came over the land of Northumbria . . .

. . .whirlwinds, lightning storms, and fiery dragons were seen flying in the sky."

". . . the ravaging of heathen men destroyed God's church at Lindisfarne . . ."
—Anglo-Saxon Chronicles, 793 A.D.

and Voyageurs . . .

"Keep every thing as secret as you can from your men,"
one bourgeois advised an inexperienced clerk,
"otherwise these old voyagers will fish all they know out of your Green Hands."
—*The Grand Portage Story*, by Carolyn Gilman

ॐ 1 ॰

June 1779
The lake-country wilderness northwest of Lake Superior.

VOYAGEUR JEAN-LUC TROTIN paddled solo through the notorious Hell's Gate Rapids along the fur-trade route. He was an experienced voyageur, but recent rains had swollen the river, and he found himself in serious trouble before he had negotiated half the route. He knew he should never have tried the river, but this was the plan.

Just as the bow of his birch bark canoe came off one standing wave, it punched through a second wave that followed too closely for his bow to ride up and over. Water folded over the canoe's gunwales. It was cold as ice, and the weight of it threatened to swamp the canoe.

Jean-Luc knew that if he was going to make it through the rapids, he couldn't afford to take on any more water. He also knew that he would. It was a vicious cycle: the more water that washed into the canoe, the lower the canoe rode, making it all that much easier to take on even more water. The weight of the chest tied down in the bottom of the canoe didn't help either.

Jean-Luc knelt just to the rear of the canoe's center thwart, the heavy wooden chest directly in front of him under the thwart and lashed to it. The chest contained the most valuable cargo ever brought into the northwest during the fur trade, and it had been charged to his care while they lined the canoe up the rapids.

Fearing for his life, Jean-Luc tried to back-paddle to gain more control in the rapids, but the mad torrent would have none of it.

The bow of the canoe launched over another wave and slammed down on the rising slope of the one just beyond it. Spray blasted Jean-Luc's face as the impact parted the water with the sound of *boom-woosh*. To make matters worse, if that were possible, the wave was pointed like a rooster tail.

Jean-Luc leaned and paddled madly. He missed the peak of the rooster tail, and his canoe rode up on its side incline. The canoe started to roll dangerously to the left. When all the water in the bottom of canoe also sloshed to the left, the roll accelerated. The wooden chest shifted, but its ropes held.

In a flash, Jean-Luc slapped the paddle blade down hard on the water, hoping the impact would right him a bit. But he felt little resistance as the blade dropped through foamy, aerated water. Jean-Luc thought he was finished as he watched the gunwale about to go under.

Suddenly, the canoe jolted as the underside of its hull hit a submerged rock. The canoe was thrown to the right as it rode up, then off the side of the rock. In an instant, everything started shifting to the right, and the canoe rolled in the opposite direction. With lightening reflexes, Jean-Luc plunged the paddle blade straight down in the water and pulled hard toward the canoe. The maneuver held the canoe, and it stabilized.

But Jean-Luc was not out of trouble. He was still in the heart of Hell's Gate Gorge with too much water in his canoe. He looked over the mad torrent of white water, scouting the steep banks and rock bluffs coming up downstream. He spotted his one and only chance to save himself, a rock bluff on the right, behind which was a safe eddy. If he missed it, he knew he was a dead man because there would be no avoiding a cataract at the bottom of the rapids.

The Devil's Cauldron was a small waterfall, all things considered. At low water levels it was even considered a run-able drop for an experienced voyageur. But at the present high water level it was a monster. Fellow voyageurs who had dared the monster had been swallowed up by the rapids, held under by the back-circulating water, only to be spit out long after their spirits had gone on to meet their heavenly patron, St. Anne.

Jean-Luc made a couple powerful, far-reaching sweeps with his paddle in a grave attempt to get the canoe headed toward the right-side bank. But the canoe was carrying a lot of water, making it difficult to maneuver.

Jean-Luc realized there was more water in the canoe than the wave had dumped in. He glanced around the interior of his hull. He noticed the oil cloth-wrapped package, bound tightly with twine, had worked free from where he'd secured it and was sloshing back and forth. He worried that his cherished flute á bec and survival gear might be washed overboard. Although the contents of the wooden chest was priceless, he didn't want to lose his instrument, and the survival gear would make all the difference later.

But surviving the rapids was his immediate concern, and the amount of water in the canoe indicated a serious problem.

The thick birch bark skin of a voyageurs' canoe remained surprisingly supple in constant contact with the water, and the curved cedar ribs made a sturdy frame. But, Jean-Luc knew the unforgiving limits of what a birch bark canoe could take, and he feared that the collision with the rock had punctured his hull. So Jean-Luc summoned every ounce of energy from his muscular arms and paddled with all his might as he tried to accelerate the canoe faster than the current to gain the right bank.

"Sebastian!" Jean-Luc shouted out above the roar of the rapids. In French he yelled, "Yesterday you went to meet St. Anne! If today is my turn, we will still have our vengeance against Duncan McKay! And we will then make our music once again! We will make it for eternity!

"HAAAHHH!" Jean-Luc screamed out in fury and determination. It was a yell into the face of death. Then Jean-Luc rotated his broad shoulders to pull hard on another desperate stroke. But the blade of his long gouvernoy's paddle wedged between submerged rocks and snapped.

2

Present day.

IN HIS BEAT-UP, HYBRID COROLLA, Tim Malone sped through a neighborhood of older, two-story houses in Duluth, Minnesota. As he took the hard left into Lyle and Maggie Hanson's driveway, he nearly lost control as he hit a patch of ice. The glare of Tim's headlights blurred over the neighbor's snow-covered front yard and then flooded their porch for an instant, illuminating snow shovels and plastic sleds propped against the railing. He braked hard once he was on clear driveway pavement and jammed the transmission into park. The car rocked forward and back, his headlights aimed at Lyle's garage.

Tim shut off his lights, folded his arms over the top of his steering wheel and leaned forward. The house was quiet, mostly dark, but one dim light still lit up the window of the downstairs living room. Lyle's travel-worn Jeep wasn't in the driveway.

Being so late, Tim figured Maggie had gone to bed and wondered if he should wake her. Earlier in the day, she had left him an urgent voice message that Lyle had left town suddenly and she was worried about him. Tim had tried returning the call but didn't get through, so he left her a message that he should arrive around 11:30 p.m. It was now 11:45. Not knowing what was going on with his best friend was driving Tim crazy, but if he were going to be of any comfort to Maggie, he'd better calm himself. He took several deep breaths and thought of his best friend. What could be up with him?

Lyle Hanson's Ph.D. was in archaeology, with a specialty in the late eighteenth-century North American fur trade. Since graduating, he had spent a great deal of time lobbying the governments of the United States and Canada for special permits and lining up funding to conduct an archaeological recovery of voyageur artifacts along the border between Minnesota and Ontario. Lyle had found it impossible to get the international bureaucracies to coordinate on formal approval.

With patience and persistence, Lyle finally succeeded in getting each government to assign two agencies to project oversight: Voyageurs National Park and Superior National Forest (managing the Boundary Waters Canoe Area Wilderness) for the United States, and for Canada, the Ontario Ministry of Natural Resources (in charge of Quetico Provincial Park) and the Ontario Ministry of Culture.

Best of all, Lyle had hired Tim to work on the artifact recovery project. It was Tim's dream come true. Although Lyle had kept the location of his search a secret, Tim knew that it had to be somewhere along the voyageurs' highway, the historic fur-trade route along the United States-Canada border, an area peppered with wilderness lakes and rivers on both sides of the border. This was Tim's favorite place on earth, so, for him, it really didn't matter what Lyle was looking for.

The timing was also perfect for Tim. He had recently postponed his graduate studies at MIT and needed to find a temporary position. The field work on Lyle's project was scheduled to start that summer.

Just as Tim figured he had calmed enough to be useful to Maggie, he noticed a movement in the lit window. The curtains parted, then swung closed again. Maggie was still up. Tim shut off the engine, jumped out of the car and ran up the shoveled walkway. He sprang onto the porch and stopped in front of the Christmas wreath still on the front door from the holidays.

Just as Tim was about to press the doorbell, the foyer light came on. Tim listened to the retracting dead-bolt. Maggie flung open the door and looked up at him, her eyes red from crying. Tim knew then that the situation with Lyle was serious.

"Maggie, I'm sorry it's so late. I was out of town all day," Tim said as he came into a hallway. "I raced over as soon as I got your phone message."

"Oh, Tim, thanks so much for coming," Maggie said and wrapped her arms around Tim's shoulders. "I don't know what's going on . . . and I'm scared."

"When did Lyle leave?" Tim asked. "Where did he go?"

Maggie looked uncertain. "This afternoon sometime. I wasn't home. He was already on the road when he called. He said he didn't want to say where he was going on a cell. He also said he didn't want me to call him. He promised to call late tonight or first thing tomorrow but . . ."

"Maggie, your . . . your phone message said Lyle was going to quit the recovery project. Surely that's not true. Not after all his work to set it up."

Maggie stepped back, covered her mouth and pressed her eyes tight. She gave a small, quick nod. Tim's heart sank. He could see her shaking and wrapped an arm around her shoulders. He guided her back to the living room.

After a few moments, Maggie gained her composure. She looked at her watch. "Lindsey'll be staying with me overnight, but she won't be here until about one o'clock. I'm really glad you came."

On a coffee table between the twin sofas where they sat, Tim noticed a box of tissues, a cordless phone, a newspaper, and a single sheet of paper with a pencil tracing of a circular design. The newspaper looked like it was folded open to a particular article. He turned his attention back to Maggie.

"I can't believe Lyle's going to quit his project," Tim said. "This long lost cargo he's been talking about that might be at the bottom of the rapids, it . . . Lyle said it could be the greatest archaeological discovery ever made in relation to the fur trade. It literally could be a treasure trove."

"I know, I know," Maggie said. She reached for another tissue.

Tim leaned forward and rested his elbows on his knees. "Maggie, I don't know what to say. All that effort Lyle put into researching old records, crawling his way through the maze of government bureaucracies, the expense of diving gear, camping equipment . . . what happened?"

"I don't know. This is a nightmare. Lyle's worked so hard to get to this point. It would have done wonders for his career. And you, Tim. You've rearranged your life just so you could help Lyle next summer. I know you were looking forward to it." Again Maggie reached for the tissue box. She set it in her lap.

"Don't worry about me." When Maggie had moved the tissues, Tim noticed a diamond bracelet on the coffee table—white gold with lots of sparkly diamond chips. It looked very expensive. "Wow! Whose bracelet?"

Maggie picked it up and ran it through her fingers before putting it back onto the table. "My friend Lindsey's. She forgot it, so I'm leaving it out for her."

Tim wondered why anyone would forget such an expensive piece of jewelry. But that really wasn't his concern. "Anyway, Maggie, don't worry about me. If this summer doesn't work out, I'll find something else to do. But, this thing with Lyle just up and leaving. That's not like him."

Maggie blew her nose. Then she shook her head and said, "I'm not sure. It started with that older guy who lives across the border in Canada. The guy who lives in the woods and has all the Viking and voyageur artifacts."

From working with Lyle, Tim knew exactly who this was. "Cedric Twohearts."

Maggie nodded. "I had the impression he's kind of an uneducated hermit or something. Well, he's educated enough to know about this," Maggie said as she picked up the newspaper article and handed it to Tim.

He took it and read the headline: ROMAN-ERA RELIC FOUND AT HADRIAN'S WALL MAY BE PERSIAN. Tim stared at it, reading it over. Then he met Maggie's eyes. "Is this serious?"

Maggie shrugged. "Apparently, it is. Lyle certainly seemed to think so, anyway."

3

"So Lyle had told you about Two-hearts?" Maggie asked while she held her cup of tea with both hands.

"Yeah," Tim said as he put the article back down on the coffee table and then reached for the spoon in his tea cup. He submerged a lemon slice and then stirred gently. "Lyle described him as a shy, eccentric . . . as almost a recluse, sitting up in his cabin playing some antique recorder or something. He said he was pretty reluctant to even grant an interview."

"Actually, when Lyle finally did get to interview him—I guess he met him at some restaurant in International Falls—he found him surprisingly personable. He even gave Lyle a couple souvenirs to donate to a museum. But when it came to hard information about the cargo lost by the voyageurs, Two-hearts was pretty guarded and even tried to discourage Lyle from going forward with the recovery project."

"Really?" Tim asked with surprise. "Did he say why?"

"When Lyle asked, Two-hearts showed him a lead seal from the fur trade and said, 'This is the reason why.'"

Maggie reached for the sheet of paper on the coffee table and handed it to Tim. "Here. This is what the lead seal looks like. Two-hearts let Lyle make this pencil tracing of it. Notice the P and C."

Tim's expression showed surprise. "Percy and Campbell?" he asked as he looked at Maggie for confirmation.

"That's right. The very fur trade company from northern England whose voyageurs lost their precious cargo. But this seal is different from the typical in that it has a design on it. Most lead seals used on fur bales usually just had the company's initials, not much more."

"Hmm. Lyle was convinced that Two-hearts knew more than he let on. Maybe he even knows what the lost cargo consisted of and why it was brought into the wilderness in the first place."

"Those are the two key questions all right," Maggie said with resignation. "Lyle said Two-hearts has been real secretive about that lost cargo. But Lyle had a hunch that, deep down, Two-hearts wanted to cooperate. It's as if he was scared of something. He didn't come right out and say it, but Lyle even got the feeling that Two-hearts might have been threatened by someone . . . by someone else who wants to get their hands on the lost cargo."

Then Maggie lifted her head and looked squarely at Tim. "On other issues, however, we finally got a break when they made that discovery in northern England." Maggie pointed to the newspaper article. "Had you heard about this ancient silver vase or whatever it is? It has engravings on it that . . ."

"Yes, I . . ." Tim stopped. Maggie had held up her hand and was listening intently to something. One finger to her lips, she flipped off the lamp.

"What is it?" Tim whispered as Maggie tiptoed to the window and parted the curtain slightly. Tim followed and looked out over her head.

A large sedan or limo had paused in the middle of the street just in front of Maggie's house. As they peeked at it, the headlights went out. Its red brake lights were still on, just barely illuminating the exhaust coming from the tail pipe. The car's interior remained dark.

"Think it could be your friend Lindsey arriving early?"

"No. She drives a minivan. Besides, she'd just park and come in."

After a few more seconds, the car's headlights came back on, and it started slowly down the street. It turned at the corner and was gone.

Maggie pulled the shades and turned the lamp back on. "Oh, God, Tim. That was weird. Should I call 911?"

"It's late. Chances are someone was having trouble reading house numbers. It was probably some guy from another block coming home drunk and wondering why his house looked different. I don't think it has anything to do with us or Lyle. I mean, they stayed in plain sight."

"Then why did they turn their lights off?"

"Maybe they could see better?"

"Yeah . . . I . . . I guess," Maggie said, sitting down. "I guess I'm a little jumpy."

"You need to try to relax. I'm sure Lyle's okay. He's smart and careful. You know that. So, what's this article?" Tim said, picking up the newspaper in hopes of distracting Maggie.

"The vase . . . its engravings included an ancient Persian symbol."

"Yes, I'd heard about it. It made the national news."

When Maggie didn't respond, Tim looked up to see Maggie looking anxiously toward the window.

"Maggie, it'll be all right."

"Oh . . . I'm sorry," she said. She tried to refocus her attention on Tim. "Uh . . . what did you say?"

"The discovery of the silver vase. It's big news."

"Oh . . . yeah." She drew in a long breath and let it out. "Yes. When this story came out, it was right about then Lyle noticed a change in Two-hearts' attitude. Lyle mentioned sensing an urgency. For the first time, Two-hearts initiated contact by sending Lyle a letter. The letter still didn't explain the lead seal, but at least the man opened up on a couple of other things . . . a couple of bombshells actually. Two-hearts said he was familiar with the same Persian symbol as on that artifact found in England."

"Yeah, but so are a lot of other people."

"That's not what he meant," Maggie said. "He meant that he was familiar with it in terms of its being referenced on an artifact here in America. Apparently the reference is inscribed on some sort of stone. Most likely a rune stone."

Tim sat up, his interest piqued. "Seriously? A stone that he *has*? That would mean—"

"No. He didn't say he *had* a rune stone. But he claims to know where one was and what information was inscribed on it. Tim, since you've been working with Lyle, did you ever hear about the new archaeological theory of the three Nordic rune stones?"

"Well, yeah, but there's nothing concrete yet. It's just a wild theory, really. Some believe that in the 1300s, the Vikings apparently hid three stones in the mid-continent of North America. All are within the watershed that drains into the south end of Lake Winnipeg."

"Yes, that's right," Maggie said.

"But that watershed's big, most of the land between North Dakota and Lake Superior."

"Isn't one stone the famous Kensington Rune Stone? Another stone was found by the French explorer La Verendrye, if I remember?"

"That's what some say, but even that—"

"Well, Two-hearts confirmed the theory and wrote that the third stone was hidden somewhere in northeast Minnesota. He even referred to the stone by a name. He called it the Rainy Lake Rune Stone. And he insisted that it made reference to the Persian symbol."

Maggie waited for a reaction, but Tim didn't know what to make of the alleged connection between a possible third rune stone and the Persian symbol. He simply stared back at Maggie with a quizzical, skeptical look.

"I'm not kidding, Tim. The letter described how all three rune stones make a reference to something important in the history of the Middle East. For the Rainy Lake Stone, its reference to the Persian symbol is apparently in context to some event in ancient history. Does that seem plausible to you?"

"Oh . . . I don't know," Tim answered and shrugged. "For the Kensington Rune Stone, at least, it's common knowledge that some of its inscriptions relate to Christian themes. In fact, amongst the Nordic runes are the three Latin letters, AVM, meaning Ave Maria. So, I suppose that for the other two stones, if they exist, it would make some sense that the text on them could also have some Christian references."

"Anyway, the other piece of information that Two-hearts mentioned in his letter was that the Rainy Lake Stone was connected to the lost cargo."

"Connected to the lost cargo? Maggie, if that's true—"

"That's huge, I know. But that's what he claims. Anyway, after Lyle read the letter, he called Two-hearts . . . I guess he has a satellite phone out there in the woods. They spoke for a long time . . . a really long time, in fact. After that call, Lyle seemed nervous, on edge. Then this morning, he spoke with Two-hearts again. He was still on the phone when I took off for Cloquet to go to a wedding shower. Then all of a sudden, just like that, Lyle must have packed some things and took off. He was long gone by the time I got home. When he called, he said he'd be gone for a couple days because Two-hearts wanted to meet immediately in private and show him something. That's when Lyle announced that he was going to suspend the recovery project."

"Maggie, do you have any idea as to where they might be meeting?"

"He said he'd promised Two-hearts to keep it a secret. But he did mention something about pictographs of all things. I couldn't understand what Lyle was saying because the phone connection started breaking up. So, all I can do is guess. Maybe Two-hearts wanted to snowshoe out to some pictographs near Ely and show him something. Or maybe he wanted to point out something to Lyle at the Kensington Rune Stone Museum in Alexandria."

"Maybe, but if it's something that Two-hearts has and can bring with him, then they could be meeting just about anywhere."

"Well, I didn't get that impression from the context of our conversation. Maybe the next time Lyle calls he'll be able to say where he went." Maggie folded her arms and looked down. "Oh, Tim, it's all gotten so crazy. I just hope Lyle hasn't gotten himself mixed up with anything dangerous."

The room took on an air of fear as the conversation fell momentarily silent. Maggie's eyes flitted nervously back and forth, obviously playing out frightening scenarios.

"Hey . . . I think I might have an idea! Maggie, do you remember when Jessa and Shukriyah came out here last summer from Boston for a few days? We all went up the Gunflint Trail and went camping."

"Yes?" Then Maggie made the connection and her eyes suddenly lit up and zeroed in on Tim's face. "That's right! Shukriyah is from Iran! Is she Persian? Would she know about that Persian symbol?"

"If she doesn't, she knows someone who does, I'm sure. There's Omar Rahani, who's like Shukriyah's adopted uncle. I'm sure he'll be heading up to northern England where they found that artifact with the Persian symbol. He's got an archaeologist up there who works for him. Maybe this archaeologist can help us out. One of his specialties is the early history of Scotland and Scandinavia."

"Do you think either of them would know about lead seals used by Scottish fur trade companies?"

"Possibly. For sure someone there will know something about rune stones."

"I have an idea, Tim." Maggie said. She got up and headed out of the room. In a few moments, she was back. "Take that tracing of the lead seal and these two souvenirs that Two-hearts gave to Lyle when they first met." Maggie handed Tim the two artifacts.

Tim examined them one at a time. "That's a voyageur's fire steel," Maggie said as he looked at the oval-shaped rod of steel. "And the other is a navigational sun crystal used by the Vikings."

"Wow!" Tim said, knowing the objects he held in his hands were both rare and important. "Pretty generous donations if you ask me. These aren't just souvenirs, these look like genuine archaeological artifacts."

"Lyle certainly had no doubt that they're authentic. Can you send the tracing and these two artifacts to Shukriyah, and then ask her to send them to her adopted uncle? Someone has to know what these things mean."

"Are you sure Lyle wouldn't mind?"

Maggie shrugged. "Oh, no, not at all. He was going to send them to some expert at some point, I'm sure."

"Okay, I'll do it first thing tomorrow."

"Shukriyah already has my e-mail address, but make sure you give her my phone number as well. If she or her uncle have any questions I want to answer them immediately. Hopefully this Omar can get his archaeologist friend to look at the lead seal tracing. Maybe he has some inside information about additional archives and records. It's possible that Lyle didn't find out everything there is to know about the Percy and Campbell fur trade company."

Maggie paused and drew in a somewhat shaky breath. Then she offered Tim a bit of a smile. "Tim, I don't want you and Lyle to give up on retrieving that cargo lost by the voyageurs. Everything indicates that it's really valuable. We need to find out what the cargo consisted of and why it was shipped into the Boundary Waters in the first place. And, if we can recover it . . . well, that would be absolutely amazing."

∞ 4 ∞

*University of Newcastle upon Tyne
Newcastle, Great Britain*

s men and women bickered in the packed lecture hall, Alistair Groom sat quietly and contemplated the evolving turmoil caused by a mishandled archaeological artifact.

"The silver urn still belongs to the landowner!" said a well-dressed solicitor to the man standing behind the podium. "I represent that landowner, and you bloody well know that he has rights to—"

"No, he doesn't!" a man from the English Heritage office in London angrily interrupted, his face almost purple with rage. "Land ownership doesn't matter a whit, and of all people you should know it! The antiquities law was written precisely for cases like this!"

"And the law states that antiquities belong to *all* citizens," said a woman seated at a table next to the podium. She was the director of Newcastle's Museum of Antiquities. "A museum is the one place that can guarantee—"

"Then prove it qualifies as an antiquity!" a fourth voice shouted from the back of the lecture hall.

The university's head of Archaeology, Alistair's former boss, stood up from his chair near the front of the lecture hall and turned to address the crowd. "Come off it! You're the very people fighting our attempt to study and analyze the artifact. You already know that the winged symbol engraved on the urn is Persian. Are you afraid that we may bloody well confirm its authenticity?"

The man standing at the podium stretched his arms forward and held out the palms of his hands. "People! People! Please remain calm. Nothing will get resolved if we can't maintain civility."

The plea didn't work, so Alistair rose to leave. Luckily, he was seated at the end of a row along an outer aisle and his departure didn't make a scene. But he did have to shuffle by news reporters and photographers leaning against the wall. As he exited into the hallway, all the loud voices blended into a cacophony behind him.

Once out of the lecture hall, Alistair leaned against the wall. He loosened his geeky wide tie with the diagonal pastel stripes—easily a relic from the 1970s—and unbuttoned his shirt collar. As the redness in his chubby cheeks faded, he ran his hand through the wispy remnants of a once full head of strawberry blond curls. His remaining locks on top gave the impression of dozens of miniature smoke plumes rising from his scalp. The thicker hair at the back of his head was long enough to tie into a short ponytail.

Due to all the dignitaries at the meeting, Alistair had given a shot at dressing up even though he wasn't the least bit fashion savvy. On top of that, he lived alone, so no one could critique his ill-fitting, nerdy attire. The sleeves on his navy blue polyester blazer were too short, the collar of his white shirt too tight, and like his casual pants, his dress pants were hemmed for high-water. And with such a fiasco of a meeting, he wondered why he had even bothered pulling out the royal regalia, as he called them, from the far end of his closet.

Suddenly, Alistair noticed someone coming into the hall from another door. The man paused, grinned at him and said, "Had enough in there already?"

"Omar!" Alistair said with delighted surprise. "Well, I'll be! You made it after all!"

"Oh, I've been here from the start. Got in last night," Omar Rahani said as he reached out to shake Alistair's hand. A tall Iranian, Omar was impeccably dressed with a salt-and-pepper-colored sport coat of herringbone-weaved lamb's wool, a teal-colored shirt with an open collar, pleated khaki slacks with cuffs, and shiny black shoes. He had a close-trimmed goatee, and his black hair was tinged with gray around his ears, giving him a most learned look. Omar's dark piercing eyes and dignified posture always seemed to command respect wherever he went.

"I saw you sitting in there," Omar continued, "but I didn't even bother taking a seat. It was predictable that this meeting would get out of control."

Alistair nodded. "Isn't that just like you . . . so perceptive and always staying above the fray."

"Alistair, what can you tell me about that urn? Do you really think it's an authentic Persian artifact?"

"You better believe it! Omar, we're going to have to sit down and talk. This is really a most exciting discovery."

"I heard about some engravings on it. Is one of them the symbol of the guardian spirit?"

"Faravahar? The ubiquitous Persian image of the little man riding the wings?"

"Yes, yes. That's the one."

Again Alistair nodded. "Yes. That's precisely what's on the urn."

"Do you think there are more artifacts where the urn was found?"

"More artifacts—yes. Other artifacts of significance? I can't be sure. As soon as my colleagues heard rumors about the urn's discovery, they got out there as fast as possible to secure the site. Although they did notice some signs of disturbance, we don't think anything else was found."

"Have you started excavating?" Omar asked.

"I almost wish we hadn't. This time of year it's slow going because the bloody mud never dries out. But we've made some progress. A ways from where the urn was found we've discovered pottery shards, charred stones from cooking pits, your basic utilitarian items. The urn, on the other hand, is ceremonial, and I'm sure that's why it was isolated. Maybe it was hidden in a place of worship and, lo and behold, it gets found centuries later by some backhoe operator who then takes it off site. That's why we've got all that trouble in there," Alistair said as he made a thumbing gesture over his shoulder toward the lecture hall.

"Omar, there's something I need to ask you. The university wants me to take a leave from my work in Turkey and stay here to help out. I don't like the idea of asking my primary benefactor for a delay, but if I could temporarily suspend my work on your patron saint and the Taurus Mountain Chronicles . . ."

"No problem at all. Apostle Thomas can wait. Besides, won't your field crew continue the excavation work at the site of the Chronicles without you?"

"Oh, for sure. I just didn't want my involvement with the urn to cause any contractual disputes with your associates on the council. Not all of them are as flexible as you, Omar."

"Ah, but in this case, I believe they will be. The discovery of this urn changes everything for our organization. You can't imagine our excitement. We definitely want you to follow up. We want to learn as much as possible about this Persian thread of influence that not only extends here to northern England but continues across the Atlantic to the very center of the North American continent."

"To the center of the North . . . ? Oh yeah! That's right! Your e-mail mentioned some sort of Persian connection in North America. Funny this all seems to be coming out at the same time."

Omar picked up a leather briefcase that he had set at his feet when he greeted Alistair. Alistair eyed it. "It also mentioned a couple Viking and voyageur items. They wouldn't be . . . are they in there?" Alistair asked as he pointed to the briefcase.

Omar smiled. "That they are, my friend."

"And they really came from the border country between the state of Minnesota and the Canadian province of Ontario?"

"That's right. They appear to have originated from northern Europe. That's why I thought they would be easily identifiable to an expert in the early history of Scandinavia, Scotland, and . . . what's this region we're presently in? North . . . um, North . . . ?"

"You almost said it accidentally," Alistair said as he held up his thumb. "Norrr-thumbria. The land north of the river Humber. But simply completing some graduate work doesn't qualify me as being an expert. Come on," Alistair said as he gestured down the hallway. "Let's go to my office. We'll take a look at what you have there in your briefcase."

"They still let you keep an office here?" Omar asked as he started walking with Alistair.

"Oh, yeah. I think they're counting on me to come back and take a staff position."

"By the way, I'd be curious to take a drive out and see where the urn was found. Wasn't it along Hadrian's Wall somewhere?"

"Yes. Along the wall of the old Roman fort at Carrawburgh. It was found in that general area. But I would suggest waiting until the novelty wears off somewhat. Right now you'd find the area swarming with tourists, amateur archaeologists sweeping the area with metal detectors, modern-day mystics making a pilgrimage—it's a zoo."

"Modern-day mystics, huh? That can only mean one thing. Most of us in the organization have heard of a Temple to Mithras located somewhere along Hadrian's wall."

"Yes, that's right. The ruins of the Mithraeum. Hadrian's Wall is where the Romans had brought your Persian ancestors as conscripts for their garrisons. Of course, your ancestors brought their religions with them."

"And the silver urn as well?" Omar asked.

"It appears that way."

"By the way, besides the winged symbol of Faravahar, what are the other two images etched onto the urn?"

"One I haven't figured out yet. The other looks like a shooting star. And if that's the case, then I have a hunch that the urn could be connected to your organization many centuries ago."

Omar stopped mid-stride and took Alistair's arm.

"That's one reason why I'm here. The discovery of this urn is huge. I need to know how the Vikings and voyageurs are connected to this area and to the Persians who once lived here.

"But Alistair, make no mistake—the other reason I'm here is also important. I'm here on behalf of my adopted niece, Shukriyah. Her American friends want to find out the mystery behind a certain shipment sent by Scottish fur traders into the heart of North America."

5

ALISTAIR'S OFFICE WAS NARROW AND DEEP with a window in the far end wall. Loose papers haphazardly strewn about his desk gave a coffee mug the appearance of a chimney rising out of a mishmash of white shingles. Some of those papers appeared to be drowning his computer keyboard, but the keys themselves were exposed just enough to provide access for working fingers. On the opposite wall, books and archaeological specimens filled a bank of shelves above a table covered with stacks of maps, professional periodicals and file folders.

"Have a chair, Omar. Here, let me clear off part of this table so you can put down your briefcase," he said, hoping that, under all the mess, he wouldn't discover the sandwich he had misplaced a few days earlier.

Omar took Alistair's suggestion and placed his briefcase on a section of cleared table. As Omar sat down, Alistair took off his sport jacket, folded it as if that would help the wrinkles, then tossed it over some boxes in the corner.

"Well, Alistair," Omar said, "working up here will give you a chance to be close to home and get away from the burning rays of the sun of my homeland. After all, you do have that fair, Anglo-Saxon skin."

"I'm part Celtic, I shall have you know. In fact, my mum wanted to name me after her grandfather, Alasdair. He lived in the Outer Hebrides of

Scotland and spoke only Scottish Gaelic. But father made her compromise, so they settled with the more boring English name of Alistair."

"Celtic, Anglo-Saxon . . . whatever it may be, you'll still escape the dust and heat of the sites in southern India and central Turkey."

"Nah!" Alistair said as he sat down and swivelled in his chair to face Omar. He rocked back and held his hands behind his head, unself-consciously exposing the wet circles of his arm pits. "I'm in my dream job down there. I always knew what it would be like doing research on Apostle Thomas and the subsequent Syriac churches, both Antiochian and Chaldean. I knew from the start there would be no getting around spending time in the hot sun. Besides, it's a nice change from working in the cold and damp of northern England."

Alistair looked at Omar's briefcase. "So, what do you have in there?"

"Let me show you," Omar said with a grin as he unlatched the briefcase. "Let's get started with this." Omar handed Alistair an oval-shaped rod of steel with curled ends that didn't quite meet. It was designed to fit around the four fingers of a grown man's hands.

"Ah, yes," said Alistair thoughtfully. "Looks like your classic voyageur's fire steel. I've often thought that I would never make it in the wild if my life ever depended on one of these things." Alistair brought the fire steel up close to his face, lifted his spectacles and squinted at it. "Hmm, I've never seen inscribed lettering on one of these before, though. Looks like a T, an R . . . possibly an O . . . and . . . I can't quite make out the fourth letter. Another T perhaps?"

Alistair swiveled his chair back to face his desk and reached for his round magnifying lamp. In one motion he pulled the lamp toward himself and turned it on. "Yes . . . the third letter is an O. And it looks like the fourth letter is another T. The metal is too worn down to make out the others."

Alistair swiveled back to Omar and handed him back the fire steel. Omar laid it back in his briefcase and took out a second item. Alistair accepted the stone and turned it in his hands. "I'm no geologist, but this looks like a crystal of quartz . . . calcite perhaps? Oh! Wait! This is a navigational sun crystal used by the Vikings, isn't it?" The object looked like an ice cube except that it was rhomboidal, the angle between every face being slightly askew.

"I believe it is," said Omar.

"It's not authentic, is it?" Alistair held up the sun crystal to the light of the window and studied the black dot on one face.

"Oh, I would guess that it is," Omar said.

"Well, it's certainly not new. It's weathered, and the black dot's faded somewhat. Tell me again about the person who provided these items?"

"That recluse I wrote you about in my e-mail."

"Oh, yeah, that rings a bell," Alistair said as he continued to rotate the sun crystal in his hands as if it was a Rubik's Cube.

"He lives in the wilderness just on the Canadian side of the border between Minnesota and Ontario."

"How did he get hold of artifacts like this, especially the sun crystal?" Alistair held the crystal close to his face, glasses lifted, and once again pursed his brow, creating the perfect examining squint of a curious professor. Then he mumbled under his breath: "Hmm, it'd be fun to try this thing out."

"I don't know how he got it," Omar said as he reached inside his briefcase to retrieve the last item, the tracing of the lead seal. "In fact, there's not much that I do know about this individual. If you recall my e-mails, everything I do know is third-hand information from those graduate students, Shukriyah's friends back in the States. I do know that the name of this individual is Cedric Two-hearts. He's a native American Indian—an Ojibwe, to be specific—with a little bit of Scandinavian blood mixed in."

Omar held out the tracing of the lead seal to Alistair.

"And this is the last item," Omar said. "Look at the 'P & C' on top of the shield design. I was told that it stands for Percy and Campbell."

Alistair traded the crystal for the tracing. He hadn't looked at it for even two seconds when he opened his eyes wide and dropped his jaw.

"Good Lord!" Alistair said as he leaned forward in his chair without taking his eyes off the tracing. Then he looked up at Omar. "You say this fellow, this . . . this Two-hearts . . . he has the *actual* lead seal?"

"Yes, that's right. Why? What is it?"

"Omar, the P and C—I have no doubt that stands for Percy and Campbell. But this is not a tracing of one of their ordinary lead seals used on bales of furs or trade goods. This looks like the kind of seal that would have been custom made for a special, maybe one-time, delivery."

"How can you tell?"

"Lead seals from the fur trade era usually had just the company's name or initials. Simple was usually better. Take the packing firms that were here in Britain, for instance. Lead seals on their baled goods would simply have basic lettering like . . . oh, 'Isaac Whieldon—London,' for a classic example. Don't get me wrong. Some seals from those days were indeed fancy, like the official seal for the North West Company. But the standard seal used by Percy and Campbell was definitely not elaborate. Certainly not like this tracing."

"I didn't know you had such extensive knowledge of the American fur trade."

Alistair smiled. "Oh, I'm somewhat of an American history buff, all right. But my knowledge has more to do with northern European involvement with American history. In the case of the fur trade, I'm interested in the how the Scottish and Northumbrian clans were involved. That history—in fact, with both the Percys and the Campbells—goes back almost a thousand years.

"You see, the Percys had been a power in northern England ever since 1309 when Henry Percy acquired Alnwick Castle. That's just north of here, almost at Lindisfarne. The Percys have been protectors of the orthodox Christian faith for centuries . . . and they've paid dearly for it, too. Thomas Percy, the seventh earl of Northumberland, was beheaded by Queen Elizabeth I for supporting Mary Queen of Scots and Roman Catholicism in the Northern Rebellion of 1569."

"Oh, my," said Omar. "I had no idea."

"The hero of the Percy family is King Oswald, the great sponsor of Northumbrian Christianity in the early 600s. The family's patron saint is St. Cuthbert . . . yes, Cuthbert. He was a prior and then the bishop of the Lindisfarne Monastery in the late 600s. In fact, Oswald's head is in Cuthbert's coffin, which is entombed at Durham Cathedral to the south of here.

"And, speaking of things in Cuthbert's coffin . . . here, look at this," Alistair continued as he pointed to the center of the tracing. "Notice the cross with equilength, flared legs. Although some call it a Templar cross, it's correctly called a Greek cross, a *crux quadrata*. It's a religious symbol commonly used by the early Scots and Scandinavians. But in this case there's a circle at the center of the Greek cross. This design was used often by the Percys and was modeled after early, Anglo-Saxon crosses. It just so happens that this is the same design of St. Cuthbert's pectoral cross, found in his coffin. That's made of gold with inlays of garnet and shell, and it's . . . priceless."

"On the tracing," Omar commented, sounding excited, "I see that the Greek cross is superimposed in the center of this larger shape." Omar traced his index finger traced around the shield shape that was divided into eight pie-shaped wedges, with every other wedge shaded in. "What's the significance of this design?"

"It's an escutcheon. It's the coat of arms for the Scottish clan of Campbell. The Campbells were the northern equivalent of the Spanish and Portugese explorers. They even teamed up with the Vikings on their expeditions. In fact, the Campbell coat-of-arms has been found in Greenland at the western settlement of Nipaatsoq."

"Really?" Omar said.

Alistair bobbed his head. "After they made their discoveries, the Campbells needed funding in order to exploit the new lands. For that aspect of their ventures, they relied on the financial backing of the wealthy Percys. It's been a long and successful partnership.

"By the late 1700s, with the fur trade really starting to heat up in North America, the Percy and Campbell Fur Trading Company was born. Essentially the business was run by the Campbells. The Percys, as the original financial backers, simply took a percentage of the profits."

"Alistair, you said this tracing is made from a one-of-a-kind seal used on a special delivery. Would this have come from North America or England?"

"Oh, most certainly from here."

"What sort of special delivery would have been sent by a fur trade company *into* the heart of the North American wilderness? And why?"

Alistair looked up. "I have no idea. The only way to find out for sure is to . . . maybe research the Percy-family archives. But it would take a determined and patient researcher to gain the family's trust. They're a pretty secretive, tight-knit clan to this day, and they are not about to grant just anybody access to their historical records. I do know this: for the Percys to have put their mark on a special seal as depicted in this tracing, there was either something of value that they were after or some sort of threat to their interests. It's possible that the special delivery, whatever it may have been, was to take care of the situation."

"Can you even make a guess what that may be?" asked Omar.

For a moment, Alistair was thoughtful. "Well, there may have been a hint in one of your e-mails. One of these graduate students you mentioned . . . apparently one is a young archaeologist intending to recover missing freight lost by the Percy and Campbell firm?"

"That's correct."

"Maybe the special delivery was intended to buy back the missing freight. Or perhaps there was a lot of missing freight that added up over each season and they intended to re-acquire it all at once."

"Hmm," said Omar. "As I understand it, the company's voyageurs had an accident. One load in particular got lost when a canoe tipped over in a river along the Minnesota-Ontario border. Apparently the cargo was valuable, it was never recovered, and today no one even knows where it was lost because the names of the lakes and rivers have changed. Hell's Gate Rapids was a specific location back in the fur trade days, but that name was never used on any map. This archaeologist, however, believes he has figured out where it is."

"I must say, that sounds exciting," Alistair said. "I wonder if any of my former colleagues here at the university have heard about the recovery effort. I imagine they would be interested."

"Unfortunately, Alistair, there has been a change in plans with the recovery. The archaeologist has called it off."

Alistair frowned. "Really? That's too bad. What happened?"

"I'm not really sure. It was shortly after he called it off that his wife requested my help through my adopted niece, Shukriyah, and a friend of hers named Tim Malone. Mr. Malone had planned on helping with the recovery effort. But when it all fell through, the archaeologist's wife asked Malone to give me the fire steel, the sun crystal, and the tracing. Her primary question was what the special shipment could have been and why it had been shipped."

"Did the wife know that we knew each other?"

"Malone did," Omar answered. "But there was an aspect to all this that the wife knew would pique my interest. You see, Alistair, there is another wrinkle to this story. Apparently this Two-hearts fellow is very excited about the silver urn discovered over here in northern England."

"Oh? Why so?"

"Because of the Persian image of Faravahar inscribed on the urn. Two-hearts says that the same image is described on a rune stone hidden somewhere along the border between Minnesota and Ontario."

"What? No way! He's got to be joking, mistaken at very least."

"No, he's very serious. Remember when we were outside the lecture hall? I referred to a possible Persian thread of influence that may have extended to the very center of the North American continent. Well, this Two-hearts gentleman is the reason I said that. He is also the reason why the archaeologist's wife wanted you to see these artifacts, especially after she found out about your expertise in Viking history. She wanted to convince you—well, the both of us—that this Two-hearts fellow is for real. The voyageur fire steel, the Viking sun crystal, and the tracing of the fur trade seal . . . they all came from Two-hearts."

"And the husband, the archaeology graduate student . . . he has relied on Two-hearts as a source of information?"

"That's right. Alistair, there's one more thing that I need to tell you about Two-hearts' knowledge of the rune stone—apparently he calls it the Rainy Lake Rune Stone, after a large lake on the Minnesota-Ontario border. He claims that the rune stone was connected to the missing shipment that the archaeologist was intending to recover."

Alistair stared at Omar for a second or two. "Blimey!" Alistair said as he bobbed his eyebrows up and down. "Believe it or not, I think this is all starting to make sense. When was that shipment lost?"

"Late 1770s, I believe."

"Hmm," Alistair mused, "right at the time the war for American independence was being fought."

Alistair reclined in his chair, rested his elbows on the arm rests and held his fingertips together as if he was holding a ball under his chin. "Omar,

I don't know if you've looked at a map, but it does seem strange how they came up with the international border in that area."

Omar frowned. "The border? Well, you're English. The Americans fought you and your King George for their independence, yes? Do you know any of the circumstances of how the border was negotiated?"

"A little bit. Those negotiations were made in 1782 in Paris by that most colorful American revolutionary, Benjamin Franklin." Alistair smiled, and his eyes sparkled. "You wanna know something, Omar? Most of us who know anything about North American rune stones are convinced that their primary purpose was to establish a claim to the land. Maybe it would be worthwhile to do some research and find out just what old Ben Franklin and his English counterparts were really up to. Maybe they too knew a little bit about the Nordic rune stones in North America."

∞ 6 ∞

Late June, 1782
Passy, France (a wealthy hamlet on the outskirts of Paris)

JOHN JAY STRETCHED HIS ARMS out to the side, arched his back, and took a deep breath of the morning air from the brick-tiled terrace that overlooked the Seine River. A stubborn haze resisting the morning sun hung over the river. From the river bank to the terrace lay lush gardens criscrossed with walking paths and framed by bordering rows of pruned hedges.

In anticipation of being introduced by Ben Franklin to French dignitaries later in the day, Jay was already dressed in his finest gray frock coat. Below his narrow face hung a white cravat with lace fringes that matched his sleeves that flared out from under the cuffs. Covering his slender legs were leather breaches above white stockings. His pointed black shoes had large, square buckles.

"I must say, Ben, the breakfast was splendid. In fact, this is shaping up to be one splendid morning all around. Clear, warm weather. This marvelous view." Then Jay turned toward Franklin who was standing next to him alongside a sculpted stone balustrade. "But let me guess. You didn't want to come out here just to enjoy the view now, did you?"

"No . . . no I did not," Franklin said with somber resignation. Although Franklin's attire was more casual than Jay's, it had its advantage in understatement. In fact, when Franklin had first arrived in Paris, he soon realized that his appeal to Parisian high society was as a humble, peculiar, yet likable statesman from the fledgling American colonies. He had been careful to cultivate this image ever since.

"On the day before you arrived," Franklin continued, "several new employees—at least as they were described—suddenly showed up at this compound. They are undoubtedly spies for that wily foreign minister, Comte de Vergennes. If we met indoors, I would have no idea who would be eavesdropping from behind the walls and doors."

Jay pulled out his clay pipe, went to sit at a circular marble tabletop supported by a heavy fluted column. There was a folded map on top of the table. "So your friends and allies have now turned crafty, have they? Well, at least they've provided you with first-rate accommodations." Jay turned momentarily to shelter his clay pipe from the breeze while lighting it from a candle. Then he continued in a more subdued tone. "On the other hand, Ben, you certainly must have put some thought into what Adams will say about all this. I don't think he'll be very pleased."

Jay sat back in his chair and crossed his legs. He propped an elbow on the table and took a puff from his pipe as he looked over the balustrade to scan the expanse of the river valley. He sensed Franklin's uneasiness by his long silence.

Franklin leaned on the balustrade with both hands. He too looked out over the valley, but didn't appreciate it as much as Jay did.

"Ah, yes . . . Adams," Franklin said. "Our good friend, John Adams. I do admit to a concern about his arrival. And I can already imagine what he'll say: that a band of haggard, upstart revolutionaries should not be giving the wrong impression to an ally, that we should not engage in anything suggestive of royalty or extravagance." Franklin faced Jay and said frankly, "Adams should never have been appointed commissioner to these peace negotiations. His obstinacy was necessary—and infectious, I might add—when we needed to lift the oppressive yoke of King George. But now is a time for diplomacy."

Franklin took a chair opposite Jay at the table. "John, from this point on things will be quite different. It's not just one adversary anymore. Vergennes wants everybody's issues on the table at the same time. This will be like playing a high-stakes card game, each player trying to guess the strength of his opponents' hand, trying to discern the difference between a solid demand that can be backed up versus a hollow bluff."

"So true, so true," said Jay. "Just a fortnight ago when I was still in Spain, I thought our primary purpose here would be to hammer out our differences with the British on a northern and western border. Good gracious, how naive. Now that I'm here, my head is swimming with all the issues that they and everyone else want to put on the table. Spain is itching to get Britain off Gibraltar. The French want to find a way to limit our westward expansion. Empress Catherine wants the Europeans to stop raiding Russian shipping and wants to protect her North American claims on the coast of the far western sea. Um, what else? Oh yes, fishing rights off the Grand Banks."

"That sums up most of it, all right. You're a quick study, John."

"Ben, in regard to the border negotiations, you sent word that you were going to hold some preliminary meetings with the British plenipotentiary to discuss the territory west of Lake Superior."

"Yes, with Richard Oswald. We did indeed meet."

"With all due respect, Ben, I was not too pleased when I heard about that. A bit premature, wouldn't you say?" Jay asked with his pipe clenched in his teeth.

As Jay looked in the distance while squinting his eyes, Franklin couldn't tell if it was anger he saw or a reaction to the pipe smoke curling around his head.

"Perhaps," Franklin said. "But Oswald proposed the meetings, and it wouldn't have been prudent to turn him down. After all, he got our friend, Commissioner Henry Laurens, released from the Tower of London, and he does have the full trust of Lord Shelburne. With Rockingham extremely ill, it's very possible Shelburne will become the new prime minister if—Heaven forbid—Rockingham should die. If that happens, Oswald's stature and influence will only increase. And, John, there's something else about Oswald. I have this haunting suspicion that he has something up his sleeve in regard to the establishment of a border west of Lake Superior. It's as if he knows something special about that territory, has personal interests there. Although Oswald is a Scot, he doesn't even seem to have a great deal of regard for the interests of his fellow countrymen who trade for furs in that part of the continent. All this concerns me. We're at a disadvantage because we know so little about this territory west of Lake Superior. This could very well hold the most intrigue in the border negotiations. "

Franklin got up, unfolded the map and spread it out with his palms. Then he stood erect and grabbed the lapels of his frock coat. "John, for these upcoming negotiations, all we have to go by is this map . . . this map by John Mitchell."

"That's been on my mind," Jay said as he rotated his shoulders and leaned over the table to study the map. "I understand it is twenty-seven years old. Shouldn't we have something more . . . updated?"

"Precisely. That's why I've attempted to find out as much about the territory as possible. John, have you ever heard of Karl Linnaeus?"

"The famous Swedish botanist?"

"Yes. Well, I once had the good fortune of meeting a student of his by the name of Pehr Kalm. His specialty is economic plants. So I asked him what he knew about economic plants west of Lake Superior. He told me about giant pines that a grown man can't even wrap his arms around. And he told me about rice. John, did you know that the Indians harvest rice in that area?"

"You mean like they do in the Orient?"

"I would imagine. And with all the lakes in that area, rice is quite abundant. It grows so thick that the Indians harvest it in little boats that resemble the gondolas in Venice."

"All right then, we have giant pines, rice, . . . uh, furs, of course. All so very good. But with the possible exception of the furs, of what real importance is all that to the crown?"

"My question exactly. Although the Scottish members of Parliament will indeed want to protect the interests of the fur traders, their influence goes only so far and Oswald knows it. That's why I wanted to test the waters by proposing a border north of the one stated in our directive of 1779. The last time we discussed this area, I dared to throw out the possibility of a border along the forty-ninth parallel rather than the forty-fifth. Obviously, I had expected Oswald to counter with a line of latitude farther south even if it was for the simple reason of securing the most territory for the crown. But he didn't. Oswald countered immediately with a very specific and peculiar demand. He said that it was of utmost importance that the border be established south of this river here," Franklin said and pointed at a line connecting the Lake of the Woods and Lake Superior.

John Jay peered at the squiggly line Franklin indicated. "Maybe he does have the interests of the fur trade in mind and that river is the primary route that the fur traders take into the interior."

"Then why stop there? Look here," Franklin said as he moved his finger toward the right side of the map. "Why not make a counter proposal that would guarantee fur trade access from Montreal, through the upper part of Lake Huron and into the eastern end of Lake Superior? If he had the fur trade interests in mind, he would have demanded a border down to at least the forty-fifth parallel. But he didn't. He simply focused on the river between the Lake of the Woods and Lake Superior."

"Are you implying that he might be willing to sell out his Scottish brethren?"

Franklin sat back down and folded his hands over his belly. "I was starting to get that impression."

A slight breeze lifted one side of the map and started pushing it off the table.

"Maybe his motives have nothing to do with furs," Jay said as he anchored the map with his hand, re-centered it and smoothed it out. "Maybe there are precious metal deposits in the area. Gold perhaps?"

"Believe it or not, there are such rumors."

"If that be the case, we should propose a border along the river itself so we acquire access to the territory as well."

"That's probably what we should do because there are also rumors about iron and copper. I've even heard reports that the native Indians in the area use copper eating utensils."

"Gold is maybe one thing, Ben, but basic trade metals such as iron and copper are another. Even if the deposits are vast, they are too far in the wilderness to exploit."

"Yes, I'm afraid you might be right."

"By the way, what is known about these native Indians? Do they make any sort claim to the territory?"

"I really don't know. But I'm glad you asked because that reminds me of something. Let me back up once again to my friend Pehr Kalm. There was more that he had to say about this land west of Lake Superior, something other than giant pines and wild rice. John, have you ever heard of Sieur de La Verendrye?"

"Oh, yes. The explorer of the North American interior. Searched for a passage to the western sea. Didn't he establish forts that can be located on Mitchell's map?"

"He did, but I don't know if they are still in existence. At least one of the forts can likely be located on Mitchell's map. Fort St. Charles is—or was— on the shore of the Lake of the Woods. And I understand there was another called Fort St. Pierre on Le Lac Pluvieux . . . Rainy Lake."

Franklin leaned over the map and let his eyes follow his fingertip.

"My guess is that it is one these tiny lakes here," Franklin said as he tapped on the map, "where the river between the Lake of the Woods and Lake Superior widens out. Wherever it is, such forts helped establish the fur trade that the Scots now find so profitable."

Jay followed the line he traced, studying the map.

Franklin stood. "It turns out that in 1749 in Quebec, Kalm met La Verendrye. He had dinner with him and the acting governor of New France. La Verendrye told Kalm a tale so fascinating that Kalm recorded it in his journal. On one of his expeditions to the west, to where the giant pines run out and the land is covered only with prairie grass, La Verendrye found a stone tablet with carved inscriptions."

Jay's eyes met Franklin's "Inscriptions?" Jay asked. "Some sort of written characters?"

"Yes . . . in a language that he didn't recognize."

"Surely a native Indian language?"

Franklin shook his head. "Apparently not. In fact, everything we know of the Indians says that they probably don't have a written language."

"Did La Verendrye take the tablet back with him?"

"Yes. He brought it back all the way to Quebec and asked the Jesuits there to attempt to interpret the inscriptions."

Franklin took a few lazy paces back toward the balustrade and stopped. He stood with his feet apart and folded his hands behind his back. Then, without rotating his body, Franklin turned his head and looked at Jay.

"John, if I may offer a seemingly preposterous supposition, I'm not so sure that the French and French Canadian explorers like La Salle and La Verendrye were the first people of European descent to reach the North American interior."

Franklin rotated back around to face Jay squarely. Then he spoke with the conviction of someone having made a fresh discovery. "These Indians La Verendrye visited—called the Mandans, I believe—they are not all dark haired and dark skinned. Some are blue-eyed with fair hair. They live in permanent round lodges with vertical walls. They cultivate crops such as squash, pumpkin, beans, grain."

Jay concentrated on this information. "Ben, the inscriptions on the tablet—were the Jesuits ever successfully in interpreting the tablet?"

Franklin shook his head, then he slowly smiled. "Guess where the Jesuits sent the tablet for more accurate interpretation?" Franklin asked, then answered his own question when Jay's expression indicated he had absolutely no idea. "It was sent to Count Philippeaux de Maurepas, here in Paris."

"Philippeaux de Maurepas!" Jay said with surprise as he leaned over the Mitchell map, momentarily studied it, and then tapped his finger on the outline of an island in Lake Superior. "Philippeaux is the name of this large island right next to Isle Royale in Lake Superior, and Maurepas is the name of an island off the north shore of the lake. No doubt they must have been named for Maurepas."

"Not only that," Franklin added, "La Verendrye apparently had set up forts beyond the Lake of the Woods, two of which are known as Fort Maurepas I and Fort Maurepas II. And . . . guess who gave Vergennes his appointment as foreign minister?"

Franklin and Jay were silent momentarily as they stared at each other.

Jay blinked. "Well, well. The plot thickens," he said with subdued surprise. "Do you think the stone was ever successfully interpreted?"

"It's never even been *seen* since. If it did arrive here in Paris, no one is really is sure if Maurepas or his representatives even took possession of it. Maybe it got tucked away in the back of some obscure pier-side warehouse and forgotten. Maybe Maurepas and Vergennes know about the stone's existence, but think that Oswald and his fur traders have more of an idea of its whereabouts than they do."

"You don't say," Jay said wryly. "I think you are right about Oswald then. Something is indeed up his sleeve. Could it be that the stone was possibly intended to document a claim to the land? If so, perhaps Oswald knows about it and wants to get his hands on it before we do."

Franklin shrugged. "Or perhaps he doesn't know of it at all. Or he knows of it but doesn't care about it. The stone could be completely irrelevant."

"Hmm," Jay pondered. "I wish there were some way we could find out what's behind Oswald's motives. Perhaps we should entertain him and serve as much port as he's willing to consume."

Franklin smiled. "Come to think of it, maybe something like that can be arranged." Franklin paused to think for a moment as he looked toward the sky and rubbed his chin. "I've got it! It was just last week that Oswald met a very pretty young lady. It just so happened that she readily caught Oswald's attention. Furthermore, not only do I know this young lady well, but I'm quite sure Oswald doesn't know that I know her."

As Jay gave Franklin a quizzical stare, he slowly slid out the stem of his pipe across his lower lip. "Ben, are you really thinking about asking this young lady to . . . ?"

Franklin chuckled. "Well, not that! She'll no doubt be able to take care of herself. Yet, at the same time, she's clever enough to get the information we need. Yes, that's it. The more I think about it, the more I think I should ask the beautiful Genevieve Le Veillard to pay Mr. Oswald a little visit. And I'll make sure she brings along a particularly fine bottle of Bordeaux."

7

Early July, 1782
Passy, France

WITH THE GRACE OF A BALLERINA, the young Genevieve Le Veillard sprang up the steps onto the veranda of the elegant villa. Once under the veranda roof and out of the light drizzle, she threw back the hood of her black cape and went in, the green crenaline gown *swishing* at each step. Genevieve hastily made her way down the hallway that led to the villa wing occupied by the popular American.

BEN FRANKLIN WAS STANDING at a window with his hands clasped behind his back. The window was tall and narrow with the drapes held neatly to each side. Nearby was a table with two empty glasses and an in-progress chess game left in place from the previous night.

Franklin, finely dressed that morning in a brown frock coat over a beige waist coat, was mesmerized by the rhythm of the rain against the window when he heard the expected quick knocks.

Without waiting for a reply, Genevieve entered, closed the door behind her, and leaned against it with her hands behind her back holding the door handle. She suggestively pulled loose the collar string of her cape and smiled in a tight-lipped devilish grin.

Genevieve had a perfect feminine face. It was as if an artist had delicately drawn each feature just right so as not to overwhelm a fragile patina. Her hair was styled in ringlets that framed each side of her face. This girlish style was the only clue that she might be younger than what she appeared and behaved.

Franklin had turned at her knock, his hands still clasped behind his back. He gave her a glance with an expression that seemed to mirror Genevieve's flirtatious countenance.

"*Mon coeur se remplit de joie en te voyant* (My heart is overjoyed to see you)," Franklin uttered with transparent contrivance.

Genevieve's eyes flashed. "Come now. How stale. Besides, you said those exact words last time. You must strive to improve your French. Remember, if you wish to flatter a lady, make sure you vary your compliments."

Franklin stepped the rest of the way around in order to face Genevieve squarely. "Did you make any progress with Monsieur Richard Oswald?"

"Dr. Franklin," Genevieve said with drawn-out but humored condescension. "The question is an insult. Again you lose points with a lady."

She reached inside her cape and pulled out a baton-like object. She rotated two sticks around a pivot to open a pleated fan and started to walk toward Franklin with fancifully swaying hips and a mincing step. As she approached, she teasingly batted her eyelashes while fanning her face. "Who are you to underestimate me?"

As soon as she was close enough, Franklin reached for her hand and bent down to kiss it. In quick succession, Genevieve pulled her hand away, collapsed the sticks of her fan and then bopped him on the head with it.

"Franklin! How dare you! That brutish Scotsman wouldn't keep his hands off me! Ohhh, the things I do for you!"

Franklin winced so hard at the blow to his head that the bifocals he had invented slipped down to the tip of his nose. With his shoulders hunched, he brought his hand to the top of his head to try sooth his stinging skull.

Undergoing yet another dramatic mood swing—albeit not as calculated—Genevieve folded her arms and turned her pouting face away.

"Oh, Benjamin! All the way over in the carriage, I kept thinking . . . if only I could get you to do what that Scotsman wanted to do. I know you want love in your life. You once proposed marriage to Madame Helvetius. But that fool turned you down. Why don't you make a proposal to one who will accept it?"

"From me? From a man old enough to be . . . ." Franklin halted midsentence. He hesitated to acknowledge an age difference with one he found so desirable.

"Enough of that already!" Genevieve shot back as she turned on Franklin once again in anger. "I've said this before and I'll say it again. I know what I want." Then with yet another emotional shift, she looked longingly into his eyes. "Better yet . . . who I want."

Genevieve seem to resign herself as she took a deep breath and exhaled slowly. "Well, I've met with Richard Oswald as you've wished. And now you owe me, good doctor. I expect a good strong dose of time together."

"Certainly. And just think of the grand time we shall have. Once all this rain stops, we shall stroll in the vineyards, take a relaxing boat ride down the Seine. And if you're brave, someday we shall even ascend in one of those large hot-air balloons that is the talk of Paris. Yes, I promise that we shall have our time together."

Genevieve pursed her lips, almost pouting. "Those are things a man would do with his sister, and you know it. I was hoping you would take me out to a formal affair. Allow me the pride of being your escort to one of the social events you always seem to be attending. So what if people gossip? We could go to . . . uh . . . I've got it!" Genevieve said with wide eyes as she snapped her fingers. "How about the mayoral dinner party for my father in a few days?"

"My sweet dear, that could be a bit of a problem. That gala will be hosted by none other than Countess Houdetot."

"What? Again? Must she be the hostess for everything? This is intentional to keep me away from you. I just know it. That homely woman always gives me a mean look. She wants you for herself."

"I must say, you are making too much of my relationship with the countess. She has been most supportive of the American cause of independence. She sincerely wanted the colonies to prevail against the English king and has offered assistance when she can. A good woman she is."

There was an awkward pause as Genevieve sighed in frustration and hung her head. Franklin placed his curled index finger under Genevieve's chin and gently raised it so she couldn't help but look him in the eye.

"However," Franklin said gently, "what the countess can do is limited. But you, my love, are helping a great deal. Your cordial visit to Monsieur Oswald was of utmost importance."

Franklin moved his hand from her chin to stroke the spiraled curls on the side of her head. She didn't miss the opportunity and turned her head into Franklin's hand. She closed her eyes as she felt the light caress of his fingers against her cheek.

"You men and your dealings. Is this how history is made?"

"Hmm . . . I'm afraid it is, my dear," Franklin said as he became melancholy and looked away. "Through the ages the personalities will change and so will the particulars of their dealings. But the essence of political intrigue will never change. Behind each and every motive is timeless ambition and greed. Most men aren't actually conscious—truly and honestly aware—of how they are led around by their desires, blindly following them as if they had a ring through their nose."

Franklin walked off to the side and looked at the floor as he started to wax philosophic.

"These upcoming negotiations with the English delegates don't concern me as much as what our new country will do with independence once it is fully achieved. What system of government will we develop? What system can resist and thwart the very shortcomings that make up human nature. Has there ever been a system of governance that can prevent power from concentrating to any one man, to any one group, to any one family with claims to a royal bloodline? Alas . . . I confess that when it comes to the institutions of men, I am a hopeless cynic." Franklin stopped and turned to face Genevieve with a gesture of humility. "Forgive me, my dear. My mind has wandered. Before I worry about a future type of government, I should first concern myself with negotiating the peace . . . which, of course, brings me back to Monsieur Oswald."

Franklin walked back to Genevieve and placed his hands on her upper arms just below her shoulders. He gave her a sympathetic look and said, "My sincerest apologies for Oswald's behavior. I promise to make it up to you."

Genevieve paused to search Franklin's eyes for sincerity. Satisfied, she said, "All right, then. But you best sit down, my dear. You speak of motives, do you? Well, it turns out that your Scottish nemesis is quite fond of enticements—two in particular—near a giant inland lake in the heart of the American continent."

"Do you know which lake?" Franklin asked as he turned and walk toward a chair.

"Lac Superieur. He showed it to me on a map."

"He showed it to you? How . . . how did you . . . ?"

Her smile was satisfied, almost smug. "You insist on underestimating me, now don't you, Monsieur Franklin? Well, it was easy. I expressed doubt. I simply asked: 'A giant inland lake? You must be joking! Are there monsters and dragons there?'"

"Well done, I must say," Franklin said as he eased himself into his chair. "Do you know if it was the Mitchell map?"

She rolled her eyes. "Now how would I know something like that? A map is a map."

"Did he expound on his enticements?"

"Of course," she said with a flourish of her graceful arm. "And as it turns out, some of your hunches proved to be correct. But not all, however. For instance, you were right about the importance of access from Canada to the headwaters of the Miss . . . Missee . . . um, it's a long river that flows south. It was clearly shown on his map."

"The Mississippi River?"

"Yes, that's the one. Very important for king and country, says Oswald. And, you were also right about that stone with inscriptions from an old Nordic language."

"The La Verendrye Stone?"

"Yes, that's the one. The rumor you mentioned is true. The stone is stored away somewhere here in Paris. Oswald said that if there had been a way to get his hands on it, it could have been used to prove a very old Scottish claim to the land in the upper basin of the Missipp . . . the Miss . . . that same river."

"A Scottish claim?"

"That's what he said. Oswald seemed to believe that the Scots and the Norse were allies centuries ago. But pay no heed, for the La Verendrye Stone is no longer of any concern to Mr. Oswald. He has become convinced that the Count de Maurepas has hidden it for safe keeping without even knowing its significance. Instead, Oswald and his associates intend to search for a similar Nordic stone in North America near Lac Superieur. This second stone, my love, is the first of Oswald's particular—shall I say personal?—enticements in the Lac Superieur region. As with the La Verendrye stone, it too could establish the old Scottish claim to much of the territory in the heart of North America. Of course, today the claim would fall under the crown of Britain. Darling, isn't the land in the basin of the Miss . . . ."

"Mississippi."

"*Merci* . . . isn't that land called the Louisiana Territory?"

"Uh . . . yes . . . in part, at least. The . . . the land on the *west* side of the Mississippi is called the Louisiana Territory," Franklin answered, trying to fathom meanings.

Genevieve noticed the perplexed look on Franklin's face and became concerned about his naivete.

"Benjamin, I should warn you," Genevieve said, pointing at Franklin with her collapsed fan. "Oswald intends to flummox you with this one. You Americans have already agreed in principle to a western border along the length of the Mississippi. Now the only thing Oswald has to do is get you to agree to a northern border between Lac Superieur and the headwaters of the Mississippi. Once that is done, all western border issues in the mid-continent will be resolved between you and the British. Then, if the British ever get a hold of that stone near Lac Superieur . . ."

"Excuse me, my dear. Does this stone have a name?"

"Oswald called it the Rainy Lake Rune Stone."

"Rainy Lake? Isn't that a small lake to the northwest of Lake Superior!"

"Oswald indicated its location on that map he showed me. And if he and his associates ever get a hold of *that* stone, they alone might be able to put forth a legitimate claim to the northern reaches of the Louisiana Territory. And according to Mr. Oswald, the Americans would have no right to a share in such a claim once the western borders had been settled upon. In fact, the stone might nullify any border agreement you make here in Paris, as they would clearly have a pre-existing claim."

"Hmm . . . interesting . . . all so interesting," said Franklin thoughtfully. "I have a hunch why Oswald has given up on searching for the La Verendrye Stone here in Paris. France ceded the Louisiana Territory to Spain about twenty years ago after the Seven Years' War and no longer has any claim to it. Therefore, I'm sure Oswald is thinking: 'Why not let a sleeping dog lie? Why not simply trust that the French will never find out about the significance of the La Verendrye Stone?' Then, as an alternative, Oswald and his associates will put all their efforts into acquiring the Rainy Lake Stone."

Franklin noticed Genevieve tapping her foot. He had interrupted her, and, of course, she had noticed. "Oh, forgive me, my darling. Please continue."

After a moment more of huff, she did continue. "A moment ago I mentioned that some of your hunches had proved to be correct. Well, now for a hunch that was not correct. You were wrong about Oswald having a disregard for the interests of the fur trade."

"Really? So, he is concerned about his fellow Scottish countrymen after all?"

"Well . . . not quite. I offer a slight correction: the fur trade as a whole is not so important. Oswald clearly has in the forefront of his mind the interests of business associates from one particular fur trading company. They are actually from the area just to the south of Scotland. Northumbria. Specifically near Lindisfarne on the coast."

"Did he mention the name of the company?"

"Percy & Campbell, Associates. They're the ones who wish to acquire the Rainy Lake Stone. They've known about it for centuries—"

"Centuries? How?"

In a rather forceful way, since he had interrupted her again, Genevieve said, "They know about a total of *three* such stones, my dear Franklin, because it seems it was the Campbell clan who had once explored North America with the Norse."

Surprise registered on Franklin's face. Then he smiled and said, "This is all very excellent, my love. You do seem to have a knack for this kind of intrigue. And what you discovered . . . my goodness, how astonishing. It sounds like Oswald won't be negotiating strictly for the interests of the crown."

"Oh, no. His goal will also be to secure everything he and the partners in that fur company want."

"Everything? There's more than the Rainy Lake Rune Stone?"

Genevieve walked over to Franklin, put two fingers to her lips and reached for the welt that had appeared on his head. Franklin pulled back.

"Oh, my dear. Is it tender?" Genevieve said in a kitten voice. "I am sorry, you know. I do regret losing my temper so."

"Quite all right. Quite all right. Now . . . do you know what is it that Oswald and that fur trading company are after?"

Genevieve leaned forward. With her open cape draping down each side, she once again touched her lips with her hand and then gently caressed Franklin's lips. As she slid her palm over his cheek, she raised her eyebrows and resumed her flirtatiousness as when she entered the room.

"Riches, my darling," she said with a flourish. "Riches are the second enticement in the Lac Superieur region."

"Riches! My goodness! Gold deposits, sil . . . ?" Franklin stuttered as he glanced down Genevieve's ample cleavage. "Um . . . silver?"

"A chest full of rubies and emeralds," Genevieve said as she kept her hand on his cheek and caressed his cheekbone with her thumb.

"Again, excellent work," Franklin said as he reached up and rotated her palm downward so he could kiss the back of her hand. "I trust that you never raised any suspicion."

"Oh, no. The Bordeaux took care of that. In fact, I found out even more about these jewels and how they will affect Oswald's negotiations. The jewels were lost about three years ago by a bunglesome company clerk and his crew. Therefore, a northern border between the two countries must be so situated as to allow the British—meaning Oswald and the Percy and Campbell company, of course—access to the area where the treasure was lost. It's a king's ransom in worth, and they are determined to retrieve it."

"Did Oswald give any hint at all as to where it was lost?"

Genevieve stood but continued her flirtatiousness.

"Franklin, Franklin, you silly man. Had I asked something like *that*, then most certainly suspicion would have been raised. As I said, he did mention a crew, and he also mentioned that they are waiting for a drought so they can search for it when the water is low. No doubt, then, it must have been lost in a river."

"Why on earth would they take a treasure like that into the wilderness?"

"What I gathered is that it was intended to purchase the Rainy Lake Stone. Apparently the native Indians have it in possession and—unlike the Count de Maurepas—have a better idea of the stone's importance."

"I see. Even a king's ransom is a pittance compared to the potential wealth the company and England could realize in that new land's resources."

"So, my love, you are hereby forewarned," Genevieve said as she tapped Franklin's nose with her index finger. "If Oswald can obtain the Rainy Lake Stone, it would not only give Percy and Campbell exclusive rights to trade for furs in the territories around Lac Superieur, it could also serve as justification to nullify any border agreement you make with the British here in Paris. The heart of North America could still end up in British hands. However, in case the stone is *not* found, then Oswald at least wants to establish the border no farther north than where they believe the treasure was lost so they still have the freedom to look for it."

Once again, Franklin pondered the stakes involved.

"And . . ." Genevieve said, suddenly abandoning her flirtatious demeanor and looking at Franklin hard. ". . . one thing more. Oswald said something very odd. He said that the Rainy Lake Stone makes reference to a Christian relic."

Franklin's brows now bunched over his nose, pushing his glasses down again. "Christian relic?"

Genevieve nodded. "Honestly. A Christian relic that dates back many centuries. Even, he indicated, before the time when the Norse made their raids on the Lindisfarne Monastery in Northumbria."

Franklin was struck dumb by this news. Genevieve looked toward the window as she thought about a sudden a revelation. "You know something, my dear Benjamin? It just dawned on me. Lindisfarne in Northumbria seems to be the connection to all of this. According to Oswald, the stone refers to a Christian relic that originates from somewhere near Lindisfarne, and he and his Percy and Campbell associates are from that part of Britain as well."

Genevieve was silent for a few seconds as she continued to watch Franklin, who was still deep in thought. Suddenly, she broke out of her trance-like state and said, "Well, there you have it, my love. Those are Oswald's enticements in the region near Lac Superieur. Besides the potential riches of the region, the Rainy Lake Rune Stone and the lost jewels are personal enticements that are quite dear to him."

"Two final questions about the lost jewels," Franklin said. "Have there been any attempts at recovery?"

"Oh, yes. But Oswald said it was a vast stretch . . . again, making me think it was a river. And to make matters worse, they've lost a life in that failed recovery effort."

"That's too bad. Whatever happened to that bunglesome clerk who lost the jewels?"

"Oh, they aren't going to let him slip away. They treat him kindly but close, so they can keep their eye on him. Deep down, Oswald said that his business associates suspect the clerk of complicity in the theft of the jewels. Oswald even had a name for the clerk. With much disgust, he made reference to: 'Duncan McKay, that conniving little rat!'"

෨ 8 ୧

Five Years Earlier

As an aristocrat, the young Duncan McKay looked the part and acted the part of an impeccable gentleman and a man of privilege. But then, what else could be expected from someone whose Scottish bloodline descended from a wealthy Highlander clan?

The advantages of his bloodline, unfortunately, would go only so far. He was a second-born son, so uncertain just how he would end up making his way in the world. But what was certain, however, was the arrogant attitude that the young McKay harbored. He felt he was as worthy an heir to the family business and high social status as was his older brother, and if it was his destiny to do so, he would prove his worth by merit. In his mind, there was one obvious place where he could go to prove it: North America. The New World. The land of boundless opportunity for anyone willing to put in a little sacrifice.

But even in starting a new venture across the ocean on another continent, McKay found having the right surname was still an asset.

McKay's father was a wise business man who had always maintained good connections with influential people. So, when McKay was ready to strike out on his own, his father was able to land him a position as a clerk with Percy & Campbell, Associates. The Percys were the financial backers of the small firm. They were from Alnwick, Northumberland, just to the southeast of Scotland near the North Sea coast. Percy and Campbell was one of the North American fur trade enterprises that would eventually merge to form the mighty Northwest Company. Mighty enough, in fact, to rival the great Hudson Bay Company.

Steering his son into the fur trade was not a random choice for the elder McKay. It was, in fact, the result of his shrewd foresight into the consequences of the American revolution.

As soon as the American colonies decided to wage war for their independence, McKay's father was certain that the governor of Quebec, Guy Carleton, would suspend licenses for the western fur trade if the rebellion wasn't put down within the first year or two. Being a loyal Tory, the governor would not want to risk any trade goods, particularly muskets and gunpowder, falling into rebel hands that may be out west. As for the likelihood of any rebels or rebel sympathizers actually being in the western territories, well, it wouldn't matter to the governor. And McKay's father knew that.

Yet, the senior McKay also knew the determination and character of the men who had a great deal invested in the lucrative fur trade. Nevertheless, in such a situation, the odds would be against them if they acted separately. It was clear to the senior McKay that the independent, licensed traders would have to form an alliance, a united front, if they wanted to successfully petition the governor to continue granting the yearly fur trade licenses. And such an alliance would have another benefit as well. Merging into a one large company would finally put a stop to the constant bickering over territorial trading claims.

So McKay's father gambled on the Americans prolonging the war, if not winning it outright. If the gamble paid off and his son was positioned on the ground floor of a merger of the disparate fur trade companies, it would only be a matter of time before his son would become a shareholder, thus securing his future.

But first, the young Duncan McKay had to learn the business of the fur trade. In fact, if some day he was going to deal with the heirs to such powerful families as the McTavishes, the McGillivrays, and the Frobishers, the inexperienced McKay would have to learn the business thoroughly from start to finish. And this meant venturing into the heart of the continent, or the *"pays d'en haut"* as the French voyageurs called it. The wilderness of rocks, trees, and water that lay to the northwest of the giant inland lake, Lac Superieur.

Indeed, venturing into the interior to learn the trade could definitely be done by any young ambitious man with a sense for adventure. The renowned Scottish explorer, Alexander MacKenzie, was fifteen years old when he joined the fur-trading enterprise of Gregory, McLeod and Company in 1779. It took him only six years to make partner. David Thompson was fourteen when he joined the Hudson Bay Company as an apprentice in 1784.

IN THE SUMMER OF 1777 Duncan McKay left Montreal and arrived at Grand Portage, the post on the northwest shore of Lake Superior used as a staging point by a variety of fur-trade enterprises.

Grand Portage occupied a very unique location within the continent's interior. From Grand Portage by water, a traveler could reach either Hudson's Bay, the Arctic Ocean, the Pacific Ocean, or the Gulf of Mexico with the longest overland portage being only twelve miles.

Although McKay wouldn't have to travel to the far-off Pacific Ocean, he would travel deep into the interior of North America. As a clerk on the fast track to becoming a proprietor for Percy and Campbell, he wouldn't be staying year-round at any one particular post the way most clerks did. He would, instead, travel for his first few seasons between Grand Portage and various company posts in the interior.

When McKay left Grand Portage for the first time that summer and went deep into the wilderness northwest of Lake Superior, he traveled with an expedition of *"hivernants,"* voyageurs who spent each winter at posts in the interior. These were sub-traders, year-round contract employees, whose main job was to transport goods into the interior to barter for furs, and then haul out the furs.

Jean-Luc Trotin, one of the high-ranking voyageurs called a gouvernoy, kept a wary eye on the young McKay. Trotin was a *"métis,"* a son of a French voyageur and an Indian mother. His narrow eyes were almost Oriental. His lower face formed a V that angled up from a pointy chin and flared out into pronounced cheekbones. Long, black stringy hair hung over his ears and seemed to accentuate a black, pencil-line mustache.

It always annoyed Trotin when young, green clerks were sent into the interior to be in charge of a seasoned brigade of voyageurs. The inexperienced clerks often felt they had to prove themselves and would refuse sound advice, the consequences of which were to force the entire brigade to take foolish risks and face unnecessary dangers.

Trotin wondered how McKay would even take to the north country. If it got to him, Trotin knew the Scotsman would be no trouble at all as he would have only one thing on his mind: looking forward to heading back east in the spring, never to return.

At first, the young McKay did indeed fear that he had made a big mistake in getting into the fur trade. The North American wilderness greeted him with hot, humid weather and swarms of mosquitoes. He felt vulnerable not sleeping in a protective shelter, especially when the first wolf howled and he heard stories—however exaggerated—of bears raiding campsites.

But nothing had prepared him for his first violent thunderstorm. When the sky started turning dark and white caps formed on the lake, the brigade paddled hard for the shore and pulled up their loaded canoes as far up the bank as they could.

First came the roar of a powerful wind. The tree tops whipped and tossed violently. McKay stayed near the canoes at first so he could experience the unchecked brunt of the tempest head on. When he looked down the shoreline into a neighboring bay, a fast-moving, slanted gray wall approached as if it were a closing stage curtain. A voyageur tapped McKay on the shoulder and signaled with his thumb in the direction of the woods. McKay wisely followed.

Everyone huddled under the trees and shrubs for protection. But it wasn't enough. When the gray wall hit, the driving, horizontal rain lashed them, and stinging pellets of hail drove through the tree branches, forcing them to cover their heads with their arms. Then for a split second, an orange bright glow lit up the woods just a short distance away. Almost simultaneous was a deafening concussive explosion, like cannon fire, that made McKay jump, then cringe. McKay had never experienced anything like this in Scotland.

Over time McKay began to realize that the north country offered more than its temperamental side. In the long run, its mystique and harmony eventually worked its spell. The beauty of the landscape seemed to surpass even that of the heather-shrouded hills back home in Scotland. On clear days, the northern lakes would turn to the same vibrant blue as the sky. At the horizon where water met sky was a dark-green band of spruce and balsam. When the sun was low, cedar trees with their curving trunks growing near the water's edge would reflect perfectly in a mirror of calm water. Towering over the forest canopy were the contorted limbs of majestic white pines that yielded in the direction of the prevailing wind, creating a horizontal drift of branches. McKay often spotted majestic eagles perched in those twisted limbs.

McKay had no idea how many lakes were in the north country, but there seemed to be thousands, each filled with pristine water and contained within rugged granite outcrops. And thanks to these outcrops, good campsites were plentiful. They looked for peninsulas where a cross wind kept the bugs away. But an ideal campsite was often a bedrock plateau with enough soil to support a stand of red pines and clear of underbrush. The first time McKay walked into one of these stands, he was immersed in color as the sun was setting over the lake behind him. The scaly reddish bark of the massive pines protruding from a floor of orange needles fluoresced in the evening sunlight. As he turned and looked between the silhouetted tree trunks, the lake sparkled as if a million diamonds graced its surface.

More than anything else, the call of the loon really put McKay in the grip of the north country's spell. The first time he heard a loon call pierce the silence one dark and still night, he jumped up in a panic and stumbled his way through the darkness to reach the shoreline. McKay stood there for a minute or two, but there was only silence. From the east-facing shoreline, he looked out over the lake, staring into a very faint twilight of identical tone in both the sky and in the water.

"It is only a duck," a heavily accented, baritone voice said from behind.

A surprised McKay looked back and tried to stare into the shadows, but he couldn't see anything. Then a dark shape moved and started coming toward him. At first McKay could only make out the black outline of a man's head and upper torso. A tiny point of light in front of the head appeared, got brighter, and disappeared. Finally at close range, McKay could see who it was. It was Jean-Luc Trotin smoking his pipe.

Trotin must have been up awhile since he was dressed for the cool night air. He wore a Phrygian cap and a long hide coat. The coat had a collar and epaulets embroidered with Ojibwe Indian designs. Beaded fringes dangled from the shoulders and forearms.

Trotin came to stand near McKay, removed the pipe from his mouth, and continued to speak in a softer voice. "It is a black-headed duck called a loon."

"An astonishing sound, I must say," McKay said. "When I first heard it, I tried to make sense of what I was hearing. I even wondered if it could be you playing your . . . your . . ."

"Flute á bec?"

"Yes. And I've heard you play it at night out on the water. But this . . . this wail was quite different and seemed to be quite far away."

The signature call of the north country repeated from across the lake. This time McKay relaxed yet remained mesmerized as he listened. As the drawn-out wail echoed over the water and faded into the surrounding wilderness, McKay suddenly felt insignificant amongst all that was in the vast universe.

"So . . . that's a black-headed water bird called a loon. What else do you know about this loon?"

"Well, it has a white necklace and a speckled back," Jean-Luc said, "and it can swim under water. In fact, there's a legend that says that the loon's necklace came from an old, blind Indian chief," Jean-Luc said. "After the loon restored his sight by bringing him along on a deep dive, the chief threw a necklace of jewels around the loon's neck to express his gratitude. When the jewels fell from the necklace, they spilled across the loon's back where they remain to this day on every loon."

McKay and Jean-Luc stood in silence for a moment, spellbound by the peaceful night.

"That was the legend as I heard it as a child. But some have now added to it," Jean-Luc continued. "There are some who now say that the loons are multiplying the jewels. One day the jewels will be gathered up and given to a brave warrior. He will hide the jewels somewhere on the shore of one of these lakes. Then there will be a period of great suffering. But after that, when the people are no longer sick or hungry or in great need, a future great chief will find the jewels and distribute them among his people. On that day his people can finally accept the jewels because they no longer desire them. Then they will be happy forever. Of course, it remains to be seen if that legend will come true."

Once again the two men looked out on the darkening lake, but the tranquility of the evening was about to be spoiled.

"Mr. Trotin," McKay said, agitated. "I'm glad we have this moment alone because there's something I've been wanting to discuss with you. Yesterday morning when the wind was strong, I announced that we should start out, but you countered my command and advised that we stay put."

"Well, yes. The wind was bad enough where we were. On the open lake, we would have been hit hard by high waves as soon as we rounded Lone Tree Point. Even later on when the wind died down and we finally did get going, you certainly must have noticed the size of—"

"Yes! Yes! The waves were big even then! You were right! But that's not the point, Mr. Trotin. The point is that you were so bold as to give me your advice in front of all the men and risk humiliating me."

Trotin was dumfounded by McKay. "Sir, I'm sure the men thought nothing—"

"I don't care to hear any speculation as to what the men did or did not think, Mr. Trotin. The next time you have any expert advice you wish to share, you shall do so in private. I am a reasonable man. Simply ask to see me privately whenever you have matters of importance to discuss, and I will listen cordially. Understood?"

Trotin didn't answer right away. He didn't like being ambushed by the sudden reprimand.

"All right, then," Jean-Luc finally said in a quiet yet assertive voice. "As you wish . . . in private it shall be."

As McKay turned and started to make his way back through the darkness, Jean-Luc took a deep breath, closed his eyes, and exhaled slowly.

"Oh! And one more thing, Mr. Trotin."

Jean-Luc turned to look into the shadows but could only see a partial outline of McKay's silhouette.

"I don't take kindly to men who sneak up and startle me as you did just a bit ago. I trust that too will be understood, Mr. Trotin."

McKay's silhouette turned and moved on so Jean-Luc didn't bother with a reply.

After that exchange, Jean-Luc was in no mood to turn in. Instead he sat down on a large rock. In fact, whenever the night was quiet and still, he often would stay up late into the night and listen to the nocturnal sounds of the forest. But this night he needed a sign. He prayed and hoped for a special sign of what the future would bring.

Miraculously, Trotin received a response. As he was looking down into the calm, mirror-like water of the lake, studying the reflection of the stars that comprise "the Moose" constellation, more commonly known as Pegasus, he suddenly noticed the reflection of a streak of light shoot across the sky. In the time it took him to look up, the shooting star had disappeared. But in looking up at the sky, he noticed another light off to his left. He stood up and shifted his head so he could look through the trees.

The northern lights were starting to grow, a rare sight to see in the summer. Fluorescent lime-green spears started shooting up in alternating locations on the northern horizon. The spears slowly extended upward and stretched into long bands that eventually reached high above the treeline. The bands oscillated back and forth like wave-tossed rushes in the shallows of a lake. As some bands faded, others increased in intensity, so much so that their color turned red.

Long ago as a boy, Jean-Luc had learned some aspects about native Indian astrology from his mother. One of the things she had told him was that a shooting star foretold sickness. But she also said that the northern lights dancing in the sky was a good omen. The spirits were pleased, and good fortune was to be expected.

On this evening, Jean-Luc had seen both. The first thought that came to his mind was that maybe . . . just maybe . . . the days of catering to the demands of mean-spirited fur-trade clerks like Duncan McKay would soon be over.

But then Jean-Luc had a more sobering premonition when he thought about the legend that he had just told McKay. What if the loons were done multiplying the jewels and Jean-Luc was that brave warrior who would run off to hide the jewels? If that were so, what suffering were his people about to endure before good fortune could be expected?

9

AS SOON AS THE LAKES IN THE NORTHWESTERN interior lost their ice in the spring of 1778, Duncan McKay and his brigade of *hivernants*, the Percy and Campbell voyageurs in the North American interior, embarked on their long journey back to Grand Portage, the mid-continent staging post on the shore of Lake Superior. McKay had made it through his first winter at an interior trading post and was now returning with a cargo of furs to be exchanged at Grand Portage for supplies and trading items.

The first winter had not exactly been a baptism by fire so much as it had been an internment in snow, ice, and loneliness. Next year, McKay vowed, he would be more emotionally ready to endure the bitter cold, the isolation, and the boredom due to long hours of darkness.

But for now the sun was high, the air was warm, and they were on the move toward the southeast. As McKay sat in his privileged position in the middle of a *canot du nord*, the twenty-four-foot voyageur canoe used in the interior, he enjoyed the continuous scenery of the rugged wilderness shoreline. It felt good to hear once again the hypnotic sound of water lapping the canoe hull as the vessel cruised through the crisp, cold sky-blue water. He watched tiny whirlpools pass by each time the voyageur in front of him lifted his paddle out of the water to begin another stroke.

By mid-summer, the Percy and Campbell brigade and those of other fur trade enterprises started arriving at Fort Charlotte near Lake Superior. The fort was named after the wife of Britain's King George III and was situated on the Pigeon River. Although the river flowed into Lake Superior, its gradient steepened downstream from the fort, a large number of rapids and waterfalls making it unnavigable. Therefore, Fort Charlotte was the trail head of the true grand portage, "the great carrying place" after which the Lake Superior voyageur meeting place was named. The grand portage was an eight and one-half mile long trail—or about sixteen "poses" as measured by the voyageurs—that descended into the Lake Superior basin to the namesake post on the shore. The grand portage was where the voyageurs, paddlers for much of the time, became human mules. And it wasn't just an issue of the portage length.

Unlike all other portages encountered by the voyageurs in the northwest, loads had to be carried over the grand portage in both directions. In the course of about a week, voyageurs had to trudge both down and up the trail with at least a couple loaded packs held in place on their backs by tump lines strapped across their foreheads. Bales of fur would be carried down the trail to the Grand Portage post, and supplies and trade items for the following winter would get carried back up the trail to Fort Charlotte. The one saving grace was that the canoes didn't have to be portaged and were left at Fort Charlotte.

At about the same time in the spring that the *hivernants* had left their winter posts in the northwest, their counterpart voyageurs from the east, the *"mangeurs de lard"*—or pork eaters—had left Montreal and headed west. Their mission was to transport supplies and trading items to Grand Portage. Since their journey required them to traverse Lake Huron and Lake Superior, they paddled thirty-six-foot *canots des maîtres*, more sea-worthy canoes that could withstand the huge waves of the two great lakes.

The *hivernants* regarded the *mangeurs de lard* as less worthy. After all, they were only seasonal voyageurs who had the luxury of paddling long distances of open water for days on end. The year-round *hivernants*, on the other hand, had to contend with back-breaking portages practically every day.

The *mangeurs de lard* arrived at the Grand Portage post at about the same time as the *hivernants*. This mid-summer annual meeting of the two groups of voyageurs was called the "Rendezvous," and it symbolized what Grand Portage had become by the 1770s. It was the gateway to the west.

Once all the bales of fur, supplies, and trading items were weighed, tallied by company clerks and proprietors, and then portaged, the two groups of voyageurs would throw a party to celebrate their annual Rendezvous.

And what a party it was.

The celebration of the Rendezvous actually got going when the voyageurs first started arriving at the Grand Portage post in mid-summer. With various fur-trade enterprises constantly coming and going over the peak of the mid-summer, there always seemed to be at least one party going on somewhere on the grounds of the post at all times.

But for those voyageurs who had finished portaging their goods and were set to depart, they were the ones who had cause to celebrate with the most exuberance. There were games and contests, feasting, the sound of bagpipes, dancing to fiddle and flute music with Indian wives and daughters of fort employees. And rum, of course. There was always lots of rum consumed by the voyageurs at the great Rendezvous.

Except for one man, that is.

Certainly Jean-Luc Trotin liked his rum. But during most evenings of the Rendezvous, after he had played two or three dance tunes on his flute á bec, Trotin preferred to sit back and watch the rival pork eaters drink up first. And when he noticed that they had drank plenty, he would insult the nearest pork eater his size or larger. A fight would be inevitable. The routine was always the same: a little pushing and shoving at first, and then before you knew it, Trotin and his opponent would be wrestling in the dirt.

Whether he won or lost didn't matter. Trotin was only interested in "hustling" his opponent. The Rendezvous was the one time in the year when a voyageur would be carrying coins and other valuables, and Trotin was an expert pick pocket. He found that he could supplement his income nicely, earning himself the nickname of Hustler amongst his comrades.

Late in the evening—or, more accurately—very early the next morning when Trotin noticed the eastern horizon begin to lighten and the stars starting to fade, he would quit "hussling" and finally imbibe whatever rum was left.

More often than not, he had to nurse a few bruises. If he could, he would slip away in the dark and sneak into the company's warehouse on the outside of the west-side stockade. Sometimes there were stacks of blankets destined for the interior. There he was assured undisturbed sleep on a makeshift bed for at least a couple hours.

By first light, when the rum was all gone and the music had died down, all the other voyageurs would either be too tired or too drunk to dance or fight anymore. Only scattered laughter around dying campfires punctuated the quiet, as the more seasoned voyageurs would spin their tall tales of the North. By sunup, all festivities would be over, and the fort grounds would be quiet except for those voyageurs starting to rise to take care of another day of fur-trade business.

And so it was with the Rendezvous of 1778. It would end as it had started—all too quickly. Soon the two groups of voyageurs would go their separate ways: the *hivernants* back into the northwestern interior, and the *mangeurs de lard* would return to Montreal with a cargo of furs ultimately bound for Europe.

In about three months, Duncan McKay would be settling in at an interior trading post for his second winter in the northwest. But before McKay and his *hivernants* departed from the Grand Portage post, two shareholders with Percy and Campbell asked Duncan McKay to meet privately. They wanted to discuss a special assignment for him. McKay was to carry out their new orders in the northwestern interior.

10

DUNCAN MCKAY WAS FEELING PROUD after his private meeting with the two Percy and Campbell shareholders. McKay had been in the fur trade for only about a year, yet the two shareholders certainly must have taken a liking to him, McKay thought. Otherwise they never would have trusted him with a mission so important.

The two company officials had told McKay that they had chosen him and his brigade of voyageurs to transport a very special trade good into the interior. It was a wooden chest. Its contents were to be kept secret, and, therefore, the chest would only be vaguely referenced in the official bill of lading. The officials had made it very clear to McKay that he was never to discuss the contents with his voyageurs.

McKay regarded the special assignment as his big opportunity to prove his worth. Indeed, the shareholders had taken notice of McKay's capabilities, but they also knew it was risky to put such huge trust in an inexperienced clerk. In fact, they never would have done so had it not been for two ill-timed events that threatened a long-awaited plan.

The wooden chest had been accompanied all the way from England by a special Percy and Campbell agent. He had been assigned to guard the chest during its entire transit. Once he arrived at the Grand Portage Rendezvous, the agent was to meet a company officer from the interior accompanied by a brigade of voyageurs. The officer, commonly referred to as a wintering partner, would then escort the agent and the wooden chest into the interior. Finally, the wintering partner would make the necessary arrangements to carry out the transaction during the following fall or winter.

But the wintering partner had had an accident just before he was to leave his post on the Rainy River to travel to Grand Portage. In no condition to try to make it to the Rendezvous, his injuries did require that he be evacuated at some point before the following winter.

If that wasn't bad enough, a second unfortunate event occurred when the company agent traveling with the chest became extremely ill while at Grand Portage. He, too, was in no condition to travel.

That's when the two shareholders at Grand Portage devised the alternate plan of having McKay and his brigade transport the wooden chest to the Rainy River post. Once there, McKay was to meet with the injured wintering partner before he was evacuated. The wintering partner would inform McKay who he was to meet in order to make the final plans for the transaction. The wintering partner's Indian interpreter would assist McKay.

It had become quite apparent to McKay as to the extent of his responsibility. He was the one on whom the shareholders were ultimately relying to carry out the business transaction.

Before McKay departed from Grand Portage, he asked the two shareholders about the item for which he would be exchanging the chest. All they would tell him was that the wintering partner at the Rainy River post would tell him in due time. McKay's first order of business was to get the chest safely to that wilderness post. As the shareholders knew that the chest was going to draw the attention of the voyageurs, this would be no mean feat.

As always, McKay's voyageurs found that the miserable side-effects of the Rendezvous quickly wore off once the trudging of the Pigeon River portage commenced in earnest. When they were ready to make their final carry, they discovered that the rumors were true regarding a peculiar wooden chest with mysterious contents. It had been placed among the goods at the beginning of the portage trail.

The style of the chest itself only added to the mystery of its contents. The slightly convex lid was hinged in the back and secured by two wide leather straps with buckles on the front. A metal front latch on the lid was sealed with a special lead disk similar to that used on bales of fur.

The lead seal was imprinted with the company's initials, "P & C," above a shield-shaped figure. Like a pie, the shield was divided into eight sectors with every other sector filled in with etching. At the center of the shield was a Greek cross.

As the men began to portage the wooden chest, it soon became obvious that it was a heavy and awkward load. That also caused curiosity.

Unlike the typical packs designed for comfortable carrying, the wooden chest had sharp edges and corners, and its flat, rough-hewn surfaces produced slivers sharp enough to pierce through clothing. When successive voyageurs attached their tump lines to the chest, they found that they could carry the chest only so far before the weight of it caused too much pain. Before long, the men complained incessantly about the chest.

But the grand portage finally ended, and the men could rest at Fort Charlotte. The fort provided a welcome respite to the weary voyageurs after such grueling work. For one last time before venturing far into the interior, the men could revitalize their bodies with fresh vegetables and pork, delicacies that they would not see for a long, long time.

Plus, arriving at Fort Charlotte meant that the wooden chest could finally be placed in a canoe. The next portage, of course, was not that far away. Nonetheless, with the grand portage behind them and once again being on the water doing what they love best—paddling at a cruising rate of forty strokes per minute—the voyageurs' mood improved immensely.

After Fort Charlotte, the next important landmark for the voyageurs was the *"hauteur de terre,"* the height of land. It could be reached within a couple days if the weather held and there were no head winds to fight. The voyageurs always looked forward to portaging over the height of land and setting up camp on North Lake, the beginning of waters that flowed to the west and north. This locale provided the psychological beginning of the great North American interior. To emphasize that point to anyone crossing over the height of land for the first time, everyone—*bourgeois* included—was obliged to partake in a special rite of initiation. Initiates would kneel by the water and be showered from a drenched cedar bough dipped in the water. Then they would swear in French to keep two promises: never to let a new-comer cross over the height of land without performing the same initiation, and never to kiss a voyageur's wife without her permission. Once an initiation was over, a musket shot was fired, and everyone would shake the initiate's hand and break out the rum to celebrate.

McKay had been initiated the year before and, therefore, he already could proudly boast, *"Je suis un homme du nord."* He was already a true northman. As there were no newcomers on this year's expedition, there was no need to perform the ceremony. But that didn't stop the voyageurs from breaking out the rum anyway. Crossing the height of land was always a reason to celebrate. Unlike the Rendezvous, it was a time when class distinctions were ignored, and everyone joined in the celebration, even the *bourgeois* . . . even McKay.

But on this trip, the voyageurs had an ulterior motive for the celebration. The voyageurs were especially eager to reach the height of land because of that damn wooden chest. They had carried it through all sixteen poses of mosquito-ridden woods back on the grand portage. At this particular height-of-land celebration, the voyageurs wanted McKay to have more than his share of rum. They wanted him to talk. They wanted to find out just what was in the wooden chest. It was McKay's most precious, most guarded piece of cargo . . . and his voyageurs had sensed it.

Sure enough, on the morning after the celebration on North Lake, McKay woke up not only feeling terrible but also a little worried about what he might have said the night before. He couldn't recall too much of the evening after he had gotten drunk, but he did recall just enough to know that he had indeed discussed the wooden chest.

ONE AFTERNOON ABOUT A WEEK after they had left North Lake, the brigade decided to make camp early because of a particularly tough series of portages. It seemed that whenever they were on a portage, they were either trudging through muddy swamps, fighting their way over windfalls across the trail, or slipping on steep muddy trails.

But that day there was another incentive to quit a little early. They were approaching an area burned by a forest fire a couple years past, and those areas were prime for blueberries. Further, it was early August, right when ripening blueberries should be at their peak.

McKay remembered the blueberry patch from the previous year. When the brigade stopped near the burned area, the first thing he did was to grab a pail and drape a towel over his head in an attempt to deter the deer flies. As the voyageurs unloaded gear and started to set up camp, McKay headed out alone for the blueberry patch.

McKay didn't get far when he remembered that the blacksmith back at Grand Portage had forged a blueberry picker and had asked the brigade to try it out. The box-shaped metal container was little bigger than an ale mug. It had closely spaced tines meant for scooping the berries off the low-lying vines. McKay decided to retrieve it so he could give it a try.

When McKay reached the campsite, he saw something that stopped him dead in his tracks. He discovered Jean-Luc Trotin rummaging through his personal gear.

"What are you doing?" McKay shouted from a distance away. He dropped the pail and strode across the camp to the man.

Trotin slowly stood up and watched in embarrassed anguish as McKay closed on him. McKay stopped and looked closely at his gear spread out on the ground. As far as he could tell, it appeared to be pretty much as had he left it. He squatted down to study the wooden chest, but he didn't notice any sign that it had been tampered with. Then McKay stood and faced Trotin with his feet apart and tightly clutching the ends of the towel still wrapped around the back of his neck.

"Just what in Heaven's name are you trying to steal, Mr. Trotin?"

"Medicine, sir. It's for Sebastian Bouvette. He's quite ill. I . . . I assume you know that, don't you sir?"

"Of course, I know that! He always seems to be ill! If you really wanted my medicine, you could have asked for it, couldn't you?" McKay paused a second just for effect and stared coldly at Jean-Luc. "Or, was it really something else that interested you? The chest perhaps?"

"No, sir. Honest. I'm not interested in the chest. I didn't ask you for medicine because Sebastian said that he had asked you earlier. He said you refused to give it to him."

"Of course, I turned him down. If I kept giving him all my medicine, I'd run out in no time. It has to last the winter."

"He's gotten worse."

"Has he now? Well, maybe I shall go see him and reconsider. But first things first. You were about to steal from me, weren't you?"

"But I didn't, sir."

"But that was certainly your intent. In going through my packs . . . well, if not theft, you're at least guilty of trespassing now, aren't you?"

"Sir, I know I used poor judgment. But I'm fearful about Sebastian's condition. He needs help."

McKay continued staring coldly at Jean-Luc, trying to detect any hint of guilt. But Jean-Luc held eye contact, finally convincing McKay that it was indeed only the medicine that he was after.

McKay's stern gaze suddenly turned worrisome. "He doesn't have the pox, does he?"

"No sir," Trotin said reassuredly.

McKay finally relaxed, kneeled down and threw open the flap on one of his packs. He lectured McKay while searching for the medicine. "All right then, Mr. Trotin. We shall go see Mr. Bouvette and bring the medicine. But as for you, this matter must be dealt with. I should send you back to Grand Portage, you know? But, as I once told you, I'm a reasonable man. I recognize that this is a first offense. Being as Mr. Bouvette's illness is a circumstance to be considered, I don't feel it necessary to have word of your transgression sent back to Grand Portage by currier."

When McKay found the medicine, he pulled the top flap back over his pack and then looked up at Jean-Luc with another cold stare.

"However," McKay said as he stood up, "upon our return next year to Grand Portage, I do intend to inform the company's wintering partner about your trespassing. Between now and then, Mr. Trotin, you will have a long time to ponder what consequences he shall render for this violation."

McKay turned in a huff and started walking in Bouvette's direction. No sooner had Jean-Luc begun to follow when McKay abruptly stopped, turned around and pointed a finger at Jean-Luc. "And one more thing, Mr. Trotin. If the company shareholder should consult with me, I shall suggest more than just a fine be rendered. I shall recommend that he take away your privilege of transporting that . . . that God awful-sounding whistle or whatever it is you carry! And that goes for Mr. Bouvette's privilege of transporting his bloody violin! Extra items such as those take up precious cargo space and require special care on portages. It's a privilege that should never have been granted in the first place!"

To have to put up with such a mean-spirited clerk was one thing for the voyageurs. But for Duncan McKay to threaten to take away their music was another. Music was sacrosanct to the voyageurs, and his threat could easily come back to haunt him. Especially now. Especially after the celebration at North Lake. The rum had done its trick on McKay, and the voyageurs knew how to hurt him.

In his drunken stupor back at North Lake, McKay had revealed that the wooden chest was full of rubies and emeralds.

11

EVENTEEN SEVENTY-NINE, THE SAME YEAR Alexander McKenzie joined Gregory, McLeod and Company and Duncan McKay had been in the fur trade nearly two full years. In the high-water months of the early summer, a more seasoned Duncan McKay was making his way out of the interior after his second winter. But McKay was not looking forward to the Rendezvous at Grand Portage. He dreaded it, in fact. Duncan McKay had failed in his mission with the wooden chest.

As hard as he had tried, he had not been able to execute the business transaction. Through his interpreter, he simply couldn't persuade the other party to accept the chest and its valuable contents. For some unexplained reason, the other party had decided to back out of the deal.

Although McKay was returning to Grand Portage with plenty of high-quality furs of otter, lynx, marten and, of course, the prized beaver, the young McKay was also coming back with the wooden chest. And he was not looking forward to the reaction of the company shareholders.

But McKay's immediate concern with the chest fiasco was the precarious predicament it would cause with his voyageurs. He had told his men that the cumbersome chest was on a one-way trip into the northwest interior. Now here they were returning with it.

To McKay's surprise, the men had taken the news quite well when they learned that once again, on every portage, they would have to wrestle with the ponderous load. Their reaction was at once a relief—and a concern. Why the nonchalant acceptance now when last year they cursed the chest relentlessly?

But for the moment, McKay was witnessing something mesmerizing. His voyageurs were standing in the middle of an ancient swamp that was now an open grassy meadow in the middle of the forest. They were singing a haunting three-tone hymn of the Lord's Prayer.

> *Notre Père qui es aux cieux!*
> *Que ton nom soit sanctifié;*
> *Que ton règne vienne;*
> *Que ta volonté soit faite . . .*

Never before had McKay's Scottish protestant ears heard his catholic voyageurs sing the Lord's Prayer. And even though he didn't understand French very well, it was absolutely spellbinding.

The hymn was sung as monks would chant in a monastery. It was a drastic change from the conventional melodies the Voyageurs sang while on the water. When paddling, they had a vast repertoire of cheerful, rhythmic songs to keep their strokes in synch during the long tedious summer days in which the sun was above the horizon in excess of twelve hours a day.

But on this morning the voyageurs were not on the water. Instead, they had to attend to a solemn occasion that called for a solemn tune. And the hymn of the Lord's Prayer was perfect for the funeral of Sebastian Bouvette.

McKay had been asked not to be immediately present at the graveyard ceremony as the voyageurs were like a family and wanted to grieve with some degree of privacy. But McKay did observe from the perimeter of tall spruce trees that provided a cathedral-like feel for the occasion. As he looked on, he noticed that the featureless, flat-gray sky set the right mood for the occasion. Furthermore, there wasn't even the slightest bit of breeze. All was quiet. It was as if the woods and the birds and animals were in mourning as well. Even the mosquitoes were at bay thanks to the cool, crisp morning air.

When it looked like Bouvette was about to be lowered into the soft black soil, the voyageurs huddled around the grave and began singing the hymn. The surrounding woods seemed to amplify an echo of the near-monotone melody—haunting and filled with an eery beauty as well.

When the ceremony ended, McKay wondered why a particular detail had been left out. There had not been the customary breaking of Bouvette's paddle. Although McKay had not seen this simple but sacred rite before, it certainly was a well-known tradition. Everybody knew that when a voyageur died, it was an established custom to break his paddle and bury it with him.

Under the circumstances, however, McKay felt too uncomfortable to approach his men and ask about this. He could only surmise that the custom was reserved for the more upstanding voyageurs, not those with the character flaws of Sebastian Bouvette.

Bouvette had been an addict. Whenever there was an allowed occasion to celebrate with rum, Bouvette always seemed to take more than his share. And sometimes McKay would discover that the rum had been broken into, but he had never quite been able to prove Bouvette had done it.

But a liking for rum was the lesser of Bouvette's afflictions. He had a consuming desire for hallucinogenic wild mushrooms and was willing to gamble with his life in trying to distinguish the poisonous ones from the ones that would give him his coveted high. Some semi-poisonous mushrooms gave Bouvette his high in small amounts, but too much would make him sick.

A voyageur's diet was risky enough with the amount of cured meats and pickled foods he consumed. Not surprisingly, ailments such as stomach ulcers and—much worse—stomach cancer were frequent maladies. With the addition of toxic mushrooms to Bouvette's diet, it was only a matter of time before he became so ill that he couldn't recover.

As a contributing member to the business of transporting furs and trade goods, Bouvette had at times been more of a burden than an asset. When he was strung out, he had trouble carrying his minimum load across portages. But even more humiliating to him and disturbing to his comrades, he couldn't effectively paddle. And in the typical seating arrangement of a loaded twenty-four-foot canoe, the loss of power was noticed.

In each canoe a highly skilled gouvernoy sat high in the stern with his long paddle. In front of him sat two, side-by-side paddlers called *milieux*. Cargo filled the middle unless it was the expedition's lead canoe and a couple of company officers happened to be along. They, of course, would sit in the middle with plenty of room to stretch their legs and under no obligation to paddle. Rounding out the rest of the crew, an *avante* sat in the bow and another pair of *milieux* sat just behind him.

Whenever Bouvette was languishing, it didn't take long for the gouvernoy to notice a side-to-side imbalance in stroking power. He would then give the command, "*Allumez*," which meant to "light up," and re-arrange his men so that one of his stronger paddlers sat on the same side as Bouvette. If the stronger paddler had to come from a different canoe, the progress of the entire expedition would come to a halt as they beached to have an early break, or a "pipe" as they called it. In that case, the voyageurs would curse Bouvette, as they knew they would have to go that much longer without being allowed to smoke their pipes.

Nevertheless, Bouvette had been well-liked by his comrades. He provided laughter around the campfire and had a seemingly endless supply of tales to spin for the mostly illiterate gang of north country bushmen. When McKay wasn't around, Bouvette would crack everybody up with animated imitations of their clean-shaven *bourgeois* and his funny-sounding Scottish brogue. Regardless of his shortcomings, the brigade would indeed miss Bouvette.

But more than anything, they would miss Bouvette's violin. Jean-Luc Trotin would miss his accompaniment the most.

With his flute á bec, Trotin often teamed up with Bouvette to serenade their fellow voyageurs with just the right tunes for the occasion at hand. At the end of a long day of paddling when the stars came out after sunset, Trotin and Bouvette—who looked so much a like that they could pass for brothers—would paddle out on the still water and play slow but beautiful melodies that echoed across the lake. An altogether different occasion was the festive annual Rendezvous when Trotin and Bouvette would whoop it up with fast-paced dance tunes.

But Trotin had long anticipated that a day would come when he would no longer have his partner with whom to play musical duets.

In fact, the previous summer when Trotin had brought Duncan McKay to see the deathly ill Bouvette at the campsite near the old forest fire burn with the blueberry patch, Trotin thought that was the end for Bouvette. Once they examined Bouvette and privately discussed his condition, they both felt that it was unlikely medicine could do any good, especially for someone whose body was so compromised by years of abuse.

The difference was that Jean-Luc Trotin wanted to administer the medicine regardless. He wanted to try anything that might save his friend. But McKay, on the other hand, made an executive decision and announced that he would conserve the remaining medicine for future medical situations that weren't so hopeless.

That was a huge mistake for McKay.

Bouvette somehow beat the odds and survived. Had McKay been willing to administer some medicine, it not only might have helped to alleviate Bouvette's suffering, but the gesture of compassion would have done wonders for boosting the morale of McKay's men. By refusing to give Bouvette any medicine at all, it only incensed his voyageurs. McKay was not well liked the way it was, but, from that moment on, all voyageurs in the brigade deeply despised him.

After Bouvette recuperated, his comrades told him about McKay's decision to withhold medicine. It didn't take long for McKay to notice the way Bouvette looked at him and knew he had found out. From then on, McKay always slept with one eye open and never got into a situation where he had to be alone with Bouvette.

But here it was, almost a year later, and Bouvette was sick once again. This time Bouvette wouldn't beat the odds. Bouvette was dying of small pox. During his final feverish night, he started to convulse, lost consciousness and died surrounded by his comrades. A funeral with full voyageur honors was in order. Duncan McKay felt some small relief that he no longer had to watch his back.

In the afternoon after the funeral, the sky was still bland and overcast as the expedition got underway. It was quiet on the water—the voyageurs were in no mood to pace their paddle strokes with lively singing. With no wind, the water was like glass. A very strange phenomenon in the mid-day.

As McKay sat in his usual position in the middle of the canoe, he thought about Bouvette's funeral. Suddenly a wolf howled somewhere deep in the forest. It was a lonely, hollow wail.

The recent events were starting to have an effect on McKay. Not only the wolf howl but the haunting hymn of the Lord's Prayer earlier in the morning, the quiet hush of the wilderness on a still day, and the rhythmic dips of paddles by a muted brigade of voyageurs in mourning. Times like these made McKay think that he could very well go mad in the north country.

ಸಿ 12 ಆ

LATE IN THE NIGHT, DUNCAN MCKAY was standing in a forest holding the valuable wooden chest. With only a crescent moon in the sky, the surrounding woods were dim. But all around McKay a warm brilliance was cast by the extraordinarily bright diamonds on four sides of the chest.

His voyageurs sure had struggled with the chest over portages. But to McKay it seemed small and light. *They would complain about a blue sky and a wind at their back*, he thought as he easily held the chest in his two hands. His gaze locked on its alluring iridescence. "It's beautiful!"

The ground was covered with short grass and scattered low shrubs. Countless tree trunks, colossal and straight, surrounded him. As the tree trunks continued up and up, they gradually grew darker and darker, eventually blending into the sky's infinite blackness.

McKay heard a distant howl. He lifted his head and listened. Another howl. Then another . . . and another. Before long it sounded like a chorus. Then, just as suddenly, the howling stopped, leaving his ears aching for sound.

McKay looked in every direction. Off in the distance he spotted movement between the trunks. A second or two later he caught another glimpse of something moving in the dark. A four-legged figure with a tail bounded from side to side as it made its way toward him. It stopped. McKay saw the dark silhouette of a head, neck, and pointed ears motionless and erect. Two points of light—no doubt its eyes—looked directly at him. The figure hunched again and bounded closer. McKay was getting scared.

He looked around and detected the movement of more dark shapes. Each one seemed to take two or three hops back and forth before stopping to look at him with glowing eyes like stars in the woods, then hop a couple more times in his direction.

McKay started running. The bounding figures broke out into a full run, chasing him. McKay ran as hard as he could. He saw a light up ahead between the tree trunks. As he neared it, he saw that it was a cabin. He broke out of the trees and looked back. Nothing. The wolves had stopped chasing him.

McKay turned to study the cabin. The windows were filled with welcoming yellow light. The roof was thatched and had a chimney at both gable ends. McKay could almost be back home in Scotland.

He walked toward the door, made of vertical wooden boards held together by upper and lower cross boards. A diagonal bracing plank extended between the cross boards.

McKay didn't bother knocking. He reached for the black, cast-iron handle, turned it downward and pushed in the door. The hinges creaked as if the door hadn't been opened in a long time.

The large main room was stark, bare, and felt oddly hollow. It wasn't so welcoming after all. Two men sat behind a table lit by a single candle. McKay recognized the men as the shareholders in the Percy and Campbell fur-trading company. A fire was crackling in the fireplaces at each end of the room. The Percy family coat of arms hung over one mantle. A flag of St. Andrew's cross—the flag of Scotland—hung above the other one.

The man on the left leaned back and folded his arms across his chest. "You failed in your mission," he said. "With that chest of jewels you're holding, we trusted you to conduct a transaction of utmost importance. But you have come back with it, Mr. McKay. And now you shall suffer the consequences."

The man on the right side got up and went to unlatch a door on the back wall of the room. A voyageur stepped out. It was Sebastian Bouvette, and he was holding a knife.

McKay turned and bolted out the front door, but he didn't get far before coming to the edge of a deep, narrow gorge. McKay heard the low rumble of a cascading river far below. He turned and saw that Bouvette had caught up with him. McKay was trapped.

Bouvette stood a distance away, his outline silhouetted by the light coming from the cabin windows and open door. Bouvette remained still with his arms at his sides, then slowly started raising the knife over his head. The shiny blade glistened.

Something distracted Bouvette and he looked to his right. He lowered the knife back down to his side. A double line of torches was approaching from out of the forest of giant trees. They were Bouvette's fellow voyageurs. The two lines of voyageurs split around Bouvette and encircled him. They raised their torches as four other voyageurs lowered a stretcher and placed it at Bouvette's feet.

Bouvette eased himself down on the stretcher and gently reclined until his head rested on the canvas. One of the four voyageurs placed a violin on top of Bouvette and then folded Bouvette's arms over it. The four voyageurs then lifted the stretcher up to their shoulders and start following the two lead men, one holding a torch and the other holding a makeshift cross high above his head. The remaining voyageurs lowered their torches and fell in behind in two lines once again, and the entire procession headed back in the direction from which it came.

Two voyageurs marching abreast took up the rear. The one on the near side held a flute á bec. He turned his head slowly and looked back at McKay with a ghostly, expressionless face. It was Jean-Luc Trotin. The one on the far side was a drummer who started pounding out a slow beat: *bomp . . . bomp . . . bomp*. The beat accelerated faster and faster: *bomp-bomp-b-b-b-b-brrrr*. Then just like that, the drumming stopped.

As the voyageurs entered the forest, they started a single-tone chant with an intermittent inflection that established a constant rhythm. The chant became an echo once the entire procession was within the forest. Before long, the torch light grew dimmer and dimmer, and the sound of the chant faded. Finally, McKay glimpsed only an occasional flicker as the torches receded deep into the forest.

The chest! The chest was gone!

McKay got down on his knees and felt around on the dark ground in his immediate vicinity. Nothing. He looked in the direction the voyageurs had gone, but it was completely black and silent. Still on all fours, he looked in the direction of the cabin. He could make it out in the light of the crescent moon, but its windows were black now. McKay was alone and didn't know where to go or what to do.

But then McKay noticed a soft orange glow. His surroundings resolved, and details became distinct by the dull, wavering intensity of a campfire's embers. He pulled his hands off the ground, perched himself up on his knees and looked around in confusion.

As soon as McKay figured out where he was, he quickly reached to his side for the wooden chest. His hand landed on the coarse wooden grain of the featureless, homely container. He felt for and then grabbed the lead seal. *Still here*, he thought, feeling a great sense of relief. A ruffed grouse started drumming somewhere deep in the woods: *bomp . . . bomp . . . bomp-bomp-bomp-bomp-brrrr*. It stopped abruptly and the dark woods fell silent again.

Earlier that evening, McKay and his voyageurs had been sitting around a large bonfire talking and laughing—a nice change in mood after starting the day with Bouvette's funeral. As the night progressed and they all eventually got sleepy, everyone simply decided to turn in for the night right where they were. It was a clear and starry night, so they abandoned their normal routine of crawling under an over-turned canoe.

When McKay awoke from his dream a few hours later, all that was left of the fire was a waning glow from dying coals. A low moon, three or four days beyond full, had risen over the lake and threw down a bright path of light that shimmered on the lake's smooth surface. The only other sounds besides the grouse were a couple of the snoring voyageurs, the constant rhythmic hoot of an owl, and an occasional *plop* of a fish rising to take an insect from the surface.

McKay eventually lay back down, adjusted a rolled blanket under the backside of his neck and studied the scene overhead. Subtly illumined tree branches, pulsating in synch with the light from the dying embers, framed a dazzling scene of the Milky Way high in the sky. The bright stars of Vega, Deneb, and Altair—the Summer Triangle—seemed to sparkle with a brilliance equal to three candles.

Ah, the beauty of the North, McKay thought. *It shows forth when needed most: at the end of a very strange day. Perhaps I didn't treat Sebastian Bouvette as well as I should have. But what's in the past is in the past. He is gone, and his funeral is over. Guilt serves no purpose any longer. I deserve to relax. And, starting tomorrow I shall do so.*

But McKay was deceiving himself. Tomorrow was not to be just another day. Although tomorrow may not prove to be as strange as the dream he had just had, he knew it definitely would prove to be a challenge.

Tomorrow was when the expedition would reach Hell's Gate Rapids.

~ 13 ~

THE FUNERAL OF SEBASTIAN BOUVETTE had been a distraction for Duncan McKay. It temporarily relieved him of the constant worry about the wooden chest, clearly the most valuable commodity in his charge. But at times this worry bordered on paranoia. He was suspicious of the voyageurs and continued to wonder why they weren't complaining about the wooden chest as they had the year before. And now McKay was coming upon a reason to have his worry grow into intense anxiety.

As his brigade approached the landing for the portage around Hell's Gate Rapids, McKay got close enough to make out two crosses at the beginning of the trail. The crosses were made of birch tree branches lashed together. Not too far from the crosses was a low waterfall where the rapids emptied into the lake. It was the notorious Devil's Cauldron. The sound of its thundering cascade got steadily louder as the brigade approached. The current from the Cauldron was so strong that the voyageurs had to fight a sideways drift as they beached their canoes.

McKay and his brigade were heading east toward Grand Portage and, being west of the height of land, were going upstream. The plan for the heavy wooden chest, however, was to line it up the rapids in a canoe.

In lining a canoe—or tracking, as it was sometimes called—two voyageurs would be on the river bank or in the shallows making their way upstream on one side of the river. One voyageur would have a rope tied to the bow of the canoe and the other would have a rope attached to the stern. The trick was to have the bow angled toward the opposite shore, then the force of the current could counteract the pull from the ropes, thereby keeping the canoe mid-stream. However, in case the canoe got off course or there was an obstruction, a third voyageur would be alone in the canoe using a pole to push against the bottom or to negotiate around rocks.

At Hell's Gate Rapids, the hardest part of lining would be getting the canoe around Devil's Cauldron. It might even require a short carry. But once they accomplished that, there were no more waterfalls for the remaining length of the rapids.

This wasn't the first time that McKay had been at Devil's Cauldron, but it was the first time that he paid close attention to the crosses. As soon as he could, McKay stepped out of his canoe into the shallows. The voyageurs took notice. Rarely did a *bourgeois* get his feet wet.

McKay immediately walked up the rocky shore to stand in front of the crosses where the portage trail started into the woods. The crosses were memorials to two voyageurs who had risked running the rapids at a high water level and lost.

Whether hot because of the temperature or because he was nervous, McKay unbuttoned his double-breasted waistcoat as he stared at the crosses and listened to the background roar of the rapids. He harbored a dread and a foreboding as he waved his fisherman's cap around his head to keep the black flies away. In fact, he was starting to obsess with the thought of death. When he tried to get a look at the rapids, tree branches and brush obscured his view. All he could make out was a mist rising above the violent chaos of churning white froth.

The hymn of the Lord's Prayer sung at Sebastian Bouvette's funeral came to mind: *Thy kingdom come, Thy will be done, On earth as it is in heaven . . .*

McKay started to have second thoughts about the canoe lining plan. Besides, he really didn't trust his voyageurs. He had a hunch they knew of the contents of the chest, so he didn't like the idea of letting the chest out of his sight.

On the other hand, McKay also had to maintain morale. He remembered all to well how bitterly the men had complained about carrying the chest over the Grand Portage. Although not as long as the Grand Portage, the Hell's Gate Rapids portage was longer than countless others on the fur-trade route.

So McKay tried a soft approach in proposing a change in the plan.

As all the voyageurs were still gathered on the shoreline, unloading the canoes, he walked back to his bustling crew and diplomatically expressed his reservations about lining the chest up the rapids in a canoe. The voyageurs' response was immediate. They dropped their packs, circled McKay and registered a vehement protest. McKay quickly acquiesced and had to put his trust in the voyageurs concerning the wooden chest. After all, he reasoned, the canoe would be constantly tethered to the two men on shore.

The impromptu shoreline meeting ended almost as soon as it began. The voyageurs went back to unloading their packs and the bulging bales of fur. When they were done, McKay watched as Jean-Luc Trotin and two other voyageurs got back into a nearly empty canoe and pushed off to paddle as close to Devil' Cauldron as possible. The wooden chest was underneath the center thwart and lashed to it.

Without even moving his feet, McKay looked over his shoulder at the crosses. From a distance, he scrutinized them one more time and thought of the hymn: . . . *Give us this day our daily bread* . . . He looked away and started to follow two voyageurs with packs on their backs. As they started up the trail and walked past the crosses, McKay concentrated on looking straight ahead without even so much as a sideways glance at crossed birch branches.

Since the trail diverged from the rapids, McKay had to bushwhack his way back to gorge every once in a while so he could check on the three voyageurs lining the canoe. He would watch from one vantage point until the three voyageurs made their way past his location, and then would hurry to another vantage farther up the gorge.

From the first vantage point, McKay noticed that the two men on shore had a hard time walking along the steep, rugged bank. Every so often they had to work their way around crags or climb over huge boulders while trying to concentrate on their lining technique. Their task was precarious as the current was strong right up close to the bank in a number of places. If one of the men happened to fall in the river at such a place, he would immediately be swept away. With that realization, McKay started to wonder if portaging the chest and the canoe wouldn't have been easier.

The fact of the matter was, however, the canoe was being lined at a good pace, and things appeared to be proceeding just fine. But if the technique was safe, McKay wondered, why hadn't they placed a full load of gear in the canoe? Besides the wooden chest, there was only a canvas covering some items on the floor in the forward half of the canoe. Maybe with more gear, McKay thought, the canoe would have ridden too low in the roiling water.

McKay shrugged. All he really cared about was that the canoe lining process was safely progressing.

Near the upstream end of the gorge, the rapids below came back into view from the trail, and McKay could wait for the three voyageurs without doing any more bushwhacking.

One by one, the three voyageurs appeared from around a bend in the river. They had somehow maneuvered the canoe through or around the last major obstacle, a set of standing waves just around the bend. The three were constantly shouting orders back and forth in French as they slowly negotiated the final stretch of slippery rocks on shore. Although his French was poor, McKay recognized a couple commands shouted by the one in the canoe, Jean-Luc Trotin, the capable gouvernoy.

"Let out some line at the bow! Pull the stern in!"

Suddenly the lead man on shore slipped on a sloping section of wet ledge rock and slid into the water. As he fell he let go of his rope.

The current immediately grabbed the bow of the canoe and rotated it broadside to the current. The fallen lead man quickly surfaced and thrashed about to find footing in the chest-deep water. He made a lunge in a vain attempt to grab the rope. But it was too late. The rotating canoe had pulled the rope out into the current and out of his reach. All he could do was save himself by staying close to shore.

The canoe kept rotating all the way around and started heading down stream. The second man on shore held fast to his rope hoping to pull the canoe into shore to his downstream side. But the rope wrapped around a boulder and held the canoe by its stern right in the middle of the main current. The canoe was dangerously close to going under as the river's wild turbulence licked the canoe's gunwales as it diverted around the stern.

"*Laisse la corde!*" Jean-Luc shouted from the canoe.

McKay grabbed a tree branch and looked on in horror as he understood the command: "Let go of the rope!"

As the second lineman on shore let go of his rope, the canoe started heading downstream. Jean-Luc dropped his pole and got low on spread knees. He reached down to grab a stowed paddle and deftly started to maneuver the canoe in the strong current and twisting hydraulics. If anyone could make it, it would be Jean-Luc.

But McKay knew that for even Jean-Luc, the odds of getting through the rapids without swamping were virtually nil. Jean-Luc was in peril, not to mention that the cargo was likely doomed as well. There were very few places to beach a canoe within the gorge. And the water level was high and the current swift and powerful.

As Jean-Luc disappeared around the bend in the rapids, McKay took off back down the trail. He had never run so fast. He tripped on some exposed tree roots and gashed his shin on a wedge of rock protruding from the worn trail. Ignoring his injury, he bolted back up and continued at a run down the trail.

McKay came head on with some voyageurs carrying packs and a canoe. As he sidestepped them and ran off the trail through some bracken ferns and thimbleberry, he yelled out what had happened. The voyageurs all dropped their loads, grabbed some rope and started running behind McKay.

McKay finally reached the beginning of the portage trail. He came to a sudden halt in front of the birch-branch crosses. For a split second that could have been eternity, the fateful words of the Lord's Prayer raced through his mind: . . . *And forgive us our trespasses, as we forgive those who trespass against us.* McKay tore through the brush toward the Devil's Cauldron.

McKay burst from the brush and slipped on some moss-covered cobbles. He got up as fast as he could and stumbled his way to the water's edge. Other voyageurs followed close behind with coiled ropes and came up alongside

McKay. Although they looked up the rapids and out on the lake, they mainly focused on Devil's Cauldron where there was a back-circulating hydraulic at the base of the low waterfall.

Suddenly an arm appeared and rotated back under. Then a human torso wrapped with a red sash surfaced for a split second. Lastly, a foot appeared and disappeared just as quickly.

All the voyageurs sprang into action. They tried throwing their ropes out to the waterfall and started yelling, "Jean-Luc! *Empare—toi de la corde*! (Jean-Luc! Grab the rope!)" A couple of the voyageurs hurriedly tied a stick to the end of their rope in order to launch it out farther.

Everyone kept hollering, but the strong voices of the voyageurs could barely be heard over the booming roar of the river.

Seconds turned into a minute, then another minute.

Eventually one of the voyageurs quit throwing his rope, dropped to his knees and started to sob. One by one, the other voyageurs quit yelling and stopped tossing their ropes. They all stood still . . . very still.

With his head bowed, the voyageur who fell to his knees started to cry out, "Jean-Luc! . . . Jean-Luc! . . . *S'il vous plaît, mon Dieu, pas le Hustler!* (Please, God, not the Hustler!)"

Out in the lake where the current had dissipated, McKay noticed the end of a broken canoe barely protruding above the surface. It lazily rotated in the slowly churning dark water and dragged a lining rope on the surface. He looked down near his feet. The blade-end of a broken paddle rocked back and forth in the small waves that lapped the stones at his feet.

McKay turned and started to head back toward the brush. His mouth hung open and his eyes were dazed. Jean-Luc Trotin, the Hustler, was dead.

∞ 14 ∞

Present Day
Tim's Malone's apartment—Duluth, Minnesota

IM GOT BACK TO HIS DUPLEX late in the afternoon. The day had gone by quickly considering the news he had received the night before when he had been over at the Hanson's house. Not only had Maggie Hanson informed him that there would be no archaeological recovery in the Boundary Waters over the coming summer, but she had told Tim that her husband, Lyle, had suddenly left town.

Because of the news, Tim hadn't slept well the previous night and was extremely tired. He kicked off his shoes, lay down on his couch, and started thinking about his day. As Maggie had requested, Tim did send his friend Shukriyah a package containing the fire steel, the sun crystal, and the tracing of the "P & C" lead seal. But throughout the day, his mind had been preoccupied with wondering if Lyle was safe. Maybe he was letting his imagination run a wild, but Tim wondered if Lyle hadn't unwittingly gotten mixed up in some dangerous intrigue with his ambitious proposal to recover the lost voyageur shipment.

Of Vikings and Voyageurs

Tim had been looking forward to the recovery project and was quite dejected that it was now likely cancelled. How great it would have been, he had thought, to work up in the Boundary Waters and be able to stay up there for an extended period of time. On days off, he and Lyle could venture off to fish hidden lakes deep in the wilderness. Or they could simply enjoy the peace and solitude of their campsite by burying their nose in a book, only looking up to check on a bobber floating nearby.

As he put his hands behind his head and yawned, he reminisced about past canoe trips with Lyle. He recalled sitting under a rain fly one rainy afternoon talking about anything from the *Tao of Physics* to what type of lure the fish seemed to be hitting. And when they weren't talking, they simply listened to the sound of the rain falling on the ground outside the perimeter of the rain fly. It sounded just like frying bacon.

But then it got quiet.

Zzzzzzz . . . ip. Zzzzzzz . . . ip. Tim remembered being startled by the shrill sound of the tent-flap zipper.

"What are you doin', Lyle?" Tim asked.

"Gonna do some casting," Lyle said as he sat with his feet out the tent opening, pulling on his hiking shoes. "It's early morning and looks like it's about to rain again. Perfect conditions for the fish to be biting."

When his shoes were tied, Lyle scooted out of the tent and turned around on all fours. "Ya' comin', Tim?"

"Nah, I need some sack time."

"Suit yourself," Lyle said as he threw the hood of his rain parka over his head.

Once again Tim heard the obnoxious zipping sound as Lyle closed the tent flap. He next heard Lyle shuffling on the turf. When Lyle started walking away, the sound becomes fainter with each step.

Pop. Pop. The smallest rain drops make a clearly audible sound on taut nylon.

"Here comes the rain," Tim thought from his warm sleeping bag.

"Hey, Tim!" Lyle shouted from down at the shoreline. "You're missing out! The fish are really biting!"

Pop . . . pop-pop . . . pop-pop-pop-pop. The rain started coming down heavy.

"Forget it," Tim thought in his semi-consciousness.

The next thing Tim knew was the sound of a breeze through the trees. There was still the sound of drops on the tent, but the sound was sporadic, mostly drops coming off trees as they shook in the wind. Tim lifted his head and looked around. It was brighter inside the tent, but Tim didn't know if it was because the sky was clearing or because it was later in the morning.

"Well, I suppose," Tim muttered to himself. "Time to get up and see how many fish Lyle caught."

Tim crawled out of the tent with his hair mussed and his hiking shoes untied. The sky was still overcast. When he looked toward the lake, he saw something very peculiar. He stepped off a couple ledges of faulted bedrock and made his way down to the water's edge. Some scattered bulrushes and horsetails protruded from the calm water near shore. A light rain started up again. The smooth surface of the lake became pocked with tiny concentric circles.

Tim saw his canoe floating empty, rotating ever so slowly about thirty yards out. Tim looked around. A fishing rod and tackle box were left on the smooth bedrock near shore

"LYLE!" Tim shouted. He looked down the shoreline, craning his neck to check out every nook and cranny and shoreline shrub. Then he turned to look in the other direction.

A ringing sound behind him startled Tim. He turned around and looked at the tent.

"What the heck?" Tim said to himself. "We didn't bring an alarm clock."

T<small>IM SUDDENLY SAT UP ON THE COUCH</small> in a cold sweat. His telephone was ringing from the end table behind him. His apartment was bright with the late afternoon sunlight streaming through the windows. Tim sat up, shifted around, and swung his feet to the floor before answering the phone.

"Hello," Tim said softly and slowly. His head was down and his eyes closed as he rubbed his forehead with his other hand.

A gentle-sounding female voice greeted him on the other end. "Hello, Tim. My name is Lindsey Melburn-Davis. I'm a close friend of Maggie Hanson's. I hope I'm not disturbing you."

"Uh . . . no. That's . . . that's fine," Tim said in a groggy voice. "I was just taking a nap on my couch. We . . . we've met, haven't we?"

"Yes, we've met. It was at Lyle and Maggie's house. In fact, I'm over at Maggie's house right now. I understand you were here last night?"

"Yeah . . . um, last night. I was there . . . late . . . late last night."

"Maggie said I just missed you. Anyway, she asked that I call you. I have some bad news, Tim. Lyle was in a car accident last night."

"What?" Tim asked as he quickly came to and leaned forward. "Where did this happen? How is he?"

"It happened on Highway 27, just east of Alexandria. He's going to be okay, but he sustained serious injuries."

"Serious injuries?"

"Yes. He's been brought to the county hospital in Alexandria, and they have him heavily sedated."

"Were there any other people involved? Other cars?"

"Yes. I understand the Highway Patrol reported skid marks from other cars. But they left the scene. Lyle's car ended upside down in the ditch."

"Upside down? Oh, God!"

"I guess once his car hit a bank of plowed snow off the edge of the shoulder, his car flipped. On the other hand, I guess deep snow in the ditch may have had some cushioning effect. So it could have been worse."

"How's Maggie? Is there anything I can do? Should I came over?"

"Thanks, Tim, but I don't think there's anything that you can do right now. She's strong and holding up well under the circumstances. She's upstairs packing right now. As soon as she's done with that and I make a couple more phone calls, I'm going to take her to Alexandria. My husband's already down there."

"Would it be okay if I came down or does Maggie want to limit visitors at this point?"

"Well, I'm thinking it might be okay if you came tomorrow afternoon sometime. I got a feeling that Maggie would really appreciate it by then. Um . . . let's see. How about this? First thing tomorrow morning I can give you a call from the hospital and give you an update. Then I can confirm if a visit tomorrow will still be a good idea."

"Yes. Please do that. Please call as soon as you can."

"All right, then. We'll plan on that."

"Thanks so much for calling, Lindsey. And please give my regards to Maggie."

"Will do, Tim. You take care."

"Oh! Lindsey, wait! One more question."

"Sure, Tim. What is it?"

"Has Maggie been able to figure out why Lyle took off just like that? Took off without even telling her where he was going."

"Alexandria seemed to make sense to her. She mentioned the Kensington Rune Stone Museum. And she also mentioned some guy's name whom she thought—uh . . . I think I better let you go, Tim," Lindsey said in a softer tone of voice. "I think Maggie is coming downstairs. Anyway, she mentioned some guy named Cedric."

"Two-hearts? Cedric Two-hearts?"

"Yeah, that's it. I'll call you tomorrow morning, Tim. I need to get going."

15

The Next Day

AT THE COUNTY HOSPITAL IN ALEXANDRIA, Tim walked down a hallway that led to the new wing housing the Intensive Care Unit. The ICU family waiting room was at the far end where the hallway turned left.

Tim saw the waiting room door open and watched as a Highway Patrol officer came out and went the other way down the hallway. Tim didn't want to think too much of what that meant as he continued at a brisk pace. When he reached the waiting room, he was concerned about invading privacy, so he opened the door just enough to peek inside.

The room had white walls that were adorned with prints of modern art. Large windows let in the bright afternoon sunlight. Padded chairs with wooden arms lined up along one wall, and two sofas separated by an end table took up the opposite wall. The end table was covered with magazines and a telephone. Half-filled plastic beverage containers and a game of Scrabble sat abandoned on a round table in the center of the room. A soap was playing on a television suspended high in the far corner of the room. The sound had been turned way down.

Maggie and her friend Lindsey were sitting together on one of the sofas. As Maggie fidgeted with the number keys on her cell phone, Lindsey tapped her on her shoulder and pointed at Tim. Wrapped around Lindsey's wrist, Tim noticed the diamond bracelet that had been on Maggie's coffee table. When Maggie looked up and saw Tim, she jumped up and ran to him to give him a long, hard hug. Lindsey also got up and followed Maggie.

"Thanks so much for coming, Tim. It really means a lot." Maggie stepped back and gestured toward Lindsey. "I'm sure you've met my friend at some point. Lindsey Melburn-Davis."

"Oh, yes," Tim said as he reached out to shake her hand. "Now I remember. It's been a while and I was asleep when you called, so I was struggling to place you when we spoke on the phone. Thanks so much for keeping me informed."

"Quite all right," Lindsey said graciously. "It's unfortunate that we had to get reacquainted under these circumstances."

"Say, Lindsey," Maggie said. "Now that Tim is here, feel free to catch up with Lyle's relatives if you're hungry."

"Oh, I'm doing fine. I really am."

"No, really. You should go eat. You haven't had a decent meal all day. Besides, I got a lot of stuff I need to go over with Tim, and it's going to be rather boring, I'm afraid to say."

"Well . . . I guess I could go for a bite. Can I bring back anything for you, Maggie?" Lindsey asked.

"No thanks. I still don't have an appetite. The most I might need is something to drink, and I can get that from the vending machines down the hall. I'll be fine."

"All right," Lindsey said as she slipped past Maggie and looked at Tim. "It's good to see you again. Thanks for coming."

As Lindsey left the room, she slowed down at the doorway corner before heading down the hallway. She glanced back. Tim was taking off his jacket and Maggie was returning to her same place on the sofa. As neither one noticed her, she stopped momentarily and studied Tim suspiciously before starting down the hallway.

"The nurses needed to do a number of things for Lyle," Maggie told Tim as he sat down on the end of the sofa, "like change his bandages or measure his blood gases or . . . God only knows what. I can't keep it all straight anymore. It's been so much. Anyway, it was a good time for Lindsey and Lyle's family to go and get something to eat. You just missed them."

"How's Lyle doing? Is he awake?"

"No, they're keeping him sedated. He has some internal injuries, some broken bones, a broken jaw. We've been told that he might have to be transferred to the Twin Cities. But at least he's stable. He looks worse than he really is. His face is all puffy and kind of purplish, and he has all those tubes and wires and IVs poked into him."

"And how are you holding up?"

"Last night and the drive down here were awful. But I'm better now."

Tim watched as Maggie's expression suddenly became serious.

"Well, that's not exactly true," she said. "Tim, there's something I need to tell you. Remember when we talked about the possibility of Lyle coming to Alexandria to meet with that older guy who lives in the north woods? That Two-hearts fellow?"

"Yes."

"Well, it's true. And now I'm kind of worried that Lyle got himself mixed up in something. I'm not sure what to make of the accident. A Highway Patrol officer was here just before you came."

"I saw him leave. Did he tell you what happened?"

"The site is still being investigated, but he had an initial assessment. It looked to him as if someone had tried to pass Lyle with an oncoming car too close. The passing car side-swiped Lyle. That's why Lyle ended up in the ditch. Skid marks from the oncoming car show that it swerved toward the shoulder on the opposite side to avoid a head-on collision. But I don't know, Tim. I keep going over all this in my mind. What if it was intentional? Could it have been that the passing car cut it close with an oncoming car to make it look like a mistake? Or maybe both cars were working as a team?"

"Maggie, we need to be careful about jumping to conclusions," Tim said with a touch of self-consciousness. He too was a little suspicion of the accident. But he felt compelled to find some way of consoling Maggie. "The patrol will conduct an objective, professional investigation, so we need to be patient."

"How come the other two cars didn't stop?"

"Well . . . things happen pretty fast sometimes. Before they know it they're far down the road. They didn't get a scratch and maybe didn't notice the car that hit the ditch, so they just keep going. Then if they find out later that someone got hurt, and they get scared to come forward because they realize that they left the scene of an accident. And who knows? Maybe they had been drinking? Then for sure they wouldn't want to come forward. At least not right away."

"The officer did say that it can take a while before people come forward. He said it takes a little time before their guilt finally compels them to do the right thing."

"I think he's right. Let's be optimistic and give it a little time. By the way, Maggie, how did you find out that Lyle came here to Alexandria to meet Two-hearts?"

"Two-hearts left a letter at the lobby desk here in the hospital. He obviously knew something happened when Tim didn't show up for their meeting. His letter is one of the reasons why I've become even more suspicious about the accident. Here, I'll let you read it."

Maggie retrieved an envelope from her purse.

"I confess that I was quite surprised after I read this," Maggie said as she handed the envelope to Tim. "The writing in Two-Hearts's previous correspondence had been short and to the point. All along I had assumed that since this man lived like a hermit in the north woods, he must be uneducated and rather hardened by his isolation. But this letter paints a different picture. Although it's also to the point—in fact, very much to the point—it does show that he's kind and sensitive. And with the exception of some spelling errors, he seems fairly intelligent as well. He's a little bold in asserting his suspicions perhaps, but he sure seems to have a lot of information.

"Look, Tim, while you read the letter, I'm going to get a drink from the water fountain down the hall."

As Maggie got up to leave, Tim removed the letter from the envelope, unfolded it and started reading.

Of Vikings and Voyageurs

Dear Mrs. Hanson,

My name is Cedric Two-hearts. You may have heard Lyle mention me. I am so sorry about his accident. I shouldn't of asked the nurses about him because I'm not related, but at least I found out that he is not critical and should recover. Thank goodness!

Lyle and I were going to meet at the Kensington Rune Stone Museum here in Alexandria. We were to talk about the wooden chest lost in the fur trade. He has researched it a long time, and I have important information for him. We were also to talk about the Viking rune stones in this part of North America.

One of these rune stones was near the Ontario/Minnesota border. My people call it the Rainy Lake Rune Stone. As happened with the Mandan Indians on the western plains, some Vikings also settled among Indians in the Rainy Lake country. Although I can only trace my Ojibwe Indian heritage back to the seventeen hundreds, I can trace my Viking heritage all the way back to the thirteen hundreds.

When Lyle gets better, tell him the Rainy Lake Rune Stone has two important connections—the wooden chest he wants to find and the silver urn found recently in Scotland. I have interest in the silver urn because the Rainy Lake Stone speaks of it with runic inscriptions. If we could find it, I think the Rainy Lake Stone would give us more information about the urn. That's why I needed to show Lyle certain runes on the Kensington Stone.

I asked Lyle to meet in secret on short notice because I think I've been watched in the past. Spied on, followed, things like that. Rumors about the wooden chest have been around for decades, and I believe some people would do whatever it takes to get it. Maybe this isn't the time say this, so I sincerely apologize, but I do hope Lyle's accident was really just an accident. I hope it's just my imagination that says it might not be, and the Highway Patrol investigation will tell you it was.

My hope for the wooden chest has always been that no one out for personal gain should get it. That's why I was willing to help a legitamate professional like Lyle find it.

So there you have it. This story is so much more than just about some long-lost voyageur chest. The real value is the history.

I won't be leaving Alexandria right away. So, if possible, please leave a note at the hospital lobby desk telling me of Lyle's progress. I know it's not my fault, but part of me feels responsible.

When Lyle gets well enough, ask to him to send a letter. He knows I keep a post office box in Atikokan, Ontario. I hope he gets well soon. My prayers are with you.

Sincerest Regards,
Cedric Two-hearts

Maggie walked back to the waiting room as Tim was folding the letter and stuffing it back into the its envelope.

"By the way, Tim, how's Jessa been?" Maggie asked as she sat back down in the same place on the sofa. "She still gonna come stay in Minnesota for a while?"

"Yeah, she arrives in a week."

Maggie noticed that something was missing in Tim's answer. Normally Tim would sound excited when discussing the arrival of his girlfriend. But his gaze drifted as he rested his hands in his lap and nervously slapped an open palm with the envelope several times.

"Looks like the letter got you thinking, Tim. So, what did you think?"

Tim was careful to avoid any talk about the accident being intentional. He didn't think Maggie needed to believe that someone had been out to harm Lyle.

"Two-hearts mentioned the accident investigation," Tim said. "The Highway Patrol needs to complete the investigation before we jump to any conclusions."

"I'm more curious what you think about this lost cargo—what he calls the wooden chest—and the talk about the rune stones."

"Oh . . . yeah. Um, he did make a statement that really caught my eye. He said something about having 'important information.'"

"Exactly! And his information about the Rainy Lake Rune Stone—I've become just as curious about that as I am about the lost cargo. You know, Tim, after reading his letter, I kind of wish I could meet Two-hearts in person."

"Yeah, but the way he stated things gave me the impression that he really wants to keep his distance. I don't know if it's because . . ." Tim caught himself before he brought up anything about sinister people after the wooden chest that Maggie might construe as a threat. ". . . uh, if it's because he is really shy or what. Maybe he doesn't think he should intrude on you at such a time. You know, he's a stranger and all."

"Oh, that's no big deal," Maggie said with a wave of her hand. Then she paused momentarily as she collected her thoughts. "Tim, I have a favor to ask."

"Sure, Maggie. What is it?"

"I once asked Lyle what he would do if he got sick or disabled and couldn't go up into the Boundary Waters to recover the cargo lost by the voyageurs, the wooden chest, as Two-hearts calls it. You know what he said? He said he hoped you would pick up the baton. He thinks you have as much love for archaeology as you do for physics. And of course, you love the location of this project: the Boundary Waters."

Tim smiled enigmatically.

Maggie waited, then said, "So, what do you say, Tim? Would you please continue with what Lyle's been trying to do? I don't want to see it stop and neither would he. He even told me so."

Tim held his silence as he thought about the possibility that someone had intentionally side-swiped Lyle. Taking on the project would take on the danger.

"I have to face facts here," Maggie continued. "Not only might Lyle's injuries prevent him from going up in the Boundary Waters this summer, he's probably going to be totally incapacitated in the short term."

"Maggie, I don't think Lyle's benefactors nor the governments of Canada and the U.S. will let just any amateur take Lyle's place. Having him out of the picture could change everything."

Maggie pressed her eyes and held up her hands as if signaling someone to stop. "Forget about bureaucracies and funding and all that stuff for just a minute! Let's focus only on a personal level for now. I want to know what Two-hearts was going to tell Lyle. What was his 'important information' about the wooden chest? What if he knows what was in the chest and why was it shipped? And what about the Rainy Lake Stone? Where is it? Can it be found? What's its connection to the silver urn? But above all, Tim, why would Two-hearts say that this story is more than about a treasure chest?"

Maggie paused, watching Tim. The last thing she wanted to do was badger him if his heart was no longer in the project.

"Tim, I'm sorry. I certainly understand if things have changed for you as a result of Lyle's accident. Maybe a break would be good for everybody. Maybe in two or three weeks, I can start looking into things on my own."

Tim studied Maggie's deep, contemplative look. Tim had seen that look before. In that gaze a 100-pound woman had about 1,000 pounds of determination. But she didn't know what she was getting into. She couldn't be prepared for the danger that might just be part and parcel with the quest.

"No, Maggie. You tend to Lyle. I'll keep going with this. I'm into this all the way, and I'm not going to stop now. The letter from Two-hearts raised more questions than it answered. In fact, if Two-hearts is going to be coming back to the hospital lobby, it even crossed my mind to hang out down there until he showed up. I would love to have a long talk with him."

Maggie's face, so tense and drawn with what had happened to Lyle, suddenly relaxed for a moment, and tears of gratitude came to her eyes. "Great! That's what I was hoping to hear, Tim." She reached into her purse and retrieved a slip of paper. "But you won't have to wait in the lobby. I found this piece of paper among Lyle's belongings. It's a phone number. Two-hearts brought a cell phone with him."

16

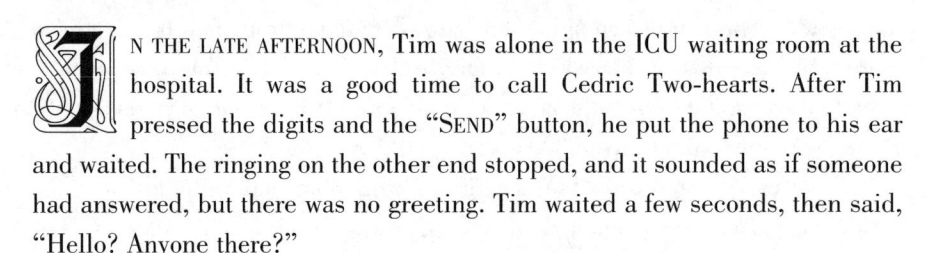

IN THE LATE AFTERNOON, Tim was alone in the ICU waiting room at the hospital. It was a good time to call Cedric Two-hearts. After Tim pressed the digits and the "SEND" button, he put the phone to his ear and waited. The ringing on the other end stopped, and it sounded as if someone had answered, but there was no greeting. Tim waited a few seconds, then said, "Hello? Anyone there?"

"Who is this?" a soft and worried voice asked on the other end.

"Tim Malone. Is this Cedric Two-hearts?"

Again, there was only silence.

"Mr. Two-hearts? Are you there?"

"Do you know whose cell phone you're using?" Two-hearts asked with a slow but hard Canadian dialect.

"Oh, geez! I'm sorry. I should have explained. Yes, I have Lyle Hanson's cell. I'm a close friend of his. Maggie—Lyle's wife—gave me the phone to use. I'm at the hospital. Your cell phone number was one a piece of paper among Lyle's stuff. She thought you might know Lyle's number and might not answer an unfamiliar number. She asked me to thank you for your letter."

Another pause. Then in a much warmer voice, Two-hearts said, "It's quite all right, hey. How's Lyle doing?"

"Well, he got banged up pretty bad. He'll have to have a number of surgeries—in fact, he's in surgery right now. He's got a nasty break—his leg will require a metal plate . . . let's see, what else? . . . a broken jaw, cracked ribs. Recovery is going to take a while. He'll need therapy. The important thing is that he's going to be okay."

Tim waited for Two-hearts to make some response, but there was only an awkward silence.

"Um, I hope you don't mind my calling you," Tim said in an attempt to keep the conversation going. "Maggie encouraged me to do so."

"You said your name was Malone?"

"Yes."

Again there was silence. With the impression of who he was talking to, Tim had trouble squaring the image of someone so shy having written such a letter to Maggie.

"Ohhh-kay. Okay," said Two-hearts slowly. "I think I heard Lyle mention the name Malone. He said he had put together a team . . . I think he said you were his longtime canoe partner. You'd be his closest assistant. You must be in the same line of work, hey?"

"Well, sort of. I'm not a trained archaeologist, but I was planning on helping Lyle this summer up in the Boundary Waters."

"Ah yes, the recovery of the trea . . . uh, the wooden chest."

Tim was shocked. Was Two-hearts about to say treasure?

"Well," Two-hearts continued, "this is good that you called me. I've been thinking a lot about Lyle. I feel terrible, hey. Especially for his wife. How is she holding up?"

"Quite well, under the circumstances. Again, Lyle shouldn't have any permanent damage and will eventually get back to normal. Just knowing that has been a big relief for Maggie."

There was another long silence. Tim was beginning to see that he should just wait for Two-hearts.

"Any word about what caused the accident?" Two-hearts asked.

"Nothing official yet. A Highway Patrol officer came to visit Maggie. His initial assessment was that there was no foul play."

Tim held his breath in expectation of a real long silence.

"Well . . . that's good," Two-hearts said in a quick reply.

For some reason Tim expected Two-hearts to say more about the officer's accident assessment. But Two-hearts didn't. Tim finally decided to get down to business as Two-hearts obviously didn't play games and said only what has to be said.

"Mr. Two-hearts, I under—"

"Cedric. You can call me Cedric."

"Oh . . . all right. Um, Cedric, I understand you and Lyle were going to—"

"What was your first name again?"

"Tim. My first name's Tim."

Tim waited a second or two for some sort of acknowledgment, but he got none. After a pause, Tim simply continued. "Anyway, I understand you and Lyle were going to meet and discuss rune stones and the special cargo lost by the voyageurs. Maggie has asked me to continue on with Lyle's work. She said that's what Lyle would want. I agree. So, I was wondering how you'd feel about working with me until Lyle gets better."

More silence. But this time it didn't feel awkward. He had been straightforward with Two-hearts, and it was now up to him to decide whether he wanted to cooperate. That should certainly take at least a moment of thought.

"Yah, that would be all right, I guess," Two-hearts said meekly. "So your first name is Tim?"

"Yes."

"Come to think of it, you must be the Tim who can help out a lot, hey? I spoke with Lyle while he was on his way down here. I told him I'd like to find out the history of that silver urn found in Scotland. It's got a Persian symbol on it, so it must go back a couple thousand years, hey? He said his friend Tim could help out with that."

Tim smiled. "Yeah, that's me. I know this astrophysicist who lives in Boston. She's from Iran—she's Persian."

"Did you say she's an astrophysicist?"

"Yes, she is."

"She would know her constellations then."

"Very much so. Technically she's not an astronomer, of course. She studies the physics of massive stars and other celestial bodies like galaxies. But she does know the night sky like the map of her hometown."

"A person like that would come in handy for deciphering some pictographs I know about."

Tim got confused. How can knowledge of astrophysics or astronomy be of any help in deciphering pictographs?

"Okay, okay." Two-hearts was sounding more trusting of Tim and started to relax. "I'm finally putting two and two together. There was another time a while back when I first talked to Lyle about these pictographs. I think he might have mentioned you back then too. Betcha any money he had said the name Tim when he spoke of someone who knew an astronomer in Boston. And sure enough, you are the same Tim Malone who was going to work with Lyle this summer. It all makes sense now."

"Yeah, that's me."

"Boston is far away."

"Shukriyah—the astrophysicist who lives in Boston—said she wants to come out here to visit. She was out last summer and met Lyle and Maggie. She loved it so much that she wants to come back."

"So, she's coming here?"

"Yes. By the way, Mist . . . uh, Cedric. This is an amazing coincidence that you and Lyle had mentioned Shukriyah. Maggie and I were also curious about the Persian symbol on the silver urn. We were also curious about the tracing that Lyle made of your Percy and Campbell seal. I sent the tracing to Shukriyah and asked her if she could get her uncle to help out. He knows a Scottish archaeologist who's an expert in medieval Scotland and Scandinavia. I thought that, between them, they might have some insight into both the silver urn and the Percy and Campbell Company, which has its roots in Scotland."

Silence. Tim closed his eyes and slowly shook his head. *What's with this guy?* he thought to himself.

"The tracing of the lead seal," Two-hearts finally said in a hushed and mysterious way. "You must know I have the actual lead seal."

"Yes, I do."

"When I spoke with Lyle before he left Duluth, I revealed something about the lost wooden chest."

Tim's interest was piqued. He wondered if the information about the wooden chest had anything to do with Lyle suddenly wanting to cancel the recovery project. Though he was tempted to ask, he took a cue from Two-hearts and just waited.

"Well, now Lyle got in an accident," Two-hearts continued. "It makes me think about the tragic history of the wooden chest. It's like there's been a curse on it for hundreds of years. The curse hit Jean-Luc Trotin and his family especially hard."

What the hell is Two-hearts talking about? Tim wondered. *Who was Jean-Luc Trotin?* Maybe Two-hearts was assuming that Lyle had explained this Trotin character to him, but he didn't know how Trotin or his family was associated with the wooden chest.

"So, for your sake," Two-hearts went on, "maybe it's best I don't say too much about the wooden chest for the time being. I know this won't make sense because there's no such thing as a curse, but I just want to play it safe for now and not talk about the Percy and Campbell seal or anything else to do with the wooden chest. For now, I just want to leave this issue with the chest and Hell's Gate Rapids alone. On the other hand, I did come all the way down here from Ontario. So, if you have time to meet, even tonight yet, I can show you what I was going to show Lyle at the rune stone museum. I wanted to show him the runic codes for the Greek letters Chi and Rho. Chi and Rho were also said to be coded on the Rainy Lake Rune Stone. And I'm sure Chi and Rho are also on the silver urn. This should be pointed out to that Scottish archaeologist because Chi and Rho are the connection to Lindisfarne."

Tim was ready to jump at this new opportunity. "Boy, that would be great. Yes, let's get together. But isn't the museum closed in the evenings?"

"As it happens, they're experimenting with expanded hours in the off-season. We should still have enough time if we go soon."

"Okay, let's do it."

"Can you be there in half an hour?"

"Sure, I can do that. I just need to find Maggie and let her know that you and I are getting together. She should be excited to hear that."

"Do you know where to go?"

"I think so. Isn't it at the north end of Broadway near Lake Henry?"

"That's right. Just past Highway 27 on the west side."

"All right. See you in a half an hour."

"I'll be there."

Tim didn't waste any time. He found Maggie and told her that he was going to meet with Two-hearts, and she was glad.

❧ 17 ☙

It was dark when Tim started driving north on Broadway, a main thoroughfare through Alexandria. Broadway was busy with end-of-the-work-day traffic, and Tim had trouble containing his excitement.

When a pair of headlights seemed to be following too close, Tim didn't think anything of it at first. Then high-beams started flashing on and off in his rear view mirror. At first, Tim only wondered if it might be someone he knew or just an impatient homeward-bound person impatient with the heavy traffic. But as Tim came to a stop at the next traffic light, the car following him bumped the rear bumper of his Corolla. It wasn't a hard hit, but Tim got scared.

The traffic light turned green, and Tim accelerated slowly, wondering what he should do. As he approached the next intersection, he maintained a slow speed even though the light was green. Again, the car behind him flashed its high beams a couple times.

The traffic light was still green as Tim neared the intersection. The trailing car honked, but Tim held his crawl. Then the traffic light turned yellow. The adjacent lane was clear, and Tim hoped the car would pass in order to speed through the intersection. But the trailing car stayed behind him.

The light turned red, and Tim decelerated. He kept a close eye on the car stopped on the cross street. Just when he saw the first movement of that car,

Tim stomped on his gas and laid on his horn. He accelerated and swerved left in the middle of the intersection in order to avoid the car about to crash into his right front fender. The oncoming car's brakes screeched, and the driver blasted his horn.

Tim swerved back to the right and looked in his rear-view mirror. Traffic from the side street filled the intersection, effectively keeping the trailing car stopped at the red light.

Tim raced up to the next intersection and turned right in order to get out of sight of the car that had been following him. He made a few more turns at random intersections, hoping to prevent the mystery car from finding him again.

Eventually he found himself on a quiet and dark residential street and pulled off to the side between two parked cars. He turned off his lights and shut off his engine. After a minute or two of looking in his side view mirror without noticing approaching headlights—or the red-and-blue strobe lights of a police car, for that matter—he took a deep breath and finally relaxed. He reached for his cell phone and selected Two-hearts' number from the speed dial list.

"Hello."

"Cedric, this is Tim Malone. I'm going to be late. I've had a little problem. Somebody was following me really close. They flashed their brights, honked. They even bumped me slightly."

"Bumped you? Where did this happen?"

"While coming north on Broadway."

"Where are you now?"

"I'm parked on some street in a residential neighborhood. I went through a red light to get away from them. Then I just started going any which way, turning down random side streets to lose them for good. A minute ago, I pulled over on a . . . wait a minute. Cedric, I see headlights coming in my side view mirror. Hold on."

Tim put his phone down on his lap and slid down in his seat as he waited for the car to make it down the street. When the car got close, its headlights shone so brightly in the side-view mirror Tim had to look away. The car passed by without slowing, so Tim put the phone back up to his ear.

"Cedric, you still there?"

"Yeah."

"Sorry about that. A car came down the street, and I'm just a little paranoid. It kept going."

"It's all right. Hey, you don't have to worry about being late. The Kensington Rune Stone Museum is closed."

"It is?"

"Yeah. Turns out it's only open on a couple evenings during the week. That other car . . . could they have been high school kids who mistook your car for one of their friend's?"

"I don't know who the hell they were."

"If they were following you and meant to do you harm, they wouldn't have made their presence known like that, especially not on a busy street."

"Well, with all due respect," Tim said with frustration, "it's a little nerve racking thinking about what might have happened to Lyle."

"Yeah, I understand, hey. But we still got to keep our wits. When I got to the museum, I too wondered if I was in trouble. I went to read the hours posted on the door, and when I went back to my car, a big black car with dark windows pulled up and parked behind mine about fifteen or twenty yards back. I think it was a Cadillac, maybe a limo even. They turned off their headlights, but no one got out. I got into my car, started the engine, but I stayed put and didn't turn on any lights. For what seemed to be the longest time, that limo just sat back there and no one got out. Finally it just drove away. So, I'm a bit nervous myself. But to be honest, I have no idea what the people in that limo were really up to. It might not have had anything to do with me. Maybe they also wanted to go to the museum and were talking to each other about what to do next when they saw that the museum was dark."

Tim was glad to hear Two-hearts talk. At that point Tim felt he was beginning to gain Two-hearts' trust. Tim was also feeling less anxious about the car that had followed him. It easily could have been some mischievous kids just cruising the main drag.

"Yeah, you're right," Tim conceded. "I guess I'm a little on edge. So, what do you want to do now? Are you still parked in front of the museum?"

"Yeah, I'm still here."

"Do you want to meet back at the museum tomorrow?"

"Uh . . . let me think. First, let me say something. Earlier you asked to work together. Well, if you're sincere, you best listen to everything I'm about to say, hey? Listen carefully . . . very carefully. And then . . . well, then get ready for a series of adventures. I'm going to need you to prove yourself. Follow?"

"Yes!" Tim said enthusiastically. "I follow."

"Okay. For the time being, forget about the wooden chest. Curse or no curse, we'll get around to this issue with Hell's Gate Rapids later on. When we do, we'll need the help of that astronomer friend of yours. She'll need to look at those pictographs I mentioned."

"Sure . . . um, should be no problem," Tim said hesitantly. He was dumfounded as to the significance of the pictographs. "Like I said, she said she wants to plan another trip out here, so I'm sure it can be arranged."

"Good. But for right now, we need to start with first things first: and that's the Rainy Lake Rune Stone and the silver urn. Since I won't be able to point out the coded runes on the Kensington Stone, I'll try to point you to some book that shows them. The coded runes are similar to those on the Rainy Lake Stone. They represent the Greek letters Chi and Rho, meaning Christ the Anointed. If I can find such a book, I'll photocopy the coded runes or sketch them, then get them to you one way or another. Send them on to your Scottish archaeologist friend and ask him to compare them to what's inscribed on the silver urn, hey?"

"When we spoke earlier," Tim said, "you described Chi and Rho as the connection to Lindisfarne."

"That's right. Lindisfarne seems to be a focal point in my heritage. It's one of the places—maybe the first place—where the Vikings became exposed to Christianity. Your Scottish friend likely knows about Chi Rho from the Chi Rho page of the Lindisfarne Gospels. If the silver urn is inscribed with Chi Rho and he's recognized it, then maybe—just maybe—he might have made a connection to history further back. Remember, the silver urn has the Persian symbol on it, hey? The man on the wings. The Rainy Lake Stone might say more about that."

"So, you're talking about ancient history then?"

"I'm talking about Biblical history."

"Biblical history?"

"Yes!" Two-hearts said emphatically. "Why else would the Vikings have revered the silver urn so much that they would write about it on a rune stone, hey? We're not quite sure where the Rainy Lake Stone is today, but it has been passed down among my people what the stone says. In the same way the Kensington Stone talks about the Biblical Holy Grail in coded runes, the Rainy Lake Stone talks about the Silver Urn. You see, when the Vikings got exposed to Christianity, they became fixated on Christian relics brought to England from the Holy Land."

"Cedric, what's the Biblical significance of the silver urn?"

"I don't know. That's forever been a mystery to my people. And now that the urn has been found in Scotland, it is time to find out, hey? I hope your Scottish friend can help. But, better yet, it would be best if we could find the Rainy Lake Stone itself."

"Do you have a guess where it might be?"

"Unlike the Kensington Stone, which stayed buried in one spot till almost the twentieth century, the Rainy Lake Stone's been moved from place to place after white men came to the country. White men wanted to get their hands on it and were even willing to pay dearly for it, hey? But my ancestors wouldn't sell the stone. They even broke it down so it'd be easier to transport to various hiding places. It was originally a big, heavy block. It was slate . . . you know, with flat layers cemented together."

"Yes, I'm familiar. I'll bet you any money it was Virginia slate. An extensive formation of that is found in northeast Minnesota."

"That may be. But the color of the slate in the Rainy Lake area must be different, because the color of the rune stone is a unique, light color. Anyway, the stone's layering made it easy for them to cleave off the inscribed face into a thin slab that made it easier to transport. Finally, after many many years, the slab was placed in a final hiding place far away from the fur trade route. It was hidden in a location sacred to native Indian tribes for centuries. Unfortunately there are lots of sacred places. But, we do at least have this clue. It's said to be a mysterious place but also a strategic one. It's a place where the compass needle does not know which way to point and where the rain does not know which way to flow after it falls to the ground. That's what's been passed down anyway."

Tim tried to comprehend the clue.

"And that's your first adventure," Two-hearts said. "Understood?"

"Yes, Cedric. Understood."

"Good. I'll give you my post office box number in Atikokan. You give me your contact information—your fax number, e-mail address—anything you have. Then you'll get your sketch of the coded runes on the Kensington Stone."

A<small>FTER THEY EXCHANGED CONTACT INFORMATION</small> and Tim hung up, Cedric pressed the "E<small>ND</small>" button and folded his cell phone. He sat in his car, looking toward the dark museum. He pondered his advice to Tim: to forget about the wooden chest for the time being, to deal with Hell's Gate Rapids later, and that an astronomer would be needed to decipher the pictographs. The pictographs were a clue. Two-hearts, in fact, knew more about the location of the wooden chest. But he wasn't ready to divulge this. According to the legend that had been passed down, a great chief was supposed to find the jewels. So Two-hearts resolved that if anyone else would find them, they would have to do so mostly by their own effort. Besides, his own interest was in finding the rune stone in order to solve the mystery of the silver urn. More importantly, Two-hearts had never even met Tim Malone. But not having met Malone didn't bother Two-hearts as much as what had happened to Lyle Hanson. Two-hearts was feeling uneasy. Lyle Hanson's accident was bothering him. Although Two-hearts had been followed and spied upon over the years, never once did he suspect that the De Beers Diamond Syndicate would resort to violence.

≫ 18 ≪

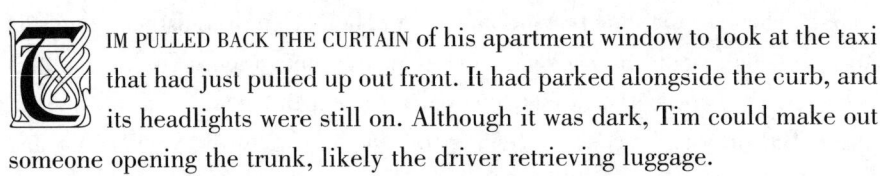

TIM PULLED BACK THE CURTAIN of his apartment window to look at the taxi that had just pulled up out front. It had parked alongside the curb, and its headlights were still on. Although it was dark, Tim could make out someone opening the trunk, likely the driver retrieving luggage.

Tim would have preferred to pick up Jessa at the airport, but he'd had a conflict at the time her airplane was scheduled to arrive. In her typical easy-going, accommodating style, Jessa simply told Tim that she'd take a cab to his apartment.

Although Tim had good intentions to tidy up a bit before Jessa arrived, the apartment was still a mess. He went into high gear, picking up newspapers, stacking magazines, and grabbed a plate and glass off the floor and brought them into the kitchen. By the time Tim walked back into the living room, he heard the doorbell and became conscious of the sound of another person coming up the porch steps. Maybe the taxi cab driver was helping Jessa with her luggage, Tim thought, as he made his way toward the door.

Suddenly Jessa appeared from around a wall that separated the front entry from the living room. She looked great. Her dark eyebrows contrasted well with her peachy skin and rosy cheeks. Her auburn hair was pulled up in her signature bun, giving the tight strands on the sides of her head a grain that was as rich as mahogany.

"Stop right there, Tim. I got a surprise for you," Jessa said as she lowered her suitcase and guitar case to the floor. She had a big smile on her face as she opened her arms to Tim and looked back toward the door.

"A surprise?" Tim asked as he suddenly stopped in the living room and gave Jessa a look of anticipation.

"That's right. But first things first."

Jessa launched herself at Tim, kissed him on the lips and gave him a long hard hug. As Tim held Jessa and rested his chin on her shoulder, he could hear the taxi drive off just before someone in the entry closed the door. Whoever it was shuffled in a bit and dropped their bag on the floor.

"I don't believe it!" Tim said as he pulled back and looked Jessa in the eye. "Is it . . . ?"

"How long can you put up with two people in this small apartment?" Jessa asked with a big smile.

"Shukriyah!" Tim said loudly as he went quickly toward the entry.

Just then Shukriyah came around the corner. Her dark hair fell down each side her head, framing an elegant face worthy of Persian royalty. Her olive skin complemented hazel-colored eyes and full lips. Her appearance was reminiscent of the disarming face on the Nefertiti sculpture.

"What on earth . . . ?" Tim attempted to ask before he gave Shukriyah a bear hug.

"Great news!" Shukriyah said. "I'm all done! I've finished my courses. I defended my thesis. That's it! So, when Jessa said I should come out to Minnesota and surprise you, I jumped at the chance."

"You're done for now?" Tim said as he stepped back and raised his index finger in front of Shukriyah. "Done until you start a Ph.D. program somewhere?"

"Well . . . perhaps. But I came out here because I need a break from astrophysics for a while. I can't wait to visit all the places I missed last time."

"It's not the best time of year. Usually winter is a pretty season. But this year it's kind of brown everywhere with the lack of snow."

"I don't know about Jessa, but that's fine with me. I'll take what I can get. I'm just eager to kick back and do some sight seeing. Soak in the hot tub at some motel."

"I'll be more than happy to accommodate you gals wherever you want to go."

"Got any ideas?" Jessa asked

"I'll start thinkin' on it. Hey, you two! Take off your coats and sit down. Can I get you anything? A beer, a wine cooler, a soda?"

"Got anything that's diet?" Jessa asked as she threw her coat on the sofa and sat next to it.

"How about diet cola?"

"That works."

"Shukriyah?"

"Yeah, a diet cola sounds good," Shukriyah said as she took a living room chair.

After a couple minutes, Tim came back in the living room gingerly carrying a cluster of two glasses of diet soda and one glass of Mountain Dew.

"Thank you," Jessa said as she carefully took one of the glasses of soda from Tim's hands. "By the way Tim, what's the latest on Lyle? How is he?"

"Well . . . considering that he got banged up pretty bad, his prognosis is actually quite good. It's just that the recovery—"

"Thanks, Tim," Shukriyah softly interrupted as she took her drink from Tim's hand.

". . . his convalescence will be long, that's all. But Maggie seems more and more upbeat each time I talk to her."

As Tim sat down, he fell silent momentarily and stared at the ice cubes in his glass. Softly, he said, "Things have certainly changed, that's for sure. I don't know what's going to happen next summer with the recovery project." Then he perked up and looked at his guests with a sort of eager half smile. "But I do have some good news about Lyle's project," Tim said. "Just today I received a fax from Lyle's Canadian contact. You recall that guy named Two-hearts, don't you."

"Yes," Shukriyah said. "I forwarded his items to Omar. That tracing of the 'P & C' symbol, the Voyageur fire steel, and that . . . that crystal thing used for navigation."

"So it's true then?" Tim asked. "Did Omar's friend confirm that the Vikings used that crystal for navigation?"

"Oh, yeah. Omar said he recognized it right away."

"You know, Shukriyah, this is an amazing coincidence that you came out here. There are a couple reasons. One: I need your talent. Two-hearts said he needs an astronomer to decipher some pictographs up in the Boundary Waters."

"What are pictographs? Are they similar to . . . to Egyptian hieroglyphics or something like that?"

"Something on that order. They're small drawings painted on protected rock faces. They seem intended more for communication than for art. Apparently the native Indians drew them long ago."

"That sounds rather exciting. I'd love to solve an ancient puzzle related to astronomy."

"And two: I need help again from Omar's archaeological friend in England. I'd like him to see that fax from Two-hearts."

"Should be no problem. I'm sure he'd be happy to help."

"Tim?" Jessa asked, "the last time we spoke, didn't you say that Two-hearts gave a clue as to where some rune stone may be hidden?"

"Oh, yeah! How could I forget? The Rainy Lake Rune Stone. Two-hearts actually gave me a clue where it may be hidden."

"Can you fill me in?" Shukriyah asked. "Is the Rainy Lake Rune Stone a tablet inscribed with Nordic runes? Similar to the . . . the, um?"

"The Kensington Rune Stone."

"That's it. You even went to inspect the Kensington Stone with—?"

"With Two-hearts. But we didn't see it. The museum where the stone is was closed. Two-hearts wanted to show me runes with special markings. Coded runes, I guess. And that's what his fax is all about. I'd like Omar's friend to see these coded runes."

"Why don't you scan them, and then I'll use your computer to e-mail them to Omar?"

"That sounds good. Anyway, after Lyle got hurt and went in the hospital, Two-hearts wrote a letter to Maggie and said that the Rainy Lake Stone might have information about the silver urn found in England. So, Maggie asked me to get in touch with Two-hearts. I called him and . . . well, let me just say that I had to struggle to gain his trust. But when I finally did, I asked if he had any idea where the Rainy Lake Stone might be. He didn't know for sure, but he knew this much. The stone is a thin slab of slate. It's at a sacred and strategic location. The location is a mysterious place because the rain water doesn't know which way to flow and the compass needle doesn't know where to point."

The three fell silent as they puzzled over the clue.

"Rain water doesn't know which way to flow . . . must be a round hill," Shukriyah speculated.

"As for the compass needle not knowing which way to point," Tim added, "I wondered if that meant it could be somewhere along the Iron Range. But the Iron Range is a hundred miles long or more."

The three fell silent again.

"Hey! I know where it is!" Tim said excitedly. "It's got to be near the Giant's Ridge Ski Hill just north of Biwabik. If rain water falls there, it doesn't know which way to go because of the Laurentian Divide that separates the Hudson Bay and the Atlantic Ocean watersheds in northeast Minnesota. Just west of the ski hill is the Pike River. It flows north into Lake Vermillion. From there, the drainage goes up to Rainy Lake, then to Lake of the Woods, Lake Winnipeg, and finally it all ends up in Hudson Bay. On the east side of the Giant's Ridge Ski Hill water flows to Sabin and Wynne lakes. They're end to end, narrow lakes that are part of the Embarrass River. At that point, only a few miles separates the Pike River from the Embarrass River, which flows south to the St. Louis River, which continues flowing south until it empties into Lake Superior. Lake Superior, of course, eventually empties into the Atlantic Ocean.

"So that's got to be it. Rain water falling in the Giant's Ridge area doesn't know where it'll end up, north or south. As for a compass needle not knowing where to point? Well, like I said, Giant's Ridge lies right along the Iron Range."

Tim looked at the two girls. They looked somewhat taken back by his explanation.

"Shukriyah, you want to soak in a hot tub somewhere. Well, I know just the place. There's a real nice lodge at Giant's Ridge, so how about if I call for reservations?"

"What if they're booked up?" Jessa asked.

"With a winter like this? Nah! They might not even have all their ski runs open."

Shukriyah wasn't so sure. "I don't know, Tim. Are you sure you want to go up there on such flimsy information. I mean . . . what are we going to do once we're there? We can't exactly start asking around if anyone's seen a missing centuries-old rune stone. People'll think we're nuts."

"I don't know how else to do this. I know I'm right about how the water flows there, so we've got a shot of at least being in the right area. There's the underground mine tour at Soudan. Maybe someone there's seen something that'll help. And the Bois Fort Tribe runs a casino near Tower. If we poke around enough places up there, maybe we'll get lucky and run into some old timer who can pinpoint exactly where the 'rain water doesn't know which way to flow.'" Tim glanced back and forth between his two guests. "So what do you think?"

Jessa and Shukriyah looked at each other, considering.

"Sure," Jessa said. "It's sure better than speculating from here."

"It all sounds exciting," Shukriyah said, "and rather important too."

"Great!" Tim said. "I'll check into reservations right away. We'll head up there tomorrow. We'll stop at Maggie's on our way out of town. She'll be thrilled to see you guys again."

Tim looked at Shukriyah. "But first, if I scan that fax from Two-hearts, can you e-mail it to Omar?"

"Sure thing."

19

Maggie Hanson's house

"OH, ONE LAST THING, LINDSEY," Maggie said. "There's a wedge of chocolate amaretto cheesecake in the fridge. Please help yourself."

"That sounds good. I just might take you up on that," Lindsey said. "After all the hospital cafeteria food I've been eating—and I'm sure I'll have more today—I really don't want to come back and be tempted by any more rich, fattening food in the house.

"Okay. Everybody all set?" After Maggie got unanimous consensus, she looked at Lindsey one last time. "Thanks again for watching the house, Lindsey."

"No problem at all. Say hi to Lyle."

"Nice to have met you, Lindsey," Jessa said as she turned to follow Maggie out the front door.

"Nice to have met you too," Lindsey said. "I hope you all have a nice time up at Giant's Ridge."

"I'm sure we will," Tim said as he and Shukriyah also followed Maggie out the door.

As the foursome gathered in the driveway near their cars, Lindsey watched out the living room window as Tim, Jessa, and Shukriyah each gave

Maggie a hug. When both cars had backed out the driveway and driven away, Lindsey remained at the living room window. She looked at her Hamilton wrist watch. The daylight flooding through the window made the diamonds on the case sparkle. She folded her arms and calmly stood still while admiring the outdoor scenery.

After a couple of minutes had passed, Lindsey saw a limo pull up and park in front of the house. Two men got out and looked at the house.

20

University of Newcastle upon Tyne, Newcastle, Great Britain

"AM I TOO EARLY?" OMAR SAID after rapping a couple of times on the open door of Alistair's office.

"That's okay," Alistair said while continuing to look at his computer screen and manipulate the mouse. "Just one minute. Have a seat . . . while . . . I . . . there. All done."

Alistair swivelled in his chair to face Omar directly and folded his arms. "Sorry ole chap, but our Internet service is still down. I never did receive that e-mail you forwarded from Shukriyah."

"Quite all right," Omar said as he opened his briefcase. "I assumed that might still be the case, so I downloaded Shukriyah's attachment onto this CD. Here you are."

"Thanks," Alistair said as he took the disk from Omar and placed it on his desk.

"Ready for lunch?" Omar asked.

"Um, could we please wait just a bit, Omar? I'm expecting a call."

"Oh, sure. No problem."

"I said I was expecting a guest—you—in about ten minutes and that we were going to leave. But you're early so I'd like to wait about five more minutes."

"By the way," Omar said as he sat down. "Shukriyah was pretty excited. Her e-mail explained that the attachment shows some coded runes from the Kensington Rune Stone."

"Ah, yes. I know a little bit about that."

"What can you tell me about the Kensington Rune Stone?"

Alistair's expression became thoughtful. "The sad and sordid tale of the Kensington Rune Stone," he said. He leaned back and his chair squeaked. "Found in the American state of Minnesota in 1898, it was inscribed with Nordic runes in the year 1362." Alistair pursed his lips. "I regard that stone as one of the most important artifacts ever found in North America not to be recognized as such."

"Really?"

"Indeed I do."

"You know, I've heard that it's been controversial from the start."

"Oh yes. That's what happens when something gets removed from an archaeological site prematurely. Similar to the silver urn found over here near Hadrian's Wall." He sighed. "The conditions didn't get documented, and the artifact is, therefore, out of context. Its authenticity is endlessly questioned regardless of what the evidence."

"Is it true that some of the text on the Kensington stone has some religious significance?" Omar asked.

"To a certain extent, yes. But the first reaction one might have is that the stone is simply informational. It just tells a story about how ten men in a particular expedition got killed. But why would that be the sole motivation for someone to do all that chiseling in a stone?"

Omar shrugged.

"In those days, chiseling in stone was a good way to establish a permanent record. Being that the Kensington stone was found in a strategic area of North America, near the divide between the north and south continental watersheds, it makes sense that the stone was likely intended to document a claim to the land."

Omar knitted his brows. "Would you also say the same about that stone discovered by the French explorer named La . . . La Ver . . ."

Alistair nodded vigorously. "Pierre Gaultier de Varennes, Sieur de La Verendrye. Yes. Yes. It's possible that stone too had been intended as some sort of claim to the land. He found it in the western plains of North America in about 1740, brought it to Jesuit priests in Quebec, and from there it got sent to Paris. It's never been seen since."

"What has me puzzled," Omar said, "is that the Two-hearts fellow not only knows about the Kensington Stone and the stone found by La Verendrye, he also knows about a third stone, the Rainy Lake Stone."

"Hmm . . . that is interesting, isn't it?"

"Alistair, do remember telling me about the blonde-haired, blue eyed Mandan Indians who lived along the Missouri River in what is present-day North Dakota?"

"Yes. La Verendrye documented their existence and so did the Lewis and Clark expedition. Possible descendants of Viking explorers, I'd say."

"I told you that Two-hearts claimed some Scandinavian blood himself. Well, maybe I should be more to the point. He specifically claims to be descended from the Vikings."

Alistair fell momentarily silent as he gave Omar a half confused, half surprised look. "Well," he finally said, "I guess that explains how he may have gotten the navigational sun crystal."

"What do you know about these Viking explorers who apparently reached the interior of the North American continent and left the rune stones? Were there documented expeditions?"

"The most well known is the Paul Knutson expedition. Commissioned in 1354, they departed in 1355. If they reached the center of the continent, I don't know, but if they did, they likely sailed across Hudson Bay."

"Why wouldn't they have gone up the St. Lawrence Seaway and through the Great Lakes?"

"Let me show you," Alistair said as he swivelled in his chair, leaned back and reached for a globe on his office table. He held it up to so that is was level with Omar's face and positioned so the North Pole was straight up.

"We usually look at a globe or a map of the Earth like this," Alistair explained with his index finger a few inches away from the equator, "with the equator directly before us, half way between the north and south poles."

Alistair tilted the globe so that the axis of the Earth was pointing at Omar's right shoulder. He rotated the globe so that Omar would see Greenland directly to the left of the North Pole.

"But this is the Earth from a Viking perspective. Imagine you are the captain on a Viking long boat. You are approaching the land mass we now know as the North American continent—and if I may add, probably an enticing land mass considering that during an earlier episode of natural global warming, even Greenland was . . . well, green."

Alistair placed his index finger near the southern tip of Greenland and slowly moved it toward the coast of northeast Canada.

"Now, if you wanted to explore the coast of the continent, it would be a toss up which way you'd want to go once you hit the shore of what we call the Canadian province of Labrador. Of course, we know for a fact that there were Vikings who sailed left and established the settlement at L'Anse Aux Meadows.

"However, it would have made just as much sense for an expedition to sail into Hudson Bay," Alistair said as he traced his finger along the northern coast of the Quebec province and down into Hudson Bay. "And if you're looking to establish land claims, you might look for large rivers that emptied into Hudson Bay. The larger the river, the larger the land mass it drained, and the more land on which to stake your claim."

Alistair returned the globe to its stand. He swivelled to face Omar and started to draw an imaginary line with his finger from eye-level down to his lap.

"I would guess that, from Hudson Bay, the Paul Knutson expedition went south up the Nelson River to Lake Winnipeg, and crossed the lake to reach its southern end. Once there, they would have found that two large rivers emptied into the lake: the Red River from the south and the Winnipeg River from the southeast. A third river from the west, the Assiniboine, merged with the Red River near its mouth on Lake Winnipeg.

"Again, the volumes of these three rivers would have indicated the size of the land mass being drained. So, the Viking explorers went up each. If they split up, separate exploration parties followed each river with the intent of staking a land claim at the height of each watershed. In each case they marked their claim with an inscribed stone . . . or so the theory goes."

"But don't the stones also have some religious significance?"

"The Kensington stone certainly does," Alistair said as he grabbed a pencil and tablet from his desktop, and then leaned toward Omar.

"Besides runic inscriptions, the Kensington Stone has these three Latin letters." On the corner of his desk, Alistair positioned his tablet next to Omar and began to write. "A . . . V . . . M . . . means *Ave Maria* or Hail Mary. Sometimes it's simply AV, which has been found on grave crosses in Greenland.

"Now, the stone says that the Viking party was comprised of eight 'Götalanders' and twenty-two Norwegians. Knowing the stone's text has at least some religious connotation, the inscriber was likely one of the Götalanders. Gotland is an island in the Baltic Sea near Sweden. It received heavy Christian influence from the Cistercians, a monastic order established in 1098 in France.

"Being from Gotland, the inscriber would have known about coding runic text. And on the stone, there are several runes—including the M in 'AVM'—that are altered. If you take just these altered symbols, you can come up with some pretty fascinating interpretations. For instance, the altered characters in the first four lines of the stone spell out, in Swedish, 'Gral är'. In English, it's 'Grail is.' Until they decipher more of the coding, no one will be able to come up with an answer to the question of what exactly the grail is."

Alistair suddenly looked at his watch.

"You know, I'm getting hungry. What do you say we go have lunch?"

"Are you going to give up on that phone call?"

"Yeah, he can leave a message and I'll call back this afternoon. I'll also look at your CD sometime this afternoon. It'll be interesting to see."

๑ 21 ๛

The next morning.

LOUD KNOCKS ON THE DOOR OF HIS HOTEL SUITE startled Omar. Although he had slept unusually late, it was still rather early for anyone to come unannounced. In a white tank-top T-shirt and boxer shorts, he quickly walked to the door to look through the peep hole. It was Alistair Groom.

Omar barely got the door open, when Alistair barged in, clenching his fists as if holding ski poles. His coat was hanging over one forearm.

"Get your arse out of bed, Omar!" Alistair said excitedly as he took long, fast strides into the main room, threw his coat over the back of a chair and turned around. "A couple things have happened!" He opened up his fisted hands as if he was showing the length of a fish he had caught. His shoulders heaved as he tried to catch his breath. "It's an absolute . . . absolute miracle. I got . . . a phone call . . ."

"Getting a phone call is no miracle," Omar said as he calmly shut the door, "unless it was a wealthy widow asking you out on a date."

Alistair looked up and pointed his finger at Omar to acknowledge the witty remark. "Hah, hah," he said sarcastically between breaths.

Omar gave Alistair a look that showed both concern and curiosity.

"My goodness, Alistair, did you run all the way here? You better sit."

"Nah." Alistair slowly stood erect and loosened a couple buttons on his shirt. "I'm all right."

"You didn't take the stairs, did you?"

"When I got to the lobby, I . . . could see . . . all . . . these people . . . waiting for an elevator." Alistair held up his hands, took one last slow, deep breath, then flopped his hands downward. "I figured you're only a few floors up."

"You certainly could have called me."

Alistair rolled his eyes. "Come off it. You know me . . . how I get when I'm excited. I can't use the phone." Alistair grinned. "Besides, you know how I love to have face-to-face conversations with men in their underwear."

"Well, you're the one who barged in here unannounced," Omar said as he headed toward his bedroom. "Help yourself to a glass of water."

"Thanks. I could use one."

"So, you said you got a call?" Omar called so Alistair could hear him from the bedroom. "Is that one of the things that make up your miracle?"

"Oh, yes. That's right," Alistair said in a similarly loud voice as he walked into the kitchen. "After we had lunch yesterday, my field supervisor in Turkey—you remember Hasan—well, he called . . . uh . . . say, Omar, why don't I wait until you come out so I don't have to shout?"

"Turkey? Good Lord! I'll be right out!"

Alistair poured himself some water and returned to the main room. Within seconds, Omar hurried out of his bedroom buttoning a white shirt whose untucked tails draped over charcoal gray trousers. He was in his stocking feet.

"Cappadocia?" Omar asked with piercing eyes that would appear hostile to anyone who didn't know him. But Alistair knew better, or didn't notice, and calmly raised the glass to his lips to take a couple gulps of water.

"Yes." Alistair wiped his lips with the back of his hand. "Hasan called yesterday. He said they found it, Omar. Those pages of the Taurus Mountain Chronicles that record the second visit of the Magi in the mid-first century. Man alive, Omar, I barely slept a bloody wink all night."

Omar froze. He paused in the act of buttoning his shirt. He eventually abandoned the job and strode to Alistair. He planted his hands on Alistair's shoulders. "This is really it then?" Omar asked softly but with dead seriousness. "You've finally succeeded?"

Alistair could barely contain himself. The eyebrows on his beaming face rose and he grinned even wider, his head bobbling.

Upon seeing Alistair's confirmation, Omar held his clasped hands to his lips and closed his eyes as if in thankful prayer.

"To be honest, Omar, it's you and your organization who have succeeded," Alistair said as he placed his glass on the table. He extended his arms out from his sides, palms up. "After all, you're the ones who hired me. This was your dream before it was mine."

"This is a miracle," Omar said softly. "I must make some phone calls. Then I need to get down to Turkey right away." He looked at Alistair with pleading eyes. "I know you had said that the university wants you to stay here in Newcastle. But, under the circumstances, would you reconsider and come with me?"

"I've already made the arrangements. Anyone can see that the silver urn will be hopelessly tied up in messy politics for the near future."

"What about the excavation site near Hadrian's Wall?"

"Fiddle sticks! Every bloody archaeologist in England is flocking there. I'd rather avoid it completely, thank you. If any issue needing special attention comes up, my colleagues will know how to get a hold of me."

Omar was pleased. "Excellent! I'll go make those calls and then get hold of my pilot. I'll let him know that you'll be a passenger."

"Wait one second," Alistair said. "You haven't let me tell you about the other thing that happened."

"That's right! I almost forgot!" Omar said. "Does it involve the CD I gave you?"

"That's what I was getting to next! Let your phone calls wait. This is big." Alistair's eyes were intense. He gestured up and down as if he was making simultaneous Karate chops. "The file on that CD . . . the sketch from that Two-hearts fellow. You won't believe it!"

"What?" Omar asked excitedly.

Alistair beamed. Omar could only smile. Alistair behaved like a young child discovering presents under a Christmas tree.

"This is a bit involved, so hang with me. The file was a sketch of two coded runes on the Kensington Rune Stone. One rune is X-shaped and the other is R-shaped. Both runes have been altered with punch marks, and they're close to each other on the fourth line of the stone."

"Alistair, let's sit down at the table and go over this carefully."

Alistair nodded and moved to the chair on which he had thrown his coat. "Now, most people in my field know about coded runes, and, as we discussed yesterday, at least a few of us know about the coded runes on the Kensington Stone. But it never dawned on me until I saw the sketch from Twohearts: both of these coded runes on the Kensington Stone are altered with two punch marks. Two!" Alistair said as he held up two fingers. "Let me show you. Do you have something I can write on?"

"Sure. Here," Omar reached inside his briefcase on the table. He pulled out a pen and a tablet of paper.

Alistair drew an X with two dots on top and a little dash on the inside of the upper right leg.

"There's a punch at the bottom of each leg . . . here . . . and here. And the R-shaped rune is pretty much a Roman R with two punches on the vertical stave . . . like so. When I looked at these two runic characters and considered their possible Greek counterparts, that's when it hit me like a ton of bricks." Alistair looked into Omar's eyes. "Do you see where I'm going with this, Omar?"

Omar nodded. "The Greek letters Chi and Rho. The commonly used first two letters in the Greek word for 'Christ the Anointed.'"

"Exactly!"

"But Alistair, your runic character is R-shaped. The Greek letter Rho looks like the Roman letter 'P.'"

"I know. But maybe they figured that their runic 'R' had the same sound as the Greek letter Rho. And more importantly, the slanted leg on their runic 'R' resembles . . . here, let me get it."

Alistair turned and reached into an interior pocket of his coat. He pulled out five folded sheets of paper.

"First—a quick question," Omar said as Alistair started unfolding four of the five sheets of paper and spreading them flat on the table. "The practice of altering runes to resemble Chi and Rho . . . might that be an influence from that monastic order you had mentioned in your office yesterday?"

"The Cistercians? Not in my opinion. The way I see it, the monks in the monasteries of the British Isles were using Chi and Rho long before the Cistercian Order was even established. And the Vikings had been on the British Isles since the early 800s. Look at these. This one is a copy of the Chi-Rho page from the *Lindisfarne Gospels*." Alistair smoothed out the first folded sheet with his palm. "This next one is a copy of the Chi-Rho page from the *Book of Kells* . . . and this third one is from the *Codex Aureus*. Notice anything?"

"Clearly Byzantine design elements," Omar replied.

"I'd say it's more Celtic with possible Byzantine influences. But nevertheless, you're getting warm in regard to the design elements. Can you be more specific?"

"Uh, design elements notwithstanding, I see there's also the Greek letter Iota in addition to Chi and Rho."

"True. But that wasn't my point—not yet, anyway. In each case, notice the letter Chi. There are large circles and dots at the end of the legs."

"The way I see it, if representing Chi was the Vikings' intent, then the X-shaped rune was the perfect choice to use as a code for the Greek letter Chi. Its standard form already had an umlaut—two dots—on top. By adding two more punches on the feet of the lower legs, the character resembles the decorative Chi used in the gospel manuscripts of Celtic Britain.

"Now, let's look at the letters Rho and Iota designs on the gospel manuscripts. Do you notice anything with those?"

"Oh, yes!" Omar said as he picked up one of the sheets. "The Iota is superimposed on the circular part of the letter Rho. The combined letters can be construed as representing the Roman letter 'R.'"

"In fact, when it comes to historic Chi-Rho symbols, there's even a precedent for substituting a Roman 'R' for the Greek Rho." Alistair handed

Omar the fourth sheet of paper showing a historic Chi-Rho symbol within an oval.

"I got to hand it to you," Omar said. "You've given this matter a lot of thought."

"I'm absolutely convinced that the author of the Kensington Rune Stone thought his Runic 'R' resembled the combined Rho and Iota on the old English gospel manuscripts."

"But one question, Alistair. Why would the Vikings have taken an interest in Christian lettering on old English manuscripts, and then adopted it no less?"

"Oh, but they certainly had the interest all right. So much so that they stole the *Codex Aureus*. Granted, I'm sure they valued it, since it was made with gold leaf. But over time, the Vikings certainly would have been influenced by the design of the lettering. Eventually, it was some alderman or magistrate or—whatever he was—some official named Alfred who was able to ransom back the *Codex Aureus* from the Danes.

"By the way, I have my own little theory about another theft involving the *Lindisfarne Gospels*. And this should be of interest to you, Omar. What I've been able to gather from my research, some rogue monk at the Lindisfarne Priory might have illuminated a fifth gospel. If he did, I'm convinced that it was the Gospel of Thomas. And I'm absolutely convinced that the Vikings stole it as well."

Alistair rubbed his chin, and his eyes darted from one side of the table to the other as his mind raced. "Well . . . actually, it might be more accurate to say that the Vikings were *allowed* to steal it. You see, when the Vikings invaded Lindisfarne, the monks saved the four canonical gospels when they fled. I suspect that they left the Gospel of Thomas behind on purpose because so many in their order regarded it as heretical."

"Hmm," Omar said. "All very intriguing. But let's get back to the Chi and Rho. It still seems quite a jump to equate the punched X and R-shaped runes to the Chi-Rho lettering on the English manuscripts."

"You think so, do you? Well, I took a hard look at the sketch from Twohearts and considered the information that got passed down to him from generation to generation. One: the Rainy Lake Stone has a Chi-Rho symbol—either explicit or in code. And two: the stone is connected—maybe even makes reference—to a very special silver urn in England. So I went back and studied my close-up photos of the silver urn . . . and that's when the light came on." Alistair started sketching furiously. "Look here. Inscribed on the urn is what appears to be three crossed bars that resemble an asterisk. On the upper part of the vertical stave is a loop . . . kind of like . . . so. The engraving is somewhat crude and was most likely not original. Some of us had disregarded it as some sort of amateur design that was not much better than high-class vandalism."

Alistair rotated the drawing and slid it toward Omar.

"However, after looking at the file on that CD and then taking a closer look at Chi Rho designs . . . well, isn't is obvious now?"

"Sure enough," Omar said. "A Chi Rho symbol."

Alistair paused and looked eagerly into Omar's eyes. Not able to contain his anticipation, he held his pen between two fingers like a cigarette and nervously drummed it on the table.

"Well, Omar, if the engraving on the silver urn is indeed a Chi-Rho symbol, then I take it you've figured out the implications."

"I can think of only one group of Persians," Omar said softly as he stared down at Alistair's sketch of the Chi-Rho symbol. Then he lifted his eyes and returned Alistair's gaze. ". . . only one group of Persians who would have cherished an item with Chi-Rho and the symbol of Faravahar."

"Of course," Alistair said. "*Your* organization. The ancient order of the Magi. Now do you see why I didn't want to wait for that elevator and ran up the stairs instead?"

"Yes, I do. And now I feel the same way. I must call my pilot at once."

"Wait. I have one last sheet of paper. Think about that sketch I just showed you. The sketch of the Chi-Rho symbol that's on the silver urn. Now look at this." Alistair unfolded the fifth sheet of paper, flattened it out and slid it in front of Omar. "The upper part of the symbol for the Assyrian Church of the East, which is a Syriac Chaldean church within the St. Thomas Christian Group, has a pair of crossed keys and a shepherd's crook. Some claim that it is intended to represent Chi Rho."

Omar stared. He stood and said softly, "Alistair, when can you be ready?"

"I'll need to stop by my office to grab a few things. Then I just need to go back to my flat and pack. Should need about a couple hours or so."

"All right. I'll give you two hours."

Omar practically sprinted to his bedroom. He had just turned the corner when he suddenly stopped and looked back at Alistair.

"One last quick question," Omar said. "I never would have thought about early English monks using Byzantine-like design elements and having a Gospel of Thomas in their possession. What do you make of that? Possible influences from the ancient Syriac churches?"

"Could be," Alistair said as he folded up his papers.

"Through Persians conscripted by the Romans?"

Alistair grinned. "Could be." He stood and grabbed his coat from the back of his chair. "I'll see you in a couple hours."

∽ 22 ∾

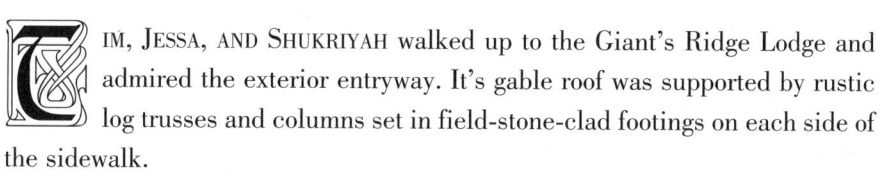

Tim, Jessa, and Shukriyah walked up to the Giant's Ridge Lodge and admired the exterior entryway. It's gable roof was supported by rustic log trusses and columns set in field-stone-clad footings on each side of the sidewalk.

After they checked in at the front desk and received their card keys, Tim picked up on the friendly, approachable nature of the receptionist. He attempted to make some small talk and inquire about the Giant's Ridge locale. With no other waiting customers, the receptionist seemed willing to speak with Tim and was able to elaborate about what she knew. But when Tim asked about Ojibwe legends of a place where "the rain water doesn't know which way to flow and the compass needle doesn't know where to point," the woman drew a blank.

"That specific phrase doesn't ring a bell," the receptionist said. "But there is a legendary place right near here at the south end of Wynne Lake. It was buried by fill, and the Bois Forte tribe wants it excavated. I guess it was a sacred place on the Embarrass River long before white man came to the area. I don't know if there were burial grounds there or if it was an old village or what."

"Why did it get filled in?" Tim asked.

"It was right next to an iron ore deposit, so it got filled in by mining operations. In fact, the fill dammed up the river. That's how Wynne Lake got formed. Today, the lake drains around the dam through a diversion channel dug out by the mining company."

"Is the tribe taking any action to get the sacred area excavated?" Tim asked.

"Actually, I think they're getting close to making a deal with the property owners. There sure are lot of people and organizations behind the effort. It even has the support of the Minnesota Historical Society."

"Who can I talk to who knows more about this sacred place?"

After thinking a moment, the receptionist's face brightened. "Oh, I know who would know something," she said. "At the Fortune Bay Resort Casino on Lake Vermillion is a supervisor named Angel Gray Feather. I used to work for her before I got this job. Not only is Angel up to speed on what the tribe's doing, but she knows several retired miners who are regulars there. One of them is a third or fourth generation miner who sure knows a lot about the mining history down here in the Biwabik area. But be warned— he's kind of an ornery fellow."

The receptionist's face grew quizzical. "His name is Milo . . . uh, Milo Mar . . . well, I can't remember, but Angel sure would."

The receptionist looked at her watch. "In fact, if the retired miners are still keeping the same schedule, then they're probably there right now. If you left right away, I'm sure you could catch them. Just ask for Angel and she would be happy to point them out for you."

Tim looked at Jessa and Shukriyah. "What do you say?"

"Better take advantage of the opportunity," Shukriyah said.

"Yeah, let's just leave our stuff in the car and head up there," Jessa said.

Tim turned back toward the receptionist. "We appreciate the information. Thank you."

"I tell you what. You might as well take a few minutes to bring in your luggage. In the meantime, I'll call Angel so she knows to expect you. She should be working today, but it's best to make sure. And besides, she can check to see if Milo is there."

Once the receptionist had spoken with Angel—who confirmed that Milo was at the Fortune Bay Resort Casino—Tim, Jessa, and Shukriyah hopped back in the car. Not even an hour had passed by the time they pulled into the large parking lot at Fortune Bay.

The architecture of the massive, sprawling facility repeated the north woods theme as at Giant's Ridge, albeit more subtly, with shallow-angled green roofs and field stone facades. Brown-colored struts protruding from underneath the roof eaves seemed intended as a Native American design accent.

They had no problem finding Angel. She was talking with another employee when she saw them coming. "I'll get back to you in a few minutes," Angel said to the employee. She turned her attention to Tim, Jessa, and Shukriyah.

"Hi! I'm Angel. You must be the three from Giant's Ridge."

"Yes, we are. I'm Tim. This is Jessa and Shukriyah."

"Welcome to Fortune Bay," Angel said with a smile. "I understand you're interested in the sacred grounds buried at the south end of Wynne Lake. Specifically, a place where the rain doesn't . . . doesn't know which way . . ."

". . . which way to flow, and the compass needle doesn't know where to point," Tim said.

"Yes, that was it. Well, first, I should tell you I have good news and bad news. The good news is that it's essentially a sure thing that the site at Wynne Lake will get excavated. The bad news is that it's not going to happen any time soon."

Tim shrugged. "Well, we're not even sure yet we have the correct site. That's why we'd like to find out from someone if they have any information about the site. Was it ever described as a place where the rain doesn't know which way to flow and the compass needle doesn't know which way to point?"

"Well, Milo Maranich should know. He and the other retired miners are in the lounge, so follow me this way. I'll be honest with you," Angel said as they started walking, "Milo can get a little . . . well, a little short tempered if he's had a few too many. But they haven't been in the lounge all that long, and when I told him what you're looking for, he seemed interested in helping. He likes it when people ask him about the old days of mining."

When they got to the lounge, Angel approached the miners but then stopped and looked around. "Where's Milo?"

"He didn't go far," one of the retired miners said. "He'll be back."

Angel turned toward Tim with her finger up. "I tell you what. Just as you came in, I was giving instructions to an employee. Let me finish with that real quick and I'll be right back." Angel took off at a fast walk.

"Where you all from?" one of the retired miners asked.

"Duluth. We just came up today."

"Are you staying here at the lodge?"

"No. We're staying at Giant's Ridge."

"Well, speak of the devil," another retired miner said. "Angel should of waited a bit longer cause here comes Milo now."

Milo Maranich was thin, slightly hunched over, and walked with short steps. He wore old fashioned, horned-rimmed glasses, and a circular object protruding in his shirt pocket was likely a snuff can. His ashen-gray complexion was creased with deep wrinkles. The absence of smile lines implied that his cold expression was the norm. He kept his distance by standing behind his seated, fellow retirees.

"Mr. Maranich? My name's Tim Malone. Did Angel already explain the reason why we're here?"

Maranich didn't answer right away. He eyed Shukriyah from head to toe. "Yeah . . . she explained," Maranich said as he bent over between two of his seated friends and picked up a half-empty glass of beer from the small table.

"Um, we were wondering if the south end of Wynne Lake was ever known as a place where the rain water doesn't know which way—?"

"Let's take this outside," Maranich said abruptly, almost rudely. "I need some fresh air." As he started for the exit, Tim gave Jessa and Shukriyah a confused, almost apprehensive look, and then started to follow.

When everyone got outside and stood under the portico, Tim tried to continue. "That location on Wynne . . ."

Suddenly, Maranich threw his beer on Tim, and tossed his glass sideways. It shattered against the stone cladding on a portico support column. He got up close to Tim and put his finger in his face.

"Now you shut up and listen to me, you stupid punk! What the hell do you think you're doing by bringing an A-rab up here? Huh?"

Shukriyah's eyes became fierce, and she took a step toward Tim to get ready to help.

"And another thing . . ."

Before Maranich could say another word, the glass door flew open.

"Milo!" Angel Gray Feather said sharply, a furious look on her face. "What on earth are you doing?"

Maranich turned to face Angel. "God damn it, Angel, stay out of this!" He stuck his arm straight out and pointed at Shukriyah. "Terrorists have no business being here, and you know it. This is a Christian country, and we need to keep it that way."

Angel let go of the door and stomped over to Maranich, coming to within an inch of his nose. "You unbelievable bastard. Now you listen to me. Number one, she's my cousin. How do you think they were able to look me up? Number two, what are you going to do about me? I'm not a Christian. My people were here long before your white Christian ancestors ever got here."

As Maranich looked at Angel, shock coming over his face. He slowly looked at Shukriyah with humiliation, then back at Angel.

"She's . . . she's your cousin? Angel, I had no idea."

"Look Milo, this is the last straw. You're no longer welcome at Fortune Bay. Insulting a guest is one thing—something you've done numerous times. But now you've assaulted one." Angel pointed toward the parking lot. "Leave. I want you off this property right now."

"Angel . . . won't you at least let me apologize?"

"Leave! Now!"

As Maranich walked away, Angel glanced at Tim and Shukriyah.

"I'm so terribly sorry. Milo is known for his crabbiness, but I never suspected he was capable of this."

Tim pulled his wet jacket away from his body and undid the zipper.

Angel added, "Look, let's go inside so I can write down your name and address. I'll send you a check to cover the cost of a new jacket. In fact, if you can stay, dinner will be on the house for all three of you."

Angel looked at Shukriyah. "I know saying you were my cousin was an awkward way to handle the situation. But that's what came to mind on an impulse."

"Oh, don't feel bad about that. It was very effective, I must say."

Angel looked at the broken glass. "I need to get a hold of someone in Maintenance to clean this up."

Tim eased off his jacket. "Well, I guess any information Mr. Maranich had would have been pointless anyway. If I understand you correctly, excavation of the fill at Wynne Lake won't take place for quite some time."

"Yeah, that's right," Angel said.

Jessa put her hands around Tim's shoulders.

As Angel held the glass door open for Tim, Jessa, and Shukriyah, a dark limousine out in the parking lot started its engine and slowly pulled away.

ಖಿ 23 ಡ

I T WAS MID-DAY WHEN TIM DROVE into Duluth from the Iron Range. The driving had lulled Jessa and Shukriyah to sleep. Even as Tim passed through successive starts and stops at various traffic lights on the outskirts of town, his two passengers showed no signs of waking. Eventually, when Tim had to make some sharper turns into his neighborhood, he finally noticed them stirring.

"Are we in Duluth already?" Jessa asked with garbled enunciation caused by a yawn. She arched her back and stretched her arms toward the windshield.

"Yeah, pretty close to my apartment, in fact."

"How did you hold up driving? Are you tired?"

Tim smiled. "No, not at all."

The talking finally woke Shukriyah in the back seat.

"Still with us back there?" Tim jokingly asked as he looked at Shukriyah in his rear view mirror.

Shukriyah groaned, stretched and shifted in her seat.

"Oh, that felt good," Shukriyah said. "I had a dream about the Soudan underground mine. That sure was a unique state park."

"It really intrigued you, didn't it?" Tim asked.

"Sure did. But I sure wish they'd give public tours of the caverns where they're doing cosmic particle research."

"Hey, I have an idea. Now that you're through in Boston, apply to the Physics Department at the University of Minnesota. You could move out here and end up spending a lot of time in the underground mine."

"Well, that's a thought now, isn't it?"

Tim made the turn onto his street.

"Here we are," Tim declared. "Home at last."

"Tim!" Jessa suddenly said. "Look. There are people on your porch. One of them looks like a police officer."

Tim felt a spurt of adrenaline hit his stomach. *What's this all about?* "That's a police officer all right. And that must be his squad car out front."

Tim parked, and the three hurried out of the car and up to the porch. The police officer was talking with Tim's neighbor, Mr. Adams, a retired man in his late sixties who lived in the adjacent duplex.

"Hello, Tim," Mr. Adams said solemnly. "I'm afraid I have some bad news."

"What happened?"

"When I came home, I noticed your door was slightly ajar. I looked closely and noticed the jamb was splintered."

Tim gaped. "Someone broke into my apartment? When?"

"We're not exactly sure," the police officer said. "According to Mr. Adams, I understand that you've been out of town, correct?"

"Yes. May I go in?" Tim asked.

"Certainly. Go right ahead," the officer said as he stepped to the side.

Mr. Adams called after Tim. "I phoned the landlord. He said he'll have someone over this afternoon yet to fix your door."

"That's great, Mr. Adams. Thanks for doing that."

The older man smiled. "Let me know if there's anything else I can do. I'll be home the rest of the day."

"All right. Thanks again."

Tim walked into his living room. As he looked around, the officer came in, followed by Jessa and Shukriyah. The officer tried to empathize with Tim.

"It's a feeling of personal violation, isn't it?"

"It sure is. Someone I don't know rummaged through my personal stuff."

"Do you have insurance, Mr. Malone."

"Renter's insurance."

"Good. You'll need to come up with a list of what's been taken."

"To be honest, things don't look that bad," Tim said. "The drawer's open where I had some cash and a small camera. My DVD player's gone."

The officer said, "Whoever it was wanted to get in and out rather quickly. They certainly didn't bother to trash the place."

Tim turned and looked at Jessa and pointed in a far corner of the room.

"Well, Jessa, at least they didn't take your guitar. Maybe they didn't know how valuable it was." Tim smiled. The beat-up guitar wasn't worth much.

"Well, it's mighty valuable to me," Jessa said.

"Mr. Malone," the officer said. "I'm pretty much done with my report. I'll let you look around and make a list of missing items. Your insurance agent is welcome to call me for a copy of my report. My name is Officer Plascowitz."

Tim turned to him. "Sooo . . . that's it? Just a report?"

"I'm afraid so, Mr. Malone. The fact is . . . well . . . there's just not much that we can do."

"I . . . I suppose there isn't. Um, thanks . . . thanks for coming over."

After Officer Plascowitz left, Tim walked slowly through the rest of the apartment. After a few minutes, he came back into the living room and found Jessa and Shukriyah sitting glumly.

"Anything else stolen?" Shukriyah asked.

"Yeah, they took a depth finder from the same place where I keep my fishing gear. But a GPS unit was right in the same area and in plain sight. I don't know how they missed that."

His two guests looked quizzical at this information.

"I don't know," Tim said as he stood with his hands in his pockets. "Whoever it was, maybe they were particular in what valuables they . . ."

The look on Tim's face grew anxious.

Jessa picked up on his uneasiness. "Tim? What is it?"

"Um, do you guys remember what I said about the possibility of Lyle's accident being . . . well, not an accident? And that car in Alexandria bumping my car from behind?"

Jessa and Shukriyah certainly remembered, but remained quiet as they stared at Tim. It was obvious to them that Tim was about to draw a frightful implication.

"Oh God! What if this burglary is connected to those incidents?"

With startling urgency, Tim went for the phone on his coffee table.

"Tim, who are you going to call?" Jessa said anxiously as she stood next to him.

"Maggie. I better find out if anything strange has happened at her place. Maybe Lindsey's seen something while Maggie's been visiting Lyle."

Shukriyah also walked nervously over to where Tim and Jessa were standing.

"Hi, Maggie," Tim said when she answered her phone. "It's Tim . . . Yeah, we had a good time. How's Lyle coming along? . . . That's good . . . No, no luck with the rune stone yet. Maggie, I got some news . . . Well, it's bad, I'm sorry to say. My apartment got broken into . . . Yeah, it really sucks . . . Yeah, a police officer just left . . . The front door's damaged and some things are missing. But to be honest, I'm surprised they didn't take more. Look, Maggie, I need to ask you something. Is everything okay at your house? Have you noticed anything strange or out of place? . . . How about Lindsey? Has she reported anything to you? . . . All right . . . Yes, I think you should call her. Even if it was something seemingly benign, some stranger snooping around the neighborhood, someone walking back and forth in front of the house or whatever, Lindsey should tell you about it . . . Good . . . Oh! Certainly. Sorry for having interrupted. I better let you go then . . . Nope, that's all I had. Just remember to ask Lindsey . . . Yup, they're both right here. Sure, I'll say hi. Talk to you soon."

Tim put the phone down and turned to Jessa and Shukriyah. "Maggie hasn't noticed anything out of the ordinary at her place. She said she would call Lindsey and ask her if she had noticed anything peculiar." Tim's expression relaxed somewhat as he rubbed the back of his neck. "You know something," he said, "I don't think I want to deal with this right now. What do you say we get out of here? I'm thinking about going down to the lake shore."

"Tim, you're going to have to deal with this sooner or later," Jessa said.

"Then I'll deal with it later."

"I suppose you're right," Jessa said. "Getting away from here for a little while might alleviate the shock of it. Shukriyah, are you up for a walk?"

"Yeah, I'm game," Shukriyah said.

"I'll bring you guys down to a place called Brighton Beach," Tim said. "Whenever I need to escape for a spell, I go down there to slow down and relax. This time of year the wind off the lake can be rather cold—especially today. But a cold wind in my face maybe just the thing I need right now."

"Do we dare leave here with the door broken like that?" Jessa asked.

"I'll ask Mr. Adams to watch the apartment. Besides, the landlord is sending a someone to repair the door, so it'd be nice to clear out of here just to be out of his way."

Tim, Jessa and Shukriyah walked out of the apartment and climbed back into Tim's car. As Tim looked in his side view mirror and pulled away from the curb, a black limousine half a block behind him also pulled away from the curb.

LINDSEY MELBURN-DAVIS PICKED up her cell phone, selected a number on her speed dial list and put the phone to her ear. "Shel. It's me, Lindsey. I got a call from Maggie Hanson. She asked if I've noticed anything suspicious while I've been watching her house . . . Oh come on! What do you mean don't worry about it? That's easy for you to say."

~ 24 ~

ON BRIGHTON BEACH AT THE EAST END OF DULUTH, Tim, Jessa and Shukriyah huddled shoulder to shoulder on a picnic table situated just within the trees about twenty yards away from Lake Superior. Although a cold winter wind was blowing off the lake, the three were determined to experience—if for only a few minutes—the sights, sounds, and feel of a Lake Superior gale.

Four-foot-high rollers pounded a dark gray shelf of gabbro protruding from the shoreline. Every once in a while a wave crest followed a trough just right and broke on the ancient bedrock with a base-sounding *ka—POOM*. The explosion of spray came back down and laminated the bedrock with a thin layer of ice as pure as glass. If the spray shot up high enough in the air, the wind could take the finest droplets far enough so that the three stubborn onlookers could feel a cold mist pepper their faces.

Finally the intrepid threesome had had enough. As they got off the picnic table and headed back toward Tim's car, they noticed a black limousine pulled over on the narrow pavement of the access road that paralleled the shoreline. Tim's car was parked in a turn-out just ahead of the limousine. Although the windows of the vehicle were tinted, they assumed that it was occupied as exhaust could be seen coming from the tail pipe.

As the threesome approached, the front passenger door of the limousine suddenly opened. A tall man wearing black gloves, a scarf and a full-length, button-down coat stepped out. His gelled dark hair was combed straight back and was long enough to form upturned curls just above his collar.

"Mr. Tim Malone?" the man asked in a voice loud enough to be heard above the whistling of the wind.

Tim, Jessa, and Shukriyah all stopped in their tracks and studied the man with suspicion. Tim didn't say a word.

"Are you Mr. Malone?" the man asked a second time. Though he took a few steps in Tim's direction, he stopped well before it began to feel like a threat to Tim.

"Yes, I am," Tim finally said, studying the man. Tim watched the man shiver in the brisk wind. He looked far from dangerous, and Tim began to believe that the man meant no harm.

"My name is Nigel Easterbrook," the man said, hunching into his collar. "I work for a Mr. Shelby Harrington of the De Beers Diamond Group, their Investment Trust Division. I'm sorry about what happened to your apartment, Mr. Malone. I understand that you had a burglary."

Tim didn't recognize his accent. Australian, maybe. Possibly South African.

"How did you know about the burglary?" Tim eventually asked.

"We think we might know who did it."

"Who, then?"

The man equivocated. "At this point we have no proof, so I have to be careful about making reckless accusations. But I will say this: De Beers has its own reasons for finding the people who robbed you."

"People? You think it was more than one person? Is it an organized burglary ring of some sort?"

"Well, that's where . . ."

"Just what's going on here? How did you find me? No one knew I was coming here. Did you follow me from my apartment?"

"Please, sir. Everything can be explained if you would be willing to meet with Mr. Harring—"

"If you were sitting in your car when the police officer was still at my apartment, why didn't you come forward then? Why didn't you—"

"Mr. Malone!" Easterbrook said sharply, his hands raised in front of him. "Please! I'm here to help. I believe we have a mutual interest in finding these people. We suspect that the burglary might be a disguise to hide more sinister intentions. We suspect that the people who went into your apartment might be the same people who ran Lyle Hanson off the road."

There was a stunned silence for a couple of seconds as Tim continued to stare at Easterbrook, this time with a look considerably more hostile. Easterbrook opened his coat and eased out what looked like a wallet. "Here, allow me to show you my ID."

Without taking his eyes off Tim's intense gaze, Easterbrook opened it and held it out. Tim sidled close enough to get a good look at Easterbrook's identification.

"Mr. Malone, if you would be willing to meet with Mr. Harrington, then he can explain everything in more detail. We not only know what happened to Lyle Hanson, we know about Mr. Two-hearts. We know about the lost cargo of the voyageurs as well, and we know that you were going to help Lyle Hanson recover that cargo next summer."

Tim continued to stare at Easterbrook. "Lyle Hanson is one of the best friends I ever had," Tim said.

"I understand, Mr. Malone," Mr. Easterbrook said gently. "And with your help, we might be able to catch the people who put him in the hospital. We don't believe what happened to him was an accident."

"Where is this Mr. Harrington? When does he want to meet?"

"He'll meet with you at your convenience, sir."

Tim felt conflicted. He didn't trust this man or the man he worked for. With what had happened to Lyle, the incident he had experienced on his way to the museum, the break in at his apartment, there was reason to be cautious. On the other hand, Mr. Easterbrook had not threatened him in any way and getting some answers was very seductive. "Well, based on everything you seem to know, I think I would like to have a talk with this Mr. Harrington but in a public place. Can that be arranged? Can we meet now?"

Mr. Easterbrook visibly relaxed. He smiled. "Most certainly, sir. He's at the Kitchi Gammi Club. I can call him. All of you, in fact, are welcome to come along."

Tim turned and looked at Jessa and Shukriyah, who in turn looked at each other. When he noticed their reluctance, Tim went to Jessa and kept his back to Easterbrook as he spoke. "What do you think?" he asked. "Do you think this is bogus? Do you want to come with me?"

"Not so fast," Jessa said with a hushed and concerned tone. "I don't know if this is such a good idea. He might have been the one to hurt Lyle and break into your apartment."

Tim cast a glance at the man, who was now hopping from foot to foot, trying to stay warm. "I think this guy's on the level. Besides, I want to find out what's going on."

"Well," Jessa said with a sidelong glance at Easterbrook, "to tell you the truth, that guy doesn't look very dangerous." Jessa looked at Shukriyah and then back at Tim. "I tell you what . . . you go to your meeting. Bring us back to your apartment. We'll wait for you there. If you're not back in . . . say, an hour, we'll call the cops."

Tim turned to Easterbrook. "It'll just be me," Tim said. "But I need to drop my friends back at my apartment first."

"May I offer a suggestion? If your friends feel comfortable driving your car back themselves, I would be happy to chauffeur you to meet with Mr. Harrington and bring you back."

Tim looked at Jessa.

"Yeah, that's okay," Jessa said. "Then we'll have a car. We'll straighten up a bit, then."

"Okay," Tim announced to Easterbrook. "I'll ride with you."

Easterbrook looked at Jessa and Shukriyah. "Ladies, might I recommend that, while in the apartment, it might not be wise to discuss our encounter here or where Mr. Malone has gone."

Tim, Jessa, and Shukriyah exchanged confused looks with each other. Then it dawned on Tim. "What's going on?" Tim asked. "Do you think the apartment is bugged or something?"

Again Mr. Easterbrook equivocated. "We . . . we just don't think it's a good idea to take any chances right now. Mr. Harrington will explain. I know you have no reason to trust me, but your own safety could be at stake."

Tim looked at Jessa and Shukriyah. Jessa nodded, but whispered, "One hour. Then you either show up or call or we're calling the police." She then addressed Easterbrook in a louder voice. "Sounds like you're serious, Mr. Easterbrook. We won't say anything."

"Thank you," Easterbrook said. "We think it's for the best."

Tim reached in his pocket and gave Jessa his keys.

"Tim?" Jessa asked, "Are you really comfortable with this?"

Tim's pounding heart made him smile. "Not particularly," Tim said. "But, hey, I might as well take the one and only chance that I might ever get to ride in a limo." He leaned to Jessa's ear. "But just in case," he whispered, "write down the license plate number."

≫ 25 ≪

AFTER A DRIVE ALONG SUPERIOR STREET through Duluth's east end, Nigel Easterbrook pulled up in front of the Kitchi Gammi Club, a large English-style brown brick mansion. The building faced Lake Superior, the obvious source of the club's Ojibwe name, Big Water. The slate roof presented a strong aesthetic balance with the double-peaked gables facing the street at each end of the building. The front yard was graced by massive leafless elms, their skeleton-like upper branches swaying in the gusts coming off the lake. The yard was defined by a wrought iron picket fence divided into equal lengths by a colonnade of stubby, concrete-capped brick pillars.

With a polite prompting by Easterbrook, Tim strode up a short walkway framed by two nineteenth-century-style lamp posts and the brown dirt of two flower beds awaiting next spring's plantings.

Up a short flight of steps, Tim came to an arched double door with leaded glass. The double door was inset within a gray masonry archway with terra cotta design. Flanking the door on each side were two sculpted, gargoyle-like Indian figures, each with a lantern gripped in their hands. The Indian figures made Tim think of Two-hearts. Since Easterbrook had mentioned Two-hearts at Brighton Beach, Tim was expecting his name to come up in the conversation with Shelby Harrington.

Easterbrook went ahead and led Tim through the arched doors and a second doorway in the foyer. Inside, Easterbrook turned to face Tim. "May I take your coat, sir?"

"Sure," Tim said as he started to unzip.

"Mr. Shelby Harrington will meet you in the large room at the end of the hall," Easterbrook said as he pointed down the hallway.

"Thank you," Tim said as he handed over his coat.

Easterbrook nodded and headed in the opposite direction.

As Tim walked down the red carpet of the elegant hallway, he kind of felt like Dorothy going to visit the wizard. The hallway's tunnel-like, barrel-vaulted ceiling was segmented by evenly-spaced arched bands, each displaying a gold-colored bas-relief of grapes, oak leaves and scroll work. Both ends of each ceiling band arced down to a pilaster adorned near the top with a triad of candle-shaped lights. Paintings of historical community leaders hung on the walls of dark-stained, chestnut panels.

At the end of the hallway, Tim came to the doorway leading into the large room. Above the door there was an interlocking K and G inside a circle. Tim thought it resembled a baseball team's insignia.

Tim found the room to be the size of a small ballroom. Being essentially empty, he assumed it was used as such. His sense of awe, a feeling that had never left him since he got out of the limousine, prompted him to stop just inside the entry. He felt as if he was forbidden to disturb the room's museum-like ambience

Tim looked around. The ceiling had large beams with a bowl-shaped chandelier in the center. A floor of wide oak boards was mostly covered with three huge Persian rugs.

The right side of the room was dominated by a fireplace containing a lazy fire. The fireplace, a gray molded affair, had a little decoration at the outer edge. A poker hung on the left side of the surround, and a long-handled broom leaned against it on the right. The wall above mantle was paneled with light oak.

In front of the fireplace two large, wing-backed chairs had been placed at opposing angles. Pleated skirting around the lower part of the chairs hung to the floor.

The only other piece of furniture in the voluminous room was a long buffet table against the opposite wall, underneath a large, leaded-glass window. A bronze statuette of a seed sower was centered on its polished surface. On the left wall hung a painting of the Duluth harbor. Tim estimated the scene was late the 1800s as sailing ships were docked at Minnesota Point.

When Tim's gaze returned to the fireplace, he startled and took a sudden step back. Just like that, a diminutive man had appeared motionlessly next to the nearer of the two wing-backed chairs as if some sort of apparition. One hand rested on the chair and the other held a cane. He wore an Inverness Cloak—more commonly referred to as a Sherlock Holmes cape—with a hound's-tooth pattern. It was unbuttoned but held together with a silver lanyard below his neck.

The man's eyes looked enlarged due to magnification through ultra-thick glasses. Although Tim intuitively knew that the man was looking at him, the man's magnified eyes didn't seem to be focused on anything in particular. With his erect posture and the far-off look, the man could have been a mannequin for all Tim knew.

"Timothy Malone, I presume."

"Yes, sir." Tim said, hearing his voice shake.

"Shelby Harrington, London office of De Beers Group."

"Oh . . . hello, sir."

"Pardon me, but I didn't mean to startle you," the man said in a lilting British accent. "Sitting as I was in this chair with its back to the door, I'm sure you couldn't see me when you came in."

"That's quite all right."

"Won't you please sit down? Now that you've arrived, I'm sure Nigel has summoned a waiter."

"I'm pleased to meet you, Mr. Harrington," Tim said has he came over and extended his hand.

"Tah tah!" Harrington said as he raised his open right palm up to the side of his head. "Pardon my eccentricities, Mr. Malone, but I avoid shaking hands in order to minimize my exposure to infectious germs. I am sorry to say that I am haunted by my phobias. I chose to meet in this large room because my claustrophobia acts up whenever I meet new people."

Tim sat down, suddenly aware that the fire was kicking out a great deal of heat. He glanced at Mr. Harrington, bundled up in his cloak and looking like it wasn't quite enough.

Harrington saw his look and smiled. "Low blood pressure. I'm always freezing. But the staff here is lovely. They accommodated me with this lovely fire."

Harrington had a spot of whiskers on his chin and a mustache long enough to be parted and combed to each side. Its dark reddish color matched his hair, which resembled Albert Einstein's in that it was high and full and went every which way. As Tim watched Harrington hang his cane on a wing of his chair, sit down and cross his legs, he assumed that the man had been raised and groomed to be a proper English gentleman.

"Well, Mr. Harrington," Tim said, "I understand from Mr. Easterbrook that you already know a lot about me. About the burglary of my apartment. About my best friend being in a car accident . . . that is—if it really was an accident."

"Alas, it is true, Mr. Malone. I do know much about you. I have requested this meeting to recruit your cooperation in a plan . . . a plan to catch the people we suspect are involved."

"Uh, one second, sir, but . . . but can we back up here? I don't mean to pry into your business—well, maybe it's my business too—but how on earth did De Beers ever get involved with all this?"

"Yes-yes-yes. By all means, a thorough explanation is definitely in order." Harrington looked high up the fireplace, gathering his thoughts. "Um, let's see . . . how best to explain all that should be explained."

As he concentrated, Harrington used his thumb and index finger to twirl the end of his mustache.

"Mr. Malone, have you ever heard of a famous diamond called the Koh-I-Noor, 'The Mountain of Light?'" Harrington took off his thick, round glasses, pulled out a white handkerchief from a vest pocket and shook it open. He raised his glasses to his open mouth, exhaled and proceeded to wipe the lenses with the pristine linen. "I fear that most people—especially most Americans—have not."

"I guess I'm a typical America then," Tim said, noticing the difference in Harrington's appearance without the thick glasses. His eyes not only looked smaller and droopy, but they gave his face a totally different, tired appearance. "No, I've never heard of 'The Mountain of Light.'"

"It's a diamond that has been worn by British queens and princesses going back to Queen Victoria in 1850. It is stored among the Crown Jewels in the Tower of London."

Harrington re-hooked his glasses around the back of his ears. "How about any other famous diamonds, Mr. Malone? The Orloff? The Star of South of Africa? The Hope Diamond? The Regent? The Regent was once worn by Marie Antoinette and Napoleon. Heard of any of those diamonds?"

"I've heard of the Hope Diamond."

"Well . . . I shall tell you a tale about another diamond, one so grand that its fame and value would have rivaled any one of those other diamonds."

"Uh . . . with all due respect, Mr. Harrington, what do diamonds have to do with Lyle Hanson's accident and the burglary at my apartment?"

"Patience, young man. That's exactly what I'm telling you. And coincidentally, it is a story that starts out with a burglary as well."

Tim sighed. He had the impression that this was going to take time, and he only had one hour before Jessa would call the police.

"In the fall of 1955, Harry Oppenheimer, the chairman of De Beers Consolidated Mines in South Africa, was presented with the most magnificent diamond ever found in a De Beers mine. It was a canary diamond with a shade of color classified as vivid yellow, which is the most valuable in the classification range. Since Mr. Oppenheimer believed yellow was a sign of good luck, he named the diamond Spero Optima, 'I hope for the best.' That was the favorite motto of Harry's father, the previous chairman, Ernest Oppenheimer.

"As of early December in that year, the stone was still uncut. It had not even been appraised. Naturally then, it had not yet been insured. Nevertheless, Harry decided to give it to his wife, Bridget McCall Oppenheimer, as an early Christmas gift.

"Then, on the evening of December 5th, there was a burglary at the Oppenheimer home in Johannesburg. When Bridget Oppenheimer opened her safe the following morning, she found missing sixty-three pieces of jewelry . . ." Harrington leaned toward Tim, pointed his index finger upward, and looked at Tim intently. ". . . and the Spero Optima."

Harrington paused for effect.

"Was it ever recovered?" Tim asked.

"No," Harrington said as he sat back. "To this day it has not been recovered. And that it was stolen has never been publicly acknowledged by the Oppenheimers."

"Never acknowledged? Why on earth not? I assume they acknowledged the theft of the jewelry."

"Oh, yes. Since the jewelry was insured, it was reported missing, an investigation got underway, and it wasn't long before all sixty-three pieces were recovered. Unfortunately for the Oppenheimers, they had assumed that if the jewelry was ever recovered, then the Spero Optima would be recovered as well."

"So they caught the burglars?"

"Hmm . . . interesting question. There were three individuals involved with the crime in one way or another. Percival William Radley and Donald Ernest Miles were the likely burglars. And then there was an Australian by the name of William Lindsay Pearson. He double crossed the other two by making a deal with the insurance company's private investigator, Dudley Strevens, who had come to Johannesburg all the way from London." Harrington leaned on his arm rest and gave Tim a sidelong glance. "Obviously a very high profile case. The press gave it a tremendous amount of attention."

Harrington straightened and stared into the fireplace. "To make a long story short," he continued, "the government figured they had an open and shut case and thought they could easily convict the burglars. But then things started to fall apart for the government . . . and the Oppenheimers. As the proceedings of the case got underway, the extraordinary wealth of the Oppenheimers became publicly known. And that's excluding the estimate value of the Spero Optima. It didn't help that Bridget Oppenheimer—the fine woman she was—had made a mistake . . . a public one, at that. She said that as a result of the burglary, she had been left with as much jewelry as the average city typist.

"You can imagine what happened. By the time the trial for Miles got underway, he had become a folk hero. At the end of his trial, when the jury came back with a verdict of not guilty . . . well, jiminy crickets!" Harrington threw up his arm in disgust. "The people in the court room began to cheer and clap and stomp their feet!

"Well, as you may have already guessed, no one was convicted. And to add insult to injury, Pearson collected the insurance company's award for the return of the jewelry. The award was equivalent to $56,000.

"So, everything was recovered except the Spero Optima?" Tim asked.

"Exactly. And as a result of all the negative publicity surrounding the trial, the Oppenheimers were in no position to pursue recovery of a diamond that had not been reported missing in the first place."

"What do you think happened to it?"

Just then a waiter appeared in doorway. He was wearing a black bow tie and black vest over a white shirt.

"Oh, yes . . . would you like anything?" Harrington asked Tim. "A cup of coffee? Perhaps a mug of hot cocoa on this blustery day?"

"A cup of tea would be nice."

Harrington relayed the request to the waiter.

"With a slice of lemon," Tim added.

"Oh, and with a slice of lemon," Harrington said.

"Anything for you, sir?" the waiter asked.

"Uh, no thank you," Harrington said as he flicked up the back of his hand as if there was a fly buzzing about his face.

The waiter politely nodded and left.

"Oh, if I had known you weren't going to have anything, Mr. Harrington, I wouldn't have made the waiter make a fuss just for me."

"No, no. Quite all right. Quite all right. I don't want anything right now. When you and I are done here, Nigel and I are going to brave the elements and walk down to a restaurant called the Pickwick. We were intrigued by its English-sounding name. You no doubt have heard of the English author, Charles Dickens?"

"Oh, of course."

"His work, *The Pickwick Papers* was a precursor of sorts to what I regard as Dickens' masterpiece, *A Christmas Carol*. When I inquired about the restaurant with the staff here, they confirmed that the establishment indeed has the distinctive decor of an English pub. It should make me feel right at home."

"Good choice, Mr. Harrington. The food is excellent there. So . . . what happened to the Spero Optima?"

"Pearson got hold of it. He was the most intelligent and the most cunning of the three criminals. For one, in his negotiations with Strevens, he would have found out that the Spero Optima had not been included in the insurance claim. And two, being a yellow uncut stone, he likely convinced Miles and Radley that the stone wasn't worth much. Most unsophisticated blokes might simply assume that all good diamonds are clear like glass."

"What happened to Pearson?"

"After he collected the insurance company's award, he wasted no time in leaving the country. You see, he was from Australia and likely running from something. I'm sure he figured it was only a matter of time before the police would learn about his shady past from Australian authorities and then have a reason to hold him. So off to Great Britain he went.

"But the Oppenheimers were certainly not about to let go of the Spero Optima just like that. And they were not about to pay the likes of William Pearson a handsome award. So the Oppenheimers did a couple things. First, they put out a notice describing the stone and its rare color, the vivid yellow similar to the color of honey. The notice not only went to Great Britain, but worldwide. It wasn't long before every reputable jeweler on every continent knew to be on the lookout for the Spero Optima. And they all knew, of course, that cooperating with De Beers was in their best interest.

"Secondly, the Investment Trust Division of De Beers set up a team dedicated to the perpetual pursuit of the stone. That, Mr. Malone, is where I come in."

Tim took a couple of seconds before he understood what Harrington had meant. "Really? You're still looking for the diamond after all this time? And what . . . you think the stone's over here, somewhere in Minnesota?"

"No. But that which can leverage the stone's return is." Harrington reached into a watch pocket of his vest and pulled out a small, flat polished agate that had a smooth, ground depression in the center. He held it between his thumb and forefinger and began to rub the depression. When he became conscious of what he was doing, he stopped rubbing, looked down at the agate and chuckled. "Years ago someone gave me this worry stone as a gift—obviously someone who knew me well. They said it was a Lake Superior agate. I didn't know a great deal about the greatest of the Great Lakes, so I located it on a map of North America. Being in the heart of the continent, I simply assumed that I'd never see it. Well, here I am, Mr. Malone. The lake is right outside the window. And I must say, it's lovely environment you have here along the lake."

"I certainly think so. I like agates, too. You have a real nice one there."

"Thank you," Harrington said as he turned over his worry stone and studied it. "But I digress. It's just that anytime I discuss William Pearson and the Spero Optima, I get angry and start rubbing this agate.

"So . . . getting back to Mr. Pearson," Harrington said as he resumed rubbing the worry stone with slow, steady strokes of his thumb. "He was in a pickle, you see. There was no place where he could sell the Spero Optima. He was even afraid to sell it on the black market. Being alone and not connected with any mob, he certainly would have risked being killed. But the very act of introducing himself to a legitimate jeweler would likely prompt a call to the police.

"Pearson did have a temporary advantage, though. He had no urgent need to unload the Spero Optima. He was fairly well off for the time being, especially with the award from the insurance company. So he bided his time and kept his eye out for creative ways to cash in on the Spero Optima.

"He finally got his chance when he heard about the lost treasure of the Voyageurs. The treasure lost back in 1779 by the Northumbrian fur trading company of Percy and Campbell. The treasure lost just north of here in the wilderness country between Canada and the United States."

When Harrington noticed Tim's perplexed look, he leaned on his arm rest and once again looked intently at him. "Sound familiar, Mr. Malone?" Harrington asked.

Tim returned Harrington's stare.

"So, *that's* what this is all about," Tim said. "And the lost cargo . . . it *is* a treasure, then?"

Harrington didn't answer right away. He sat back and looked into the fire. As Tim continued to stare, he could see the oscillating flames reflected in Harrington's huge glasses.

"A treasure it is," Harrington said softly as he nodded slowly. "It is a treasure of rubies and emeralds."

≈ 26 ≥

THE WAITER RETURNED CARRYING A SILVER TRAY supporting a teapot covered with a fitted quilt insulator, a cup and saucer that looked like fine china, a dainty, shiny spoon on an embroidered napkin, as well as scones, and a small bowl of lemon slices.

"Will you be needing milk or sugar for your tea, sir?" the waiter asked after he set the tray down on the buffet table under the large window.

"Uh, no thank you," Tim answered.

The waiter made a slight bow and left the room with the brisk pace and erect, formal posture of a professional butler.

"Time to stretch a little," Harrington announced as he got up, "so pour your tea, my good man, pour your tea."

Harrington took his cane in hand and began to stroll about the room. He walked with a slight limp. Tim, handed such a deliberate cue, headed for the buffet table.

"So, this is the Duluth harbor," Harrington commented as he stopped to look up at the painting on the wall opposite the fireplace. "I understand ships come here from all over the world. It's like a seaport, is it not?"

"Not *like* a seaport," Tim said as he prepared his cup of tea. "It *is* a seaport."

"The painting has an interesting perspective," Harrington commented. "The scene is mostly sky."

"Rule number one for an artist: don't center your subject," Tim said as he poured his tea.

"I must say, it looks like a well-protected harbor." Harrington continued to study the painting. "Speaking of harbor paintings, did you know that on the night the *Titanic* went down, there's a legend that the ship's designer, Thomas Andrews, was last seen in the first-class smoking lounge, staring at a painting of a harbor. I believe that harbor was Plymouth Sound in Cornwall."

Harrington took his eyes off the painting and faced Tim. "How about Lake Superior, Mr. Malone? Have ships gone down in Lake Superior?"

From the buffet table, Tim was looking at the painting while holding his saucer and cup of tea. He had submerged a lemon slice with the spoon and was squeezing it against the bottom of his cup. The symbolism was not lost on Tim as he looked down at his sunken lemon slice through the steaming, tinted tea.

"There certainly have," Tim said. "Probably the most famous shipwreck is the *Edmund Fitzgerald*. It sank in November 1975, with twenty-nine men on board. If you think the waves are big on the lake today . . . well, the lake can get a lot angrier. Angry enough to take down a 729-foot freighter."

"What was she carrying?"

"Iron ore pellets."

"I wonder if the voyageurs ever had one of their canoes swamped in Lake Superior.'

Tim considered. "At least on Lake Superior they used Montreal canoes, which were larger than the canoes used in the interior. They paid attention to the lake's moods . . . maybe better than ship captains do today."

"It's still an open boat," Harrington said as he strolled back toward the fireplace. "So the odds are that a canoe or two got overwhelmed by waves, wouldn't you say? And just think of it: no life jackets for the men, the loss of precious cargo that had come from far far away."

"At least they would have been on Lake Superior in the summer months. The water's still really cold, but there's a better chance of survival than in November. As for the cargo, if they were heading west toward Grand Portage with trade items, much of it was probably metal goods, like muskets and pots and kettles. That would have all sunk. On the other hand, if they were leaving Grand Portage with bales of fur, I suppose there's a possibility that those would have floated."

"But scattered all over the lake in a matter of hours."

"Yeah, I suppose."

"Hmm . . . it looks like our fire is dying out," Harrington said as he stopped near the fireplace and noticed the last glowing embers. "Shall I ask for more wood?"

"Not for my sake, Mr. Harrington," Tim said as he returned to his chair. "But, thank you."

"Very good. It feels toasty enough in here, I suppose." Harrington replaced his cane on the wing of his chair and sat down, wrapping his cloak about himself carefully. "Well, similarly speaking, Mr. Malone, the greatest lost treasure of the voyageurs can be attributed to a small-scale shipwreck . . . a canoe wreck can it not?"

"I guess that's one way to put it. In this case, the canoe would have been the smaller North canoe used on the lakes and rivers in the interior." Tim gently sat down to avoid spilling his tea. "Mr. Harrington, how did Pearson hear about the lost treasure?"

"He came to the conclusion that if he was going to find a way to trade on the Spero Optima, he would have to offer up something else in addition. Some sort of service or whatever. Well, why not offer what you're good at? So, he started looking for opportunities that would afford him the chance to indulge his lust for treasure-seeking, for striking it rich with the next big find, for making the next big score whether it was illicit or not. And all it took was a little research into companies with a history of trade and commerce, especially if they had been denied a large insurance claim."

"As Percy and Campbell had?" Tim asked in anticipation.

"As the Percys had. The Percy half of Percy and Campbell had been the financial backbone of the company. They were from Alnwick, Northumbria, and they have had quite a legacy in English history going back many centuries. To this day, they are still a family of significant means.

"But back in 1779, they made a bad assumption about how goods and commodities are insured. You see, company assets used in conducting the fur trade business were insured. But that was not necessarily true for a collection of private valuables being taken secretly into the wilderness."

"So, the Percys were the sole owners of the treasure?"

"Yes."

"Did they get anything at all from the insurance company?"

"Not a single shilling. The insurer of the fur trade company told the Percys that their claim would fall under their—well, what we know today as a homeowner's insurance policy. The grantors of that policy, in turn, said that if the treasure was being transported by company representatives who had recorded it as cargo in the company manifests, then the treasure was being used to conduct company business.

"To sum it up, the claim was denied and the treasure was a total loss. By the early to mid 1800s, with the fur trade in its last days, all hopes of recovering the treasure had been abandoned. It was about a hundred years later, when . . ." Harrington pointed his finger up in the air and looked at Tim to see if he could complete the sentence.

". . . when Pearson came on the scene," Tim said obligingly.

"The smart, shrewd, calculating William Pearson. And it didn't take long for him to see two things that would work to his advantage. One: the Percy clan was probably one of the few dynasties in the British Commonwealth as powerful as the Oppenheimers. In other words, they wouldn't have anything to fear from the Oppenheimers. Two: he realized that in the mid-twentieth century, the chances of finding the treasure had increased due to the advent of modern equipment, like the metal detector and scuba gear, which had been invented by Jacques Cousteau and Emile Gagnan in 1943.

"So, sometime in the late 1950s, he approached the Percys with a proposal. If he could—"

"Excuse me, Mr. Harrington, but how did De Beers know all of this? Had they been following Pearson all along?"

"Oh, yes. Very good! We knew of his every move. Of course, he soon figured that out."

"And his proposal to the Percys was . . . ?"

"If he could have full rights to the treasure, plus a stipend for equipment, travel, and living expenses—enough to get started and to live on for a few years—he would hand over the Spero Optima to the Percys." Harrington sat back and smiled. "Well, a deal like that would certainly put De Beers in a bind. At least with Pearson hanging on to the Spero Optima, we thought we would be able to wait him out. Not being a rich man, we figured that he'd settle for a small pay off sooner or later. The Percys, on the other hand, certainly wouldn't have to. They would be able to sit on the Spero Optima indefinitely."

"Did De Beers try contacting the Percys?"

"Of course. We tried. But the Percys wouldn't admit to even having met Pearson, much less having any knowledge of the Spero Optima. Nevertheless, it soon became obvious that a deal between the Percys and Pearson had indeed been struck. Pearson changed his name and gave us the slip. Of course, we knew that he was bound for North America, specifically to the border region between northeastern Minnesota and Ontario. But we were never sure of his exact whereabouts."

"How did he know where to start?" Tim asked. "Did the Percys give him clues? Did he have any contacts?"

"A century and more had passed since the heyday of the fur trade. The Percys were no longer associated with anyone with intimate knowledge of the wilderness. In fact, the treasure itself had slipped into legend with fading details. No one even knew where Hell's Gate Rapids was. A lot of—"

"Excuse me. You know about Hell's Gate Rapids?"

"We know about it. Yes. We don't know where it is any more than the modern-day Percys. As I was about to say, a lot of the place names have changed. To the best knowledge of the modern-day Percys, the treasure could have been lost anywhere between Lake Superior and Lake Winnipeg. I suppose it's possible that they still had records in their family archives, but the records would have been useless if they weren't accompanied by eighteenth-century-era maps.

"So, Mr. Malone, as far as we can tell, Pearson was basically on his own when he started looking for the treasure. However, if he was anything, he most definitely was resourceful. By making the right connections, he was eventually able to hook up with two mineral prospectors working the wilderness. They were two World War I veterans, Russell Blankenburg and Benny Ambrose."

"Benny Ambrose?"

"You know of him?"

"Yes," Tim said. "He's a Boundary Waters legend. He and Dorothy Molter were the last private citizens allowed to live out their years in the Boundary Waters Wilderness after it had been made federal land. Ambrose lived on Otter Track Lake, and Molter lived on Knife Lake. Molter sold homemade root beer to canoeists who stopped at her cabin."

"I understand Blankenburg was somewhat of a legend himself. In our attempt to get to know the border country, we've pored over maps, we've had the Canadian government fly us over it, and we've driven to the end of nearly every road that leads to the wilderness. One of those roads was the Gunflint Trail in the extreme northeastern corner of Minnesota. Near the trail end was the famous Gunflint Lodge. In fact, Nigel and I and Brody—that's our driver—stayed there. Well, lo and behold, the owners told us that Blankenburg established that lodge in the 1920s."

Tim said, "Being almost a pioneer, I imagine he got to know the wilderness like the back of his hand."

"That's one of the reasons why Pearson . . ." Harrington gave Tim a sidelong glance. ". . . or whatever name he was going by—wanted to work for Blankenburg, even if it was only temporarily. Pearson needed to learn how to navigate a canoe and how to survive in the wilderness."

"Had you been following Pearson all this time?"

"As best we could. By using aliases, he could always stay a step ahead of us. For instance, when my predecessors inquired with Blankenburg and Ambrose, they didn't even know who my predecessors were talking about at first. Not that it mattered. Pearson was already long gone."

Tim said, "Mr. Harrington, I'm impressed with what you know."

"Well, with the Percys holding onto the Spero Optima, we've had to concentrate all our efforts on this . . . this saga, if you will, of the lost treasure. We couldn't let Pearson get his hands on it."

Harrington paused, and emotion worked at his face. "Mr. Malone, this treasure was so important that we suspect it even influenced the treaty negotiations that ended the American revolution for independence. And this is where I shall tell you a little interesting tidbit about myself. It almost makes me feel that my part in all this has been predestined. My mother's side of the family is descended from Henry Strachey. He was a highly regarded undersecretary of state in the colonial office back in the early 1780s. By the fall of 1782, the treaty negotiations with the American commission were already underway in Paris when Strachey was ordered to take part. Under the administration of Lord Shelburne, Strachey was to assist Richard Oswald, a Scotsman that many in the Prime Minister's cabinet no longer trusted to act alone. It didn't take long for Strachey to figure out that Oswald had personal motives. He was more concerned with the business interests of Percy and Campbell and the treasure than in England's interests.

"But a good deal of progress had already been made in the negotiations and, so to speak, the die had been cast. According to Strachey's personal diaries handed down to his heirs, the most famous of the American commissioners, Benjamin Franklin, had insisted that the border to the west of Lake Superior be placed no farther south than where it is today. It didn't take Strachey long to figure out what had happened. Somehow Franklin had learned of Oswald's motives. Although Strachey could never prove it, he figured Franklin had someone spying on Oswald, or perhaps had planted a mole in his Paris office.

"Think about it, Mr. Malone. Between the Lake of the Woods and the Pacific Ocean, the border follows the forty-ninth parallel all the way. But at the Lake of the Woods, the border breaks southeast toward Lake Superior, following a zig zag canoe route used by the voyageurs. I don't know about you, but to me it sure seems like an odd border placement. That is, unless, you have an ulterior motive for such a border."

"Yeah, but didn't the present-day border get established well after 1782? My understanding is that the negotiators in Paris didn't have accurate maps of the land west of Lake Superior. In fact, in helping Lyle with some of his research about the chest, I learned that, for the border description agreed upon in Paris, only six specific places west of Lake Huron are named. One of those places, Isle Phillepeaux in Lake Superior, doesn't even exist. And the location of a place called Long Lake has never been positively identified."

"Granted," Harrington conceded. "They did not have good maps in Paris. However, even when better maps did become available, Britain and the United States nitpicked over the precise border placement until it was finally settled once and for all by the Webster-Ashburton Treaty of 1842.

"In fact, what I find peculiar is that in 1803, the Northwest Company willingly moved their trading post from—"

"Uh . . . excuse me," Tim said as he signaled his interruption with a finger pointing up. "Wasn't it the Northwest Company that absorbed Percy and Campbell?"

"Not exactly. About twenty years earlier, several fur trading companies—including Percy and Campbell—all merged to form the Northwest Company. Then in 1803, they willingly moved their trading post from Grand Portage to Fort William in present-day Thunder Bay in order to vacate American territory. Yet, they made quite a fuss about keeping the old canoe route itself, accessed from Grand Portage, within British territory even though they had started using a new route going up the Kaministiquia River."

"Hmm . . . that *is* interesting," Tim said. "Sounds like the lost treasure might have had quite an influence on many events. Even going back to Paris, you think the treasure's existence was really known by Ben Franklin?"

Harrington waved a hand in dismissal. "Who knows for sure? All I'm saying is that a valuable treasure got lost somewhere along the original canoe route used by the voyageurs, and that the international border happens to follow that route.

"But I must say, Mr. Malone, that's probably been a good thing for us . . . and a bad thing for Pearson, if you think about it. Not being an American citizen and not Canadian either, Pearson was constantly hindered by two different governments with two different sets of exploratory regulations. And it didn't help him any when the land on both sides of the border became protected wilderness territories with even tighter regulations."

Harrington nodded. "Pearson never did find the treasure. We're sure he died but don't know exactly when."

"Did he have children?" Tim asked just before he leaned over to place his saucer and cup on the floor beside his chair.

"Yes. And his heirs have been just as determined to find the treasure. They no doubt believe in the legitimacy of their rights to the treasure, and they are just as shrewd and cunning as Pearson himself was."

"Have they made any progress?"

"None. And they really never had hope of making any. Pearson himself had already researched a number of possibilities for the treasure's location. He searched the most logical rapids and made a number of dives, in fact. But he never found anything. Time wore on and the years turned to decades.

"Then at some point the Pearsons learn about a Mr. Two-hearts, a native Indian living in the Canadian wilderness near the border, and a Mr. Lyle Hanson, an archaeologist who has been researching the treasure's location. And that's when the Pearsons begin to feel threatened."

At that moment everything came together for Tim. His eyes widened. "My God!" he said as he leaned forward in his chair. "So, it's the Pearsons who are behind all this?"

27

"THEN LYLE'S ACCIDENT WAS NO ACCIDENT!" Tim proclaimed. "It was Pearson's relatives, wasn't it? Lyle was run off the road on purpose by these people, wasn't he?"

"Well, we think—"

"And at Brighton Beach, Mr. Easterbrook said that he thought he knew who burglarized my apartment! It was them, wasn't it?"

Again, Shelby Harrington tried to give Tim an answer. "As I was about to say—"

"And in Alexandria, were they the ones who bumped my car from behind? And . . . and Two-hearts! Mr. Easterbrook also said he knew about Two-hearts! Two-hearts said someone followed him to the Kensington Rune Stone Museum! It was them, wasn't it?"

"Mr. Malone, please! Please slow down! I shall attempt to explain."

Tim gripped the armrests of his chair to contain himself and stared intently at Harrington.

"The answers to your questions are: Probably. Probably. Not likely, and no, they didn't follow Two-hearts."

Tim gave Harrington a confused look, then smiled sheepishly. "Sorry, Mr. Harrington," Tim said as he sat back. "So . . . what do they want?"

"Information. Mr. Malone, I understand what you've been going through. And I shall propose a plan to catch the perpetrators. But first things first. Your questions deserve to be answered. First of all, we do think that it was Pearson's descendants who ran Lyle Hanson off the road. We also think they burglarized your apartment, and I shall give my theory as to the real motive in a minute. As for your car being bumped from behind in Alexandria, I highly doubt they would have done that as it would have served no purpose. Lastly, as far as Mr. Two-hearts being followed to the museum . . . well, that was Nigel and Brody."

"What?"

"Trust me, there was no malicious intent. We've known about Mr. Two-hearts for a some time. We've wondered if he was the only person alive who might have even the vaguest knowledge of the Hell's Gate Rapids location. But our attempts to contact him were clumsy, and I think we scared him off. He lives in a remote part of the wilderness and is distrusting of outsiders. He never responded to our attempts to communicate, probably thinking we're after the treasure."

"Aren't you?" Tim asked.

Harrington looked at Tim, his bespectacled, magnified eyes fixed on his own. It made Tim wonder if Harrington had taken offense to his question.

"Ah . . . let's see. How shall I put this?" Harrington looked high up the fireplace in concentration. "Please understand, Mr. Malone, the only item we feel we have a right to is the Spero Optima. As for finding the treasure, we have no capacity for an undertaking such an operation as that. Our primary goal is to prevent the Pearson heirs—let's refer to them as the Pearsons—from ever getting it."

Tim picked up on Harrington's subtle evasiveness. "But if Lyle found the treasure," Tim said, "it would likely become government property."

"A more acceptable outcome than the Pearsons acquiring it."

"Had you ever thought about making an offer to the Pearsons for their testimony? They could testify that a deal had been made with the Percys involving the Spero Optima."

"Not only would the Pearsons be implicating themselves in the illicit scheme, they would be double-crossing the Percys. Besides, after so many years of so much effort, I'm convinced they have their heart set on finding the treasure as if they've always had a right to it."

"How much do the Pearsons know about Lyle's research into the treasure chest? Do you think they ever spied on him?"

"I'm sure they have," Harrington said easily.

"And also on Two-hearts?"

"At first, we simply thought that the Pearsons knew about him but didn't believe he knew much about the treasure. That thinking sure changed when Mr. Hanson was run off the road. Convinced as we are that the Pearsons did it, they acted precisely then for one obvious reason: they figured out that Mr. Hanson was on his way to Alexandria to meet with Mr. Two-hearts, and they wanted to prevent the meeting. The Pearsons must have felt that valuable information of some sort was going to be exchanged."

That comment made Tim wonder if Harrington was trying to bait him. He thought about the letter that Two-hearts had given to Maggie at the hospital in Alexandria: *Lyle and I were . . . to talk about the wooden chest lost in the fur trade. He has researched it a long time, and I got important information for him.*

Until that moment, Tim hadn't taken that part of Two-hearts' letter all that seriously. But now it perplexed him and made him very curious as to what Two-hearts really knew. Maybe Lyle didn't know everything about the treasure after all.

Tim looked at the dying embers in the fireplace and contemplated what he could risk divulging to Harrington. He decided he wasn't ready to tell Harrington that Two-hearts had 'important information' regarding the treasure.

"Well, Mr. Harrington, Lyle has figured out the location of Hell's Gate Rapids but he has been keeping it a secret . . . even from me, so far. He was going to go up there this coming summer and start work on recovering the treasure. He invited me to be part of his crew."

"My hat goes off to him," Harrington said. "If he really did figure out where Hell's Gate Rapids is, he has accomplished something no one else has in a very long time. And he was able to gain the trust of Mr. Two-hearts."

Tim folded his arms, mulling over what he knew as the puzzle pieces began falling into place. "So . . . everybody was in Alexandria at the same time," Tim said. "Besides Lyle, there was you, Two-hearts, and the Pearsons."

Tim looked over at Harrington. "Do you think the Pearsons also would have harmed Two-hearts if they had the chance?"

"We did become concerned about that. So when Brody spotted Mr. Two-hearts at the hospital, he kept—"

"You guys were at the hospital?"

"Of course," Harrington said with a subtle tone of pride. "We spotted you when you stopped by. You spent considerable time talking to Mr. Hanson's wife in the Intensive Care visitor lounge."

Harrington's candid disclosure was probably intended to promote trust, but Tim felt uneasy about his spying abilities. "Hmm . . . knowing that I've been watched by the Pearsons is bad enough. Knowing that you've been doing it too kind of gives me the creeps," Tim said with disdain. "What were you going to say about spying on—oh, excuse me—*spotting* Two-hearts?"

Harrington apparently didn't pick up on his change of tone. "When Brody spotted Mr. Two-hearts at the hospital's information desk, he kept track of him."

"Oh, yeah? For the safety of Two-hearts or for the selfish interests of De Beers?"

Once again, Harrington's magnified eyes fixed on his own, except this time with anger. Harrington had stopped rubbing his worry stone and, instead, was squeezing it tightly. "Mr. Malone! Please! We aren't like that! Look, Mr. Hanson got hurt badly and we didn't want to see that happen to anyone else. I invited you here in trust and peace. Please reciprocate."

Tim felt no need to capitulate, but he'd gain nothing in an adversarial atmosphere. "Yeah, you're . . . you're right, Mr. Harrington. I . . . uh . . . I was out of line. But, you've got to realize that this whole thing is still quite a shock. At this point, truthfully, I have no idea who to trust. Put yourself in my shoes."

Harrington shifted in his chair and heaved a sigh. "Well . . . no, I'm sure this can't be easy for you to accept. Perhaps all this has been too much, too soon."

"I've been trying to tell myself that anyone with bad intentions would hardly have invited me to this fine establishment and then been as forthright as you have, Mr. Harrington. Please continue."

"Well, as I was about to say, Brody kept track of Two-hearts. Later on, he and Nigel followed Two-hearts to the Kensington Rune Stone Museum. Nigel didn't know why he went there—it was closed, after all—but I think I've now got it figured out. He was going to meet you, wasn't he Mr. Malone?"

"Yes. That night was when my car got bumped from behind. I got spooked and drove off. I hid down some residential street and called Two-hearts. He told me that the museum was closed so we cancelled the meeting."

"Ah, now I get it," Harrington said, smiling slightly behind his mustache. "Anyway, Mr. Malone . . . your question about the Pearsons wanting to harm Mr. Two-hearts . . . well, we've been speculating how the Pearsons regard Mr. Two-hearts. Perhaps they concluded that Mr. Two-hearts knows something peculiar about the treasure. Something in addition to its location. Why else would Mr. Hanson have agreed to meet him in Alexandria?"

"Well," Tim said as he thought again about Two-hearts' letter to Maggie, "I guess that does make sense."

"So, I think we can relax," Harrington said. "The Pearsons won't harm Mr. Two-hearts if they think he might have valuable information."

Harrington leaned on his elbow and changed his tone of voice. "And with that assumption, Mr. Malone, I have an idea. An idea that is the essence of the proposal that I had mentioned. A proposal that would require your cooperation."

"Okay, Mr. Harrington. I'll listen. What's your proposal?"

"We're convinced that the Pearsons staged the burglary of your apartment. After all, didn't it look staged to you? When there is a back door, it's pretty clumsy for a burglar to break into the front door, wouldn't you say?"

"Come to think of it, yes. I guess I was also surprised by some of the expensive items they left behind."

"Exactly. The Pearson's real reason for wanting to break in was to plant a bug. They hope you will be discussing information about the treasure, especially its location. Now, we can use special equipment to confirm whether a bug has actually been planted, but assuming it has, then we have an opportunity to set a trap for the Pearsons."

"What do you have in mind?"

"While in your apartment, you will pretend to be talking to someone on your phone. It could be a real person on the other end pretending to be an archaeologist on Lyle Hanson's treasure recovery team. Either way, you will discuss receiving a letter with a map. Tell this person in a clear voice that the map gives a detailed description of where Hell's Gate Rapids is located."

"Who sent the letter and map?" Tim asked.

"Perhaps the letter and map could have been sent from either Mr. Twohearts or from Lyle Hanson. If the letter is from Mr. Hanson, he might be informing you that he doesn't expect to be well enough to work on the recovery next summer. Therefore, he has chosen to reveal to you the location of Hell's Gate Rapids."

"That seems logical. Then what?"

"Invite the other person to come over sometime and look at the map. Being excited, the other person will propose to come over that same evening. With a tone of disappointment, you'll say that you are about to go out of town overnight. You say that you will be back tomorrow and, therefore, the following evening will work out. Then simply end the conversation by announcing something like, 'It's settled then, see you tomorrow night when I get back.'

"At that point, the Pearsons will believe that you will be out of their way. And you should indeed get into your car and drive away, most likely to meet us at some arranged location. Then, some time that evening, the Pearsons will break into your apartment to steal the map. The police will be laying in wait, and we'll spring the trap."

"And my door gets broken down again?"

"We'll pay for it," Harrington promised. "In fact, we will reimburse your landlord for the repairs today, and we'll compensate you for any items that were stolen and not covered by insurance."

"What about my neighbor?"

"No doubt, something will have to be arranged with him. Do you know him well?"

"Fairly well."

"Then tell him you've been invited to the Kitchi Gammi club for dinner and that you're allowed to bring a guest. He will certainly be safer away from his flat. A number of such details must yet be worked out. In fact, we might even have to prepare a script for your phone conversation. But for right now, I simply would like to know if you are agreeable to the plan in principle."

"How will this plan help you get the Spero Optima?" Tim asked.

"To avoid jail, we're hoping the Pearsons will make a plea bargain by confessing to everything. Hopefully we can even get them to confess to their illicit deal made with the Percys long ago. That definitely would put us in a much better bargaining position against them."

"Illicit deal or not, the Pearsons still could argue that their claim to the treasure is legitimate, nonetheless."

"Burglars who have bugged someone's home will have a rather hard time convincing anyone that they have a legitimate claim to anything. Simply put, Mr. Malone, we would be in a much better position with the Pearsons if they are facing criminal charges. And if their car can be connected to Mr. Lyle Hanson's accident, then the Pearsons might be faced with more serious criminal charges, in which case, all of us would be in a better position."

"Yeah, I think you're right. Your plan does sound pretty good, Mr. Harrington. But before I decide to go along with it, would you be able to confirm if my apartment has been bugged?"

"Of course. We'll need to establish that first."

"Well . . . everything in your plan seems pretty well thought out. But . . . but I guess I would like some time to think it over."

"By all means do," Harrington responded re-assuredly. He reached inside his coat. "Here's my card. Please call when you've had plenty of time to think about my plan."

When Harrington stood up, Tim took the cue and did likewise.

"Thank you for your willingness to meet so spontaneously, Mr. Malone."

"You're welcome, Mr. Harrington. It's been interesting to say the least."

"When the gentleman back at the check-in desk sees you, he'll summon Nigel. He and my driver, Brody, will then take you back to your apartment. I'm sure you must have things to do as a result of the break in."

"That's for sure. I hope the landlord sent someone to fix my front door." Tim started to reach out with his right hand. But as soon as he remembered, he halted his hand and withdrew it self-consciously. "I'll . . . um. I'll be in touch, Mr. Harrington."

"I look forward to hearing from you," Harrington said with a slight nod. As Tim left the room, Harrington went to the window to wait for Nigel and Brody to escort Tim down the front walkway. As he waited, he pulled out his cell phone, selected a number on his speed dial list, put the phone to his ear, and pulled out his pocket watch.

"Shelby here," Harrington said as he looked at his pocket watch. "Malone just left. I think it went as well as one could expect . . . No, I don't think he doubted my story. But as far as buying into the plan, he said he wants to think about it. He's a skeptical young lad . . . Very well . . . Yes, good day to you too."

28

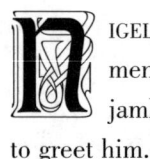

NIGEL AND BRODY DROVE AWAY after they dropped Tim off at his apartment. When Tim walked up to his door, he stopped to inspect the door jamb before walking in. Jessa and Shukriyah rushed into the entryway to greet him.

"Wow! The door's fixed," Tim said. "That was fast."

"They just finished about ten minutes ago," Jessa said. She hesitated, then said, "So, how did it go?"

Tim motioned the two women out on the porch. Nigel had reminded him not to talk about anything related to the treasure while in the apartment. But at this point, Tim had started to wonder if it was Harrington himself who was competing for the treasure.

"Look, I don't know about this guy I met. He knows way too much and it gives me the creeps. For all I know, he could even be behind Lyle's accident."

Tim pulled out Harrington's card. "Shukriyah," he said, urgency in his voice as he looked at Harrington's card. "I need to find out anything I can about a Shelby Harrington of the De Beers Diamond Group. Would you be willing to contact Omar and ask him if his organization can find out if this Harrington guy is legit?"

"Certainly."

"Thanks. I want to call Two-hearts but not from here." Tim looked to the street to see where the women had parked his car. "Look, I'll explain all this later, but could you guys go inside and . . . just make small talk, relax and listen to music . . . do whatever you'd like but don't refer to me. I'm going to grab my cell and go back out to my car."

As soon as Tim climbed back into his car, he dialed up Two-hearts' satellite phone. After a couple rings he got an answer.

"Gosh, am I glad you answered," Tim said with relief. Then he started talking fast, almost as if he was in a panic. "I got some big news. I just had one heck of a conversation with a guy from De Beers Diamond Company."

He waited for a response, but none came. Tim closed his eyes and shook his head. *Man, I hate it when you do this.* Then he remembered the delay that can happen with a satellite phone. "Cedric, did you get all that?"

"Yah. Remember when you complete a sentence, don't add any after thoughts, hey."

"All right. Sorry about that."

In his usual relaxed manor, Two-hearts took his time to formulate a response to Tim's news. What he expressed seemed to reflect more of a realized expectation than a surprise. "So . . . De Beers approached you, did they?"

"Yes. Look, Cedric, I gotta be blunt. I want to find out just what's going on with that lost wooden chest. I know in Alexandria you told me to forget about it for the time being. But the circumstances of Lyle's accident are suspicious. Now my apartment's been broken into. I'm afraid I'm caught in the middle of something big, and I have no idea who to trust anymore."

"Your apartment got broke into?"

"Yes. This Harrington guy from De Beers thinks the real reason behind the break-in was to plant a bug . . . a listening device."

"What was that guy's name again?"

"Harrington. Shelby Harrington."

"Okay . . . okay. I knew De Beers was mixed up in this, but I never knew any names."

"Harrington wants to set a trap to catch some bad eggs named Pearson."

"Pearson?"

"Yes. He says it's the Pearsons who want the wooden chest, not him. But if the Pearsons get it, then he can't get back this very rare diamond. Look . . . it's a long story."

"I haven't heard any of this before. But back up a minute. I got a couple questions. First, how's Lyle?"

"Good. He's still got a couple surgeries ahead of him, then a long road of recovery and physical therapy, but he's going to be okay."

"Okay. Glad to hear it. Now, did you have any luck with the Rainy Lake Rune Stone?"

"No. Finding that'll be like finding a needle in a hay stack. That's another reason why I'd rather focus on the wooden chest."

"All right . . . all right. Just hold on a minute." Two-hearts paused, and Tim thought he might be considering if he could trust him. Two-hearts finally said softly, "The treasure's been a secret for over 200 years. If it's destined that an Ojibwe chief won't possess it according to legend, then at least I want it to end up in responsible hands."

"I can understand that," said Tim.

"There seems to be too many people close on your trail ready to snatch the treasure away from you the first chance they got. I don't know if De Beers' intentions are innocent, and now there's new adversaries by the name of Pearson. I can't say I like this at all."

"I'm not real happy about this either."

"Okay, but I only know clues. And I'll only give you one to start out with, because if that one can't get solved, then the others are meaningless, understand?"

"Yes," Tim said, holding his breath. "I understand."

"Remember those pictographs I mentioned?"

"Yeah. You said we'll need an astronomer to decipher them."

"That's right. The pictographs are on North Hegman Lake, north of the town of Ely, Minnesota. You'll need the help of that astronomer friend of yours to decipher the meaning of the pictographs during the spring equinox. And that's coming up, hey, so the timing's good. If you succeed, that'll help you solve the next clue. So there's no sense in me telling you anything more at this point until the pictographs are figured out."

"All right. I've never seen them, but I know where the Hegman Lake pictographs are."

"Good. There's another bit of information I can give that doesn't relate to the location of the chest. You remember the Percy and Campbell lead seal I got?"

"Yes."

"Well, it's from the wooden chest itself."

There was silence as Tim tried to absorb what Two-hearts had just said. But nothing immediately clicked for Tim. "All right. I got it. The pictographs on North Hegman Lake, and you have the lead seal that was on the wooden chest."

"That's right. You first solve those pictographs, then get back to me and we'll take the next step."

Tim had been uncertain for so long that the excitement he was just starting to feel seemed almost alien. He smiled. Maybe there was a solution to all this somewhere along the line.

29

A Restaurant in Duluth

"Tim, don't you get it?" Maggie asked in friendly frustration. She slid forward, sat erect, and opened her hands in a pleading gesture. "Two-hearts has the very lead seal that was attached to the treasure chest. Now come on!"

Tim put his index finger to his lips. "Um, I'm supposed to be embarrassed now, aren't I?"

"You're about to be. Just think of this question: if Two-hearts has the lead seal, then how was it recovered if it was in the river?"

Tim threw his head back on the backrest of their booth. "Well, it could have been . . ." Tim paused. His whole body gave a little jerk and his eyebrows rose almost to his hairline. "AHHH! How humiliating! *That's* the secret of Hell's Gate Rapids. The treasure never got lost *in* them! How could it have if Two-hearts has the very lead seal that was on the chest?"

Maggie, Jessa, and Shukriyah giggled.

"And to think I've been bragging to my friends and relatives that I'm dating an MIT graduate student," Jessa said in jest.

"Hey, we're talking archaeology here," Tim said as he looked at Jessa out of the corner of his eye and shrugged. "My specialty is in particle physics. What can I tell ya'."

Then Tim leaned forward and rested his elbows on the table. "You know, it's no wonder why Lyle called off the recovery. Where Two-hearts says he 'explained things in full,' he must have told him that the treasure was not at the bottom of any river. And he must have wanted Lyle to keep it a secret because he suspected De Beers was after the treasure."

"Well, one thing is for sure," Shukriyah said. "The clue that the pictographs are supposed to provide has taken on a new twist. The pictographs obviously won't point to the location of a rapids."

"Yeah, that for sure is a new twist," Tim said.

"Hmm," Maggie said, thinking. "Tim, I just thought of something. The spring equinox is late in March. I doubt if we'll be able to get out on the ice."

"With the winter we've had, I expect we'll be able to paddle out there."

"Maggie, I have a question," Jessa said. "If the pictographs do give a clue to some place other than a rapids, then how did the rumor ever get started that the treasure was lost at the bottom of a rapids? You told us Lyle had done such exhaustive research of manifest records. He even went up to Winnipeg to research the . . . um . . . was it the Percy and Campbell archives or the North West Company?"

"The Hudson Bay Company archives," Maggie said. "Percy and Campbell got absorbed into the North West Company, who eventually merged with the Hudson Bay Company."

"Anyway, wouldn't it have been the Percy and Campbell officials themselves who made detailed entries about an accident in the rapids and that a valuable wooden chest got lost?"

Maggie's initial response was only a dumfounded look. "You know, that's an excellent question," she said. "The company clerks, proprietors . . . whomever . . . obviously all were convinced that the treasure ended up somewhere in the bottom of Hell's Gate Rapids. They also recorded that when the treasure was lost, a high-ranking voyageur named Jean-Luc Trotin drowned in the rapids."

"Jean-Luc Trotin?" Tim asked with surprise. "Two-hearts mentioned that name in Alexandria."

"I wonder why the company officials were convinced that the treasure went to the bottom of the rapids?" Maggie asked.

≈ 30 ≈

June 1779
On the Voyageurs' Highway, Northwest of Lake Superior.

AT THE BREAK OF DAWN ON THE MORNING that followed Sebastian Bouvette's funeral, Jean-Luc Trotin stood on an outcrop of granite that sloped down to the quiet lake. Although it was a bright morning with an azure-blue sky overhead, the rising sun had to fight through thick shrouds of heavy white fog that hung over the lake. Along the shoreline to each side of Jean-Luc, fingers of the white fog reached onshore and into the trees, giving the woods a ghostly aspect.

As birds chirped along the shoreline, two of Jean-Luc's comrades, Edouard and Henri, came down through the bright mist to join Jean-Luc. Edouard was the brigade's guide, an avante—farthest forward-sitting voyageur—who was always in the lead canoe.

"Beautiful morning, gentlemen," Jean-Luc said in French. He looked at Henri and placed a hand on his shoulder. "I trust you slept well last night."

As Henri was mute, he simply nodded a confirmation.

"And you, Edouard?"

"Better than Mr. McKay," Edouard answered. "Did you hear him talking and thrashing in his sleep."

"I did. I did indeed. Another nightmare, I'm sure. He was even crawling around on all fours. I think our mean-spirited little bourgeois is going crazy. He should be ripe for our little scheme."

"It was shortly after I heard McKay snoring again that I saw you get up and light a torch from the campfire embers. Then I heard you launch the canoe and paddle out in lake."

"You could hear me?" Jean-Luc asked with a look of concern.

"Well, a number of us were lying awake simply wondering when you were going to head out. But don't worry, you were quiet. McKay was sound asleep and wouldn't have heard you. So tell us, Jean-Luc. What did you see? Did you see your signal down at the other end of the lake? Are your relatives camped down there as we had planned back at the Rainy River post?"

"Yes, I saw their distant fire. I've been waiting for this day ever since my relatives told me that McKay was trying to trade the treasure chest for the inscribed stone of Rainy Lake. Glory be to the wise chiefs who turned him down. No company bourgeois, in fact, no Englishman, should ever be allowed to buy the stone. But, when the wise chiefs turned him down, I realized where and how I could fix McKay for good. So I arranged for my relatives to follow us day by day. They are now camped exactly where we had agreed. And last night I used a torch to return their signal."

Jean-Luc placed a hand on Edouard's shoulder.

"Today is the day, Edouard. Today we will get our revenge on McKay when we arrive at Hell's Gate Rapids. And with the recent events, with Sebastian's passing, I know that Providence is on our side. This opportunity is God-given."

"Your relatives will pick you up?"

"Yes. Here's the plan. When the two of you release the lines at the top of the rapids, I will paddle through the gorge and eddy out at Last Chance Cove. From there I will bushwhack through the woods on the other side of the rapids. Then tonight after sunset my relatives will meet me on the other side of Devil's Cauldron."

"Jean-Luc, why don't we stop at Last Chance Cove on our way upstream? If we have a rope long enough, we can stay attached to you as you paddle-ferry the canoe across the rapids into the cove. You can get out, unload the wooden chest, and then shove the canoe back out into the rapids. We can simply tell McKay that there was an accident."

"He'd never accept it. He must witness the accident himself if he is to believe it. Besides, as we progress upstream, McKay will leave the trail and come through the woods as often as possible to check on us. He won't want to let that wooden chest out of his sight any more than he has to. We simply can't risk unloading it when he might see us. Plus, if we have our accident at the top of the rapids right under his nose, we'll know for sure that he'll never see me eddy out at Last Chance Cove and unload the chest."

"But if we release you at the top of the rapids, you'll have to face the stretch of standing waves between the rock walls. If you run to the either side to avoid them, the current will likely smash you into the wall no matter which side you take."

"Then I run the waves! Listen! Don't worry about me! You just concentrate on your part. The hardest lining will be at the rock walls. The canoe can easily get pinned if we're not careful. And both of you must be careful not to slip off the wall."

"Jean-Luc," Edouard said, hoping to talk Jean-Luc out of running the rapids. "I'm worried. All the rapids are higher than normal this year."

"Then I die trying!" Jean-Luc snapped and glared at Edouard. Jean-Luc held out his open hands in a pleading gesture. "Do you want to know something, Edouard. I am in debt to the company. Of all the gouvernoys in the fur trade, how many do you know who are still in debt to their company?" Jean-Luc didn't wait for an answer. "I am the only one because of crooked bookkeeping that I cannot prove. No, Edouard. Today is the day that I paddle Hell's Gate Rapids!"

Edouard and his comrades were all too familiar with Jean-Luc's steely stare. Whenever their gouvernoy gave them "the look," no one ever challenged him further.

"Yes, Jean-Luc," Edouard said meekly.

"Even if I die," Jean-Luc continued, "at least the treasure will go to the bottom of the rapids and the company shareholders will blame McKay not only for losing the treasure but also for my careless death. But enough of that. I know I can paddle the rapids, even at high water. I'll use the shortest canoe in our fleet. All I need is for you and Henri to do your part. Once we're near the top of the rapids and are back in view of the portage trail, I'm certain that McKay will be waiting for us there."

Jean-Luc's glance passed between Edouard and Henri.

"What are the others saying? Do they trust my intentions?" Jean-Luc asked.

"Of course," Edouard answered. "Had it been anyone else taking the treasure, they may have had suspicions. But no one in the brigade would ever have suspicions of you, Jean-Luc. Besides, they've all figured out that the jewels are as good as worthless to a voyageur anyway. It would raise suspicion if any of us suddenly left the fur trade and went back to Montreal. The whole scheme would be exposed as soon as we tried to hawk the jewels. Believe me when I say . . . vengeance on Duncan McKay will be plenty of reward for all of us."

Henri nodded in agreement.

"All right then," Jean-Luc said. "One last time. Let's go over what each of you must do. Henri, the location where the portage trail comes back alongside the rapids. You know exactly where that is, right?"

Henri gave confirmation with a simple nod.

"At that location, there will be a few large boulders in the main current. Edouard will whip his bow line up and over the boulders. Then, Henri, you will do the same with the stern line. That's when my canoe will be in position. All you have to remember, Henri, is to keep the stern line low to the water so it catches around one of the boulders. Be sure to hang on to your rope tightly. I will holler when I want you to let it go."

Then Jean-Luc looked back at Edouard.

"Edouard, after the stern line is in position, I'll give you a little nod and quickly slide my hand up and down the high end of my pole. That will be my signal. There are plenty of narrow little inclines right there for you to slip and fall on. Choose one of them for your fall, and then let go of your bow line as you go down. When you get your head back above water—don't worry, the water won't be over your head—then panic for a second or two, or pretend like you're hurt. Whatever you do, make sure you let the canoe pull your rope far enough out into the river as it starts to head downstream. Then you can pretend to make a hopeless lunge for the rope. For this scheme to work, two things must happen. Not only must McKay witness everything for himself, he must also be convinced that it was all an accident."

Jean-Luc looked into Edouard's eyes for any sign of confusion or doubt. "Okay?" Jean-Luc asked.

"Okay," Edouard said softly, hanging his head.

Once again, Jean-Luc placed a hand on Edouard' shoulder. "Don't you worry, Edouard. I will make it. I must make it." With that, Jean-Luc turned and walked away.

Edouard stepped closer to Henri. "Have you noticed that Jean-Luc doesn't look well" I think he's trying to hide the fact that he is sick."

Henri nodded.

"As soon as we stopped to set up camp last night, he got out of the canoe, went in the woods and threw up. And then I saw him shivering."

With both index fingers, Henri started poking at various points on his face.

"Yes, I too fear that Jean-Luc is coming down with the pox. If he gets lesions in the next two or three days, then he'll know for sure. Henri, maybe that's the real reason why he's so willing to run the rapids. But if he's weak, he'll have a much harder time making it."

ɞ 31 ҩ

Later that Day in Hell's Gate Gorge

A<small>S</small> E<small>DOUARD</small> <small>AND</small> H<small>ENRI</small> <small>LINED THE CANOE</small> around a bend toward the upstream end of the Hell's Gate Rapids, Jean-Luc noticed Duncan McKay come into view on the portage trail high above the river. Jean-Luc had to subdue his hatred for the man and concentrate on keeping the canoe out in the current with the bow angled away from Edouard and Henri. With rushing water on each side, Jean-Luc constantly used his pole to position the canoe and frequently yelled out instructions over the river's roar.

When the threesome came near the boulders that protruded from the current, Jean-Luc braced the canoe with his pole so Edouard could let out some slack and whip his rope up an over them one at a time. Once Edouard's rope was on the upstream side of the first boulder, Jean-Luc braced his pole for Henri. Henri also let out some slack and whipped his rope over the boulder. The coordination of the three experienced voyageurs made a difficult maneuver look easy.

Once Henri's rope was on the upstream side of the boulder, Jean-Luc kept one eye on it to make sure that it would catch the boulder once the bow was free. When everything was set up just right, Jean-Luc shouted out two final instructions so the bow of his canoe would swing toward the opposite shore once the bow line was released.

In French he shouted, "Let out some line at the bow! Pull the stern in!"

Then Jean-Luc gave Edouard a little nod and quickly slid his upper hand up and down the pole. At that signal, Edouard appeared to slip, and he dropped his rope. The canoe instantly rotated broadside to the current. Jean-Luc leaned as far as he could over the downstream gunwale so the current wouldn't cascade in over the upstream gunwale and roll the canoe under.

The canoe swung all the way around and started accelerating downstream. Henri still had a hold of the stern line. When his line wrapped around a boulder, it snapped taut and jolted the canoe to a sudden stop mid-stream. Water quickly built up around the stern end as the current diverted around each side of the canoe. Although the canoe appeared perilously close to getting swamped, the situation was stable. Nevertheless, Jean-Luc feigned urgency.

"*Laisse la corde!*" Jean-Luc shouted from the canoe.

Henri let go of his rope and watched as the canoe started to drift with the current. Jean-Luc threw his pole overboard and got low on his knees in the middle of the canoe. He reached for the paddle he had stowed under the canvas in the bow section. His first, worst challenge would be the series of standing waves right around the bend in the rapids.

The bow of Jean-Luc's canoe rode up and over the first wave. But as the bow descended the downstream slope, the upward slope of the second wave followed too closely. The canoe punched through the second wave instead of riding up and over it, and water gushed in over the gunwales.

Another wave was pointed like a rooster tail. Jean-Luc's canoe rode up the wave's sloping side and was just about to tip over. A sudden collision with a submerged rock saved him but sent the canoe rolling to the other side. Jean-Luc's quick, skillful white-water maneuvering saved the canoe a second time. The collision with the rock, however, had likely resulted in hull damage and more water was probably leaking into the canoe.

Jean-Luc was now in the heart of Hell's Gate Gorge and his situation was dire. As he tried desperately to keep control of his water-laden canoe, he looked downstream, scouting the steep banks and rock bluffs. On river-right he spotted his one and only chance to save himself: Last Chance Cove. If he missed it, he knew that his fate would be to end up in Devil's Cauldron at the bottom of the rapids. So Jean-Luc made a couple powerful, far-reaching sweeps on his left-side in a desperate attempt to get the canoe headed toward the right-side bank.

"Sebastian!" Jean-Luc shouted out above the roar of the rapids. "Yesterday you went to meet St. Anne! If today is my turn, we will still have our vengeance against the evil McKay! And we will then make our music once again! We will make it for eternity!

"HAAAHHH!" Jean-Luc screamed out in fury and determination. It was a defiant yell into the face of death. Jean-Luc rotated his broad shoulders to pull hard on a desperate stroke. But the blade of his long gouvernoy paddle got wedged between submerged rocks and snapped.

Jean-Luc threw down the handle end of his broken paddle and reached under the canvas for a spare one he had stowed. Within the time that it took him to retrieve the spare and get it in the water, the canoe had swung almost broadside to the current. He quickly extended his paddle behind him on his left side and kept prying against the stern-end hull.

Once the canoe was re-oriented correctly, Jean-Luc resumed the hard strokes on his left side. Not only did he have to align the canoe in an optimum position to eddy out at Last Chance Cove, but he also needed to be going faster than the current.

Last Chance Cove was created by a huge rock formation that jutted out into the current. The water behind it was quiet. The abrupt transition between the river's current and the quiet water was called the eddy line. Jean-Luc's only chance was to cross that eddy line just right and get the bow of his canoe into the quiet water. If his canoe approached the cove at the wrong angle, the swift current would simply carry the canoe past the cove and down the rapids for an inevitable plunge into Devil's Cauldron.

As Jean-Luc approached the cove, he had the right angle and good momentum. After one last powerful stroke on his left side just before his bow reached the eddy line, his bow crossed the line, and he swung the blade end of his paddle across the canoe without switching hands. With his right hand now high in the air holding the paddle's handle, he leaned out and extended his left arm over the right gunwale giving the canoe a dangerous pitch. Then he stabbed the quiet water behind the bluff with the blade of his paddle.

Jean-Luc pulled with all his might to bring the bow of his canoe farther into the quiet water. The stern of the canoe, still within the river's current, swung downstream like an errant compass needle looking for north. As the stern swung, Jean-Luc had to rotate his paddle blade for optimum pull into the quiet water. Once the canoe was oriented with the bow pointing almost straight upstream, Jean-Luc pulled hard on three or four strokes to bring the canoe completely within the quiet water.

He had done it. Jean-Luc had successfully eddied out at Last Chance Cove. He made a few final strokes to beach his canoe on a tiny sandy shore between the wall of rock that formed the cove and a smaller outcrop of rock. When the canoe stopped, he threw his paddle on shore and jumped out. As soon as he had his feet on shore and had pulled the canoe farther onto the beach, he instantly fell to his knees.

Although no time could really be wasted, Jean-Luc was completely out of breath. He rolled over and flopped flat on his back to steal a moment or two of rest. He closed his eyes and felt his chest heaving. The roar of the rapids was soothing and for some reason seemed to come from all directions. Maybe it was because he was flat on his back, he thought. Or maybe it was because he was lightheaded due to illness and exhaustion. He felt as if he could easily drift off to sleep.

Jean-Luc knew he had to keep his wits. He opened his eyes but the white clouds above appeared blurry against the blue sky. Every muscle in his body ached and was stiff from a fever-induced chill. He shook his head and tried to concentrate on what he must do next. His most important task, surviving the rapids, was now complete, and there was no doubt that he would prevail. But a highly unpleasant task remained. After a minute or so, Jean-Luc slowly sat up, then got to his feet.

The first thing Jean-Luc did was to untie the wooden chest from the canoe thwart. With its "P & C" lead seal still well-secured, he hoisted the chest out of the canoe and limped on shore as he held the awkward box against his thigh and leaned backward. In his weakened state, the chest felt heavier. After he let the chest plop to the ground, he returned to the canoe and looked down inside to study the remaining contents. Since the canoe was sitting at a pitch on the sloping sand, all the water had collected in the stern.

But in the bow, Jean-Luc stared at the loathsome canvas. After hesitating momentarily, he slowly reached down to grab an edge of the canvas. But he quickly pulled his hand back and paused again. He closed his eyes with dread while his hand tightened into a grip in mid-air. Then in one sudden motion he reached down and peeled the canvas back toward the stern. He rolled the canvas back under successive thwarts, then yanked the entire canvas out and threw it on the beach.

Inside the canoe lay the body of Sebastian Bouvette.

Jean-Luc studied his friend's face. Aside from the small pox lesions, Sebastian looked oddly content. Almost serene. Maybe he too was relieved, Jean-Luc thought, that they had not swamped in the rapids.

Jean-Luc turned his attention away from the corpse as he fished a bulky oil cloth-wrapped package out of the water in the stern. The oil cloth was tied tightly around a pigskin bag tied at the neck. He brought it up the beach and stood before a log at the edge of the woods.

Jean-Luc undid all the knots and reached inside the pigskin. He first pulled out his two most valued possessions and placed them on the log. Then Jean-Luc pulled out a metal pot. Inside the pot was a rawhide package of pemmican—a mixture of dried bison meat and melted fat pounded into a paste and then pressed into a cake. Also inside the pot was his clay pipe and a twist of tobacco. Although everything was dry, the stem of his pipe had broken.

The pemmican was the only food Jean-Luc would have until after sunset when his relatives were to meet him. It wasn't much, but since he started having trouble keeping food down, he thought the pemmican was all he'd bother taking. And if by chance he did get hungry, he knew he could supplement the pemmican because his mother had taught him to recognize wild edible plants. The trick was not to delay searching until one was so hungry that foolish risks would be taken. Years ago in one particular desperate time of hunger, Jean-Luc found out that he was one of the lucky voyageurs who could tolerate rock tripe, a black spongy-looking lichen that could kill some people who ate it.

Later that day, sometime after it got dark, Jean-Luc's relatives were to meet him near the point where Devil's Cauldron emptied into the lake. Although he had his fire steel, he wouldn't dare light a fire that evening just in case McKay would order his voyageurs to stay put for the evening and camp somewhere in the area. Jean-Luc had one of the more unique fire steels among his fellow voyageurs. His had been stamped with 'TROTIN,' although the steel was worn down to the point that only the T, R, O, and part of the second T were legible.

Finally, Jean-Luc was ready to deal with the cadaver of Sebastian Bouvette. Still feeling groggy, Trotin took a few strained deep breaths. With the empty metal pot still in hand, he walked back down to the canoe. Putting the pot down, he removed his knife and placed it by the metal pot. He took off his red sash, reached down to run the sash underneath Bouvette, and tied it around Bouvette's mid-section. Lastly, he went down to the stern end to retrieve the handle of the paddle that had snapped in the rapids but was still floating inside the canoe.

"Sebastian," Jean-Luc said solemnly in French as he laid the broken paddle on top of Bouvette. "We did not do the customary breaking of a paddle at your funeral yesterday. Your comrades and I agreed to save that ceremony for today. A paddle broke while we ran the rapids, so here is only the handle. The blade end has already preceded you downstream.

"I am sure St. Anne, the patron saint of all travelers, has already met you at Heaven's gate. When you enter, search the golden shores and hold a good campsite for me. Just make sure that there are no long portages. Then we shall make our music once again.

"And please . . . please understand what I must do next in case your body washes on shore. Your death has simply provided us with too great an opportunity to pass up. We were always afraid that McKay might become suspicious if he never saw my body. But you have solved that for us, Sebastian.

"May the Lord forgive me for what I am about to do," Jean-Luc said in closing as he touched his hand to his forehead, his stomach, and then to both shoulders. "Amen."

With his dark hair, Bouvette looked a lot like Jean-Luc. And it wasn't by chance that he had been dressed in clothes similar to what Jean-Luc wore. But Jean-Luc couldn't take the chance that McKay might see Bouvette's body up close and recognize his face.

Jean-Luc walked a short distance behind him and picked up a boulder. He brought it back to the canoe and raised the boulder over his head with both hands. For a moment he hesitated while holding the boulder above his head. Then he slammed the boulder into Bouvette's face. He repeated it. Again . . . and again. When Bouvette's face was disfigured to the point that it could be mistaken for his own face—or almost anyone's—Jean-Luc stopped pounding. Then he threw the boulder off to the side and dropped to his knees. He placed his forearm on the canoe gunwale, buried his face in the crook of his arm and wept.

When Jean-Luc composed himself, it was finally time to give Bouvette his send off. Jean-Luc took the metal pot and started bailing the water that had collected in the stern. When most of it had been emptied, he gathered up the long lining rope still dangling in the lagoon and threw it in the stern. He moved forward to do the same with the bow rope, part of which was caked with beach sand.

When the last of the bow-end lining rope was in the canoe, he pushed the canoe off the beach and back into the miniature lagoon. He waded into the water, spun the canoe around, then positioned it right behind the rock bluff that formed the lagoon. The canoe was now just behind the eddy line of the swift current and ready to launch.

Jean-Luc cupped his hand around the black pitch-sealed, spruce root lacing on the canoe's stern curvature. With his other hand firmly gripping the gunwale, he rocked the canoe back and forth a couple times. After the last back pull, he placed both hands on the stern curvature and leaned into it with his shoulder. With all his might he pushed the canoe out into the current. For a moment he watched the canoe that bore the body of his comrade. As it caught the current and sped downstream on its way to Devil's Cauldron, it began to toss and bounce in the turbulence. Jean-Luc couldn't stand to watch the canoe overturn so he turned back toward the sandy beach.

"Bon voyage, Sebastian," Jean-Luc said as waded through the quiet water of the lagoon.

When he got back on the beach, he walked up to the log where he had left his two most valued possessions. Although Jean-Luc was more concerned with how the flute á bec fared the trip down the rapids, he certainly was eager to inspect both items.

≈ 32 ≈

*North Hegman Lake near Ely, Minnesota,
Just inside the Boundary Waters Canoe Area Wilderness.*

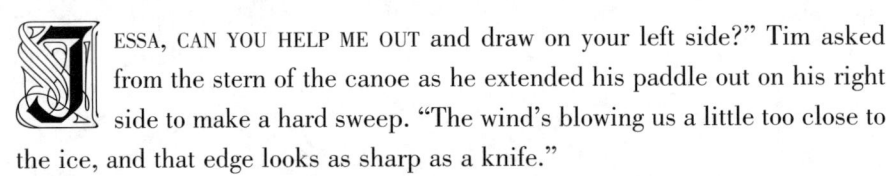

"JESSA, CAN YOU HELP ME OUT and draw on your left side?" Tim asked from the stern of the canoe as he extended his paddle out on his right side to make a hard sweep. "The wind's blowing us a little too close to the ice, and that edge looks as sharp as a knife."

"Oh' yeah, I see what you mean," Jessa said from the bow. "We're a little too close." She reached straight out with her bent-shaft paddle, speared the water with the blade and then pulled in toward the canoe's hull.

"I imagine the Kevlar hull is tough enough not to cut that easy," Tim said. "But I'd rather not find out in water this cold. Let's paddle ahead to where the ice looks broken up."

Maggie and Shukriyah followed in a second canoe. The foursome were making a day's journey to North Hegman Lake near Ely, Minnesota, just inside the Boundary Waters Canoe Area Wilderness. They were on their way to examine pictographs on a large rock outcrop on the suggestion of Cedric Two-hearts.

Two-hearts' latest communication included information about the voyageur Jean-Luc Trotin—nicknamed "the Hustler"—who paddled solo down Hell's Gate Rapids with a wooden chest. Of course, that chest became the legendary lost treasure of the voyageurs. But contrary to what everyone had believed for over 200 years, from the fur trade company officials up to William Pearson, Pearson's descendants, and even Lyle Hanson, the treasure was not lost as a result of Trotin's canoe over-turning in the rapids. When Tim asked, Two-hearts admitted that Jean-Luc Trotin had survived the rapids and ran off with the treasure.

Two-hearts went on to say that the Hegman Lake pictographs were the first key to figuring out where Trotin had hidden the treasure. Two-hearts passed along three aspects of the clue that had survived through a number of generations.

One: the clue involved native Indian astrology.

Two: the pictographs revealed the clue every year during the spring equinox.

And three: the phrase, "the direction of the chase," is the only known specific information.

As Two-hearts had recommended to Tim when they spoke in Alexandria, Shukriyah had come along in hope that she could apply her astronomy skills in figuring out the meaning behind the pictographs.

The two canoes were headed in an easterly direction and had just come out of a narrows that squeezed North Hegman Lake. As the larger eastern portion of the lake opened up before the four paddlers, they came upon a massive floe of black ice. A breeze out of the northwest kept the floe toward the southeast, fortunately keeping a water route to the pictographs open.

For late March, it was odd that they could be paddling at all on a lake in northeastern Minnesota. A very mild winter had resulted in numerous record ice-out dates throughout the state.

When they reached the area where the ice was broken up, they stopped paddling and listened. As they bobbed up and down on the small waves passing under the canoe, they became entranced by the tintinabulation of countless ice shards clinking together. It was as if they were in a breezy ballroom with a hundred crystalline chandeliers.

Maggie and Shukriyah paddled up alongside Tim and Jessa, and the foursome let their canoes drift closer to the tinkling ice. Jessa used her paddle to push against a basketball-size chunk of ice. As the chunk rotated, its multiple crystalline surfaces sparkled.

"The ice looks like honeycombs," Shukriyah observed from the other canoe.

"Yeah, like a bunch of elongated hexagons all stuck to each other," Jessa added. "It's so beautiful. Just like diamonds: perfectly clear."

"You know," Maggie said from the stern of the other canoe, "we should go back and get that large cooler. This ice could pass as the lost treasure of jewels. It'd be nice to take a chunk back with us."

"Not a bad idea," Tim said, "but the fact of the matter is, guys, it's time to push on ahead. So far fate has been on our side with this northwest breeze keeping this part of the lake free of ice. We should be able to paddle right up to the pictographs with no problem. But if the wind switches, we'll have to hightail it out of here right away before the ice blocks our way out."

As they started paddling toward the pictographs, the rock outcrop was visible in the distance as a mostly gray, weathered mass that sort of resembled a giant pillow, a description that could fit countless other outcrops in the Boundary Waters. But this outcrop obviously was special, and the foursome got quiet as they headed for their destination. There's a certain sense of respectful anticipation when approaching a place that conveyed a mysterious message from so long ago.

As they drew closer, the outcrop seemed to loom like a bastion. They soon could make out details. The upper portion of the lake-facing wall rolled inland with a smooth curve. Its lower portion was mostly jagged and irregular and sliced by thin fissures. Isolated, pinkish-toned surfaces on the lower portion appeared to be raw, unweathered granite, and were framed by vertical stripes of black lichen. It was one of these surfaces part way up the wall upon which the pictographs had been painted.

Anticipation rose as they paddled up to the base of the lake-facing wall. Before long they were close enough to make out the pictographs. They got as close as they could, stopped paddling, and held the gunwales of each other's canoe as they studied the aboriginal-like outlines of a man with his arms spread, a wolf, a moose, and people in canoes.

Since the northern end of the lake necked down to form another narrows, they had some protection from the wind, and the water was calmer, allowing them to study the pictographs without quickly drifting away. For several minutes, they simply stared in silence as Tim and Maggie made an occasional correction stroke to keep the canoes near the cliff face.

"Well, why don't we beach somewhere," Tim said as he finally broke the silence. "We'll have some lunch. Shukriyah can study her star chart. Then I guess we wait for sunset."

Tim searched the upper part of the outcrop. "But I don't know about eating lunch on top of this bluff . . . you know, being consecrated or sacred ground."

Tim surveyed the surrounding shoreline, then pointed at the most ideal spot. "Let's paddle over there and climb up on that dome-shaped rock knoll."

When the two canoes approached the shoreline below the rock knoll, the bow paddlers grabbed some leafless branches of overhanging sweet gale. As Jessa knew how particular Tim was about scratching the gel coat on the hull of his canoe, she maneuvered the bow ever so gently into the rocky shallows until she was close enough to hop out between two patches of remnant corn snow. Shukriyah did the same and then held her canoe steady so Maggie could work her way forward and climb out.

After everyone had disembarked and the canoes were lifted up on shore, Tim and Maggie tied the canoes to trees using bowline knots. They all climbed toward the top of the knoll with their day packs, water bottles, and life jackets to use as seat cushions.

It didn't appear as if anyone else had ever walked up on the knoll. Unlike a well-worn campsite with exposed tree roots and patches of bare soil, the knoll's granite surface was sprinkled with crunchy lichens and scattered, low-lying wisps of delicate woody stems. One species of lichen looked like grayish brown corn flakes.

Down the backside on the forest-side of the knoll, large white pines stood in old snow as if guarding the knoll against invaders. But a number of jack pines appeared as if they had breached the barrier to establish a foot hold in the shallow duff that made up the knoll's perimeter crown. Upon seeing the jack pines, Tim surmised that a forest fire must have passed over the knoll at one time.

As the girls found a large rock to sit upon and started poring over the diagram of the pictographs and the star chart, Tim walked along the lake-side edge of the knoll to avoid walking on the crunchy lichen. When he found a bare surface of rock large enough on which to spread out, he threw down his life jacket and sat down to start munching on a baloney sandwich and some trail mix. When he surveyed his surroundings, he spotted a vigilant gray and white whiskey jack jay perched in a nearby tree, obviously hoping for Tim to share a morsel or two.

All was right with the world, Tim thought. As he soaked in the wilderness surroundings, he was reminded of "The Pipes of Pan," the first chapter in *Open Horizons*, a book written by the wilderness writer and Ely native, Sigurd Olson. When one was immersed in nature as Tim was right then, it was as if he were listening to the Pipes of Pan, engrossed with a childlike sense of wonder all too easily dulled by adulthood.

And "listening to the Pipes" was an apt analogy as Tim became acutely aware of the sound of the breeze as it passed through the high canopy of the surrounding pines. It's a lonely yet beautiful low-tone howl that is somehow more ominous and haunting than the sound of wind through broad-leaf trees.

The opposite shore was a horizontal gray band accented by splotches of green conifers. On this day, the landscape seemed almost tundra-like, being still in winter dormancy. Yet, by mid-summer, the woods would be more like a steamy jungle. The vegetation would grow thick and lush, and the mosquitoes would swarm so that protective gear had to be worn on portages no matter how hot.

Tim turned his attention again to the wind as he realized that he needed to discuss something with the girls. Although the wind was still coming out of the northwest, he started getting nervous about staying till after sunset. The wind could change, and the last thing Tim wanted was to be stranded out on the lake after dark. It also looked possible that the constellations might be obscured by clouds.

As Tim opened a small bag of M&M's, he heard the sound of three pair of feet coming his way.

"Hey, there's something I need to discuss with you guys," Tim said as the girls approached. "I've been doing some thinking. I'm a little nervous about staying out here till after sunset. I know we have our head lamps, but having at least some twilight out on the lake would be a big help, and this time of year there isn't much. The possibility of dealing with ice floes in the dark is making me uncomfortable. I think it's a little too danger—"

Tim stopped mid-sentence and cocked his head up when he became aware of smirks on the girls' faces.

"Well, we don't have to stay out here till after dark," Shukriyah said with an unmistakable tone of assuredness. "We no longer have to make a field orientation of the pictographs with the spring equinox constellations—"

"'Cuz we got it all figured out!" Maggie said as if on cue.

Tim simply stared, surprised yet pleased and instantly eager to hear more.

"Well, if I may offer a slight correction," Maggie said. "We don't claim to know where the treasure is *hidden*—not yet, anyway. But we're convinced we've figured out the meaning of the pictographs."

Maggie turned to Shukriyah, who took this as her prompt to explain.

"We're convinced that the man in the pictographs diagram is what the native Indians had called the Great Wintermaker, what we know today as the constellation Orion." Shukriyah pointed out for Tim a particular sky location on her star chart. "The seven marks above the Great Wintermaker's shoulder represent the seven brightest stars of the Pleiades. Just after sunset around the time of the spring equinox, the Great Wintermaker is dominant in the southern sky. As a ritual to signify his upcoming departure for the summer, the Great Wintermaker is watching a great annual chase in the heavens right at the time of the equinox. That's when the wolf—the constellation Leo—rises above the eastern horizon and chases the moose—the constellation Pegasus—down to the western horizon.

"Now, as an observer of the diagram stands at the cliff face and looks at the moose, the observer will realize the direction of the hidden treasure by knowing where the moose disappears. Where the moose finally drops below the horizon is in the northwest. In fact, that's the direction the observer's facing, and that's the direction where the treasure's hidden."

"Higher up in the diagram," Maggie said, "there's an 'X' that we suspect represents the Lake of the Cross . . . Lac La Croix, which is northwest from here. We're convinced that the treasure is either hidden along the shoreline of Lac La Croix or somewhere between here and there."

"Well that really narrows it down a lot," Tim said sarcastically.

"Oh, come on!" Shukriyah fired back. "You got any better ideas?"

"No, but that's not the point. I came out here expecting that a clue to the treasure would be obvious. But it sure doesn't seem so based on what you're telling me. We shouldn't have to come up with ideas for what the clue *might* mean. Look . . . with all due respect to Two-hearts, I don't know if we should be too quick to swallow—hook, line, and sinker—everything that he has to say. All my life it's been pounded into my head that these pictographs in the Boundary Waters and the Quetico are perhaps a thousand years old or more. To suggest that some voyageur painted the them in the late 1700s is pretty radical."

"See, I told you he'd be stubborn," Jessa said to her female comrades.

Tim shook his finger at Jessa. "Guess who just volunteered to carry the canoe across the portage to the parking lot."

"But, Tim," Maggie said, "the very essence of a clue is that it's not supposed to be obvious."

"All I'm saying is that with your take on the pictographs, it sure seems like a little skepticism is healthy."

"Tim, let me tell you something about the age of the pictographs in the Quetico Superior." Maggie said and sat down. "For one thing, the most logical pigment used for the pictographs paint is vermillion ochre. It was made of mercuric sulfide brought in by the voyageurs in the late 1700s. Back then, travelers made detailed descriptions of the Picture Rock Cliffs on Crooked Lake but they never made mention of any pictographs. Surely they would have described them if they had existed at that time. The fact that they didn't is probably because they were made *later*."

"Okay, okay" Tim said as he gave some ground, "but you've got another slight problem here. Trotin didn't exactly leave you a signed and numbered print. My point is still valid. You're taking it on faith whatever Two-hearts says. Everything Two-hearts seems to know comes from oral history."

"Granted, we are taking it on faith," Maggie acknowledged. "But if Trotin did indeed do the painting, there's a possibility that he left a hint of who he is and who he represents. The pictographs show three canoes, two of which have two people in them. Those canoes might be Trotin's way of representing his comrades in the fur trade. But there's only one person in the third canoe. That, my doubting friend, might be Trotin's way of representing himself when he went down Hell's Gate Rapids all by himself and stole the treasure."

Tim considered. "I guess you do have a point. There are some things that fit," Tim said as he nodded. "Still . . . a lot of it is speculation. But I confess, what you're saying sounds pretty compelling."

"Two-hearts said something else," Maggie continued. "Trotin was apparently known for being the author of at least a few pictographs. The ones on Darky Lake in the Quetico, not too far north of here across the border, have a very similar style to the ones here on Hegman Lake. And Lac La Croix is not too far west of Darky Lake. Apparently, Trotin spent a lot of time in this area after he got out of the fur trade."

"You know, that brings up a good point," Tim said. "If it's true that Trotin did hide the treasure in this area and spent time here, then wouldn't you think that Hell's Gate Rapids would also be in this area? Lyle had never even wanted to give me a hint. I had the feeling that he wasn't going to tell me where it was until the day our recovery team left town."

"Hey, let me tell ya'. He had even kept it a secret from me—his own wife! All I knew for sure were two things. The treasure was lost on a water route somewhere along or near the present border, so the rapids had to be east of the Lake of the Woods. And two, the treasure got lost in the early part of the summer, which means that the brigade of voyageurs and the clerk Duncan McKay had to be on their way to Grand Portage but were likely west of the height of land at North Lake. In other words, the rapids could have been anywhere in between the Lake of the Woods and North Lake."

"But if all that water flows west, why would Trotin have run a rapids while heading east, upstream?" Shukriyah asked.

"I don't know. This whole thing with the treasure is sure one big puzzle."

"Well, if it was anywhere near this area," Tim said, "the Basswood River is not too far north. And divers did find voyageur relics there back in the 1960s. But in some ways it doesn't seem to fit. After trying to glean hints from Lyle, I've always imagined Hell's Gate Rapids to look something like the gorge just upstream from where the Vermillion River empties into Crane Lake."

"My guess would have been the Granite River over on the Gunflint side," Maggie said. "Relics were found there as well. There's a rapids with a Devil's Cauldron-like drop near the point where the river empties into Lake Saganaga. But the early names of many lakes and rivers in that area have been changed or long forgotten since the voyageur days."

"Such as?" Tim asked.

"Well, the Indians used to call Rose Lake the Lake of Talking Cliffs because two paddlers could hear their own echo out on the lake. Hungry Jack Lake got that name in the white settlement days when some party was bringing provisions up the original Gunflint Trail by horse and wagon. A man named Jack was on the east shore of the lake waiting for the party, but they got delayed by heavy snows. When they finally arrived, one of them yelled down from Honey Moon Bluff and asked, 'Are you hungry, Jack?'"

"Hey!" Tim said as he perked up. "What about the more northerly voyageur route through the center of the Quetico? You know, around the north side of what was called Hunter's Island: from Lac La Croix, up the Maligne River to Sturgeon Lake, and southeast to Kawnipi and Saganaga? Somewhere between Sturgeon and Kawnipi Lakes there's a heck of a rapids skirted by Have-a-Smoke Portage. And Canyon Falls is near the southeast end of Kawnipi, and that's basically a set of rapids that runs through a gorge."

"Yeah, that route is certainly a possibility," Maggie said. "There are any number of good choices."

"Or how about the far northern edge of the Quetico?" Tim asked. "Did the voyageurs ever go up the Namakan River and go through Beaverhouse and Pickerel Lakes?"

"If they did, that would have been a completely different route going northeast away from the border. And they wouldn't have gone that way until 1803 when the North West Company abandoned Grand Portage and started bringing their furs to Fort William in present-day Thunder Bay. Even then, I think they still got up to Pickerel primarily by way of Lac La Croix, Maligne River, and Sturgeon Lake."

Maggie paused and a thoughtful look came over her face. "Uh . . . come to think of it, even the Sturgeon—Kawnipi—Saganaga route around Hunter's Island is doubtful. Lyle wouldn't have needed U.S. permits for that route."

"He would have if his point of entry was still on the U.S. side," Tim said.

"Oh, yeah! Good point!" Maggie acknowledged. "Boy, that route sure does add a host of possibilities. Hmm . . . you know, when I found out that the location of Hell's Gate Rapids had become a moot point, I never thought to ask Lyle where it was. I mean, he certainly can tell us now. It'd sure be interesting to finally have that mystery solved."

Maggie leaned back and became reflective. "But . . . solving the bigger mystery," she continued, "the mystery of the hidden treasure location. The real location."

"So, where do we go from here?" Shukriyah asked as she stood looking between Tim and Maggie. "By looking at the maps of this area, it sure looks like there's a lot of room to hide a treasure between here and Lac La Croix. The length of shoreline on Lac La Croix itself must be in the hundreds of miles."

"You know, I just thought of a problem," Tim said. "Two-hearts said that he'll give the next clue once we've solved the clue on the pictographs. But what if our interpretation is wrong? I don't know what he'll do in that case. For all I know, he might tell us to go back and keep working at it."

"Does he know himself what the interpretation is supposed to be?" Jessa asked.

"He seemed to imply that he does. I guess if he tells us that our interpretation is wrong, then yes, he knows. And if that's the case, he probably also knows exactly where the treasure's hidden."

"Well that's cruel," Maggie said. "Why would he toy with us like that?"

"Because it would be a break with tradition. Apparently, legend says that a latter-day Ojibwe chief is supposed to find the treasure."

Maggie perked up. "Hey! Now it all makes sense. At first, Lyle had a really hard time getting to know Two-hearts and gaining his trust. But things changed after they met in International Falls. Maybe Two-hearts noticed Lyle's dark features and discussed ethnicity. If they did, Lyle would have told him that he is one-quarter Ojibwe."

"Perhaps, but Two-hearts seems like the kind of guy who'd be easy going with anyone once he got to know them."

"Whatever transpired in International Falls," Maggie said, "that's when Two-hearts seemed to become more cooperative. He even gave Lyle those souvenirs—the fire steel and sun crystal."

"Well, we're sure benefitting from the relationship Lyle established. In fact, when Lyle got hurt on his way to meet Two-hearts, I'm sure some guilt prompted Two-hearts to continue his cooperation with us."

Tim looked at each of the women. "Even though Lyle may have some Ojibwe blood, he's not a chief. Any of you know of a chief who can join our quest?"

"I know someone who certainly has the attributes of a good chief," Shukriyah said. "That's Omar, of course."

Tim flicked up his eyebrows and pointed at Shukriyah. "Actually, that's not a bad idea. I could see where Omar could quickly gain Two-hearts' respect."

Maggie became contemplative. "You know something you guys? Deep down, I got a hunch that Two-hearts wants us to find that treasure. When I think back to the letter he left for me at the hospital in Alexandria, he no doubt saw Lyle as the best way to deal with it. He himself is not a chief and doesn't want to deal with it. He obviously doesn't want it to fall into private hands. But with Lyle, he must have recognized an opportunity to get the treasure in the public domain . . . the one sure way that the treasure would not benefit just a few people but all people."

Maggie looked at Tim. "So what do you think? Do you want to approach Two-hearts with our interpretation?"

"I think so. It's our only option. I'll tell Two-hearts that it's our best guess. Then I'll see whether he gives us the next clue. So . . . what do you all say we pack up and paddle back to the car?"

❧ 33 ☙

South Hegman Lake, north of Ely

TIM AND JESSA BEACHED THEIR CANOE at the landing for the portage trail leading back to the parking area. They disembarked, unloaded their gear, and pulled their canoe onto higher ground to make room for Maggie's and Shukriyah's canoe, which was also about to reach the landing. Feeling relieved to be on solid ground, Tim stretched his back and let out a big yawn.

As Jessa helped Maggie and Shukriyah gently beach their canoe, Tim put on a day pack, prepared to hoist his canoe onto his shoulders. Once it appeared that everyone was all set to go, Tim rolled his canoe up onto his shoulders and started up the incline leading away from the lake. Once the trail leveled out, it was an easy hike all the way back to the parking area.

On most portages to a the lake, a person reaches a point where they first glimpse the blue, sparkling water of the lake. They feel an instant relief knowing they'll soon be able to drop their load. The portage back to the parking area had a similar point where the parking area first came into view. Tim felt that same sense of relief when he first glimpsed his Corolla.

Suddenly, Tim's foot caught in mid-step, and he fell forward. One knee smashed onto the ground. As he put out his hands to catch the rest of his fall, his palms scraped on the gravelly trail surface. The forward tip of the canoe thrust against the cold, hard ground with a bang. With his head still under the canoe's hull, a percussion of Kevlar reverberated into a surround-sound roar.

As quick as he could, Tim rotated, threw the canoe off to the side with one arm, and looked back. As soon as he saw the thin, taut wire, he shouted to Jessa and Shukriyah as they hurried toward him. "Stop right there!"

Tim thrust his arm straight out and pointed. "There's a wire stretched across the trail!"

Jessa and Shukriyah froze. A little farther back on the trail, Maggie slowly let down her canoe.

Tim ushered them all off the path into the trees. From there each peered out, looking for assailants. "Do you see anyone?" Tim asked.

He looked back. Maggie looked scared. Jessa and Shukriyah looked more confused than anything. Overhead a gray jay studied him, squawking. Typically, jays liked to harass people, both to let the forest know where they were and to beg for tidbits. The only jay calling was right over his head.

Slowly Tim got to his feet, and the women came up behind him. "You're bleeding," Jessa said.

Tim glanced at his hands and knees. Luckily, his abrasion-resistant leather gloves had protected his hands. But his knee was a different story. It hurt. There was blood on his pants, and he could feel it dripping down his shin. It would need attention soon.

Tim squatted down to take a close look at the wire. Jessa and Shukriyah did the same. Maggie remained standing, looking around.

"God damn it!" Tim said in disgust. "Who in the hell would pull such a dirty stunt?"

Maggie pointed toward the car. "Probably the same person who smashed your window."

The others quickly got up and looked.

Tim hurried up to the car, stopping a few feet from the broken driver's side window. Again he looked around, trying to see around the trees in case someone was watching them. The leafless trees and open woods held no assailants. There were no other vehicles in the lot.

Tim peered at the broken window and took a few tentative steps toward it. Looking inside his car, he saw a piece of paper on the front seat. Moving carefully, Tim approached, then reached into his pocket for his keys.

"Tim, wait!" Shukriyah said. "There might be another booby trap."

Tim froze and thought for a second. He went around to the other side of the car and looked through the passenger-side window. After a careful inspection of the interior, he was satisfied that all was safe and went back around to the driver's side to open the door. As a precaution, however, he unlocked the door and opened it slowly, reaching in to lift out the paper without touching anything else. Then he read the hand-written message written in large block letters.

"HOPE YOU HAD A NICE TRIP. ONE SHOULD AVOID TREASURE SEEKING. IT CAUSES A LOT OF ACCIDENTS. STOP NOW BEFORE SOMETHING REALLY BAD HAPPENS."

The others huddled close to read with him.

"Pretty slick," Tim finally said. "Not overtly threatening but definitely gets the message across. I get the impression they're not just referring to my little tumble. I'm sure they're referring to Lyle's accident as well."

The three girls remained quiet as Tim continued to stare down at the ominous warning. At last he lifted his head to take another look around the parking area, then pulled his car keys out of his pocket again. With the car door fully open, Tim put his gloves back on and swept the broken glass off the car seat and got inside.

"Cross your fingers," Tim said just before he turned the key.

The engine started, and Tim let out a sigh of relief. "At least they didn't disable the car. Otherwise we would have been faced with a long walk."

Tim shut the engine off and got out. He made another quick inspection of the remaining glass shards in the car door and turned to look down the portage trail. "Well, I guess this is the extent of the warning. We should take down that trip wire, clean up the rest of this glass, and load up the canoes and our gear."

"Should we call 911?" Jessa asked. "Maybe a sheriff should investigate the scene."

Tim considered that for a moment. "Ah, the hell with it. By the time they get here it'll probably be dark. Then what can they do? I'd rather just load up and get out of here. I still have this feeling we're being watched."

What are you going to do about the broken window?" Maggie asked.

Tim shrugged. "What can I do? It's gonna be a chilly ride back to Ely, that's all. I'm sure there's some place there we can get some duct tape and plastic."

"You have comprehensive coverage, don't you?"

"Yeah . . . but I'm getting sick and tired of making calls to insurance agents."

Tim looked intently at Shukriyah. "Speaking of phone calls, the first thing I'd like is for you to give Omar a call and ask him if he's found out anything on Shelby Harrington. If he plans to but hasn't yet, then please ask him to hurry it up."

೫ 34 ೬

Archaeological Excavation Site of the
Taurus Mountain Chronicles
Cappadocia Region of Central Turkey

OMAR GAZED OUT THE WINDOW OF THE ONE-ROOM field office while he waited for Alistair and Hasan. He had an unobstructed view down a long slope all the way to the excavation site. He stood with his hands in his pockets, listening to the monotonous hum of the air conditioner.

The field office was a sparsely-furnished pre-fab structure used only for meetings and waiting guests, such as Omar. In the middle of the square floor was an old-fashioned wooden desk with a swivel chair and five metal folding chairs. Along one wall stood a file cabinet, a water cooler, and a rack of maps. Along another wall was an old, beat up sofa with pages of a Milliyet newspaper strewn haphazardly on the cushions.

Omar's mood became reflective as he watched the archaeological activity, some of it bustling, but most of it slow. He thought how fitting it was that the hallowed Taurus Mountain Chronicles had been found in Cappadocia. In some respects, it was the near the center of the universe for the 2,000-year old order of Persian Magi.

Southeast of Cappadocia lay historic Edessa, where another hallowed assemblage of ancient items had also once been interred. Some of St. Thomas' bones had been brought to Edessa in the fourth century after being exhumed near Madras in southeast India. Later on, the bones had been taken by the crusaders and eventually ended up in Ortona, Italy.

On the other side of Turkey's eastern border lay Urmia, Iran, formerly known as Rezaiyeh. When the Magi of the Christmas story returned to Persia from Bethlehem, they built a church in Urmia that was in use at least into the twentieth century. Sometime just before 50 A.D., St. Thomas had arrived in Persia while on his apostolic journey east. He baptized a successive generation of Magi, some of whom joined him on his journey.

Urmia was also the likely birthplace of Zoroaster, the founder of the ancient, monotheistic Persian faith of Zoroastrianism, a possible pre-cursor, perhaps, to subsequent Judeo-Christian traditions. If the Apostle Thomas was the patron saint of the Persian Magi, then Zoroaster might be considered their patron saint in the ages before the Christian era.

A couple locations to the west of Cappadocia had interesting implications not only for the modern-day Magi, but also for anyone else interested in Christmas-related customs and beliefs. The tradition of gift giving had its roots in the southwest corner of Turkey. St. Nicholas was a fourth century bishop in Myra, now known as Kale.

North of Kale on the coast of the Aegean Sea lay Ephesus. Many believe that Mary, the mother of Jesus, spent her last days in Ephesus and not in Jerusalem. Omar hoped that the most recently discovered chronicles, those that document the second journey of Magi, would solve that mystery.

Ephesus could easily have been the destination of the second journey, as the Magi certainly seemed to have had an affinity for the Anatolian peninsula. After all, that was where their chronicles have been found. But wherever the destination, Alistair was convinced that the Magi would have attempted to find Mary. If she no longer lived, they would have made a pilgrimage to her tomb. Had they been successful in either case, it should be recorded in their chronicles.

The door of the field office suddenly opened behind Omar. It was Alistair. He stood momentarily in the entryway with one hand still on the knob of the door. The front of his shirt was wet with sweat, his blue jeans were dusty, and stubble on his face indicated he hadn't shaved in a few days. A hand-sized GPS/radio was clipped to his belt.

"You made it," Alistair commented.

"Yes. But that was quite the taxi bill."

"Trust me. It'll be worth it."

Omar noticed Alistair's teasing grin and knew something was up.

Alistair's attention was suddenly drawn outside. Omar became conscious of the rising sound of a car engine. It stopped and a car door opened.

"He's here," Alistair announced to someone as he motioned with his arm.

The car door slammed shut and the car drove away, its sound quickly fading.

"I didn't notice you come up from the excavation," Omar commented.

"I walked over from the mobile lab," Alistair said as he came all the way into the field office. "And Hasan just arrived. That was someone from the climate-controlled storage facility who dropped him off."

Hasan appeared in the doorway with a big smile. He was holding a round container of Cornell and Deihl pipe tobacco in one hand and a fancy-looking gray case in the other. Hasan also had the same brand of GPS/radio clipped to his belt.

"Greetings, Omar," Hasan said. "Good to see you again."

"It's good to be back," Omar said. "I take it you have good news."

"Oh, yes," Alistair said as he eased himself into the swivel chair, leaned back and put his feet up on the desk. "I'd have had champagne had it not been forbidden here. But you do like pipe tobacco, don't you?"

"Indeed, I do," Omar replied. "This must be some very good news."

Hasan placed the container of tobacco on the desk. With a closed-lip smile and shifty eyes adding a touch of dramatic flair, Hasan gracefully held out the gray case with one hand underneath, like a jewelry store clerk displaying diamond rings to an engaged couple. Hasan opened the case to show off three meerschaum smoking pipes laid in velvet-lined molds. The pipe bowls were white, carved sultan heads with turbans and beards. The pipe stems were black.

"Behold three exquisite beauties," Hasan said as he swept the back of his free hand over the three pipes. "Made by the master craftsman himself, Sadik Yanik. Never been smoked, worthy of royalty, and offered to you on this very fine day for your personal enjoyment. I trust you will be most satisfied."

"My goodness," Omar said as he leaned over the desk to admire the pipes. "Exquisite beauties they are."

"Um . . . there is a slight problem that I just thought about," Alistair said with a tinge of embarrassment. "Omar, do you remember that voyageur fire steel you showed me in my office back in Newcastle? You don't have it in your briefcase by any chance, do you? We sure could use it right now."

"We could," Hasan admitted. "Somehow we forgot the most important thing."

"Don't tell me," Omar said as he looked back and forth at Alistair and Hasan. "You brilliant fellows don't have a lighter?"

"Nope," Alistair said. "No lighter, no matches, no . . . no blow torch, which is probably for the best, all things considered. The closest fire starter I can think of is a magnifying glass back at the mobile lab."

"Well, boys," Omar said, "looks like we'll have to wait to break in these pipes."

"I tell you what," Hasan said. "I'm sure Derya has a lighter. And he wants me to come down to the pit anyway."

"Oh, I wouldn't worry about it," Omar said. "Not being able to smoke these pipes today wouldn't be the end of the world."

"It would be for me," Hasan quipped as he made for the door. "Besides, Derya just radioed me as I was on my way here. He made me promise that I'd meet with him before the end of the day." Hasan got to the doorway and looked back. "I'll be back a little later."

"Did you hear from your fellow council members?" Alistair asked Omar as Hasan went outside.

"I did. They'll spend the night in Ankara and come to Kayseri tomorrow. Then we'll all come back here, and you can take them on a field tour. Of course, they're very eager to hear about your big news."

Omar grabbed the backrest of a metal folding chair and sat down.

"Speaking of which, I haven't even heard about this big news. What have you found?"

Alistair took his feet off the desk and pulled his chair up so he could fold his arms on the desk. "Well, you already know that we found the chronicles that document the second journey of the Magi. We have yet to find the text that describes exactly where they went, but my bet is still on Jerusalem. On the other hand, the text we have read so far has solved a few mysteries. For starters, we've determined that Magi set out on their journey in 66 A.D."

"Alistair," Omar said in a taunting sort of way. "I can see it in your eyes. The big news is waiting to burst out. You might as well get to the point."

Alistair grinned in a way that conceded Omar's point. Alistair never did have much of a poker face.

"Omar . . . the silver urn found near Hadrian's wall. The chronicles refer to it."

Omar's brow furrowed as the focus of his eyes intensified.

"The silver urn was once possessed by Mary, the mother of our Lord."

For what seemed like eternity, the only sound in the office was the hum of the air conditioner.

"What?" Omar said in a soft, drawn-out whisper. He leaned forward and regarded Alistair with shock.

"The chronicles state that Mary, while in her last years, gave the silver urn to the Magi."

"You're absolutely sure about this?"

"Positive. There's no doubt."

Alistair paused so Omar could absorb what he had just heard.

Omar's eyes first flitted across the desk top, then met Alistair's. "Did the Magi receive the urn on their second journey?"

"It had to have been then."

"How can you be positive that it's the same silver urn as the one found in England?"

"By the engravings that are on it. The chronicles document that Mary's urn had two engravings. The Persian symbol of Faravahar—as you know, the man on the wings holding a medallion—and a Chi Rho symbol. That's exactly what's on the urn found that was found in England. Of course, Faravahar is the only original symbol, and the urn now has a third symbol that resembles a shooting star. But we're convinced that one was engraved much later."

Omar stared into Alistair's eyes before gazing into the distance over Alistair's shoulder. His lips parted but no words immediately came out as he tried to choose from all the questions racing through his mind. Then he asked the most important one.

"Alistair. Just what is the significance of the silver urn?"

"We don't know yet. But just imagine the possibilities. Here we have a Persian relic that shows up within the Jewish community. Omar, a connection like that could go all the way back to 539 B.C., when the Persian king Cyrus the Great conquered Babylon and released the Jews from captivity. Cyrus may have presented the urn as some sort of good will gesture. Who knows?"

Alistair suddenly looked somewhat glum. "But I must confess . . . it bothers me that this particular section of the chronicles was silent in regard to the urn's significance. There's a chance that the authors have addressed it in a later section, but my fear is that we may never find out."

"Why wouldn't they have stated something? That's rather odd, wouldn't you say?"

"I too felt that way at first. But in wrestling with an answer to that same question, this is my only theory. Maybe the significance was plainly obvious to the authors. In that case, they would have seen no reason to state the obvious."

"If that is the case, then the urn should be highly significant."

"One would think so," Alistair said as he locked his fingers together and anxiously tapped his thumbs together. "Omar, I just might have an idea on how we can crack this question."

"And what's that?"

"Your adopted niece. The one who is visiting in the American state of Minnesota."

"Shukriyah?"

"Yes. Her friends who know that Two-hearts gentleman."

"Go on."

"Two-hearts knows of a rune stone, the Rainy Lake Rune Stone, I believe it was called. Remember?"

"Yes . . . yes. Continue."

"Two-hearts claimed that the Rainy Lake Rune Stone is connected to the silver urn. Well, one of the last times when you were in touch with Shukriyah, didn't she say that she and her friends went to track down a clue to where the stone is hidden?"

"Yes . . . well, I have some news about that little venture. Number one . . . they didn't find the stone. Number two . . . when they got back from that trip, they found that the apartment of the friend with whom she's staying had been burglarized."

Omar looked at the floor and mumbled under his breath. "That reminds me. I've got to get back to her about what we found on Shelby Harrington."

Alistair stopped tapping his thumbs, leaned forward on his forearms, and looked hard at Omar. "Look, if the Rainy Lake Rune Stone is indeed connected to the silver urn, then the stone might refer to the significance of the urn. That bloody stone might be our one and only chance to find out. Omar, you must encourage Shukriyah and her friends to keep looking for it."

"All right, I'll do that. But first, there's something I would like you to do for me."

Alistair hesitated. "Oh . . . I don't know if I like the sound of this," he said with a nervous grin.

Omar waved his hand. "It's not that ominous. Just call Hasan on your radio. Tell him we're still sitting in here waiting to smoke these pipes. We need that lighter."

35

Tim Malone's apartment, Duluth

SHUKRIYAH CAME IN FROM THE PORCH and handed Tim back his open cell phone. She leaned in to his ear and whispered. "Omar's ready to talk with you now. Thanks for letting me use your phone."

Without a word, Tim took the phone, walked out on the porch, and closed the door behind him. "How are you Omar?"

"Very well, thank you. I understand you're curious about a certain gentleman named Harrington?"

"Any information you have would be appreciated."

"Well, our agent in London didn't have to work hard. In fact, he met Harrington a couple years ago."

"You're kidding?"

"Keep in mind, our agent doesn't claim to *know* him. But Harrington is who he says he is . . . Shelby Winston Harrington the third, employed by the Investment Trust Division of De Beers."

"Well, that's at least good to hear. Where did your guy meet Harrington?"

"Our agent—well, any of our agents—makes an effort to circulate among business and political leaders. Networking is part of their mission. No doubt, the officials at De Beers do likewise. They met at some social event at some club where our agent got introduced to Mr. Harrington. He seemed to think Harrington was a little eccentric. He could easily recall meeting him because Harrington was wearing white gloves."

Tim chuckled to himself. "That's Harrington, all right. So can he be trusted?"

"Our agent certainly thought so. This may not be the solid information you were hoping for, but it might give you confidence. A long-trusted contact of that particular agent knew Harrington quite well. After speaking with him, our agent was quite confident that Harrington was a man who could be trusted."

Tim sighed. "That really helps, Omar. I've been feeling a little paranoid lately. Thank you."

"While I've got you on the phone, Tim, I have a favor to ask of you."

"Sure. What is it?"

"The rune stone. My consultant, Alistair Groom, and I were wondering if you could continue looking for it."

"Well, there are a couple issues with that. If we were close to locating the stone the first time, then it's buried under a massive amount of mining fill and would be impossible to find. On the other hand, if we weren't close, then I have no idea where else to look. It'll take some pretty heavy duty research. But more importantly, I have to attend to a couple other things first. Now that I have confidence that this Shelby Harrington character can be trusted, I have a plan to carry out with him. Then—and this is for my friend, Lyle Hanson's sake—I need to look for this long-lost voyageur treasure he was working so hard to find. I hope you can understand. I regard it as an obligation to Lyle and his wife."

"I fully understand, Tim. By all means, take care of first things first. Maybe in the future there'll be a chance to turn your attention back to the rune stone."

"I hope so. Maybe a little research will uncover some other clue where I should look. For now, as you said, first things first. I appreciate your understanding."

"That's quite all right. Good luck with the plan you have with Mr. Harrington."

"Thanks. Did you need to speak with Shukriyah again?"

"No, we're all done. You have a good day."

"You to, Omar. Good-bye."

Then Tim reached in his back pocket for his wallet, took out Harrington's card, and entered his phone number.

"Shelby Harrington? Hi. Tim Malone speaking. I'm just calling to let you know that I'm ready to implement your plan . . . No, I don't think it'd be efficient to teach me. If one of your men check for the bugs, I'd . . . Yes, I have two guests staying with me . . . That sounds good. I'm sure they'd be more than happy with those accommodations . . . I'll ask Maggie Hanson to be the person on the other end of the line. She's familiar with many of the details regarding the treasure . . . A planning meeting sounds good . . . Yes . . . Okay, Mr. Harrington. I'll see you then."

❧ 36 ☙

About a week later.

"SHELBY HERE."

"Hello Mr. Harrington, it's me. It's all set," Tim said into his cell phone as he drove away from his apartment. Tim spoke somewhat nervously. "I just left my apartment a few minutes ago. Am I free to drive to the Kitchee Gammi club?"

"Yes. Nigel just called and said that no one is following you. You're in the clear to proceed here."

"Hope it's not too early. I told Maggie that I would be leaving the apartment in a couple hours, but it was kind of nerve-wracking just sitting there waiting."

"No need to worry. You're fine. Like I said, proceed over here. You can park in the lot across Ninth Avenue East."

"Tell Maggie that she did a great job with the conversation," Tim said.

"I will. It sure sounded like she came across well. How do you feel it went on your end?"

"Great! Everything felt natural."

"From listening to Maggie, it sounded like you hit all the key points."

"Oh, yeah. I mentioned that I received the map of the treasure's location. I said it was in my apartment. I told her I'd be heading out of town overnight. Oh—then Maggie asked if my neighbor was home. I said out loud that he wasn't. When she brought up the first burglary, I added that I wasn't concerned because the odds of back-to-back burglaries are really small, especially on a week night."

". . . and that you were going to leave a light on and your stereo on as precautions?"

"Yup. I mentioned that too. I felt everything slipped smoothly into our conversation."

"Splendid!"

"But what if the Pearsons don't fall for it?"

"Confidence, my good man. Confidence. The Pearson have been waiting decades to find out the location of the treasure. And now they believe that a map of the location is in your apartment. They'll show up. In the meantime, we'll relax in the club lounge while we wait for the call from Nigel."

"Okay, Mr. Harrington. I'll be there shortly."

Tim put down his cell phone and continued to make his way through the dark, residential streets. It wasn't long before he turned onto the main artery of Superior Street. About fifteen minutes after his call with Harrington, he finally arrived at the Kitchi Gammi club and signaled his intent to turn up Ninth Avenue East.

When Tim rounded the corner, he immediately noticed a limousine parked along the curb at the club's entrance. Its lights were on and someone was standing on the sidewalk alongside it. When Tim recognized Brody, Harrington's driver, he stopped in the street and rolled his window down. Brody hurried up to Tim's window.

"The trap has been sprung, Mr. Malone."

"Already?"

"We just got the call from Nigel. They knew you'd be gone and didn't waste any time. The police are apprehending the burglars in your apartment as we speak. Go ahead and park in the lot. Mr. Harrington, Maggie, and Jessa are already sitting inside the limo."

"... and Shukriyah?"

"She said she wished to wait here at the club."

"All right. I'll be right there."

Tim parked his car and ran back to the limousine. He got in and sat down on the plush back seat alongside Jessa. Brody sped away as soon as Tim closed his door.

"Well, Mr. Malone, now you can see what I meant by having confidence," Harrington said from the front passenger seat.

"Boy . . . I'll say," Tim concurred.

Tim leaned forward to look at Maggie sitting on the other side of Jessa. Maggie glanced back at Tim. "You look nervous," Tim said.

"Well, of course. Aren't you?"

"Yeah, I . . . I guess I am. This is definitely a whole new experience."

"Mr. Malone," Brody said, "be prepared to show some identification."

The suspense in the limousine steadily heightened as Brody made his way toward Tim's apartment. No one said a word.

Just as Brody made the turn onto a residential street in Tim's neighborhood, a parked squad car could be seen up ahead at the next intersection with its strobe lights flashing. The squad car was blocking the street on which Tim's apartment was located.

As Brody got close to the intersection, he put on his right turn signal and slowed down to a stop alongside the curb. Brody lowered his window when he noticed a police officer step out of the squad car. The officer approached the driver's side of the limousine.

"I understand that one of you is the homeowner?" the officer asked politely as he looked through Brody's window to study the faces of all the passengers.

"I am," Tim said from the back, directly behind Brody. He reached forward across the spacious interior to give the officer his driver's license.

The officer looked at the license for a second or two.

"All right," the officer said as he handed the license back to Tim. "I'll let them know you're here. You can proceed."

The officer spoke into a mouthpiece clipped just below his shoulder as he walked back to his car. Brody raised his window and waited for the squad car to pull forward. When the squad car stopped, Brody put the limousine in gear and proceeded to round the corner onto Tim's street.

Up ahead were three more squad cars. Two were parked on the left side curb in front of Tim's apartment. The third squad car was barricading the street at the far intersection. All three had their strobe lights flashing.

More details of the scene became apparent as Brody drove down the street. A number of onlookers had gathered on the sidewalk directly across the street from Tim's apartment. The two squad cars in front of Tim's apartment had come upon the scene from opposite directions

Brody pulled up to the curb and parked behind the first squad car in front of Tim's apartment. Nigel and an officer were standing on the sidewalk. They kept their eyes fixed on the limousine as it parked. Everyone got out and immediately focused on the entrance to Tim's apartment.

Harrington was wearing his signature Inverness Cloak and a gray felt hat with a turned-down brim. A band just above the brim held a small feather in place. He walked up to the officer as Tim, Maggie, and Jessa followed.

"Excuse me, Officer . . . ?"

"Quinn. Officer Quinn."

"Officer Quinn, are the burglars still inside?" Harrington asked as he pointed at Tim's apartment with his cane.

"Yes, they are," Officer Quinn replied. "My colleagues will be leading them out any minute now." He turned to Tim. "I understand you're the homeowner?"

"Yes, sir."

"How many burglars are there?" Harrington asked.

"Two, but they had these two accomplices." Officer Quinn gestured to the back seat of the squad car directly in front of the limousine. "We apprehended them while they were waiting in a getaway car, then we closed in on the apartment."

"Where is the getaway car?"

"On the street on the opposite side of this block. The burglars sneaked through backyards and broke into the rear of the apartment."

Officer Quinn walked up to the driver's door of the squad car and opened it so the interior dome light went on. The two accomplices in the back seat were both wearing handcuffs. A young female sitting on the side closest to the sidewalk quickly turned her head the other way. But Maggie caught a glimpse of who it was.

"No!" Maggie said in horror. Maggie stepped off the curb, quickly went to the back door of the squad and bent over to get a better look inside. When the person in the back seat continued to look the other way, Maggie pounded on the glass with the palms of her hands. The female in the back seat made a reflexive glance toward Maggie and immediately turned away again.

"Lindsey!" Maggie stood erect, placed her hands on the side of her head and began to wail. "No! Lindsey, how could you?"

When Maggie started pounding the roof of the squad car with both hands, Officer Quinn gently escorted her back to the sidewalk. Tim and Jessa rushed up to assist. Officer Quinn handed Maggie off to Jessa who put her arm around Maggie's shoulders. Maggie rested her head on Jessa's shoulder and continued to cry. As Harrington began to understand the extent of shock Maggie was experiencing, he came up to Jessa with a suggestion.

"My dear, why don't you take Maggie back to my automobile. It's warm and comfortable inside. Brody has kept the engine running."

As Jessa led Maggie to the limousine, Brody ran ahead and opened the back door. Harrington turned to Tim with utter surprise.

"Don't tell me Maggie knows the woman in the back seat of the squad car?" Harrington asked in disbelief.

"You won't believe it," Tim said as he slowly shook his head. "She's a close—uh . . . well, Maggie *thought* she was a close friend."

"Oh, my Lord!" Harrington said as he put his hand over his heart. "The poor dear. Being betrayed so. How utterly awful!"

"You know something," Nigel said as he looked curiously in the direction of the squad car, "I recall seeing that woman at the hospital in Alexandria. She was in the Intensive Care waiting room."

"Yup, she was there all right," Tim said.

"Do you know the woman's name?" Harrington asked.

"Melburn-Davis," Tim answered. "Lindsey Melburn-Davis."

Harrington turned toward Officer Quinn. "Officer Quinn. The other person sitting in the back seat? Do you know who he is?"

"It's the woman's father, Peter Melburn."

Just then the door of Tim's apartment opened. Five police officers started filing out as they escorted the two burglars in handcuffs.

Officer Quinn looked toward the apartment and pointed.

"In fact, all the suspects are related. The name of the first suspect you see is Sheldon Davis, the woman's husband. Annn . . . and the suspect coming out now is James Melburn, the son of Peter Melburn."

As the officers led the two suspects to the other squad car, Sheldon Davis, Lindsey's husband, kept his head down. He got in the car without incident. But when Lindsey's brother, James Melburn, got nearer, he seemed to recognize Tim and had no qualms about giving Tim a dirty look. Although Tim had never seen him before, Melburn started yelling at Tim as if he knew him.

"You son-of-a-bitch!" Melburn said. "The same thing that happened to Lyle Hanson should have—"

"Jim!" Sheldon Davis yelled from back seat of the squad car. "Keep your mouth shut!"

Melburn heeded the warning momentarily then turned to Tim. "That treasure belongs to our family, and don't you forget it."

Melburn continued uttering obscenities as one of the officers placed a hand on Melburn's head to coax him into the squad car. As the officers shut the back doors of the squad car, Harrington tilted his head back and closed his eyes.

"Ohhh . . ." Harrington said. "Now I get it. Peter Melburn must be William Lindsay Pearson's son! And Peter named his daughter after his father's middle name . . . Lindsay! And when William Pearson came to America and changed his name, he no doubt chose the name of Melburn after Melbourne, Australia. You see, Pearson was originally from Australia!"

Officer Quinn came up to Tim. "You can inspect your apartment, if you would like."

"Sure. Just one second. I'll be right there."

Officer Quinn turned and headed for the apartment.

"Mr. Harrington?" Tim asked. "While I look around in the apartment, will you take Maggie and Jessa back with you? I think Maggie needs to get away from here."

"You're absolutely right. Brody and I will take them back to the club right away. Nigel will wait for you until you are finished in your apartment. Then I think we all need to unwind back at the club. Find a way to debrief somehow. And with Maggie's husband still in the hospital . . . well, Mr. Malone, you're the best one to counsel Maggie right now."

"Oh, definitely . . . and I won't be long. Nigel and I will be right behind you. But don't under-estimate Maggie. She's pretty tough. She has a way of letting loose with an initial outburst, but then she rallies quickly."

Tim stared into the Harrington's thick glasses. If Tim wasn't mistaken, Harrington's eyes not only seemed to convey a sense of accomplishment, they also betrayed a hint of sentimentality from behind the usually stoic English facade.

"Your plan was brilliant, Mr. Harrington. Thank you so much."

"Now you can go forth, young man. Go forth unfettered. Go forth and find the lost treasure of the voyageurs with no more fear of the Pear . . . uh, excuse me—the Melburns."

"I certainly will. It sure would be nice if Lyle could have a speedy recovery. But even if it's slow, I've promised Maggie to continue Lyle's search and do everything that I can."

"It would be best if you could find it, Mr. Malone. Then the treasure would end up in government hands for the foreseeable future. And who knows? If you find it right along the border, then the Canadian and American governments can fight over it. Now wouldn't that be a jolly riot?"

"What about for you, Mr. Harrington? With Pearson's heirs in custody, this sure must be a turning point in your decades-long quest for your diamond."

Harrington shrugged modestly. "No doubt, our hand has just improved immensely. We'll see if the Melburns are willing to admit to their nefarious scheme with the Percys. If they do, then I say the odds of recovering our own little treasure will increase dramatically."

"I sincerely hope so, Mr. Harrington." Tim looked toward his apartment. "Well . . . I should go. See you back at the club?"

"We'll be waiting."

Harrington reached out his right hand. Tim was surprised for a second, but then he looked down and noticed that Harrington was wearing a glove.

"If Maggie can rally as you say," Harrington said optimistically as he shook Tim's hand, "then maybe we can all find a way to celebrate."

37

Tim Malone's apartment

"So you think the Melburns were responsible for everything," Cedric Two-hearts asked Tim over his satellite phone.

"I'm sure of it," Tim answered. "The burglary of my apartment. Lyle's accident. And what's really incriminating about Lyle's accident is that paint scratches on one of the Melburn's vehicles have been matched to paint residue on Lyle's car."

"Well, I guess I was wrong about De Beers, hey? After all this time, they never had evil intentions?"

"No, they didn't, Cedric. To be quite honest, they may have spied on you, followed you, things like that. But they never wanted to find the wooden chest for themselves, and they certainly never wanted any harm to come to anyone."

"Speaking of harm, just how bad did you hurt your knee?"

"Oh, it was nothing serious. For sure, it was a pretty bad scrape, but it'll be all right."

"And your car window . . . did that get fixed?"

"Yup. I got a new window."

"You know, I never did ask you. How did that trip to the pictographs work out? Did you decipher the clue?"

"I'm really glad you brought that up. Yes, we think we might have an answer. The treasure's hidden somewhere to the northwest of North Hegman Lake. Most likely somewhere along the shore of Lac La Croix."

Two-hearts didn't say a word.

Damn it! Here we go again, Tim thought.

"That's a big area you're talking about," Two-hearts finally said.

Tim shifted to the edge of his sofa and supported his elbows on his knees. "Look Cedric, I'm sorry if this sounds a little rough, but why are you playing this game? Why can't you just tell me the clues you know? We've sacrificed a lot here. Lyle almost died trying to meet you in Alexandria. My apartment got broke into. I tripped over that damn wire and my car window got smashed. Not to mention how upset and scared we've all been with this stuff. I don't care if you want to cooperate or not. But I've had enough of this game playing."

When Two-hearts kept silent, Tim rubbed his forehead and realized that he may have made a big mistake by losing his temper.

"Cedric, I'm sorry. Uh . . . it's just . . ."

"That's all right, hey. But now it's my turn to be frank. The way I see it, every white man's the same. He's a prisoner to his desires. And he gets mad when his desire gets thwarted. I'm sure that's why the legend says that a wise chief will find the treasure."

"Cedric . . . please. I don't want that treasure for myself. I'm doing this for Lyle, and you know that he never wanted that treasure for himself. He's a professional archaeologist and you trusted him."

There was another silent spell. But instead of being impatient, this time Tim forced himself to be patient to see if he had over-stepped his bounds with Two-hearts. Luckily he hadn't.

"Okay . . . okay," Two-hearts said in his laid-back, conciliatory manor. "You're right, hey. I always felt bad about what happened to Lyle. It was my idea to meet in Alexandria. But you're still going to have to be patient about the treasure. You're going to have to do this my way and that's that."

"Yes . . . I . . . um . . . I understand."

"Look, I'm no chief, hey. I confess that I too got desires. And this is one of them: I want to find out about the silver urn found in England. It has very special meaning . . . but what is it, exactly? Like I told you in Alexandria, if the Rainy Lake Rune Stone can be found, then it might just tell us about the silver urn."

"Cedric . . . the place we went to the first time . . . if it's the right location, then the rune stone's buried under very deep fill. And if it's not the right location, then I don't know where else to look."

"Where was it you went?"

"Funny you should ask," Tim said as he picked up an envelope from his coffee table. Its return address had a Fortune Bay Resort Casino logo. "We went up to a ski resort called Giant's Ridge. It's on Minnesota's Iron Range, and it's where we thought the stone could be. We went to the Fortune Bay Resort Casino on Lake Vermillion to ask some old miner about the clue. He ended up throwing his beer at me."

"Threw his beer at you?"

"That's right. A resort manager said she'd pay for a new jacket. And sure enough, it looks like my check just came in the mail."

"Well, there must be others up there who also know about the clue."

"That manager said the one nasty old miner was the best source. But I'm not approaching him again. I think if he'd had a gun, he'd have shot me."

"Ask that manager again. She might suggest someone else. And who knows, hey, she might get you a discount on a room if she still feels bad about your jacket."

"Well . . . after the altercation she bought us dinner in the restaurant, so I don't know if I dare expect too much more from her." Tim let out a deep breath as he thought about Omar also wanting him to search for the rune stone. "On the other hand, it sure seems like the voices of wisdom are asking me to search for the rune stone. So maybe it's the right thing to do right now. I guess I'll have to think about it."

"Put on your thinking cap and give it another try. Go up there, be persistent and ask a lot of questions."

"We did the first time."

Two-hearts was quiet a moment, then said, "I tell you what. If you promise to give it another try, I'll invite you up to my cabin. I have some artifacts I think might interest you. Would you like to see some Viking coins?"

Tim let out a surprised laugh. "Boy, would I ever. In fact, I'd love to see where you live."

"I don't know if Lyle would be up to making the trip, but you could bring his wife, your girlfriend, your astronomer friend, and even the astronomer's uncle, and his archaeologist. Then I can finally meet you all."

"That sounds great, Cedric, though Omar and Alistair are overseas right now, but, you never know."

"Hopefully there might be good news the next time we talk."

"Yes . . . hopefully. Okay, I'll give the search for the rune stone another go and keep my fingers crossed."

"That's the spirit, hey."

"Well, Cedric, you take care now?"

"Yah, sure will, hey."

"I'll be in touch."

Tim turned off his cell phone and placed it on the coffee table. He ripped open the envelope from Fortune Bay Resort Casino. Inside he found a check and a single sheet of paper. A message on the paper was hand-written.

Dear Mr. Malone,

Once again, I apologize for what happened to your jacket. Enclosed is a check that should easily cover the cost of a new one.

I have some interesting news for you. Milo Maranich felt real bad about his actions. (He still thinks that . . . I forgot her name . . . is still my cousin.) He also wants to continue coming to Fortune Bay so he can join his retired colleagues.

So, trying to get back in good with me, he offered to help you. He told me that the place you are looking for, 'the place where the water doesn't know which way to flow and the compass needle doesn't know which way to point,' is NOT near Giant's Ridge at the south end of Wynne Lake.

Milo says that the location you're probably looking for is at Hibbing Taconite. It's called the Hill of Three Waters, and there's only one other place like it in North America. He said it's a three-way continental divide.

I hope that helps. And let me know if it does, because I then might go easy on Milo if he promises to get some kind of treatment and behave.

      Good luck!—Angel Gray Feather

"Well I'll be damned," Tim muttered to himself. "Talk about providence."

Tim got up and went into the kitchen where Jessa and Shukriyah were chatting over coffee.

"Guess what, you guys? Tim said as he held up Angel's letter. "I know where to look for the Rainy Lake Rune Stone."

"Are we going back up to Giant's Ridge?" Jessa asked.

"Nope. We'll still go up to the Iron Range, but this time we'll go to Hibbing. Trouble is, I have to figure out a way to get onto the property of a taconite mining company."

ॐ 38 ☙

After Tim did some quick research on the Hill of Three Waters, Jessa and Shukriyah joined him in the living room.

"How is that area a three-way continental divide?" Shukriyah asked.

"The borders of three continental watersheds meet at one point just north of the town of Hibbing. Drainage flows in three different directions from that point: north to Lake Winnipeg and eventually into Hudson Bay, east into Lake Superior and into the Atlantic Ocean, and south down the Mississippi into the Gulf of Mexico. There's only one other spot like it in all of North America."

"And I assume they've mined iron ore in this area called the Hill of Three Waters?"

Tim thought about the implications of her question.

"Well . . . yes. And that could be a problem. The region north of Hibbing all belongs to the mining company. The property is tightly restricted for safety reasons, and the area of the Hill of Three Waters happens to be on this property. Although the immediate area has never been blasted out and excavated—or at least that's what the research tells me—I don't know if we can get access to it unless . . ."

"Unless what?" Jessa asked.

"Well, I know someone who works there. Elwyn Kipmeyer. He's a geologist for the mining company."

"Does he have the authority to let us onto company property?"

"I think so, but it's not that easy. Mine employees just can't bring friends and relatives to the mine any old time they want. There's got to be an official reason for allowing visitors to access mine property, especially where active mine operations are taking place."

There was a lull in the conversation as Tim thought about how he might approach Elwyn Kipmeyer about getting access the Hill of Three Waters.

"You know, Elwyn and I aren't exactly what I'd call real close friends, but he does owe me a favor. A couple summers ago, he and his brother wanted to go camping up on Basswood Lake in the Boundary Waters with the intent of doing some serious fishing. Elwyn asked me if he could borrow my old aluminum square-stern canoe, so he could mount his small electric trolling motor. Not only did I loan him the canoe, he and his brother had great luck fishing because I pointed out my favorite fishing holes on a map."

"Well, if people who want to visit the mine need an official reason," Jessa suggested, "then why don't you tell him about my major in Journalism."

"But your specialty is music."

Jessa rolled her eyes. "Well . . . Tim! Get with it, here."

"Yeah, yeah. I get it."

"Tell him that I want to do research on three-way continental divides in North America because I'm considering writing an article about them."

"Yeah, that's a good idea. And another thing that'll really help is if I tell him that I'll be bringing two attractive ladies."

They both hit him with questioning looks.

"Come on! He's single after all," Tim said with a shrug. "But I gotta warn you. He can be a little obnoxious. He likes to talk up a storm whenever he's around girls."

"Fair enough!" Shukriyah said enthusiastically. "Jessa and I have been warned. You should go right ahead and get a hold of your friend Elwyn. It doesn't hurt to ask."

"All right then. I'll give Elwyn a call."

ಖಾ 39 ଔ

THE EARLY PRE-CAMBRIAN LAURENTIAN MOUNTAINS have long since vanished. Once a high massif stretching along present-day Minnesota's Iron Range, they were ground down by glaciers over the following eons. And what the glaciers started, modern-day iron miners continue as they blast away at a remaining broad ridge of rock with the less prestigious name of the Laurentian Divide.

Of all the mines along the divide, the Hull Rust Mine, just north of the town of Hibbing, is the largest. In fact, being six miles long, a mile and a half wide, and 600 feet deep in places, it is the world's largest open-pit iron-ore mine.

AS SHUKRIYAH WALKED UP TO THE CHAIN LINK FENCE at the Hull Rust Mine overlook on the north side of Hibbing, she protected herself against a cold wind by holding her hands in the pockets of her coat and squeezing her shoulders up and in toward her ears. She was awestruck as she looked up and down the man-made canyon.

Shukriyah studied the exposed geologic layers on the opposite slope of the canyon wall. Bands of dull purple, brownish red, and steel gray were speckled with patches of snow that stubbornly nestled in the corners and crevices of flat ledges. Roads switching back and forth sliced the colored bands of rock and angled their way down into the canyon depths.

A yellow strobe light caught Shukriyah's attention. It emanated from the roof of a pickup truck making its way along one of the roads notched into the far slope. Against the enormous scale of the canyon, the truck appeared so tiny that she likely wouldn't have noticed it without the strobe.

With the entire scene before her dominated by the drab, muted colors of the canyon, Shukriyah had to look almost straight down to appreciate any contrasting color. Far below, a blue shimmer of open water surrounded by gray ice testified to the spring thaw well underway.

On closer inspection of the ridges at higher elevations, Shukriyah imagined that a visit in the summer would reveal a brighter scene. Dormant shrub trees and brush had somehow gained a foothold in the seemingly sterile terrain of shattered rock.

"Quite impressive isn't it?" Tim asked as he and Jessa approached. They had been looking at a 170-ton mining truck and a giant steam shovel bucket on display on the other side of the visitor's center.

"It sure is!" Shukriyah replied. "I had no idea they did mining to this extent in northern Minnesota."

Tim said, "Say, before Elwyn shows up, I'd like to ask something of you two."

"Sure," Shukriyah said. "What is it?"

"Look around!" Tim said with an eager voice as he pointed to a couple locations on the canyon rim just beyond the fence. "There's a lot slate around here. Well, guess what Two-hearts told me? The Rainy Lake Rune Stone was carved on slate. So if we get up to the Hill of Three Waters and find that the ground up there also has a lot slate, I want a chance to search around. Two-hearts said that the rune stone was cleaved into a thin slab of slate so it would be easier to carry. Maybe no one's ever found the rune stone because it blends in with surrounding slate already there."

"Makes sense," said Shukriyah.

"So, what do you want us to do?" Jessa asked.

"When we get to the the Hill of Three Waters, keep Elwyn talking. Keep him focused on anything but me. I want to turn up as many pieces of rock as possible."

"What are you going to do if you find a piece of slate with runic inscriptions?" Jessa asked. "Especially if it's big?"

Tim's eyes focused off into the distance across the parking lot. "I don't know. And since our host is now arriving," Tim said as he gestured toward an oncoming club-cab pickup, "I guess I'm gonna to have to wing it."

The pickup came directly across the empty parking lot and pulled up without bothering to align between parking stripes. Elwyn Kipmeyer jumped out without turning off his motor or closing his door. He greeted Tim with a big toothy grin and held his hand out. "Hi ya', Tim!" Elwyn said as he shook Tim's hand vigorously, so vigorously that he had to clamp his left hand on his green hard hat to keep it from flying off in the wind. "Good to see you!"

"Good to see you too," said Tim. "Elwyn, this is Jessa. And this is Shukriyah."

"Hi, Jessa. Tim's talked so much about you, I feel I know you. All good, of course . . . no—wait a minute! Mostly good. But don't you worry. The little bit of bad I heard was pretty mild."

As Elwyn broke out in a kind of machine-gun laugh, Tim sidled a glance at Jessa that seemed to mean, *See what I mean?*

"And Shu . . . uh, shoot . . . shucks . . . I know it's something like that."

"Shukriyah," she said as she reached out to shake Elwyn's hand. "Nice to meet you."

"And nice to meet you. Have you all had a few moments up here to enjoy this wonderful view?"

"Yes, we have," Tim answered. "Breathtaking isn't it?"

"Well, personally, with the visitor center building closed, it's a little too cold to be hanging around out here. So why don't we get in my warm truck and head up to the plant entrance. It's closer to Chisholm, way on the north side of the mine."

Tim climbed into the front passenger side of Elwyn's truck, while Jessa and Shukriyah got into the roomy back, Elwyn made his way through the north side of Hibbing and turned north on Highway 169. He chattered almost the entire time. "So, Shukriyah," Elwyn said loudly. "I understand you're into astronomy."

Shukriyah gave him an indulgent smile. "Astrophysics, actually. In fact, I just finished my masters degree."

At that point, most people would have offered a congratulations. But most people weren't Elwyn. "Well, I certainly would volunteer to go out under the night sky and get a lesson from you on the constellations." Without a trace of self-consciousness, Elwyn let loose again with his machine gun laugh, while Jessa and Shukriyah looked at each other and rolled their eyes.

"Uh, Elwyn . . ." Tim said with a tone of caution.

"Oh, come on, Tim. Girls like a guy with a sense of humor. Isn't that right?" Elwyn looked into his rear view mirror to see if he could get concurrence from his passengers in the back seat.

Tim had turned in his seat and gave them both an apologetic look. Jessa's arms were crossed, but Shukriyah sighed and said, "Yes, I like humor." She gave Elwyn a pretty smile that edged into a sneer for Tim.

Without noticing Shukriyah's subtle sleight of hand, Elwyn turned west on St. Louis County Road 5 and then south into the mine entrance. He slowed as he approached a guard quarters and rolled down his window. The guard on duty no doubt had been expecting Elwyn as he came out of the quarters with a clip board for Elwyn's visitors. The guard handed the clip board to Elwyn without saying a word.

"Gotta sign in everybody," Elwyn announced as he passed the clip board to Tim.

"How about hard hats and safety goggles, Elwyn?" the guard asked, sounding a little bored. "Need any?"

"Let's see, Tim's got his," Elwyn said as he then turned around and looked in the back. Jessa and Shukriyah had already noticed the safety equipment on the seat between them, so they each held up a visitor-issue white hard hat and a pair of plastic goggles.

"Nope. We're in good shape. Thanks."

After everyone had signed the sheet, Elwyn returned the clip board to the guard and proceeded down the entrance road into the mine.

It wasn't long before a large industrial complex spewing white steam loomed in the distance. Elwyn drove around to the south side of the plant and eventually made his way onto a moonscape terrain devoid of vegetation. This scraped ground was criss-crossed with interconnecting dirt roads. Elwyn stopped just before a wide, well-used road. Suddenly, a giant truck appeared over a rise in the road. The ominous sight looked like some sort of futuristic apparition rising out of the ground.

"Rule number one," Elwyn announced as he watched the oncoming truck. "Haul trucks have the right of way."

"Man alive!" Tim said. "Look at the size of that thing!"

"Yup. The driver is twenty feet off the ground. It's not that easy for him to see small vehicles like this. And if he did run over us, he might not even notice."

As Jessa and Shukriyah watched from the back seat, the passing haul truck filled their field of vision through the windshield. They mostly saw a set of twelve-foot tires roll and the guttural engine roar. Clouds of dust followed.

When the road was clear of haul trucks, Elwyn crossed it and continued on. It wasn't long before he stopped in front of a rise in the terrain covered with small trees and vegetation. Although the area may have been logged over at one time, it had never been excavated for iron ore.

"This is it, folks," Elwyn announced as he put his truck into park.

"This is it?" Tim asked with surprise.

"Yup. I imagine you expected a mountain or at least a real high hill of some sort. But no, this is all there is to the Hill of Three Waters. Put on your hard hats and goggles and we'll go see it."

With Elwyn at the head of the line, the foursome made their way up the rise and through leafless trees and brush somehow finding sustenance in the rocky soil. Patches of snow showed where the wind had failed to scrape away what had fallen. They came upon a colossal boulder that looked as if Paul Bunyan might have placed it there. Elwyn stopped and turned to the others as they formed a semi-circle.

"Legend has it that this is where a number of tribes from the western Lake Superior region—mostly Ojibwe tribes—met to discuss how they would defend themselves against the invading Sioux. The Sioux were from the plains to the south and west, and they depended on buffalo for food and clothing. But the buffalo that normally migrated up from the far south hadn't returned that year, forcing the Sioux to look elsewhere for food."

Tim signaled to Jessa by pretending to grip a pen and mimicking a writing motion. Jessa picked up on the signal and pulled a pen and small tablet from her coat pocket.

"The Sioux had come here to forested country," Elwyn said without missing a beat. "However, not only were the Sioux out of their element in the north woods, they had to contend with tribes teamed up against them."

"Elwyn, I got a question," Tim said. "I see a lot of this slate around here. I also noticed it back at the overlook. Is slate common around here?"

"Very much so. It's called Virginia Slate."

"How wide-spread is it? Is it found—say . . . up to the border, for instance? Up by Voyageurs National Park? The Rainy Lake area?"

"Oh, yeah. It's a wide-spread formation that extends up into Canada."

Elwyn looked at Jessa writing in her tablet. "How about you, Jessa? Do you have any questions?"

"Uh, no thanks. Not yet, anyway."

"The actual marker for the three-way divide is over here," Elwyn said, pointing the way.

As Elwyn lead the foursome to the concrete marker, Tim came up alongside Jessa and whispered, "If you can, think of questions to ask him."

"Like what?" Jessa whispered back.

"I don't know. Just find a way to keep him distracted."

When Elwyn came to the concrete marker, he placed his hand on it as if posing for a photo op. "Well, this is it. This is the marker for the three-way divide. It was placed here in 1953. It replaced a wooden marker."

In preparation to write an answer to a question, Jessa squatted and placed her tablet on her thigh.

B-B-BOOM, . . . BOOM, . . . BOOM, . . . B-BOOM.

"Good Lord! What was that?" Jessa asked.

"Today's blast," Elwyn said with a shrug. "That's how they get the ore. They blast the bedrock so huge shovels can scoop up the pieces and load them into those large haul trucks. The haul trucks bring the rock to the plant for processing."

"How far away was that blast?" Shukriyah asked.

"Well, far enough that we didn't hear the warning sirens, but close in terms of proximity to our location near the plant. You see, ore that was once considered too deep for economic mining is being mined today because of the high price it commands these days. Plus, there have been improvements in iron extraction technology, so lower-grade ore passed up years ago is being mined. Come on. Let's go to the edge of the woods. We might be able to see where that blast came from."

Tim hung back as Elwyn led Jessa and Shukriyah through the trees. As soon as they were out of sight, Tim ran back to the large boulder and started looking around.

"This is hopeless," he said out loud. Broken pieces of slate were scattered everywhere amongst the dead, yellow grasses.

After he searched near the large boulder, Tim looked in the thick brush and at the base of trees to see if he could spot any larger pieces of slate that looked out of place somehow. He kicked at pieces and turned over others with his hands.

Tim was about to give up. *If they had buried the rune stone*, he thought, *then there's no way I'm going to find it*. He stopped and scanned the surrounding area. Resignation overcame him as he put his hands in his pockets and billowed his cheeks to let out a slow exhale.

Something not even a yard away caught his eye. He dropped to his knees for a closer look. It was a flat piece of slate that angled into the ground. Its color was lighter than the other pieces of slate scattered all around, and he could make out two grooves that met at an angle.

Tim quickly got up and broke off a branch from a nearby tree. He dropped to his knees again, took off his hard hat and placed it beside him, and gently proceeded to scrape at the stiff ground. The soil a few inches down was finer, darker, and wet from thawing. He scooped up the loose soil with cupped hands and threw it to the side. When he had exposed a corner of the slab, he wiped his hands on his pants and swept the piece of slate with his palm.

"God Almighty!" Tim said to himself as he poked his fingernail in a dirt-filled groove, pried out a bit of caked dirt and blew it clear. "Runes!"

Tim looked back to see if the other three were coming. He couldn't see anyone, but he heard Elwyn's characteristic laugh in the distance. Tim hurriedly gouged away with the branch to remove more of the stiff soil in a wider perimeter. When the upper edges of the slate became more exposed, it appeared that the slab was small. But it wouldn't budge when he slipped his fingers underneath and pulled. The lower portion was stuck in the frozen ground.

Tim gouged at more soil and exposed all but the lowest side held in the grip of the frost. He tried to wiggle the slate back and forth and tug. But it was too late. Shukriyah and then Jessa appeared in single file out of the trees about twenty yards back. Elwyn wouldn't be far behind, so Tim grabbed his hard hat, quickly got to his feet, and walked toward them in order to get away from the piece of rune stone that was stuck in the ground. While Tim was putting on the hard hat, Elwyn's lecturing reached an audible threshold as he marched in step behind Shukriyah and Jessa.

". . . add bentonite clay so they can mold the mix into small pellets, fire the pellets in a kiln so they become rock-hard, and finally load the pellets onto trains to be shipped out," Elwyn said as he finished his explanation of the taconite pellet-making process for Jessa and Shukriyah.

The threesome stopped when they reached Tim.

Jessa raised her tablet and made a few notes. Then she put the end of her pen to her lower lip. "Uh, where do they send the pellets?" she asked.

"The trains go down to Duluth and transfer the pellets onto ships. Then the ships take them to steel plants on the lower Great Lakes." Elwyn looked back and forth at Jessa and Shukriyah to see if there would be any more questions, but they remained silent. "Well, there you have it. That's pretty much the process from beginning to end."

Elwyn looked at Tim and noticed his dirty pants.

"Looks like you've been playing in the mud. If you were hunting for agates, I got bad news for you: there aren't any around here."

Elwyn let out his signature laugh, and Tim smiled back at him, trying to look sheepish. "So *now* you tell me!"

"By the way, Tim, I'm not supposed to let visitors get out of my sight."

Tim felt caught off guard and didn't know what to say. But Elwyn had a smirk on his face, indicating he was about to make an attempt at some humor. He winked at the girls. "But without you, I had these two babes to myself." Once again, Elwyn let out his irritating laugh.

"Okay, folks, that about does it for the tour. I don't know if you were expecting something like a real high hill, something that really stands out in the broad landscape . . . but no, this is it. Pretty nondescript for a continental divide. Most people are disappointed."

"That's quite all right," Tim said. "We really appreciate you taking the time to bring us here."

After Jessa and Shukriyah had also expressed their gratitude, Elwyn looked at his watch.

"Pretty good timing. I got a meeting coming up, so I think I better bring you guys back to the mine overlook." Elwyn started out and the girls started to follow. Jessa stopped suddenly when she felt Tim's hand on her arm.

"Jessa!" Tim said in a loud whisper. "You've got to tell Elwyn that you lost your camera."

"But . . . I have it right here," Jessa said in a quiet but confused voice as she pulled her camera out of her pocket.

"Give it to me," Tim said as he grabbed the camera and put it into his pocket. He looked toward Shukriyah as she continued to follow Elwyn toward his pickup truck. "I'll explain later. Please just do as I say. Yell out to Elwyn that you lost your camera somewhere. I'll pretend to look for it around here. After a little while, I'll yell out that I found it."

Jessa gave Tim a confused look. "Uh . . . okay." Then she looked in the direction of the others. "Hey you guys!" Jessa called out as she took several steps in their direction. "Wait! I lost my camera!"

Elwyn and Shukriyah doubled back, looking at the ground from side to side as they approached.

"Do you recall the last time you knew you had it?" Elwyn asked as he came up to Jessa and glanced at the ground in the immediate area. "Any chance you left it in the truck?"

"No. It was in my pocket when we left the truck. I'm pretty sure I left it back at the edge of the clearing."

Elwyn started back to where they had been earlier and the two girls followed.

"Just in case it's around here somewhere, I'll look for it in this area," Tim announced.

As soon as the threesome was out of sight, Tim went back to the piece of slate. He got down on his knees, took off his hard hat, and picked up the same branch and gouged at the stiff soil. He tried again to work the stubborn slab back and forth.

The slate suddenly popped loose. Tim slid it out of the ground, brushed it off, and slipped it inside a large interior coat pocket and zipped up. It just fit. He grabbed his hard hat, got up, and walked to the concrete marker.

"I found the camera!" Tim yelled out.

Elwyn's muted voice shouted back through the trees. "Where are you at?"

"By the concrete marker!"

After a few minutes, the threesome joined Tim back at the concrete marker. "Here you are Jessa," Tim said as he handed over the camera. Then he pointed at a random spot on the ground. "It was right here. You must have taken out your camera and set it down to take notes."

"Yes, now I remember," Jessa said as she started taking photographs of the concrete marker. "I got distracted by the blast." She turned toward Elwynn. "Sorry for the delay, but I sure appreciate it. I'd hate to lose my camera."

"I'm glad it had a happy ending." Elwyn replied. "Well . . . assuming that we haven't forgotten anything else, we should be all set to head back." Elwyn looked at the faces of his three guests and was satisfied that everyone was ready. He assumed his usual lead position and started heading back toward his truck.

After the foursome walked out of the woods and got into Elwyn's club cab pickup truck, Elwyn drove past the plant and down the same road on which he had entered. As Elwyn came up to the guard shack, he slowed down but didn't roll his window down. The guard simply raised the sign-in clip board signaling that he would mark the check out time alongside each of the visitors' names.

When Elwyn got back to the mine overlook, each expressed appreciation once again and quickly evacuated Elwyn's pickup truck.

As Elwyn drove off, Jessa got out her tablet to finish writing a few more notes.

"You can stop writing now," Tim said with a hint of jest in his voice.

"Hey . . . I found the taconite process fascinating," Jessa mumbled while keeping her serious eyes glued to her tablet as she wrote. "So why shouldn't I finish what I've started?"

"Because of this," Tim said with a smirk. He held open his coat with one hand and, with his other hand, lifted the piece of slate out of his pocket.

Jessa's eyebrows went up and her mouth opened like an opera singer trying to hit high C.

"Goodness gracious, Tim! Is it . . . ?"

Tim smiled and nodded his head slowly. "It's gotta be part of the Rainy Lake Rune Stone."

"This is absolutely amazing!" Shukriyah said as she bent over for a close-up look. She lightly touched the grooves of the runic inscriptions. "I had no idea you found anything."

"Do you think there are more pieces still up there?" Jessa asked.

"I would imagine so," Tim said. "If there are, I think they've been scattered all through there and partly buried. It was a miracle that I found this one."

The joy on Tim's face faded. "And if the other fragments are scattered and buried, then it's likely that the rune stone will never be completely found and pieced together."

With both hands, Tim brought the stone up close to his face and contemplated the runic characters. "I don't know if Omar and Two-hearts are going to be satisfied with this particular piece, but it's all they're going to get."

ॐ 40 ॐ

Kayseri, a city in the Cappadocia region of Turkey

OMAR RAPPED THREE TIMES on the door of Alistair's hotel suite. It was past midnight, so Omar waited several seconds and knocked even harder. Finally he noticed through the peep hole when a light come on. The door opened slowly, revealing Alistair in boxer shorts and a white tank top T-shirt. His eyes were barely open and his thinning hair was mussed.

"Goodness gracious, Omar," Alistair mumbled as he stepped to the side and opened the door all the way. "You could have called to warn me that you were coming."

"Well, now," Omar said with a smirk as he walked in. "You know how I love to have face-to-face conversations with men in underwear."

"Touché, Omar." Alistair shut the door. "But I have no doubt that I'm a much more frightful sight. Make yourself at home. I'll get my robe."

As soon as Alistair returned, tying his robe, Omar wasted no time. "You must have some very important news to report. The note you left under my door said, 'Come and see me at once, no matter how late it is!!!' I take three exclamation points very seriously."

"Sit down, Omar," Alistair said as he pulled out a chair at a small table. He sat opposite him.

"Does this have anything to do with those photo attachments I e-mailed you?" Omar asked. "The photos of that rune stone fragment Tim Malone found?"

"It does. That, the silver urn, and the mid-first century Persian Magi." Alistair was groggy at first. He rubbed his face and sat hunched. "Omar, I spoke with Hasan earlier. More of the Chronicles have been translated."

Omar leaned forward. "Excellent! I was hoping to hear that."

Alistair shifted to the edge of his chair. "So, where shall we start?"

"Malone's e-mail. I'm sure you noticed his compliment for you. He's learning just how difficult it can be to find lost rune stones and treasures. He obviously would like to work with a trained expert such as yourself."

"That is a nice coincidence. I've been thinking along those same lines myself. Anyways, let's get to that later. His e-mail . . ." Alistair bent over and took a single sheet of paper from a brief case on the floor. ". . . it included photo attachments of the rune stone. This is a printout of one of those photos."

"Yes," Omar said as he took the printout from Alistair. "This is really something now, isn't it?"

"It's very exciting!" Alistair agreed.

After Omar had studied the printout, he looked across the table at his robed friend and knew he was about to put forth an astounding conclusion. At that late-hour, Alistair's scruffy appearance and his almost beseeching palms, Alistair looked like a Medieval monk about to deliver an impassioned sermon.

"Omar, the verdict's in. That the Vikings had reached the center of North America in the 1300s is now beyond all reasonable doubt."

Omar let out his breath. "I knew this was going to be huge when I saw Malone's photos." Omar looked back down at the printout. "How about these runic symbols, Alistair? Were you able to interpret them?"

"Two rows of runic characters are visible. There are only three characters in the first line, and they translate to the Roman letters of O, L, and I. The 'O' could also be 'aa.' The second line has more characters, and seems to imply something being stored somewhere or some object being kept at some location."

"Does it mean anything to you?" Omar asked.

"Truthfully, I don't know what to make of it yet."

"So, the significance of the silver urn still eludes us."

"At least we're getting warmer . . . which brings me to the latest translation of the Chronicles. Recall our discussion about the Persians who made the second journey in about 66 A.D.?"

"Yes."

"Well here's the news. The Chronicles imply that the silver urn was familiar to the visiting Persians. The context isn't exactly clear, but they definitely seemed to know what it was. You and I may not know the significance of the urn, but those first-century Persians sure did."

Omar looked puzzled.

"Omar, I now highly doubt that the Persians gave the urn to the Jewish community some 500 years earlier during their exile in Babylon. How would the Persians in 66 A.D. have known what it was? Another thing . . . the fact that the urn has an engraving of Chi Rho has started to puzzle me."

"Why?"

"I started thinking . . . what reason would there have been to engrave Chi Rho on something 500 years old? Chi Rho didn't come into use until the early to mid part of the first century. In fact, the Chi Rho engraving on the urn may be one of the earliest uses ever discovered."

"This is all very interesting. The first century puts us into the time of the New Testament."

"Exactly. Everything regarding the urn likely happened during the early to mid- first century. The Persians brought the silver urn to the Jewish community in Judea and got it back some time around 66 A.D."

"Alistair, let's go back to that fragment of rune stone," Omar said as he tapped the printout on the table. "Is there any hope at all that this one fragment can shed any light on the significance of the urn."

Alistair considered that. "It's still possible. Hasan's trying to work out some theories."

"If it does shed light on the urn, then the Vikings obviously knew the significance of the urn, didn't they?"

"That's where all this seems to be headed. If they referred to the urn on a rune stone, then no doubt they did. What's fascinating is that the Vikings seemed to have had a fixation on Christian-era relics that had ended up in England. Besides the urn ending up there, the Holy Grail's rumored to have been brought to England by Joseph of Arimathea, who was likely a reluctant member of the very same Sanhedrin that wanted Christ convicted. After all, Joseph donated his own tomb for the burial of Christ. If the Vikings referred to the Holy Grail on the Kensington Rune Stone, then it makes sense that the Rainy Lake Rune Stone could refer to the silver urn."

"That brings up a question," Omar said. "The Rainy Lake Stone apparently referred to the engraving of Faravahar on the urn. Why do you think it didn't refer to the other two engravings?"

"It may have, but that Two-hearts fellow didn't know it. Another thing is, since it's easy to describe the Faravahar image, its description would have been easy to pass down from generation to generation. It's possible that no one knew what the other two images were meant to depict."

"What's your take on the shooting-star image?"

"I believe it's something engraved by your mid-first-century Magi brethren. We've always thought that the engraving was something celestial. Well, we weren't far off. After we found out that the second visit of the Magi was in 66 A.D., I looked up Halley's comet. Guess when it appeared in the first century."

Omar gave a slight chuckle and cocked his head.

"66 A.D., of course."

"We can nail it down to some time between 63 and 66. Assuming it was readily visible in the night sky then, I'd bet a million pounds that it was the sight of Halley's Comet that inspired the Magi to start out on their second journey. Then, when they got back, they inscribed the comet onto their newly acquired urn in order to commemorate their journey."

"Maybe the comet had appeared near the constellation Perseus," Omar surmised. "If so, they went on the second journey because they thought they were acting on the prophecy of the Gift of Gold. The prophecy of peace." Then Omar gave Alistair a sidelong glance. "Only to be disappointed by the start of the Jewish Revolt in 66 A.D."

"Yeah, all that crossed my mind too."

"Whatever they were acting on, it's all so absolutely amazing," Omar said. After a moment of quiet reflection, Omar straightened and folded his hands on the table. "So . . . where do we go from here?"

"I propose we make a trip. Hasan can handle things here. He seems to manage just fine when I'm not here. In fact, even when I am on site, the field staff still go to Hasan with their questions. And that's just fine. Hasan needs experience in a leadership role."

"You want to go to Minnesota, don't you?"

"Ahh . . . so very perceptive."

"Ever since I showed you that fire steel and sun crystal from that Two-hearts fellow, I could tell that you were curious about what Shukriyah and Tim Malone are up to."

"What can I tell you, Omar?" Alistair smiled sheepishly. "Are not all archaeologists waiting to pounce on the next big find? I'll be honest. All along, I'd been wondering what other relics that Two-hearts gentleman might have in his possession. Now he's told Malone he has Viking coins and even offered an invitation to visit."

"I understand that a trip to visit Mr. Two-hearts requires an ability to paddle a canoe."

"Omar, for the profession that I'm in, surely you must know how much I have to rough it. In fact, I think you're the one who should be concerned about paddling a canoe."

"Hmm . . . you might have a point there."

"Anyway, what really got me going on the idea to travel to the States was that small piece of rune stone found by Mr. Malone. I've been driving myself mad trying to figure out the meaning of those runes. The second line states that something is being stored or some object is being kept at some location. Well, Omar, think about it in terms of the first line implying the existence of the Silver Urn."

Omar thought for a moment. He met Alistair's eyes. "You don't . . . think . . ." he stammered, giving Alistair a quizzical look. "No! You really think that the complete message would have mentioned the location of the Silver

Urn?"

"I do. Of course, a detailed description certainly couldn't have been carved in stone, but one place name would have been easy enough to etch."

"But Malone said he found his fragment in the middle of an active iron mine. Finding other pieces would be nearly impossible."

"Granted," Alistair said, "it certainly would be nice to look for the remaining pieces of the stone. But I have a bigger prize in mind."

"And that is . . . ?"

"When I first heard about the lost treasure of the voyageurs, I never believed that it could really be worth that much. Who would risk sending a fortune across an ocean and into a wilderness in the heart of the North American continent? But through the centuries, the Percy clan has been known for their desire for antiquities, rare jewels, and any valuables of a historic or religious nature.

"Well, I have new theory. The Percys didn't want to purchase the rune stone to establish territorial fur trade rights or even an international border, for that matter. I'm convinced that they wanted the stone because it would have revealed the location of the Silver Urn. And they were willing to pay dearly for the stone. They, too, must have known about the significance of the urn but didn't know where in England it was."

"So, you think the value of the lost treasure is . . . substantial?" Omar asked.

"Could be priceless."

Omar considered this. "I must say that I had been thinking . . ." Omar said. "Malone's friend and supervisor—Lyle Hanson is his name—he's incapacitated as a result of a car accident. So Malone certainly could use some archaeological expertise. He acknowledged that himself."

"Do you think it would be out-of-line to ask your council to approve a trip to the States?"

"Let me tell you, Alistair, with the success you've had here in Turkey, they'd fund your way on a cruise around the world if you asked for it."

"Well, Minnesota will do just fine. In fact, if I can swing it, I'd like to visit a few places in the Midwest relevant to Viking history. The Kensington

Rune Stone Museum is in Minnesota, of course. But I would also love to go to North Dakota or southern Saskatchewan and find out where Sieur de La Verendrye found his inscribed stone. Omar, do you know that he found his stone within a hollow of a large, standing stone pillar. The pillar was one among many found on the prairie."

"Hmm . . . any relation to all the hollows chiseled into the rock cliffs and pinnacles right here in Cappadocia? I understand they are early Christian."

"I've been curious about that myself. I've also been meaning to find out about the standing pillars in the A Coruña province of Galicia. It's a Celtic region in the northwest corner of Spain. Those pillars have hollows that face the sea. Were the pillars meant to be replicas of older pillars? Because if they are, then take a guess whose long boats once appeared off the coast of northwestern Spain."

"Vikings?"

"You got it."

"I tell you what. I'll get hold of Shukriyah and let her know that we'll be coming to the States."

Alistair picked up the printout. "And I'll carry this with me until I figure out the exact meaning of those runes. I don't care how long it takes."

≈ 41 ≥

*Lobby of the historic Fitger's Inn
Duluth, Minnesota*

LYLE HANSON SAT IN A SOFA CHAIR with his crutches resting on one armrest. As Maggie stood behind the chair covering Lyle's eyes, Tim held a book directly in front of him.

"Happy birthday!" Maggie said taking her hands from Lyle's eyes.

With Omar, Alistair, Jessa, and Shukriyah all sitting around, Lyle took the book in hand.

"Holy cow!" Lyle said as he recognized Eric Sevareid's *Canoeing with the Cree*. "Is this a collector's . . . ?" Lyle didn't have to complete his question once he opened the cover and saw Sevareid's signature. "It sure is!"

Lyle looked over his shoulder at Maggie. "Where did you find it?"

"Tim ran across it in a rare-book specialty store. It's from all of us."

"Wow, thanks a million everybody!"

"Sorry I didn't gift wrap it," Maggie said. "I've been in an absolute tizzy trying to get ready for the canoe trip."

Lyle noticed seven treats on the large square coffee table. "And what's all this?"

"It's your birthday cake. Alistair brought it all the way from Istanbul."

Lyle put the book down and reached for a wedge of baklava on a small paper plate, along with a plastic fork and napkin.

"Mmmm . . . this is wonderful!" Lyle said after he took a bite. "It's so much better than any baklava that I've ever had. My impression has always been of a pastry over-sweetened with honey with some crushed nuts thrown in for authenticity. Thanks for bringing the real McCoy."

"You're very welcome," Alistair said. "And happy birthday."

"Thank you," Lyle said. "Go ahead, everyone. Dig in."

Jessa handed Maggie one of the paper plates and a fork and napkin, and everyone enjoyed the special treat.

"Shukriyah, you've been in Istanbul," Omar said. "Have you ever had baklava like this?"

"No, I haven't. And I agree. It's excellent. Who makes it?"

"It's called Güllüo lu baklava," Alistair replied. "It's quite popular in Istanbul. Whenever I'm over there, it's the first thing I buy when I arrive and the last thing I buy when I leave. When Omar and I were about to leave to come here and meet all of you, I convinced him that we should load up."

Alistair and Omar had just checked into Fitger's Inn a few hours earlier. Except for Lyle, the others had come to plan the details of their upcoming canoe trip. They were all going to go visit Cedric Two-hearts and were waiting to have a scheduled phone conference with him.

Lyle put down his empty paper plate and picked up *Canoeing with the Cree*. "Let's see now . . . when Eric Sevareid and Walter Port were planning their canoeing expedition from Minneapolis to Hudson Bay, some thought they were young, foolish kids." Lyle paged through the beginning of the book until he found what he was looking for. "Oh yes, here it is. Page 16. It seems they fulfilled that description somewhere on either the Minnesota River or the Red River. Sevareid describes how their canoe, which they named *Sans Souci*— 'Without Care'—floated away from them when they didn't secure it well enough on the river bank.

"Folks, I don't know quite how to put this, but all of you are about to go on a canoe trip with someone who went over a portage—without care!—and did something even more foolish."

"No! No! No!" Tim said waving frantically in Lyle's direction. "Don't tell that story!"

Lyle grinned and continued. "On a portage on one very memorable canoe trip in the Quetico, Tim went ahead carrying a pack and the canoe."

Tim groaned and rested his forehead on his hand.

"When Tim came to the edge of a swamp, he noticed that a trail veered off to the side. Now—to his credit, I must say—he had checked the map before he left and had remembered that the portage trail appeared to curve around a swamp. So, he followed that trail veering off to the side . . . and followed it . . . and followed it. Eventually, he came to the end of the trail and put down the canoe and pack on the lakeshore.

"Well, everybody, you are all hereby informed," Lyle said with his finger pointing up, "that Tim portaged the pack and the canoe back to the very same lake we had just paddled across."

"Now, wait just one minute," Tim said as everyone had a good laugh at his expense. "Isn't there always just one portage trail between two lakes? Who would ever have even dreamed there was a portage trail that looped back to the same lake?"

"Uh, the sun was out, Einstein," Lyle said.

"Hey, while I was on that trail I was under a canoe. And being in June, the sun nearly straight overhead anyway. And then when I finally dropped your blasted ten-ton fiberglass canoe—plus a stuffed Duluth pack—I was just so doggone tired that I just headed back down the trail like a zombie. The combined load I had just hauled was easily over one hundred pounds."

He got no sympathy, not even from Jessa. "Like I've said before, I better watch it when I tell people that I'm dating an MIT grad student. They're not going to believe me."

"All right, all right. I admit that was pretty bad." Then Tim noticed the cell phone on the coffee table and seized his chance to change the subject. "You know something, I think it's close enough to when we're supposed to call

Two-hearts." He grabbed the cell, leaned back in his chair, and pointed at Lyle. "I'm glad you're not going on this trip."

Tim selected Two-hearts' phone number from his speed-dial list. As the phone on the other end started ringing, he turned and noticed a smirk on Shukriyah's face.

"Caught you snickering at me," Tim said to Shukriyah. "When we set up camp the first night, I'm going to hide food in your tent so the bears will visit you."

Shukriyah's humorous mood quickly vanished. As Tim put the phone to his ear, she looked at Lyle with concerned eyes. "Will there really be bears where we're going? What do I do if one comes into my tent?"

"Don't play hard to get," Lyle said.

"Lyle!" Maggie said, shocked, as Lyle burst out laughing. Then she said, "Shukriyah, it's nothing to worry about. Bears are rarely a problem as long as you use common sense with your food. And excuse my rude husband. He was more polite when his jaw was broken. *Then* he couldn't speak."

Two-hearts answered his phone, and Tim held up his hand to signal silence.

"Hello, Cedric. Tim Malone here. . . . I'm fine. . . . Yes, everyone's here. . . . I'm going to turn on the speaker phone and put it . . . go ahead . . . We'll have to . . . go, ah . . . okay, we'll have to be patient with the satellite transmission delay. Now just a second, I'll put my phone down so all of us can talk to you.

"Cedric, can you hear me?"

"Yes, I can hear you. Did you receive the map of where I live?"

"Yes, I did. Thanks. We should be able to find your place just fine. Besides myself, the five others who will come to visit are all here. Omar Rahani, Alistair Groom, Jessa Hallberg, Shukriyah Maqadma, and Maggie Hanson. And there's another special person in the room. A wise guy, but nevertheless, a special person. Lyle Hanson is here too."

"Lyle's there? Lyle, can you hear me?"

"Yes, I can. How are you, Cedric?"

"I'm just fine. The more important question is: how are you?"

"I'm getting stronger week by week. I can move around on my own pretty well. And in a way, I'm a new man because I have some man-made materials in me: metal alloy plates, plastic composites, who knows what all."

"Well, it's good to hear your voice, hey. Can Maggie hear me?"

"I'm here, Cedric."

"Maggie, for a long time there's been something I wanted to tell you. The night I asked Lyle to meet me in Alexandria, that was the night I told Lyle that the treasure was not in the rapids. I told him to keep everything a secret, even the place where we were meeting. Well, I just want to say I apologize."

"Thanks, Cedric. But the fact that Lyle got hurt certainly wasn't your fault. And it turns out that you were wise to keep everything a secret. The person I thought was a close friend was in fact my worst enemy. She was spying on me. So it was a good thing I didn't learn anything from Lyle. My friend's family found out enough the way it was. They were so desperate that they followed Lyle to Alexandria."

"Okay . . . okay. Well, Lyle, now your friends can look for this treasure for you without looking over their shoulder all the time."

"Yes. That's a big relief."

"There have been many others who have tried to get there hands on the treasure for their own personal gain. So, I think it's time that some legitimate folks like yourselves find it once and for all for the public good."

"Cedric?" Tim asked. "How far back does that go? When did rumors of the treasure's existence first get out?"

"I guess it goes all the way back to the fur-trade days. Ever hear of the explorer David Thompson?"

"Yes, we have."

"I'm a descendant of Chief Two-hearts of the Rainy Lake Ojibwe. That's who I'm named after. Well, back in the 1820s, when surveyors for both England and America came to this wilderness west of Lake Superior to try establish the border, Chief Two-hearts was suspicious of their real intentions. You see, one of the surveyors was David Thompson. He used to be employed by the North West Fur Trading Company, and Chief Two-hearts knew that. So, when Thompson came to Rainy Lake looking at the sky through his shiny metal survey instrument, Chief

Two-hearts asked him why he was 'rambling over our waters and writing in his little book.' It's even recorded that way in the history books.

"Chief Two-hearts got even more suspicious when Thompson asked him about all the rivers and rapids in the area. That's when Chief Two-hearts became convinced that Thompson was looking for Hell's Gate Rapids so that he could make sure that it ended up within British territory."

"Do you mean to say that the location of Hell's Gate Rapids was already a mystery by the 1820s?" Lyle asked.

"Yah. Back then, place names could change in ten to twenty years. There weren't any maps to speak of. And other rapids might have been given a similar name if a death had occurred there. Besides, the fur-trade company officials probably did their best to keep the location of Hell's Gate Rapids out of the record books.

"Anyways, this whole thing with the lost treasure involved quite a turn of events by the time Thompson showed up. The treasure was intended to buy the Rainy Lake Rune Stone. But the stone was probably already taken out of the area by the 1820s. It didn't matter, hey. No one was asking about it any longer. Chief Two-hearts could see it was the lost treasure itself that had become the new attraction.

"Things were fairly quiet until 1893. That's when the Rainy Lake gold rush hit, and things got really crazy. My people never knew what to make of all the people who came to the wilderness to strike it rich. Why did they suddenly come to Rainy Lake on such flimsy rumors? Traces of gold had been found in a lot places."

"Do you think that some gold seekers were actually looking for the treasure?" Lyle asked.

"I didn't mean it quite like that. Uh . . . what could of happened goes something like this. Some geologist reports in his daily log that a rock he inspected contained a trace of gold. Word gets out, but it's no big deal. People had learned their lesson with the Lake Vermillion gold rush back in the 1860s. That gold rush was a big bust.

"Now, just by coincidence, the descendants of the old fur-trade company in England hire some miners to look for the lost treasure. The miners show up in the Rainy Lake area, asking the locals about the rivers in the wilderness. The locals put two and two together, start thinking that the geologist was really trying to keep the amount of gold a secret, and before you know it, a rumor of gold spreads like wild fire. Of course, the same thing happened at Lake Vermillion. The Rainy Lake gold rush also turned out to be a big bust."

"Cedric?" Tim asked. "I recently did some research on Russell Blankenburg and Benny Ambrose. Have you ever heard of them?"

"Oh, yah. My father knew them both. They lived down near Saganaga Lake."

"That's right. Well, during World War I, when Ambrose was in the famous Rainbow Division, he had an Ojibwe friend from the village of Grand Portage. Apparently this friend told Ambrose about a legendary lost gold mine somewhere in the wilderness along the border. That's one of the reasons Ambrose moved up there. Cedric, do you think the friend really told Ambrose about the lost treasure of the voyageurs?"

There was a long silence before Two-hears replied. "You know, that's a good question. Blankenburg and Ambrose were two mineral prospectors. I suppose it's possible they had spent time looking for the treasure. And now that you told me that Pearson fella actually met them, who knows what kind of arrangement they could of had."

There was another pause.

"Say, can I change the subject" Two-hearts asked. "I got a question for the archaeologist from Scotland?"

"Hello, Cedric. This is Alistair Groom. I assume you mean me."

"Yah. What's going to happen with the Silver Urn?"

"We're quite certain that it'll wind up in the London British Museum."

"Okay."

"Now I have a question for you."

"Go ahead."

"The main reason we're coming to visit you is to discuss the lost treasure. But we'd also like to see your Viking artifacts. Would that be okay?"

"Yah," Two-hearts said. "That'd be good, especially for someone with your background. Mostly I have a bunch of coins that go back centuries."

OF VIKINGS AND VOYAGEURS

"I understand you even have some Viking blood in you. Lyle tells me that you have blue eyes."

"Yah. Not everyone believes me though. They say blue eyes could be from unknown European ancestors in the 1800s or early 1900s, or simply a genetic roll of the dice. Then I tell them about the blond-haired, blue-eyed Mandan Indians along the Missouri River. You know, where North Dakota is today. But they still don't want to believe me."

"Well, I certainly do," Alistair said. "Let me tell you about the Brokpa. They're a fair-skinned people who live in the villages of Dha-Hanu in the province of Ladakh. Ladakh is in the extreme northern tip of India, sandwiched between the Himalayan and Karakoram mountain ranges. The Brokpa are said to be descendants of soldiers from the army of Alexander the Great. Alexander went through that area 1600 years before the Vikings went to North America, so obviously such genetic traits can last a long time."

"That's good to know, hey. And in speaking of Alexander, that reminds me of something. I want to ask you about the Persians. Did I understand correctly that it was the Persians who brought the Silver Urn to northern England?"

"That's the theory. The Romans brought Persian families to northern England—maybe entire villages—as permanent conscripts along Hadrian's Wall."

"And some time later, the Vikings invaded northern England in about the same place?" Two-hearts asked.

"Correct," Alistair said. "The Vikings first invaded Lindisfarne."

"And the monks had to run away with the gospels?"

"Exactly."

"How many gospels do you think there were?"

"There are four known gospels that were illuminated by one bishop. All of them are the Biblical gospels. They're in the British Library. I'm convinced that—"

"Hold on a second," Two-hearts said.

There was a short pause, and then Two-hearts came back on. "This is nuts. I sure chose a bad option for my satellite phone service. I'm sorry to have to tell you, but I'm running out of minutes. Even though you made the call, I'm going to be hit with a big surcharge pretty quick here. So we have to hurry it up."

"As I was about to say," Alistair said, "I'm convinced that there was a separate, fifth gospel illuminated by another Lindisfarne monk—the Gospel of Thomas. I believe that certain Persians had a lasting religious influence in northern England. But unlike the other four gospels, I believe that the Vikings confiscated the Gospel of Thomas."

"I have the Gospel of Thomas."

Alistair grabbed Omar's forearm. Although everyone remained quiet, the feeling of utter surprise was palpable. For a couple of long seconds, everyone looked at each other with stunned faces. Finally, Alistair shifted forward in his seat so he would be closer to the phone on the coffee table.

"Cedric, please repeat that. Did you say that you have the Gospel of Thomas?"

"Yes. That's what I said. There are three things in my cabin that I cherish. My Gospel of Thomas is one of them."

Alistair quickly looked at Omar again and dramatically mouthed the words: ("I can't believe it!")

"Cedric?" Alistair continued. "When we come to your cabin can we also look at your Gospel of Thomas?"

"Certainly. But we better hurry up and talk about what day you will be arriving."

"Cedric, this is Tim. Our plan is to drive up to Crane Lake tomorrow and spend the night there. Then on the day after tomorrow, an outfitter will transport us to the point where we can start canoeing. We'll set up camp and then come and visit you sometime in the afternoon."

"Who is your outfitter?"

Tim looked at Maggie. "Uh . . . . Wally's Outfitting and . . . ?"

"I know Wally," Two-hearts said. "I'll let him know what's going on. It'll help a lot if he knows you're visiting me, hey."

"Then we'll see you the day after tomorrow, okay?" Tim asked.

"Okay, that sounds good. See you then."

∞ 42 ∞

*Somewhere in the Ontario Wilderness between
Quetico Provincial Park and Voyageurs National Park,
Minnesota*

THE SKY WAS GRAY, AND A COLD, FINE MIST hung over a channel that led to a chain of smaller lakes. An outfitter named Wally was kneeling on the wet, wooden slats of a dock as he made final preparations of the camping gear. His aluminum transport boat with its overhead canoe rack was tied up on one side of the dock. Three eighteen-foot Wenonah canoes, each with the company's classic color of ripe wheat, were tied up on the other side.

The dock location was a staging point for Wally's outfitting enterprise. It was a good jumping off point for canoe parties that had been shuttled from far away or across large open water. A shuttle would not only save time for a canoe expedition, it could overcome the difference of not starting out at all if the waves on a large lake were too big for a canoe.

A shed just on shore served as a supply depot for the canoe parties that Wally outfitted. And in case of inclement weather or high winds, it also served as an emergency depot for the returning parties in case Wally wasn't able to travel on the scheduled pick-up day.

Maggie, Jessa, and Omar stood behind Wally in their Gore-Tex rain suits. They were waiting for him to stuff the remaining olive green Duluth packs as Tim, Alistair, and Shukriyah were loading the first few into the three canoes.

"When you guys are at your camp," Wally said as he continued to work on his knees, "put your empty food wrappers and packaging in a plastic bag. Then if you leave camp, either take it with you or tie it up in a tree with your food pack. Oh, and another thing if you leave camp. Always be sure to have your paperwork with you: your Remote Border Crossing Permits from Canadian Customs, your Crown Land Camping Permit, fishing licenses, passports . . . anything like that."

"Does Two-hearts have to worry about any of those things whenever he crosses the border just to go into town?" Jessa asked.

"Oh, I'm pretty sure that the native Indians who live in the area have certain privileges. Authorities on both sides of the border are on a first-name basis with them all.

"Just about done here," he said. "Then you can load the rest of these packs, and we'll get you going. By the way, I see by that case that someone plays the guitar."

"I do," Jessa said. "With Maggie on her harmonica, we plan to serenade the others."

"Now that's an instrument that's practical for this country," Wally said. "Easy to pack and portage."

"It may be practical," Maggie said, "but useless if this weather doesn't clear. I was hoping for a nice sunset over a quiet lake when the acoustics are optimum."

"Two-hearts really appreciates music," Wally said. "He's been known to go into International Falls whenever there's a concert. You should consider playing your music for him when you see him. I think he'd like that."

"Cedric recognized your name when we told him who our outfitter was," Jessa said. "Do you know him well?"

"Oh, yeah," the Wally answered. "I've known him for as long as I can remember."

"Is it true he's kind of shy?" Maggie asked. "That he doesn't even like it when fishermen come on his lake?"

Wally didn't answer right away. He continued to focus on his chore at hand as he threaded another leather strap through a roller buckle.

"Oh, Two-hearts is a strange duck, all right," Wally said without looking up. "In fact, there are very few people around here who dare go onto his lake. To scare people away at the portage to his lake, he'll leave carcasses of crows, squirrels, and rabbits hanging from trees. He even ties a real hangman's noose around the necks."

Jessa gasped and Shukriyah put her hand up to her collar. Maggie glanced back at Jessa and Shukriyah with a look of concern and puzzlement.

"But . . . but when we've communicated with him, he seems so . . ." Maggie stopped mid-sentence when she noticed that Tim was smiling. Then she quickly looked down at Wally.

"I'm just pullin' your leg, ma'am," Wally said as he stood up and put his hands in the pockets of his purple fleece cardigan. "The truth is, you're going to remember this trip for a long, long time. Especially you younger folks. Us locals regard Two-hearts like kind of a . . . oh, you know, a wise guru who sits in a mountaintop cave or somethin' like that. He can never go into town, sit in a restaurant and just read a newspaper all alone. Someone will always come up to him and start asking him questions, hoping they can get him talkin'. He may not have a formal education, but he sure has learned a lot on his own."

Wally looked at the canoes and the packs he had just synched shut. "Well, these are ready to load. Any last questions about the directions?"

Tim thrust a map in front of the Wally. "Just to make sure I got this straight . . . this bay here is where you suggest we camp, right?" Tim asked as he pointed to a location on the map.

"That's right. We call it Little Pike Bay. The campsite there is a good one this time of year when there are no bugs and the nights are cold. It's sheltered from the wind fairly well."

"And after we set up camp, I know that we're supposed to paddle to Two-hearts' cabin by going into this long, narrow bay over here. Will it be obvious amongst these islands?"

"Oh, I'm glad you asked. I forgot to mention that a forest fire came through this area a couple years ago," Wally said as he moved his finger across

Tim's map. "Keep paddling until you reach the burn. You won't miss it because of all the black, charred trees that look like skeletons. That's where you'll turn into the bay."

"Did the fire threaten Two-hearts' cabin?" Tim asked.

"It threatened Two-hearts. The fire jumped across the lake. And when it did, it went down on both sides of the narrow bay toward the portage to the lake Two-hearts lives on."

"What did he do?"

"He threw a wet blanket in his canoe. Then he got ready to paddle out to the middle of his lake with the blanket over his head, if he had to. He said the smoke started to get thick enough to make him cough. But then he lucked out. The wind switched, and the rains came. In fact, the fire didn't even reach the portage going into his lake. Anyway, after you cross the portage to his lake, he's the only one who lives on it. He told me he'll leave a fire going in his fireplace. His cabin isn't visible because it's tucked in the trees, but you'll be able to tell where it is by the rising smoke."

Wally studied the faces of his six clients. "Any other questions?"

"I thought they only had weather like this in Scotland," Alistair remarked. "Do you know how long it's supposed to last?"

"Probably not long. Before we left this morning, I checked the radar, and it showed clear skies just to the west. I expect this low pressure system should leave some time later today." Wally looked at Maggie. "In fact, you just might get your sunset tonight so you can play your music." Wally paused in anticipation of more questions. "Anything else?"

"No, I don't think so," Tim said as he looked to his comrades. The five others either shook their heads or verbalized that they did not.

"That's it," Tim said as he turned again to Wally. "We're ready to go."

"Remember, use the satellite phone to call our Crane Lake headquarters if there's a change in plans. It's in the safety pack with the first-aid kit. But if we don't hear from you, I'll meet you back here at 2:00 tomorrow. Okay?"

"Understood," Tim said.

"All right then," Wally said. "Let's load these last packs so you can shove off."

Of Vikings and Voyageurs

The weather may have been inclement, but the spirits of the six paddlers were high as they started on their way.

With the assistance of Omar's long-armed strokes in the stern of the canoe, Shukriyah became impressed at how the bow's vertical edge seemed to slice through the dark water. When her scientifically astute eyes examined the lake surface constantly coming at her, she noticed that it had a strange, non-directional chop even though the air was relatively calm. Without the burden of a high-pressure atmosphere, she wondered, perhaps the water surface was free to rollick with the slightest whiff of air.

The inclement weather certainly didn't prevent the north country from displaying a melancholy beauty. The balsams on the surrounding sloping shore looked like a chorus of spires poised on risers on a stage. A cloud in the shape of a man riding a horse drifted low in the sky like a ghost. The shape of its outline seemed frozen as it floated like a single solid mass toward shore, seemingly destined to crash into the sharp spires of trees and pop like a balloon.

It wasn't long, however, before the group realized that Wally knew what he was talking about when it came to weather. Here and there, little patches of blue sky peeked through the overcast as it drifted east and started to thin.

By the time they stopped at their campsite, pitched their tents and hung their food pack on a high, horizontal tree limb, the sun came out and dappled the north country with brilliant color. The lake turned vibrant blue, and various shades of green emerged in the canopy of trees along the shoreline. The new, freshly opened leaves of poplar trees were a rich, lime green that contrasted with the darker greens of the conifers.

The change in weather made everyone eager to set out for Two-hearts' cabin. After a quick snack of trail mix, peanut butter or cheese on pita bread, energy bars, and powdered drinks of Kool-aid or Tang, they launched their canoes and paddled with renewed energy. It wasn't long before they came to the burned-over area, turned into the long, narrow bay and paddled to the portage leading to the lake on which Two-hearts lived.

The portage trail was ideal—not too long, free of hazards, and flat and wide enough to use a wheeled dolly, something Two-hearts likely did. Tim reached the other end first. He let his canoe roll sideways off his shoulders and eased it into the water. As Omar and Alistair came up behind with the other two canoes, Tim helped each by bridging one end of their canoe, allowing them to come out from under it.

Tim was placing the last canoe in the water when Maggie, Jessa, and Shukriyah joined them. As each walked toward the water's edge, they lowered their day packs and paddles while maintaining a wide-eyed gaze out over the lake. It was as if they had reached some sort of long-anticipated Shangri La.

The lake basin appeared saucer-shaped with its consistent sloping shoreline circling the entire perimeter. Almost directly across the lake from the portage, a narrow plume of smoke could be seen rising lazily above the spruce and balsams. The smoke was the most uniquely welcome sign that anyone of them had ever seen.

They all got back into their canoes and pushed out into the lake. Not a word was spoken as six pair of eyes were locked on the smoke plume. The only audible sound was that of paddles dipping into the water. It wasn't long before details on the opposite shore started becoming distinct.

Suddenly a human figure emerged from the woods. The only detail visible from that far was that the figure was wearing a red shirt. It dawned on Tim that perhaps Two-hearts didn't always live alone or that he had invited some guests for the occasion. Tim wasn't sure what to expect. He didn't even know what Two-hearts looked like.

When the distant figure appeared to take a few steps forward, it seemed as if the person was walking on the water's surface. Then an arm swung overhead. Everyone in the three canoes returned the greeting.

After several more minutes of paddling, it not only became apparent that the person was a man, but also that he had walked out on a dock that was only a few inches above the water. Even the eight supporting posts were cut low. Tim wondered if the dock had been intentionally built that way so it would be less visible from afar. Other than the smoke plume, the dock, and a barely visible narrow track used to winch a boat onto shore, there was still no indication that anyone lived within the stretch of shoreline forest directly ahead.

Eventually each of the three canoes oriented for a final approach to the dock. Tim and Jessa arrived first. As Tim eased up on his strokes, he got his first close look at the man waiting for them. He wore a red-and-black plaid, long-sleeve shirt, blue jeans held up with a wide leather belt, and mocassins with beaded fringes. Jet black hair flowed down and back on each side of his head—long enough to smooth behind his ears but too short for a pony tail.

The man's square-jawed face was reminiscent of the idealized Canadian Royal Mountie depicted on the famous Potlatch Corporation paintings. Yet, there was nothing authoritarian about his appearance. His lips were shaped in an ever-so-slight smile, giving him a perpetually peaceful visage similar to that of George Washington on the dollar bill.

Tim had been expecting someone older; that is, if the man on the dock was Two-hearts. On the other hand, if the lack of gray hair could be ignored, the man could have indeed passed for someone in his upper fifties. There was also nothing apparent about the man that seemed suggestive of anything Scandinavian. That is, until Tim got close enough and the man looked at him straight on. The stark contrast of the his bright blue eyes against dark, native skin was suddenly noticeable from several feet away.

The man squatted down, grabbed the gunwale at the center thwart and held the canoe so that the bow end was tight up against the dock. After Jessa got out with the bow rope in her hand, the man let out the bow and rocked the canoe against the dock rail until the stern came up tight. When Tim stepped out and grabbed the stern line, the man stood up and held out his left hand for Jessa to hand him the rope.

"I can take that for you," he said.

Tim followed the man as he towed the canoe closer to shore and stopped at the dock post closest to shore. He made a loop in the rope by twisting his hand inward and threw the loop over the post. He repeated the process to make a clove hitch, snugged it tight, then added a half hitch for some extra maybe unnecessary insurance. Tim tied the stern to a post with his trusty bowline, but it was just a loop that couldn't be snugged tight around the post.

The man stood up and took a few steps toward Tim and Jessa with his right hand extended. "Welcome. I'm Cedric Two-hearts."

∞ 43 ∞

After Two-hearts helped Omar and Shukriyah, and Alistair and Maggie disembark and tie up their canoes, he greeted each one with a hardy handshake. As his guests introduced themselves, Two-hearts made a point to repeat every name. When the introductions were complete, he turned to lead his six guests off the dock and up to his cabin.

Since there was hardly any open beach to speak of, the path started into the trees pretty much where the weathered dock boards ended. The path angled up to the cabin along a gradual incline. Two-hearts had laid out a uniform layer of gravel bordered with rounded stones for his path, and it was virtually canopied by overhanging balsam branches.

Alongside the path were two overturned canoes supported on saw horses. One was an aluminum square-stern, and the other was a small fiberglass solo canoe. A two by six was nailed to two nearby trees with a free end cantilevered beyond one tree trunk. Small circular marks on the free end indicated that the board had been used to mount an outboard motor.

On the side of the path opposite the two boats was a Ferris wheel-like gill net drum that didn't appear to have been used in many years. Its wood was gray and warped, its metal hardware rusty, and the ground on which it rested was over-grown with mature brush.

The top of the path came out to a level opening in the woods cleared of everything except the largest trees. For Tim, the scene instantly brought back memories of visiting his grandparent's cabin on a remote lake in northern Minnesota.

The main cabin was the largest building on the site. Made of logs stained dark-brown, it had an old roof with patches of green moss growing on the shingles. A field-stone chimney dominated the left gable end of the cabin, and the smoke plume used as a navigational target was still rising.

A small gable roof covered the cabin entry and was supported by two angled posts fixed to the exterior wall. The windows had green shutters that Two-hearts could close whenever he left for an extended period. Two-hearts hadn't yet replaced the old-fashioned, four-pane storm windows with screens.

An old-fashioned antennae was attached to the right side of the cabin. It intersected the gable roof right at its peak and extended skyward. The top of the antennae appeared higher than the chimney, but Tim couldn't recall being able to see it from out on the lake.

A more modern, sun-tracking solar panel had been perched high on a pole about five to ten yards from the cabin. If Tim felt it appeared out of place, it was only because his grandparents never had one. But he knew it was the right thing to have even if it clashed with his imaginary ideal of a wild-woods cabin. Tim knew that the solar panel could only supply supplemental energy and, therefore, guessed that a generator and a couple of propane cylinder tanks were on the backside of the cabin.

There were four other structures on the compound. The only one that wasn't made of the same dark-stained logs as the main cabin was the firewood shelter. Its three walls were made of unfinished rough boards, and it had a flat sloping roof. The shelter was completely open on the side where the roof was highest. A stump used for firewood splitting was directly in front of the open side and seemed to be growing out of a bed of wood chips.

The building closest to the path leading down to the lake had a large double door on it. Tim wondered if that's where Two-hearts kept motorized equipment and a larger boat. A building close to the main cabin looked like a sauna with its stove-pipe chimney and white lace window curtains. The third log building looked like a combination tool shed and work shop. A rusty circular saw and steel animal traps hung on the shed's outside wall beneath a low roof eave.

As everyone followed Two-hearts to his cabin, Maggie noticed the traps. "Do you still trap?" she asked.

In his unique style, Two-hearts would sometimes give a delayed response even if he knew the answer. In this case, Two-hearts stopped to look at the traps with a sentimental admiration. "Not any more," he said. "I used to help my dad trap beaver, fisher, lynx. But then he had an accident. His arm got mangled in a conibear."

"I'm so sorry to hear that," Tim said. "Isn't that the worst kind of trap to get caught in?"

"You got that right. His arm was never the same . . . and come to think of it, neither was his frame of mind. He was just too gun shy to be around traps any longer. So our trappin' days came to an end. The last time I trapped, it was only for nuisance critters."

"What animals other than bears are a problem out here?" Tim asked.

"Skunks are no fun. And you never want a family of racoons to get in your cabin, hey. Other than that, there are always the pesky little rodents."

"Ever had any problems with wolves?" Jessa asked.

"No," Two-hearts answered as he started toward the cabin. "I hear 'em howl, but I never see 'em unless I make a trip out here in the winter. Then I see 'em loping across the ice. The only ones who might have run-ins with wolves are the folks with dog-sled teams." Two-hearts opened the storm door on this cabin and pushed in a thick wooden interior door. "Why don't you all come in."

Two short wall sections forming a ninety-degree corner provided a partial enclosure of the entryway. A number of garments of the hard-working woodsman hung on a row of hooks. A short bench had work boots and mukluks stowed underneath.

A host of aromas, all wild, greeted the visitors upon entering the cabin proper. The two wall sections in the entryway steered everyone to the right toward a kitchen and eating area. Once fully inside, the cabin interior opened up, revealing one large, dimly-lit room. The interior side of the log walls were stained dark like the exterior, and small four-pane windows let in only a minimum of natural light.

The living area was separated from the kitchen by a long counter extending a little more than half way across the floor. A walkway with a parquet-style floor pattern started at the entryway and ran along the exterior wall to a private area behind the kitchen wall.

The living area was clearly the center of attention. The fire that produced the guiding smoke plume still burned in the field-stone fireplace at the extreme far left wall. It gave the room a faint but pleasant smoky fragrance that seemed like the ultimate signature of the north woods cabin lifestyle.

Over the fireplace a heavy wooden mantle supported by two half-round logs protruded from the stone masonry. Above that a pair of antique, Alaskan-style snowshoes crossed to form of an X. A dream catcher was centered in the upper v-notch formed by the crossed snowshoes. Below the snowshoes was a large single moose antler resting on the mantle. It was propped against the field stones and was centered among several smaller knick-knacks and mementos.

Except for flat stones at the base of the fireplace, the floor was made with wood-planks and was mostly covered with large, oval-shaped braided rugs. Most of the furniture appeared to be rustic. The frame of a high-back sofa was diamond willow. The sofa was flanked by a matching diamond willow floor lamp and an end table. A Hudson Bay blanket appeared more arranged on the back of the sofa rather than thrown haphazardly.

Alistair was quick to notice two large book shelves along the opposite wall in the living area. In between the shelves was an old, heavy-looking wooden desk with flat, decorative boxes on top. Alistair wondered if the illuminated Gospel of Thomas was in the book shelf and if other artifacts were in the boxes. Just as he was feeling that it might be too impolite to broach the subject of artifacts too quickly, Omar broke the ice.

"Cedric, we wish to thank you for sending the fire steel and navigational sun crystal," Omar said. "I received them just before I went to Newcastle to see the silver urn."

"Did you ever think the Viking sun crystal was connected to the Rainy Lake Rune Stone, which would refer to the silver urn?" Two-hearts asked.

"No . . . I certainly did not."

"The fire steel was clearly marked with T, R, and O," Alistair commented. "Do you know what those letter stand for?"

"Jean-Luc Trotin. The voyageur who stole the treasure."

"Is that why they called him 'The Hustler'?" Tim asked.

Two-hearts smiled. "His comrades called him Hustler because he was an expert pick-pocket."

"So, his comrades had to keep a constant eye on him?"

"Oh, no. He never stole from his own brigade. He usually stole from rival voyageurs of competing companies at the Rendezvous. If he ever took advantage of anyone in his own company, it would have been the pork eaters from Montreal."

"Was Trotin related to Chief Two-hearts?" Maggie asked.

"They say that he and Trotin may have been cousins. I'm not sure, hey. But I do know that they knew each other. When Trotin decided to hide the treasure, he left his clues with Chief Two-hearts."

"Do you know why Trotin decided to hide the treasure?" Tim asked.

"It was that curse I told you about in Alexandria. A small pox epidemic. In fact, Trotin got it himself."

Two-hearts' expression became rather sober. "Yes, small pox has quite a history on native Americans. The British used it against tribes who had befriended the French during the French and Indian War. In the guise of charity, they gave the tribes blankets contaminated with small pox.

"The disease eventually migrated west and started devastating the tribes in the Great Lakes area and the Plains Indians. By 1781 it was a full-blown epidemic. Besides Jean-Luc, there were other voyageurs who also got it. Being strong, many were able to survive it. But not so with Jean-Lucs' family. Of those who got sick, many died.

"Jean-Luc blamed himself for the rest of his life. But he believed was caught up in an old Ojibwe prophecy. Had he stayed in the fur trade, he never would have exposed his family to the disease. But once his family members were dead, he felt he had been destined to hide the treasure."

"What's the prophecy?"

"There's a legend that says the speckles on the back of a loon are jewels spilled from its necklace. Someday the jewels would be gathered up and given to a brave warrior. He would hide the jewels on the shore of one of these lakes. Then much later, after a period of great suffering, when the people were no longer sick or in great need, a wise chief will find the jewels and distribute them among his people. The chief will know his people are ready to receive them when they do not desire them. With or without them, they'll be happy forever."

"So it was when the family members suffered from small pox that Trotin figured he must be the brave warrior?" Maggie asked.

"That's right. So he hid the jewels and gave Chief Two-hearts the clues. The clues have been passed down from chief to chief. And then at long last, a wise chief must come along and find the chest of jewels."

Two-hearts looked at Omar. "You look like a wise chief, hey?"

"Me?" A surprised Omar asked as he put his finger on his chest. "No, I'm not a chief."

"Some of us regard him as a wise chief," Shukriyah said.

"I second that," Alistair said.

A rare side of Omar came out as he averted his eyes in embarrassment.

"Cedric?" Tim asked. "We've seen a tracing of the lead seal that was attached to the treasure chest. Can we see the actual lead seal?"

"Sure. Come over to my desk. I have other artifacts to show you. The fire steel and sun crystal I had sent you were not my most valuable artifacts." Two-hearts walked over to his desk and put on his reading glasses. He opened one of the decorative boxes and started taking historic coins out of circular insets. He looked at each one before handing them one by one to his astonished guests.

"These are some of the valuables the Vikings brought when they came here in the 1300s. "Here's a Byzantine coin. . . . This one is the only one I have that's an actual Viking coin. Notice the long boat engraved on it. . . . This one is an Islamic silver dirham."

"My goodness!" Shukriyah said as she took the Islamic coin from Two-hearts and studied it closely. "How is it that the Vikings got a hold of Islamic coins?"

"They traded as far away as the Black Sea," Two-hearts said. Then he looked at Alistair. "Didn't they make it over there by going through Russia down the Dnieper River?"

"That's right," Alistair said. "They traded in Constantinople and Trebizond on the north coast of Turkey." Alistair glanced at Omar. "Wouldn't that be something if we found latter day chronicles in Cappadocia that make reference to Vikings."

Omar tilted his head and gave a slight smile. "You never know."

"Here's a denier from the time of Charlemagne," Two-hearts said as he handed it to Jessa. When Two-hearts saw what the next coin was, he handed it to Alistair. "Here, you might be familiar with this one."

"Good Lord! I am indeed! It's a silver penny showing King Ethelred. It was struck in 1009." Alistair leaned toward Omar to point out a detail on the coin. "Look here . . . this inscription means, 'Ethelred, King of the English.' He died in 1016."

"Why did the Vikings have so many coins from other countries?" Omar asked Alistair.

"Rulers in England and on the continent often paid them off to keep the peace. The Vikings found extortion quite profitable. In fact, archaeologists have found more late Anglo-Saxon coins in Scandinavia than in Britain."

"Why do you think the Vikings brought all these different types of coins to North America?"

Alistair shrugged. "Anybody's guess. Perhaps they were anticipating trade. Perhaps the Vikings thought they might stay a while and wanted to bring any property that had special significance. For instance, maybe these coins were spoils of war. In fact, Ethelred did stand up to an invasion from King Olaf Trygvason at one point. By the way, Trygvason was instrumental in converting the Vikings to Christianity."

Two-hearts opened another decorative box and pulled out what at first appeared to be an over-sized coin. "And you might be interested in this, hey," he said as he handed Tim a lead seal from the fur trade.

Tim guessed at what it was right away. "Wow! Is this it?" he asked Two-hearts as he gently received the lead seal with two hands. He held it with two hands as if it was made of glass. "Is this the Percy and Campbell lead seal that was attached to their treasure chest?"

Once Tim saw the "P & C" and the shield with the Greek Cross and the Campbell coat-of-arms, he didn't wait for Two-hearts' customary delayed response. Tim whispered, "Man alive . . . it sure is."

"Attached to the treasure itself. Trotin removed the lead seal, then hid the treasure."

"That's one of the reasons why we wanted to visit you in person," Maggie said as she handed her coin back to Two-hearts. Everyone else who had a coin followed her lead and Two-hearts replaced them one by one. "We were hoping to learn the remaining clues that reveal where the treasure is hidden. Would you be willing to share that information?"

Two-hearts said nothing but reached down to pull open a desk drawer. He lifted out a bunch of papers and file folders and plopped them on the desktop.

"Trotin knew that legends and stories would get passed down among my people by word of mouth," Two-hearts said as he looked through the stack of papers and folders. "So he wrote down some things. But some papers got lost through the years. The ones that remained started to age and deteriorate. Somebody along the way attempted to copy the remaining papers before they crumbled to bits. One of the things that has sur . . . ah, here it is."

Two-hearts pulled out a protective plastic sheath with an old, yellowed piece of paper inside. "This is one thing that's survived. Do any of you read French?"

"I do," Maggie said. She took the plastic sheath from Two-hearts and looked it over before she started reading it out loud. "*'Les rubis et les émeraudes seront toujours à mon côté.'* Rubies and emeralds shall forever be alongside my name. And below that is says, 'As my name shall forever be under the cross.'"

"Can we take that to mean that Trotin is buried with the treasure?" Maggie asked as she handed the plastic sheath back to Two-hearts.

Two-hearts placed the sheath back on the stack of papers and file folders and went into one of his little silent spells. Then he responded quietly. "I don't know if I would be too quick to jump to conclusions."

Omar became convinced that Two-hearts was feeling uncomfortable and wondered if he was struggling with a desire to help but felt conflicted by his sense of historical culture.

Two-hearts turned his attention to Tim and Alistair, who were taking stock of the books on the shelves. "Do you like my collection of books?"

"I have some of the same ones," Tim commented enthusiastically. "Sigurd Olson's *Reflections from the North Country* and *Open Horizons*, Grace Lee Nute's *The Voyageur's Highway*, Bill Mason's *Path of the Paddle*."

"Cedric?" Alistair asked. "I've been really eager to ask you about your illuminated Gospel of Thomas. I believe you said it was one of your three most cherished possessions. Do you keep it here on the book shelf?"

"What do you mean by illuminated?" Two-hearts asked.

Alistair gave Two-hearts a confused look. "Well . . . if it's anything like the other Lindisfarne gospels, then isn't it decorated with sophisticated artwork?"

Two-hearts reached up to the top row of books shelf and pulled out a modern, hard cover book.

"Here," Two-hearts said as he handed the book to Alistair. "This is my Gospel of Thomas."

Alistair took it with both hands and stared at it with wide-eyed bewilderment followed quickly by utter embarrassment. He handed the book to Omar and covered his face with both hands.

"Oh my God!" Alistair said through his hands. He shook his head. Then he started to laugh. "Blimey! It's always the bloody assumptions that bite you in the arse, isn't it."

"Did you think that my Gospel of Thomas was one of the Lindisfarne Gospels?" Two-hearts asked.

"I confess that I did. For some reason, that's what I thought when we had our conference call at Fitger's Inn."

"It wasn't just Alistair," Omar said. "We all thought that you owned a historic copy of the gospel. But I must say, it was Alistair who was the most excited to see it."

"Yes . . . yes I was."

Omar walked a few paces to the side and started leafing through the gospel.

"May I ask why you cherish the Gospel of Thomas?" Shukriyah asked.

"Well, for a couple reasons. For one, my twin sister died a couple years ago."

"I'm sorry, Cedric. I didn't know."

"No, no. That's all right. She had sent the gospel to me as a gift." Two-hearts reflected a moment. "Yah . . . it was the last thing I received from her."

"May I ask the other reason?"

Two-hearts studied the faces before him. They all looked at him with a serious anticipation, clearly waiting for a response.

"Okay . . . okay." Two-hearts threw his arms out to the side. "Look, the gospel is simply 114 quotes of Christ. And as far as anything I've read, it nails it on the head as to what truth is. Everything that we perceive, every thought, everything that we are conscious of is just that . . . the content of consciousness. It's all so very temporary, very fleeting, and unreal to the core. And the perceiving of it is possible only because . . . you . . . are! The only aspect of you that is real is your uncreated being. Although it's not subject to perception by the five senses, it is something that is still—in its own way—perceivable, understandable. As a wise man once said, it's closer to you than your own skin. But it's not within the realm of space and time. It was not borne of a woman, and it never changes."

As Two-hearts was speaking to them, Omar continued to thumb through the gospel. He stopped at quote #17: "I will give you that which no eye has seen, no ear has heard, no hand has touched, and no human heart has conceived."

Omar opened to the back of the gospel. He wanted to find a quote that he recalled was the same as verses 20 and 21 in Luke 17 of the Bible. He started leafing the pages backward but didn't have to go far. The quote he was looking for was #113. "The disciples asked him: when will the Kingdom come? Christ answered: It will not come by watching for it. No one will be saying, Look, here it is! . . . or . . . Look, there it is! The Kingdom of the father is spread out over the whole earth, and people do not see it."

Omar closed the book and smiled as Two-hearts continued speaking to the others. Then he stepped closer to the gathering.

"I understand that you're an astronomer and that Tim knows something about modern physics," Two-hearts said. "Well, then both of you might know about the Copenhagen Interpretation of Quantum Mechanics. Its main point is—and I hope I'm not over-simplifying—that a conscious observer is required to impart reality to events." He gave a nervous laugh, then continued, "Oh, there are scientists who don't buy it, hey. So they've come up with the Transactional Interpretation of Quantum Mechanics, which states that for any quantum reaction to take place, one particle sends out an offer wave into the future to a target particle. That particle answers with a confirmation wave that travels backward in time. The net result is that the reaction is agreed upon, so to speak, and the reaction appears to take place instantaneously."

Tim frowned. "But . . ."

Two-hearts nodded. "But those scientists shouldn't let go of the Copenhagen Interpretation. What we call the world appears to us because of our own consciousness. No mind, no world. Simple as that."

Two-hearts looked at Tim. "It's funny that you noticed the book by Roger Penrose, *The Emperor's New Mind*. Even he wonders how important consciousness is in creating the so-called physical world we perceive."

Two-hearts reached for the book and opened it up to a book-marked page. "Let me read to you the questions he asks on page 433," he said. "'How important is consciousness for the universe as a whole? Could a universe exist without any conscious inhabitants whatever? Are the laws of physics specially designed in order to allow the existence of conscious life?'"

Two-hearts replaced the book by Penrose and reached for a yellow and black book titled, *I Am That*.

"You know who really understands it well is this guy named Sri Nisar . . . Nisarga . . . datta—kind of a hard name to pronounce—Maharaj." Again, Two-hearts opened to a book-marked page. "When asked by someone if he denied the existence of an objective world, common to all, this guy Maharaj answered: 'Reality is neither subjective or objective, neither mind nor matter, neither time nor space. These divisions need somebody to whom to happen, a conscious separate center.'"

"In other words," Tim asked rhetorically, "if a tree falls in the woods and there's no one around to hear it, does it make a sound?"

Two-hearts shared Tim's laugh. "Hey, I like that."

Then Tim turned to Shukriyah and looked down his nose. "And that covers everything on tomorrow's exam."

Two-hearts laughed again, albeit this time a little more sheepishly. "Oh . . . I'm sorry," he said. "I suppose I got carried away."

"Don't apologize," Shukriyah said. "I asked about the Gospel of Thomas, and you gave me an honest and thorough answer. I thank you."

"We all thank you," Tim said with humility. "I didn't mean to be disrespectful. It's just that the particle physics you referred to is something both Shukriyah and I have studied in Boston. However, you've given me more insight than any professor that I've ever had."

"Well, there aren't many subjects that get me talkin' a whole lot," Two-hearts said as he replaced *I Am That* back on the shelf. "But this subject is one of 'em."

Omar knew that Wally the outfitter had been dead on with his reply to Maggie. They would indeed remember their visit with Cedric Two-hearts for a long, long time.

"Cedric?" Jessa asked. "You said that you have three items that you cherish. Are you willing to show us another one?"

Two-hearts replaced the stack of papers and folders in their desk drawer and opened a different drawer. He took out a thin, foot-long object wrapped in old leather and placed it on his desk. Like a surgeon uncovering his delicate, surgical instruments, Two-hearts slowly rolled out the leather wrapping to reveal a woodwind instrument.

"I've always called this instrument a recorder," Two-hearts said. Then he looked at Maggie. "Do you know what a French voyageur would have called it in the late 1700s?"

But Jessa had training in classical music. "Flute á bec," she answered.

"Okay . . . flute á bec," Two-hearts said. "This flute á bec was owned by Jean-Luc Trotin. Music was very important to the voyageurs."

"Do you play it?" Jessa asked.

"Oh, yes." Two-hearts picked it up and ran up and down the C major scale.

"Jessa and I have instruments back at our campsite," Maggie said. "Our outfitter, Wally, had suggested that we should bring them when we visit you. I now regret that we didn't."

Two-hearts perked up. "You have instruments with you?" he asked. "What?"

"I brought my harmonica, and Jessa brought her guitar."

"Wanna know something? I've never had this recorder outside of my cabin. But I've always wanted to play it on the shore of the lake during a quiet sunset."

"That's amazing! That's the exact same reason why I wanted to bring my harmonica on this trip. Any reason why you've never done it?"

"No one to hear me." Two-hearts said with a shrug. Then he thought for a moment. "You know, it's turned into a beautiful day outside. Chances are good for a quiet sunset. You don't suppose I could come and visit you at your campsite. Maybe we can play together. We could . . . what do they call it . . . jam?"

"That's a wonderful idea!" Maggie said as everyone else voiced the same sentiment. "I'll tell you what . . . please join us for dinner. We have plenty of food with us."

Two-hearts hesitated and looked at the others.

"Oh, you don't want to pass this up," Tim said. "Maggie's an excellent outdoor chef. If it was me doing the cooking, then everyone would have to put up with pouring boiling water in a foil pouch of freeze-dried Turkey Tetrazzini."

"That's pretty close to what I was going to have tonight," Two-hearts said in a comical undertone. "All right. I'll come. I'll bring my recorder and two copies of sheet music. I'll come early and show it to you. The two of you can practice playing it before dinner. Then after dinner, just after sunset, the three of us can serenade the others."

"Perfect!" Maggie said with a big smile. "Let's cross our fingers that it stays nice out."

"Wally said he was going to suggest that you camp in Little Pike Bay. Is that where you are?"

"Yes."

"You know, it's too bad you didn't come here later in the summer or the fall. Then I'd have some real delicacies to share for the dinner. But this time of year I don't have too much. All I have is some smoked white sucker. It's the only time of year it's good. How about I bring some?"

"No thanks," Maggie said. "We want this dinner to be our treat to you."

"Well . . . this sounds real nice, hey."

"What delicacies do you have later in the late summer and fall?" Omar asked. "Do you ever harvest any wild plants from the forest?"

"Yah . . . and from the shallow water too. Blueberries are common in later summer, and wild rice in the fall. There are also bunchberries, cattail roots, arrowhead tubers, wintergreen, highbush cranberries . . . lot's of things. You can have yourself quite a feast if you fix any of those with some fish or wild game and some snapping turtle soup as an appetizer."

"I've heard that snapping turtle is quite a delicacy," Tim said. "How often do you have it?"

"A fella doesn't come across 'em too often. And they're a bugger to clean. You chop off their head in the morning, but by the end of the day they're still clawing at your arms as you're cleaning them out."

Jessa scrunched her nose.

"Well, unless Tim refuses to wash the dishes, then our dinner should be pretty much non-violent," Maggie said. "Like I said, this will be our treat to you. We want to show our appreciation for all you've done. So don't feel obligated to bring anything."

"All right," Two-hearts said. "When you take off, I won't be too far behind you."

44

"THAT WAS SURE DELICIOUS," TWO-HEARTS said after he finished his portion of the raspberry bread pudding Maggie had made in her Dutch oven. "Thank you. Thanks for the entire dinner."

"You're very welcome," Maggie said. "And thank you for joining us. It was so nice of you to come."

Having polished off Maggie's dessert, everyone simply wanted to lounge around the campsite within a grove of red pines. Each found a comfortable spot to enjoy the bright westering sun, its reflection shimmering on the nervous lake surface.

Two-hearts, Alistair, and Omar sat on one log near the fire ring enclosed with a circle of rocks. Jessa and Tim sat on their life jackets with their backs resting against another log. Maggie was also sitting on her life jacket but her back was supported by a Nada-chair, a lumbar pad connected to two straps that wrapped around her knees. Shukriyah was sitting in Tim's Therma-a-Rest Trekker chair that easily converted to a sleeping mattress by undoing a couple of buckles.

"What's that?" Jessa asked Tim as he pulled a small flat agate out of his pocket.

"It's called a worry stone," Tim answered as he held the stone up for all to see and flipped it around with his fingers. "It's a gift from Shelby

Harrington of De Beers Consolidated Mines. He wrote that he won't be needing it anymore. The Percys confessed to having the Spero Optima and promised to hold negotiations for its return."

"That sure had a happy ending," Maggie said. Then she looked at Twohearts. "And speaking of happy endings—or not so happy, for that matter—I started wondering whatever happened to Jean-Luc Trotin after he hid the treasure? Apparently he survived small pox. Then what?"

"They say that the small pox scars on his face not only made him self-conscious, he feared that he was forever contagious since his scars were permanent. Jean-Luc lived out his life as a loner. He became a sort of mysterious legend in the bush. And mysterious legends have a way of becoming the greatest of legends.

"I don't know, hey. I suppose the truth is he lived with surviving family members, or maybe even found a wife who would accept him and then lived a quiet life. All I know for sure is that he never left the bush. He was not one of the veteran voyageurs who settled in communities like Sault Ste. Marie, St. Paul, Winnipeg. Yet, in living in the bush, he could never go near a trading post for fear of being recognized by company officials. But in regards of his fellow voyageurs, the fact that he was still alive was the second best kept secret in the northwest . . . second only to the fate of the treasure itself.

"They say that Trotin did have one more consolation in his life besides making off with the treasure. He stole the treasure from an evil fur trade clerk named Duncan McKay. Trotin did live long enough to find out that he had outlived McKay."

Maggie continued, "I asked a former colleague to look up Duncan McKay in the company archives in Winnipeg. It looked like he never got promoted and he never went into the interior ever again. His name showed up year after year in the Grand Portage ledger books, though. When the company moved up to Fort William in 1803, my colleague said his name appeared in the ledger only for Fort William's first year of operation. After that, a new name started appearing."

"So, McKay never got promoted, huh? Well that sure adds up," Twohearts said. "Ever been to Thunder Bay?"

"It's my hometown," Maggie replied.

"For the rest of you, there's a hill as big as a mountain that overlooks the original site of Fort William near the shore of Lake Superior. The hill's like a palisade with vertical rock cliffs on three sides."

"You mean Mount McKay? You're kidding! Do you really think he . . . well . . . jumped?"

"I do, hey."

"Oh dear!"

"I don't know what the city tourist office in Thunder Bay would tell you about how Mount McKay got its name, but now you know the story I've been told."

"How about, Trotin himself?" Tim asked. "Do you know when he died?"

"No one really knows, hey. Word spread through the bush that he was simply no more, that's all. Someday, maybe, the story of Jean-Luc Trotin will be told no more. You see, like the Vikings who were here centuries earlier, the voyageurs had no custom of keeping a decent, recorded history, and so much has been lost. Only the North West Company kept a regular history, a history of the annual profits it made on the backs of voyageurs like Jean-Luc Trotin."

A distant loon call echoed over the lake. Everyone quieted to listen as the sound faded into the wilderness.

"Oh, my . . . that's beautiful," Shukriyah said.

"We should contact Crane Lake and tell them we want to stay out here another day," Alistair said.

"Tim?" Shukriyah asked as she studied the map on her lap. "I sure would like to bring Jordan on a canoe trip some time so he could experience all this. How well do you think he would manage?"

"No problem. In fact, you know what we could do? We could sign up for a trip with Wilderness Inquiry. They specialize in outdoor wilderness trips that accommodate both able-bodied and disabled people."

Alistair looked at his watch and then at Two-hearts. "By the way Cedric, I just thought of something. Are you aware of the hour? You'll be paddling in dark by the time you get back to your cabin."

"Paddling in the evening is beautiful. The loons are calling. There are no waves to fight. And dusk goes till quite late this time of year. Your eyes adjust quite well to minimal light. The only place that can be kind of dark is the portage, and I have a head lamp for that."

Two-hearts looked up to the sky. "Besides, the stars should be out in all their glory tonight. And if I'm lucky, the Northern Lights might even come out. It's an omen of good luck."

"Speaking of loon calls," Maggie announced, "the one we just heard was actually the kitchen bell sounding. We got to do dishes. There's a pot full of water that's been heating up on the camp stove. It should be ready now. And, we'll need more firewood if we're going to have a bonfire later on."

Everyone sprang into action. Maggie and Jessa gathered everyone's dishes. Shukriyah went to a pack to get the phosphate-free liquid soap, a scrub pad and towel. Alistair went to collect twigs and fallen branches. Tim went to get his folding saw to cut the larger branches into lengths suitable for a bonfire.

"Can I help with dishes?" Two-hearts asked.

"Absolutely not, Cedric," Maggie replied. "Same goes for you, Omar. You two just sit there and relax in the warm, evening sun."

As the others got busy with one task or another, Omar slid over on the log next to Two-hearts.

"This is quite the environment you live in."

"I feel fortunate," Two-hearts said as he looked out over the lake. Tree branches were shading his face from the sun. "It's a privilege to be able to live in the wilderness."

Omar didn't exactly want to jump to the question that Two-hearts' comment brought to mind, so he joined Two-hearts looking out over the lake.

"Cedric, if you don't mind, there's a question that's been on my mind ever since we arrived here in the lake country. With mankind's global impacts on the environment, do you see any changes to this wilderness?"

Two-hearts didn't answer right away, which made Omar wonder if his question was offensive somehow. Two-hearts looked at the ground as the sun shone brightly on his shirt. Omar regarded the seemingly dejected contemplation as a surrender to fate.

"Yah, it sure seems like there are changes," Two-hearts finally said. "Winters seem shorter. This year, the ice went out the earliest it ever has in recorded history. Summers seem hotter. Thunderstorms are more violent. In all my life I've never seen a tornado. Then two years ago I saw my first one near Kabetogama Lake. And last year some people saw one near Kettle Falls. Pine trees are more prone to disease and beetles. And where the pines have died off, deciduous trees have started to grow in their place. Some of the lakes are getting algae blooms in August. Southern animal and fish species are moving northward. Down in Wisconsin and Minnesota, I've heard that there are now poisonous snakes in the watershed of the St. Croix River."

Two-hearts raised is head to look out over the lake again. The sun rays were now below the trees and shining in Two-hearts' face. But he just squinted and didn't seem to mind. The light seemed to chase away any sign of dejection and his face washed serene again.

"If you don't mind my asking something . . . well, it's more of an observation . . . the long line of chiefs among your people must have been men of strong character. Apparently none acted on the clues to the treasure and tried to find it."

"Not just anyone can become a chief," Two-hearts said thoughtfully. "A wise chief is free of attachments and knows the meaning of having enough. He knows that a desire for wealth—in fact, wrong desires in general—can be poisonous. Once acquired, wealth can also be a burden. After all, that which is acquired must be protected day in and day out, year after year."

Two-hearts turned to look at Omar. "And you know something? I think you know that as well."

Omar looked into Two-hearts' peaceful blue eyes and watched a pleasant smile come to his face.

"I still think you look like a wise chief," Two-hearts said.

Omar looked at the ground in embarrassment and chuckled. "Oh . . . I think you can do better than someone like me."

"Back at the cabin this afternoon, I saw you looking at the Gospel of Thomas."

"Yes. Thomas is an important, historical figure in my culture. He traveled through Persia and India while doing his missionary work."

Omar then said, "This whole thing with the lost treasure these kids are looking for reminded me of one of the quotes in his gospel. So I tried to find it before we left the cabin. It is quote number 109 and uses a hidden treasure as a comparison. Its meaning is something like: if you know yourself, if you have that wisdom of immutable being, then it's like you have found your infinite treasure. And of that wisdom you can give without limit to anyone who should ask."

Two-hearts smiled. "It's funny, hey. My ancestors have known that for a long, long time. I think that's why my sister sent me that gospel."

The shimmering lake had relaxed to a flat calm that reflected the sun with an even, steady glare. Tim came to the fire pit and dropped an armload of sticks and branches. Alistair followed and dropped his load alongside Tim's.

"Is the wood wet?" Two-hearts asked.

"Not too bad," Tim said as he started breaking the thinner branches into single lengths. "It should burn okay. It's at least been dead awhile."

"Cedric, I have a question for you. While I was gathering firewood, I noticed some slate scattered around. It reminded me of our phone conversation in Alexandria when you said that the Rainy Lake Rune Stone slate would be a unique, light in color. That's exactly what it turned out to be. How is that you were so confident of the stone's color?"

Two-hearts studied the sticks and branches piled on the ground, then gazed out over the lake. "Earlier this afternoon, I told you that I had three items in the cabin I cherished more than anything else. I showed you two of them—one was Jean-Luc Trotin's flute á bec, which I brought with me tonight. Well, I also brought the third item with me tonight."

June 1779
Hell's Gate Rapid, Last Chance Cove

AFTER JEAN-LUC TROTIN HAD SHOVED his canoe back out into the flowing current, sending the corpse of his friend and comrade, Sebastian Bouvette, on its way to the plunge at Devil's Cauldron, Trotin walked up to the log where he had placed his two most valued possessions. He sat down, placed his elbows on his knees, and leaned forward to rub his forehead. He got the chills, and his wet legs exacerbated the shivering. But at least he wasn't nauseous. He hadn't eaten anything all day.

Trotin looked over at the treasure chest plopped in the sand, and wondered if he had the strength to haul it through the woods. If he didn't, he would bring it up to higher ground within the trees and have it retrieved some other time.

Although Trotin was confident that he could make it down to the meeting place near Devil's Cauldron, he knew that his condition would worsen over the next few days. In fact, he knew that his very survival was at stake.

Trotin looked at his two possessions on the log, and reached first for his flute á bec. He untied a small bundle of maple tree branches enclosing an oily leather wrapping. After Jean-Luc un-rolled the leather wrapping, he held up his flute á bec and closely inspected it from different angles. He was pleased to find it unscathed.

Next he reached for a flat, light-colored stone. He held it close to his face and softly wiped his thumb across the five strange symbols engraved on the surface. He wondered who the author had been. The piece of stone had broken off a large slab that his Ojibwe relatives in the area had in safe keeping.

Present day

TWO-HEARTS REACHED DOWN under the log he was sitting on and produced a flat, cloth-wrapped object. He placed it on his lap, unwound the wrapping, and held up Trotin's fragment of the Rainy Lake Rune Stone.

"After his run down the rapids," Two-hearts said, "Trotin had before him the very treasure of rubies and emeralds that was intended to purchase the rune stone. It's sort of ironic that also right with him was a fragment from that very same rune stone."

"May I take a closer look?" Alistair politely asked.

"Certainly."

Alistair sat down on the log next to Two-hearts and gently took the stone in hand. It didn't take long for him to translate the runic characters as . . . B . . . A . . . N . . . U . . . M.

"Mean anything to you?" Omar asked as he noticed Alistair squinting at the stone close to his nose.

"No . . . but the broken edge . . . it . . . it . . . I'll be right back." Alistair handed the stone back to Two-hearts, then got up and hastily took off toward his tent.

As everyone else looked puzzled, Tim took the opportunity to change the subject. "Cedric, while we wait for Alistair, I got a question about the treasure. Can we assume that Trotin was able to carry it down to his meeting point, and that it was taken to a place somewhere to the northwest of the Hegman Lake pictographs? Maybe as far as Lac La Croix, even?"

Two-hearts sat erect and slowly slid his hands out to his knees as he stiffened his arms. "That seems to be a darn good guess as to what the pictographs mean." Two-hearts gestured toward Maggie. "What did you ask back at the cabin? Weren't you wondering if Trotin was buried with the treasure?"

"Yes, I was. I was intrigued by the clue that rubies and emeralds shall forever be alongside his name, and that his name shall forever be under the cross. No doubt a cross on a head stone."

Tim snapped his fingers. "Hey, wait a minute! Under the cross could mean under the Lake of the Cross. Maybe he's buried somewhere south of Lac La Croix?"

Tim rushed over to Shukriyah. Maggie and Jessa followed and gathered around Shukriyah as she held open the map for all to see.

Alistair came back with his printout and sat next to Two-hearts. "What's this all about?" Alistair asked as he gestured toward the others huddled over the map.

Omar replied. "Trying to figure out where the treasure is hidden."

"Well I'll be . . . look at this!" Tim announced excitedly. He pointed at an area south of Lac La Croix. "Ruby, Hustler, and Emerald lakes!"

There was silence for a few seconds.

Maggie stood erect and looked over at Two-hearts. "Cedric, back at the cabin when I asked you if Trotin was buried with the treasure, didn't you say that we shouldn't be too quick to jump to conclusions?"

"Yah . . . that's usually good advice in dealing with matters like this."

"But we're obviously close, aren't we Cedric?"

Two-hearts stared at Maggie for a few seconds without answering. Then he thought of her husband, Lyle. "Okay . . . Okay . . . There is one last clue."

Once again, everyone stared at Two-hearts.

"Think back to the clue on the pictographs. Then think about this . . . follow the moose one more step, and on the shore of *that* lake you shall find your heritage."

All were silent.

"Remember, you guys?" Shukriyah asked. "Pegasus, the moose constellation . . . during the spring equinox it sets in the west."

Tim bent over and put his finger on Hustler Lake. ". . . follow the moose one more step . . . presumably to the west, and . . . here it is! Heritage Lake. That's got to be it."

Tim stood up and looked at Two-hearts for confirmation. Two-hearts simply stared back at him, his expression blank. An awkward silence fell over the camp.

Omar finally broke the ice. "Tim, if Lyle's lost his funding, tell him that my organization will help fund his efforts to organize another treasure recovery effort. Searching the shore of an entire lake will no doubt be much more expensive than searching a rapids."

Shukriyah immediately thought, *At long-last, Two-hearts has indeed found his chief.*

"You think your council will endorse it?" Tim asked.

"Yes, I'm quite confident. After all, the treasure is connected to the Rainy Lake Rune Stone, which is connected to the silver urn."

"Speaking of the Rainy Lake Rune Stone," Alistair said as he faced Two-hearts, "may I see that piece of rune stone again?"

Two-hearts handed over the rune stone fragment.

Alistair placed the rune stone and the photo side by side. Just as he had suspected, the broken edge on the stone matched that in the photo. He looked closely at the runic characters. The characters that represented O L I in the printout were to the left. To the right were runic characters on the stone that spelled out B A N U

M. Alistair was visibly thunder-struck. His reaction was so dramatic that Omar actually became concerned. "What is it, Alistair? Your face just went white."

When Alistair stood up slowly, it became obvious to everyone that he had something important to announce. Even the mild-mannered Two-hearts had an anxious expression as he waited for the drama to unfold. But Alistair didn't say anything, though it looked like he was trying to.

Omar walked up to Alistair and placed a hand on his shoulder. "You're frightening me, Alistair," said softly. "What is it?"

"Olibanum," Alistair said. "The Oil of Lebanon."

Omar instantly got it. His lips parted but no words came out. His eyes looked dazed. One by one he looked at all the others surrounding him. Too stunned and too emotional to say anything, he slowly turned and walked down to the lake.

Alistair waited so Omar could come to terms with the enormity of what he had just heard. Although Omar's back was to everyone, Alistair noticed him pull out a handkerchief and bring it up to his eyes. He looked at Shukriyah and nodded in Omar's direction.

As Tim watched Shukriyah approach Omar and put her arm over his shoulder, he turned to Alistair. "What is the Oil of Lebanon?"

"The Incense of the Frankish Crusaders," Alistair said.

Tim didn't get it, but Jessa seemed to. "The Incense of the Franks?"

"That's right," Alistair said as he handed the rune stone fragment back to Two-hearts. "The silver urn is the Frankincense Urn. First brought to Bethlehem, returned by Mary to the next generation of visiting Magi, brought to England by Persians conscripted by the Romans, and last but not least . . . revered so much by the invading Vikings that they make reference to it on a rune stone."

Everyone diverted their attention to the lakeshore just in time to see Omar put his arm around Shukriyah's waist. With her arm still over Omar's shoulder, she gently rested her head on his shoulder.

Two-hearts broke the emotional pall that had fallen over the camp. "So, we finally find out what that silver urn really is," he said. "It's been my dream for many, many years." He wrapped the cloth back around the rune stone.

"Well, everybody," Two-hearts said has he stood up, "the witching hour is nigh upon us."

"The witching hour?" Alistair asked.

"Yes. That time in the evening when the last of the sun's rays have disappeared below the horizon. When the lake is like glass and everything perfectly still and quiet. It was described that way in one of Sigurd Olson's books. And it's the perfect time to play our music. So, what do you say, girls? Let's get ready, hey."

Two-hearts started walking down to the lake and everyone followed. Two-hearts stopped alongside Omar and Shukriyah and pointed out his plan to Maggie and Jessa. "See those rocks sticking out of the water over there," he said as he pointed out into the bay to the left side of the setting sun. "I'll beach my canoe on the large, humped-back shaped rock and play from there."

Two-hearts swung his arm through the low but bright sun and pointed down the right side of the bay. "Jessa, see that ledge sticking out from the shoreline over there? That's where you'll be. It's nice and flat." Two-hearts pointed into the trees to the extreme right. "There's a trail that starts from the campsite over there. It follows the shoreline and will take you right to the ledge rock. You can't miss it.

He turned to Maggie next. "Maggie . . . Jessa and I will raise our hands when we're ready. I'll play the tune once through. Then when I'm done, you girls can play the tune just like you practiced before dinner. I'll be getting back in my canoe and will paddle far out, so play the tune a couple times because I would love to hear you play it from far out on the lake."

Two-hearts searched the faces of Maggie and Jessa to see if they had questions.

"Okay, we're good to go," Jessa said. Then she put out her right hand. "Cedric . . . thanks so much for coming this evening and thanks for what you are about to do. Playing an accompaniment to Jean-Luc Trotin's flute á bec will certainly be a privilege."

"The evening has been a great pleasure," Two-hearts said as he shook Jessa's hand. "I feel honored to be able to play the flute á bec for you."

Everyone else gathered around Two-hearts as Jessa went to pick up her guitar, a small folding stool, and then started out for the trail alongside the bay. One by one, Two-hearts looked each in the eye and gave a hardy hand shake. Maggie was last.

"You say hi to Lyle for me, hey," Two-hearts said. "And tell him that he sure married a hell of a cook."

Maggie reached her arms around Two-hearts' neck and hugged him. Two-hearts put his arms around Maggie, patted her back a couple times and gave her a bear hug.

Just as the sun was perched on the trees of the far shore, Two-hearts eased his solo canoe into the water, placed the rune stone fragment on the bottom and bent over to grip the gunwales on each side. He put one foot in, pushed off with the other and hopped in. As he paddled away from shore, his initial tack took him directly into the setting sun. With each backstroke, the water running off the end of his paddle blade looked like liquid diamonds falling into the lake.

The sun had just set by the time Two-hearts reached the little rock island, and pulled his canoe up. Although it was far away, the sound of the canoe hull hitting against the rock was easily audible in the evening's perfect acoustics.

As Two-hearts and Jessa got ready, everyone enjoyed the "witching hour." They looked across the lake at the silhouette of the tree line on the far shore. Combined with its symmetrical reflection in the still lake, it resembled a horizontal ink blob on a Rorschach Test. The jagged black band was bordered above and below with an iridescent yellow. Higher in the sky, the yellow cooled into a lavender that reflected at the feet of the onlookers. As Maggie stood ready with her harmonica, she turned to Tim. "Did Cedric knew where the treasure was all this time?"

Tim looked back at Maggie with an expression that at once was both suspicious yet satisfied. "To be honest . . . I simply don't know." Then he looked back out over the water.

The figures of both Two-hearts and Jessa were dark but well outlined in the twilight. Two-hearts was farther away. He stood facing across the bay. On the other side, Jessa was seated in her stool as her guitar rested on her lap. She also faced out over the bay.

As everyone on shore looked out on the lake, they could make out Cedric Two-hearts raising an instrument to his lips.

For the first time in over 200 years, the music of Jean-Luc Trotin's flute á bec echoed across a lake somewhere in the wilderness that lies to the northwest of Lake Superior.